INCANDESCENCE

Other books by Greg Egan:

Schild's Ladder
Teranesia
Diaspora
Distress
Permutation City
Quarantine
An Unusual Angle
Zendegi (forthcoming)

INCANDESCENCE

GREG EGAN

NIGHT SHADE BOOKS
San Francisco

ISBN: 978-1-59780-129-4
Printed in Canada

Night Shade Books
Please visit us on the web at
http://www.nightshadebooks.com

1

"Are you a child of DNA?"

Rakesh was affronted; if he'd considered this to be information that any stranger wandering by had a right to know, it would have been included in his précis. After a moment's reflection, though, his indignation gave way to curiosity. The stranger was either being deliberately offensive, or had a very good reason for asking. Either way, this was the most interesting thing that had happened to him all day.

"Why do you wish to know?" he replied. The stranger's own précis contained extensive details of its ancestry and sensory modalities, but Rakesh wasn't in the mood to acquire the necessary skills to apprehend it on its own terms. By default, he was already perceiving it as human-shaped, and hearing it speak in his own native tongue. Now, in place of its declared chemosensory label, he assigned it a simple phonetic name chosen at random: Lahl.

Before Lahl could reply, Viya had risen to her feet beside Rakesh and gestured toward an empty spot on the annular bench that surrounded their table. "Please join us," she said.

Lahl nodded graciously. "Thank you." Lahl's actual gender didn't map on to Rakesh's language neatly, but the arbitrary name he'd given her was grammatically female. She sat between the other two members of the group, Parantham and Csi, facing Rakesh squarely. Behind her in the distance, water cascaded down a jagged rocky slope, sending a mist of fine droplets raining down on to the forest below.

"I couldn't help overhearing your complaint," Lahl said. "'Everything has been done. Everything has been discovered.'" To Rakesh, they were seated in the open air, near the edge of a mesa that rose above the treetops of a vast jungle. The murmur of multilingual conversation from the tables around them might have been the sound of insects, if it had not been for the occasional translated phrase that Rakesh allowed himself to hear at random, in case anything piqued his interest. Perhaps to Lahl his words had come across as a distinctive aroma, standing out from a jumble of background odors.

Csi spread his hands in a gesture of apology to this stranger unfamiliar with their customs. "That's just Rakesh's way of talking," he confided. "You should pay him no attention. We get the same speech every day."

"Which makes it no less true," Rakesh protested. "Our ancestors have sucked the Milky Way dry. We were born too late; there's nothing left for us."

"Only several billion other galaxies," Parantham observed mildly. She smiled; her position on this subject had barely shifted since Rakesh had met her, but for her it was still a worthwhile debate, not the empty ritual it had become for Csi.

"Containing what?" Rakesh countered. "Probably more or less the same kinds of worlds and civilizations as our own. Probably nothing that would not be a hideous anticlimax, after traveling such a distance." A few thousand intrepid fools had, in fact, set out for Andromeda, with no guarantee that the spore packages they'd sent in advance would survive the two-million-light-year journey and construct receivers for them.

Rakesh turned to Lahl. "I'm sorry, we keep interrupting you. But what exactly does my molecular ancestry have to do with this?"

"I could be mistaken," Lahl said, "but it might have some bearing on whether or not I can offer you a cure for your malaise."

Rakesh hesitated, then took the bait. "I do come from DNA," he said. "But I warn you, I think that's a strange way to pigeonhole people." His human ancestors had fashioned descendants in their own image—who in turn were largely content to do the same—but membership of the broader DNA panspermia implied no particular cultural traits. Entirely different replicators had given rise to creatures more similar to humans, in temperament and values, than any of their molecular cousins.

Lahl said, "I don't mean to judge you by your ancestry, but in my experience even molecular kinship can sometimes lead to a sense of affinity that would otherwise be lacking. The DNA panspermia has been extensively studied; every world it reached was thought to have been identified long ago. Adding the first new entry to that catalog in almost a million years might well hold more interest for you than it does for me."

Rakesh smiled uncertainly. This was not exactly the kind of momentous discovery that people had made in the Age of Exploration, but in his blackest hours he had often imagined contributing far less to the sum of knowledge than this modest footnote.

It was a pity he'd been beaten to it. "If you've found such a world," he said, "then you're the one who has extended the list."

Lahl shook her head. "Strictly speaking, the crucial evidence was obtained by a third party, but that's not the point. We can quibble all day about the formal attributions, but at present only a fragment of the story is known. Almost everything about this world remains to be discovered, and until someone is willing to pursue the matter vigorously, the few scraps of information I'm carrying will mean very little."

Viya said, "So you're here to trade what you do know?"

"Trade?" Lahl appeared startled. "No. I'm merely hoping to find someone who can do justice to this, since I don't have the time or inclination myself."

Rakesh was beginning to feel as if he was being prodded awake from a stupefying dream that had gone on so long he'd stopped believing that it could ever end. He'd come to this node, this crossroads, in the hope of encountering exactly this kind of traveler, but in ninety-six years he'd learned nothing from the people passing through that he could not have heard on his home world. He'd made friends among the other node-dawdlers, and they passed the time together pleasantly enough, but his old, naive fantasy of colliding with a stranger bearing a surfeit of mysteries—a weary explorer announcing, "I've seen enough for one lifetime, but here, take this crumb from my pocket"—had been buried long ago.

Now that it was being resurrected before his eyes, he felt more wary than excited. He addressed Lahl respectfully, but chose his words with care. "I can't promise you anything, but if you have the time to tell us what you've learned, I'd be honored."

Lahl explained that she belonged to a synchronization clan. Its members roamed the galaxy, traveling alone, but had agreed to remain in contact by meeting regularly at prearranged locations, and doing their best to experience similar periods of subjective time between these reunions. She was on her way to the next such event, in a planetary system twelve hundred light years outward from this node. Given that the meetings took place just once every hundred millennia, travel plans could be made well in advance, and there was no excuse for tardiness.

However, for reasons she did not wish to detail, when the time had come to begin the journey Lahl had found herself on the wrong side of the galaxy, with no prospect of fulfilling her appointment by any conventional means. The communications network run by the Amalgam skirted the crowded sphere of stars that formed a bulge at the center of the galactic disk, adding several thousand lightyears to the journey compared to the straight-line distance. So she had weighed her options, and her sense of obligation, and placed her fate in the hands of the Aloof.

Viya gazed at her wonderingly. "You've been through their network?"

"Yes."

"You would have been encrypted, though?"

"That's the usual practice," Lahl said. "But I came at a bad time. There'd been an unexpected surge in traffic a few decades before, and there were no encryption keys available for my destination. Keys have to be distributed the long way around; shortages can take centuries to fill. So I had no choice. I traveled in plain sight."

"Yet you emerged unscathed?"

"I believe I'm intact," Lahl replied. She added mischievously, "Though I would think that, wouldn't I?"

Three hundred millennia ago, certain brash citizens of the Amalgam had studied the Aloof's data traffic, deciphered its basic protocols, and constructed links between the two networks. This unilateral act of bridge-building had apparently been tolerated by the Aloof, albeit with only a trickle of data passing through, since few people were willing to trust the short cut. The Amalgam had tried many times to extend its own physical infrastructure into the same territory, but the Aloof had calmly and methodically reversed the trajectory of every spore.

Csi said, "I think I would have arranged for a suitably located backup to wake, and attend the reunion on my behalf instead."

"That would have been grossly discourteous," Lahl explained. "And to have the slightest chance of pulling it off, I would have needed to start planning about sixty millennia ago. If I'd had that much foresight, I would never have ended up cutting things so fine in the first place."

The table fell silent as the four of them contemplated the risk she'd taken. The Aloof had never been known to act maliciously—even the insentient engineering spores they'd swatted back out of the bulge had been left unharmed—but their stubborn refusal to communicate gave them an aura, if not of danger, at the very least of unaccountability. Worse, the part of their network accessible to the Amalgam did not carry quantum data, so the Amalgam's standard protocols—which rendered it physically impossible for an eavesdropper to decipher a transmission, or to alter it without detection—could not be employed. That problem had been addressed, in part, by distributing matched pairs of quantum keys around the edge of the bulge via the Amalgam's own network, creating stockpiles that could be used to encrypt the classical data of travelers taking the short cut. If demand for the keys outstripped supply, though, it could take a while for the stockpiles to be replenished.

Rakesh said, "The explorer you mentioned: did she take the same route? Is that how you met?"

"Explorer?"

"Didn't you say that a third party found this uncatalogued DNA world?"

"They found evidence for it," Lahl said. "Not the world itself, as far as I know."

Rakesh was perplexed. "As far as you know?"

"The Aloof embodied me," Lahl explained, "deep inside their territory. I was shown a meteor, which appeared to be a fragment of a planetary crust ejected by an impact event. Inside, it was riddled with DNA."

"So you've met them?" Viya asked, incredulous now. "You've met the Aloof?"

"Of course not," Lahl replied. "They kept me at arm's length. They woke me in a small interstellar habitat, well suited to my customary embodiment, alone with this rock and the instruments needed to examine it. The short cut had bought me five thousand years' grace, so I had no qualms about spending a few days obliging my hosts, and satisfying my own curiosity. The cells inside the meteor were all dead, but there was enough intact genetic material to reveal that it hadn't been blasted straight off the surface of any of the known DNA worlds. It was from a mature divergent branch of the panspermia. It must have originated on a world of its own."

"Do you know where they collected it?" Parantham asked. "They would have had to travel out of the bulge, surely?"

Lahl said, "There was a map showing where they'd found it: not far from the place where I was examining it. Particle tracks in the outer layers of the rock seemed to bear that out; it looked as if it had been exposed to ambient radiation levels for about fifty million years. And as best as I could date the impact event, that was about fifty million years ago, too."

Viya frowned. "That makes no sense. For ejecta to get from a typical DNA world down into the bulge would take at least half a billion years."

"Exactly," Lahl said. "So it can't be from a typical DNA world. The planetary system itself must be deep in the Aloof's territory."

Rakesh felt a thrill of astonishment, though he was far from convinced that Lahl's conclusion was the right one. All eleven panspermias were believed to have originated at middle radii in the galactic disk, between twenty and thirty thousand light years from the center. Certainly, the worlds on which the eleven replicators were known to have thrived were confined to that zone, where the galactic chemistry favored the formation of suitable planets, the radiation levels were reasonably low, and such biosphere-sterilizing calamities as supernovae were relatively rare.

The process by which collision ejecta had spread the replicators between star systems was supposedly well understood, and though nothing ruled out the possibility of debris carrying DNA-based micro-organisms all the way down to the galactic bulge, no one would have expected them to gain a foothold there.

"Perhaps the Aloof were showing you their cousins," Parantham suggested. "Perhaps this was their first attempt to introduce themselves." It was widely assumed that the Aloof had been born in the disk, like everyone else, and migrated to the bulge before any other civilization had traveled widely enough to encounter them.

Lahl shrugged. "If they'd wished to convey something like that, they could have made themselves clearer. They deciphered my transmission and embodied me; there was nothing mysterious to them in my nature to stand in the way of communication."

Csi said, "I don't doubt that they deciphered you, but are you sure you were embodied?" He spread his arms, taking in the five of them and the whole elaborate scape. The node, in reality, was a few cubic meters of processor, drifting through interstellar space. There was no mesa, there was no jungle, nor any of the alternatives that any of them were perceiving.

"Of course I'm not sure," Lahl conceded. "And even if I was embodied, the meteor itself could have been a carefully manufactured fake, or the instruments I was supplied with could have been contrived to mislead me. But I can't see the point in that kind of deception. Why spread misinformation about the DNA panspermia among people to whom you're largely indifferent?"

"Why spread valid information, either?" Rakesh mused. "I'm surprised they didn't just lob this out of the bulge, muttering about yet another incursion by those awful disk people."

"Lob it where, though?" Csi replied. "And if the planet it came from really does lie in the bulge, this 'incursion' probably predates their own presence."

Lahl regarded them both reprovingly, as if she considered these comments to be willfully obtuse. She said, "I believe they felt obliged to tell someone, to get the word out. In spite of their refusal to communicate with us on any other topic, I believe they considered it their duty to pass this information on to us, to make of it what we will."

"As you considered it your own duty to hand the message on to a descendant of the appropriate replicator?" Rakesh suggested.

"Exactly."

Rakesh was on the verge of pointing out that it was somewhat parochial of her to assume that the Aloof would share her sense of obligation, but then it struck him that, out of all the travelers who'd taken the short cut, the Aloof might have chosen Lahl precisely because she was the most likely to understand, and act upon, their intentions.

Whatever the original cues being translated, Lahl's face had taken on a subtly challenging aspect, as if she was waiting for Rakesh to make clear to her whether or not she'd been wasting her time.

Rakesh was still unsure of the verdict himself. *Was this his calling?* He had never thought of the bulge as a place of genuine mysteries. Many individual citizens of the Amalgam were every bit as private as the Aloof; he had no idea what went on inside their homes, but his ignorance hardly transformed those places into unexplored territory. The higher the gate, the more manicured the garden.

That was the wrong comparison to make, though. The fact that the Aloof fastidiously repelled any physical intrusion into the bulge was no proof that they'd transformed, visited, or even catalogued every last one of the millions of worlds within their domain. If their refusal to engage with the cultures of the disk had its origins in paranoia, they might have adopted a policy of hypervigilance, scrutinizing every last rock for signs of life lest some interloper arise in their midst. Equally, though, stumbling across the DNA-infested meteor might have been sheer bad luck, an unwelcome find imposing obligations that they would never have actively sought.

He said, "If I took this on, where would I pick up the thread? I can't cross the bulge and simply hope to be singled out to be shown what you were shown."

"I have the habitat's address," Lahl said. "The Aloof appended it to my transmission. When you reach the bridge to their network, you could simply name that as your destination."

"With no guarantee that the request would be honored," Csi said. He was staring at Rakesh as if his friend had lost his mind.

Rakesh said, "I haven't come to any decision yet."

Now it was Parantham who was showing disbelief. She turned to Lahl. "If he won't take the address, give it to me! And none of this DNA bigotry. I can only trace my own ancestry back fourteen generations—to a *de novo* created by a rather hazily documented collaboration—so I can't promise you any mystical molecular affinity. But if the Aloof want someone to hunt down this lost world for them, I'll do it!"

"Hunt it down how?" Csi asked bluntly.

"They recorded the meteor's velocity when they captured it," Lahl said. "And they provided me with detailed maps of the region. I couldn't literally wind all the dynamics back fifty million years; the region is so densely packed with stars that their motion becomes chaotic on that time scale. But it was possible to generate candidates for closer exploration."

"How many?" Csi demanded.

"About six hundred."

Csi groaned and leaned backward on the bench, as if to extract himself from the gathering. "This is insane!"

Rakesh could not deny that, but it was an increasingly enticing folly. Uncharted or not, the center of the galaxy was an exotic, bejewelled place, and if its self-appointed guardians really were inviting outsiders in for the first time ever, that alone was a remarkable opportunity. If the reason for the invitation turned out to be a wild goose chase, or even a complete misunderstanding, that need not render the voyage worthless; it was impossible to rule out danger and disappointment, but at the very least he'd be risking much less than the galaxy-hoppers. How many millennia might he while away before another prospect the equal of this came along?

He said, "I'll take the address." He glanced at Parantham. "I assume I'm not required to go alone?"

Lahl said, "Take an entourage. Take a caravan." She held out her hand, the fist closed, then opened her fingers to reveal a glass key sitting on her palm, an icon for all the data she wished to convey to him. As Rakesh reached for it, she said sharply, "This is *your* duty now. Your burden. You do understand that?"

He hesitated. "What exactly are you asking me to promise? I can't be certain that I'll find this planet."

"Of course not." Lahl frowned, perhaps wondering what distortions her perfectly lucid chemical emanations were suffering in translation. "Succeed or fail, though, you'll see it through?"

Rakesh nodded gravely, reluctant to press her for details lest they transform this reasonable-sounding commitment into some far more rigorous obligation.

He took the key from her, and she stood.

"Farewell then, Rakesh." The scape drew her as almost literally unburdened, her bearing visibly more relaxed and graceful, as if she'd been freed of a physical load.

The four friends rose. As Lahl walked away across the mesa, Rakesh peeked at her version of the scape. A long, translucent, segmented creature pushed its way briskly through a dense carpet of decaying vegetable matter, beneath an overcast sky.

Csi called after her, "Enjoy the reunion!"

Rakesh restored his normal vision and looked around the table. Parantham was jealously eyeing the key in his hand.

Viya smiled. "You're not really going to do this?" She sounded as if she'd be unsurprised if he shook his head and casually pitched the key over the edge of the mesa.

"Of course I am," Rakesh replied. "I gave my word."

"To whom, exactly?" Csi asked. "For all you know, she was just some *de novo* that the Aloof created and spat out as bait."

"*Bait*? If they wanted visitors, all they had to do was stop turning us away. We never needed luring."

"We never would have gone in this way by choice," Csi said. "With no guarantee of integrity. Once you're in, they can send you wherever they like, and do whatever they want with you."

Rakesh said, "Why would they want to harm me? Anyway, people taking the short cut have been checked, and there have never been any violations found."

"What proportion have been checked?" Viya asked. "One in a thousand? And the data passing through the network is classical, remember. Even if the original transmission comes through intact, that doesn't prove it hasn't been copied. If you go in without encryption, there'll be nothing they can't do to you."

"All right, it's a risk, I admit it. The Aloof might be deranged sadists who clone travelers in order to torture them for eternity." Rakesh was disappointed. He had no shortage of doubts about the wisdom of his decision, but he'd expected more from Viya and Csi than this timidity masquerading as sophistication.

None of them had come to the node with the intention of staying for a tenth as long as they had. Half their time was spent debating the best way to move on, inventing one fanciful scheme after another, hunting for ways to build up momentum lest they end up stranded, or worse: slinking back to their home worlds with nothing to show for the millennia, or simply drifting aimlessly on through the network.

He held up the key. "This is what I came here for. I'm not going to sit at this table for another century, waiting for something better."

Csi adopted a conciliatory tone. "We all get bored, Rakesh. We all get frustrated. But that's no reason to fall for the first scam artist who comes along."

Parantham said, "If it's a prank, what happens? We cross the bulge, the Aloof ignore us, and we end up on the other side of the galaxy. We lose fifty millennia, but we gain new surroundings, and the minor daredevil status that comes from having taken the short cut."

"And if it's a trap?" Viya asked. "If the Aloof really do mean you harm?"

Parantham hesitated before replying; Rakesh waited gleefully to hear her pour scorn on the idea.

She said, "That's what backups are for."

2

As the work party dispersed, Roi headed for the nearest tunnel. The warm buzz of cooperation was fading, giving way to a faint sense of melancholy, and she needed to get away from the wind and the weight to a place where she could rest.

She'd lost count of the number of shifts she'd spent with this team, tending the crops at the garm-sharq edge of the Splinter. It was important work, killing the mites and weeds, keeping the crucial reservoir of food healthy and abundant. If the edible plants prospered here, where the hot, fertile wind blew in from the Incandescence, the seeds that ended up scattered throughout the garmside would give rise to enough secondary growth to feed everyone. If that ceased to happen and people were driven by hunger to feed on the reservoir itself, the initial shortfall could spiral out of control. Roi was too young to have lived through a famine, but some of her fellow workers had survived two or three. The visceral sense of satisfaction that came from acting in unison was enough to keep her working at almost any task, but this one easily stood up to the scrutiny of conscious reflection.

The tunnel dipped and weaved erratically as it wound its way up. The wind was strong but steady, a nuisance but no great complication. Away from the well-trodden path that marked the easiest ascent, a riot of vegetation colored the light of the underlying rock. Roi resisted the urge to reach out and crush the inedible varieties; most of them had their uses, and as long as they didn't crowd out the food crops they deserved to be left to grow in peace. It was a familiar part of the winding down process to be aware of the weeds everywhere, without responding to the sight of them in the manner that was second nature when she was working.

The tunnel ended in a crowded chamber, where six routes leading up from the garmside edge converged. People were coming up out of the wind after finishing a variety of tasks, and while there was no need for most of these shifts to be synchronized, some kind of social cue seemed to have nudged the timing into a rather inconvenient lockstep. Roi recognized a few members of her own team crossing the chamber, but felt no desire to rejoin them.

At the edge of the flow of bodies a group of wretched males clung to the rock, begging to be relieved of their ripeness. Roi approached them to inspect their offerings. Each male had separated the two hard plates that met along the side of his body, to expose a long, soft cavity where five or six swollen globes sat dangling from heavy cords. Not all of the seed packets were plump and healthy, but Roi made a conscious effort not to be too finicky. With her own carapace split open along her left side, she used her mating claw to reach into the males' bodies, snip the globes free, and deposit them inside herself.

She stripped all the packets from the first three donors, and they shuddered with gratitude and disappeared into the crowd. When she took two globes from the fourth male and found that she was full, she muttered a few consoling words and left him wailing for further assistance.

The ripe seed packets secreted a substance that the males found extremely unpleasant, and while unplucked globes did shrivel up and die eventually, waiting for that to happen could be an ordeal. There were tools available for severing and discarding them, but that method was notoriously prone to spilling an agonizing dose of irritant. Something about a female's mating claw—something harder to mimic than its shape and its mechanical action—sealed the broken cord far more effectively than any tool.

As Roi continued across the chamber, a pleasant haze of contentment washed over her. The seed packets were battling for supremacy, but the poisons they were using against each other had a thoroughly positive effect on her. The battle was rendered more intense by a weapon of her own: a small quantity of crushed plant material that she replenished regularly. All of her competing suitors would die, valiantly trying to out-poison this thoroughly sterile rival.

Roi left the chamber by the least crowded route, intent now on finding a quiet crevice in which to recuperate. The wind would never fall completely silent unless she traveled all the way to the narrow calm space that divided the garmside from the sardside, but it wouldn't take long to reach some veins of less porous rock that offered a degree of shelter. There was no shelter from the geographical certainties of weight, but after so long working at the Splinter's edge she didn't need much lightening in order to feel unburdened.

Ahead of her, a lone male stood idle in the middle of the tunnel. He wasn't begging for help, and as she drew closer Roi could see that he carried no seeds. A moment later she recognized something else in his appearance: the visibly laboring heart of someone who'd ventured well beyond the weight he was accustomed to bearing.

The male was blocking the easiest way ahead, so Roi, undeterred by the weeds, climbed the tunnel wall to detour around him.

"It must be something simple," he declared.

Roi paused courteously. "What must be, father?"

"Whatever underlies it all."

"Of course." Roi had no idea what he was talking about, so she could hardly dispute him.

She hesitated, then started to move on.

The male scrambled after her. "My name is Zak."

"My name is Roi." He was exerting himself valiantly to match her pace, but she took pity on him and slowed down a little. "I work among the crops, at the garm-sharq edge."

Zak chirped approval. "Valuable work."

Roi glanced behind them. If this was some kind of recruitment ambush, his team-mates were well hidden. "What do you do?"

"I doubt you will have heard of my task. In fact, lately I've been working alone."

Roi didn't ask why he remained unrecruited; he was plainly quite old, and probably in poor health. Being stranded without team-mates was an unfortunate fate for anyone, but she had no power to change that for him. She certainly couldn't recruit him into her own team, in his condition.

"I spend a lot of time in the Calm," Zak continued. "Near the Null Line."

"I see." Resting, hoping to recover from an illness? Or perhaps being weightless too long was the cause of his weakness. "Doing what?"

"Playing with some contraptions of mine. Trying to find something simple."

"I don't understand. What is it you're looking for?"

Zak said, "I'm not sure. But I'll recognize it when I see it."

They continued on in silence for a while. Roi didn't mind him accompanying her; he could hardly hijack her loyalty on his own, and she was relieved to see him heading for a level more conducive to his health.

"Do you ever wonder why we climb *up* to the Null Line from the garm and sard quarters," Zak asked, "but *down* to it from the shomal and junub?"

"What is there to ponder?" Roi replied, amused. "That's just the way it is." When Zak said nothing she added defensively, "Do you really think it's surprising? Any point you name must be above some places, and below others. So why shouldn't the four quarters be half and half?"

Zak said, "If you ascend to any other point and then continue on in the same direction, you cross between the two alternatives: the point that was originally above you is now below you. When you cross straight through the Null Line, that doesn't happen. If you go from garm to sard, the Null Line remains above you. If you go from shomal to junub, it remains below you."

Roi was tired, but she forced herself to concentrate. She might have let the matter drop for the sake of harmony, but something about Zak provoked her to disputation.

"At the Null Line you have no weight," she said finally, "so there really is no up or down. That's the difference. If any other point stayed above you as you crossed through it, your weight would have to reverse suddenly, changing completely in a single step. At the Null Line it shrinks to nothing, so a change in direction is no change at all."

"Exactly." Her answer was clearly no revelation to Zak, but he sounded pleased that she'd made the effort to think it through. "That still doesn't explain the particular pattern, though. I can see no logical difficulty with a far simpler situation: our weight always pointing away from the Null Line, or always pointing toward it. Nor can I see any barrier to more complex arrangements. Why the four quarters? When you circle around the Null Line, why should it be above you, then below you, then above, then below? Why not six changes of direction, or thirty-six?"

Roi rasped annoyance. "And if it was thirty-six, you'd be asking why not four, or six."

"Of course I would. But I don't believe it could ever be thirty-six."

"You just told me you can see no reason why it shouldn't be!"

Zak said, "I can't see the reason yet. But four is small enough to point to something simple. If it was thirty, I could believe it might be thirty-six. Because it's four, though, I believe it *must* be four."

They'd reached a junction in the tunnel. Roi moved toward the left branch, which she knew was a cul-de-sac ending in some comfortable crannies.

"Before we part," Zak said, "can I show you something?" He opened his carapace and reached into the empty seed bed to remove a rolled-up sheet of cured skin, which he proceeded to spread out before her. "This is my favorite map of the Splinter."

Roi was unimpressed. The single cross-section portrayed was covered with an absurdly regular hatching of short, straight lines which bore no resemblance to any routes she knew. And there was no hint of anything really useful, such as vegetation patterns or the lodes of dense, sheltering rock.

"Are you telling me I can get from *here* to *here*?" she asked, gesturing at two endpoints of one of the peculiar markings. But it wasn't even clear where these points were meant to be, since there were no cues to indicate how far along the Null Line, rarb or sharq, the cross-section was taken.

"It's not a map of tunnels," Zak replied. "It's a map of weights."

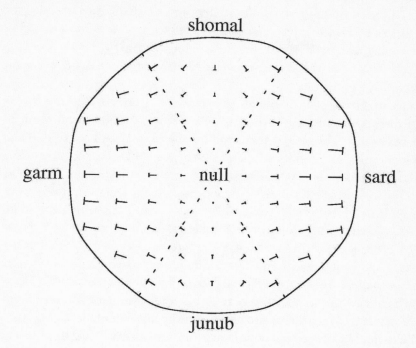

It took a moment for his meaning to become clear. The longest lines were drawn at the edge of the Splinter, where the weight was greatest. The lines' varying lengths, and the way they gradually rotated as you followed them around the center of the map, offered a plausible rendering of the way weight changed from place to place. A small crossbar on each one distinguished the bottom end from the top.

"You drew this yourself?" she asked.

"No, I copied it from a map I found in a library. That had nothing to indicate its provenance, though, and it could easily have been a copy itself. For all I know this could be the seventh or eighth generation."

Roi pondered the strange task the original cartographer had embarked upon. "Everybody knows that weight increases as you move away from the Null Line. What's the need for a map like this?"

"In what manner does it increase?" Zak demanded. "How quickly, as you move in different directions? And which way, exactly, is down, as you move between the quarters?"

Roi couldn't imagine why anyone would need to know these things with more precision than she already knew them herself. Still, there was something compelling about the stretching and shrinking and rolling of the lines. Each individual mark conveyed nothing new to her, but seeing the totality displayed in this way was curiously satisfying.

"It's pleasing to the eye," she conceded. "Like the pattern of seeds on a leaf."

"Oh, it's far simpler than that," Zak replied. "I can characterize it very easily. Suppose you travel three hundred spans shomal or junub from the Null Line. The weight there will be one vazn, back toward the Null Line. If you travel twice as far, the weight will be two vazn; three times as far, three vazn; and so on, in proportion to the distance.

"If you travel garm or sard instead, your weight will point *away* from the Null Line, and it will grow three times as fast. You only need to go one hundred spans before it reaches one vazn."

"What if you travel in none of those directions?" Roi gestured at the map. "The weight twists around. It's no longer so simple."

"It remains simple," Zak insisted, "if you know one more trick. Think of weight as a line, as it is on this map. Put aside for a moment the length and direction of that line, and ask instead for its extent along two axes: shomal-junub, and garm-sard. However far you are shomal or junub of the Null Line determines the weight line's extent along the shomal-junub axis. However far you are garm or sard determines its extent along the garm-sard axis. That's all you need to know in order to draw the line. Its extent in each direction has a simple prescription, and that fixes the line as a whole."

Roi absorbed this, then re-examined the map, which seemed to bear out Zak's claim. But if his recipe for combining the effect of travel in different directions seemed simple enough to be inevitable, it was the basic ingredients that now struck her as puzzling. Why did being garm or sard of the Null Line add three times more to your weight than being shomal or junub? Why not four times, or five? And why did "garm-sard weight" push you away from the Null Line, while "shomal-junub weight" pulled you back to it? She couldn't even guess at the answers, but she could understand now why Zak was pursuing this strange, lonely task. These patterns demanded an explanation.

"When you find what you're looking for," she said, "I hope to hear of it."

The shadow of Zak's heart grew visibly faster, as if she'd hefted a large rock on to his carapace. He said, "Why not help me in my search?"

Roi looked around again, but he was still alone. Did he honestly believe he could recruit her, unaided? She said, "I've told you the work I do."

"I don't expect you to leave your team," he replied.

"That's wise of you." Roi felt a stab of pity for him, followed by a treacherous thrill of disloyalty. It wouldn't have been the worst fate in the world if Zak had had forty team-mates waiting to ambush her, a throng of eccentric questioners to lure her away from the worthy monotony of the crops.

"What I'm asking won't interfere with your work. I only want you to take some measurements, as you travel around the edge."

"Measurements?"

"To confirm the weights." Zak began rolling up the map. "I have no idea who drew this. I can only guess about the scales they used to represent distances and weights. And what if it's not accurate? I can't just take it on faith! Even if it was correct when it was drawn, what if something has changed since then?"

Roi was still trying to wrap her mind around the notion of a solo, partial recruitment, but this last comment electrified her. "Someone told me a story once," she said, "about the weights growing stronger."

"So strong that they tore the world to pieces. Hence our name for what remains."

Roi said, "Do you believe that's true?"

Zak hesitated. "Who can say? Maybe it's simply in our nature to imagine a larger, more glorious world in the past. To console ourselves, as we confront our limitations, with the idea that we were once part of something greater."

Roi joked, "I think I'd find more consolation by imagining a larger world *in the future*."

Zak took her words perfectly seriously. "Exactly, but how? Should we hope to catch up with our mythical cousins who went tumbling away into the Incandescence?"

This was becoming too strange for Roi. "You said something about measurements."

"Yes." Zak opened his carapace again, and removed a long tube wrought from susk cuticle. As he offered it to her, the shifting light revealed a coil of metal inside, with a small, smooth stone attached to the end of it.

Roi took it, trying not to show her astonishment at how casually he was handing over this extraordinary device. "See the numbers carved along the side?" Zak asked her.

"Yes."

"The greater the weight, the further the spring stretches."

"Of course." That principle was clear, but how would she measure the exact direction? There were a number of slender rods lying against the side of the tube; Roi tugged gently on one of them, and it unfolded into a spindly leg. There were three legs, and a system of shorter rods as well.

"You need to take sights of some reference points," Zak explained. "And then record the angles between the legs and the weight tube."

"This is beginning to sound complicated."

In fact, it was beginning to sound like work. What she felt about Zak's plans, though, was nothing at all like the buzz of camaraderie. He wasn't competing with her team; he was offering her something entirely different.

"You only have to record a few numbers," Zak assured her. "I'm not asking you to do any of the calculations."

He set up the tripod and demonstrated. There were navigation signs painted on the walls of all the main tunnels at regular intervals, and Zak had devised a set of rules for choosing points on them to orient the apparatus.

"You should ask some members of the signage teams," Roi suggested. "They go everywhere."

"I did. They refused."

When she'd completed a successful measurement for herself, Roi folded up the device and stored it in her fallow right cavity, along with a roll of skin for recording the results.

They parted, promising each other that they'd meet in the same place after thirty-six shifts.

As Roi searched for a resting spot, the encounter began to seem increasingly remote and implausible, as if she'd heard about it from a friend of a friend, not experienced it for herself. Zak had spoken of plans to look for other helpers, but she didn't think much of his chances. Even now, her own conviction that she could spare the time to indulge in this charming, pointless activity was beginning to waver. Then again, she was tired, and even the thought of tending the crops with her team-mates made her feel weary.

She found an empty crevice near the end of the tunnel, and slid into the welcoming fissure. She could still hear the constant susurration of the wind, but the mass of dense rock behind her was strong enough to divert the flow away from her weathered carapace.

With her eyes pressed against the rock, her vision was filled with a shapeless radiance. Everything in the Splinter glowed with the warmth of the Incandescence; sheltered or not, she was always bathed in that same light.

Roi relaxed and let her eyes grow unresponsive. The radiance began to fade, dissolving into a colorless absence. Images of the weeds she'd sought throughout her shift marched across the emptiness. Then her body became numb, and her mind quiet.

3

Csi had organized the departure, designing a scape to suit the occasion with versions tailor-made for every participant. Rakesh found himself on an ocean-going vessel some fifty meters long, surrounded as far as the eye could see by heavy, gray-green seas. The sky was cloudless, but the sun was low and the wind relentless. There were five other people assembled on the deck: Parantham, Csi, Viya, and two old friends of Parantham, Jafar and Renu.

"We are gathered here to bid farewell to Rakesh and Parantham," Csi declaimed, "who have heard the song of the sirens, and decided, against all of our wise counsel, to follow it." Parantham smiled, perhaps at the very same reference; her own cultural background was such a mosaic that the human legend was probably just as meaningful to her as any alternative.

Rakesh tried to stay focused on the details of Csi's parting gift. The timber beneath his feet was warped, as if by decades of humidity. The salt in the air was pungent. The bodily parameters that he'd ceded to his friend's design guaranteed that the relentless swaying of the deck left him mildly queasy. All this theater was not so much a distraction as an adornment, refracting the strange truth of the event without ever trying to conceal it.

Rakesh had not anticipated how hard it would be to cut his ties and move on. When he'd left Shab-e-Noor, his home world, he'd been preparing for a thousand years. Since his youth it had been his plan to remain in the local system for no more than a millennium, and by the time the self-imposed deadline approached all his family and friends were convinced of his sincerity and had worked to make things easier. Even so, the wrenching feeling that came from the realization that one step would separate him from everyone he knew—for at least six times longer than he'd known them—had been almost unbearable. It was like marching into a white-hot furnace and being seared to the bone, losing every nerve ending, every connection, every link to the world outside his skull.

The first node he'd reached had been three thousand light years away. He'd jumped again, twice, almost immediately, after finding that nearly everyone he met had either come directly from his home world, or had visited it not long before. At the third node, in contrast, the intersecting currents of travelers had seemed thoroughly cosmopolitan, rich with complex histories and anecdotes ready to be mined.

So he'd stayed, but he'd kept himself suitably aloof, eschewing all but the most pragmatic associations, priding himself on his readiness to depart in an instant with no goodbyes. If even one in a thousand of the travelers passing through had come from a place worth visiting, he'd reasoned, it would not take long to choose a destination.

In a sense that premise had been true, but many people were returning from ageless spectacles that Rakesh had known of since childhood. Whether it was a million-year-old jungle, the immaculately preserved city of an ancestral civilization, or some delicately beautiful nebula, detailed images had already reached Shab-e-Noor long before his birth. Witnessing such sights firsthand rather than in a scape might merit a local planetary hop, but not the burning of millennia and his alienation from everything and everyone he'd known.

Other travelers took their chances as they searched for less famous, more transient pleasures. By their very nature, though, such destinations could rarely be shared: after five or ten millennia, the most energetic social or artistic renaissance would certainly have faded. Sometimes the insights of these movements could be passed on, but away from the time and place that had given birth to them, most, far from being potent memes ready to spark new revolutions, were uninspiring. Rakesh hadn't traveled thousands of light years to return home with a handful of bland, second-hand slogans.

Eventually, he'd settled into a state somewhere between cynical resignation and injured bemusement. A logical strategy might have been to make the best of the imperfect information flowing through the node to build up a list of promising worlds, and then wait for that list to include a sequence of planets that could be visited efficiently in a single grand tour. Rakesh had known people who'd done just that, and after five or ten years of planning departed happily on a trip that would take them twenty or thirty millennia. He'd toyed with his own lists, and then set them aside. His heart wasn't in it. If he was ever to break free, he needed something more: a penetrating new insight into the intractable theory of travel.

Or, as it turned out, some sheer dumb luck.

"By your own free choice, you are abandoning your loyal companions for this dangerous folly," Csi announced dryly, "so all we can offer you in return are these talismans to help you on your way."

From an ornate chest sitting on the deck beside him, Csi extracted two weighty metal chains. With Viya's help, he tied one around Rakesh's upper body, while Jafar and Renu did the same for Parantham.

Two robust, seasoned-looking planks lay on the deck, neatly slotted through a convenient gap below the guard rail to protrude over the edge. Rakesh supposed they might have been carried on ships like this for the sake of repairs. That prospect struck him as somewhat cheerier than if they'd been brought along with only their present purpose in mind.

Parantham shot him an amused look and casually hefted herself over the guard rail. Rakesh clambered over more cautiously, then crouched down to lower his center of mass, wondering at the overpowering need he felt to keep his balance and stay out of the ocean until the very end.

He couldn't turn his head far enough to face the people watching from the deck, but he called back to them, "Don't think we'll never cross paths again. It's a small galaxy, and I plan to be in it for a very long time."

Viya laughed. "Is that a threat of retribution, from the mouth of Davy Jones's locker?"

Rakesh held up a length of the iron chain to demonstrate how loosely it was tied, and rattled it dismissively. "You think this is enough to hold me down? You should know I studied under Houdini!" The ship lurched abruptly, almost toppling him. He managed to steady himself, but his heart was pounding.

While Rakesh was still inching his way forward, Parantham marched to the end of her plank. Watching her poised swaying at the edge made his stomach clench. Embodied on his home world, he'd dived into water from greater heights than this, but never from such an unsteady platform. Parantham was a native of scapespace; no doubt she was imbued with her own kind of innate prudence against physical damage whenever she was embodied, and no doubt Csi had done his best to make her experience memorably intense, but even if she was perceiving an identical scape, they were not quite together in any of this.

Parantham turned her whole body around to face the deck, but she still had to shout over the wind. "Jafar, Renu, Viya, Csi. I'll never forget your friendship. Be sure that I'm happy and certain in my choice. I hope you all find freedom, and I hope it is as sweet as this." In one fluid movement she turned back to the ocean, bent her knees, leaned forward, and dived.

Rakesh watched as she disappeared beneath the foaming water. He was shivering now. He lifted himself up to his full height and walked forward unsteadily, as rapidly as he could. Maybe Parantham had felt something close to pure exhilaration at her departure, but he couldn't, and he didn't want it that way.

He stopped a few centimeters short of the edge and turned slightly, spreading his legs to brace himself.

"To travel is to die? I won't argue with that." The wind seemed to swallow his words, but he didn't really care if he was audible or not. Over the last few days he'd made his peace individually with everyone in the node that he'd been close to. Let them violate the physics of the scape to hear him, if it really mattered. "I've died once before, and I've lived almost a century in this second incarnation. It was a strange, frustrating, maddening existence. You made it bearable, and I'm grateful for that, but don't ever forget why you died the first time. When you get the chance, move on to the next life."

Rakesh took a step forward and gazed down at the waves. He stretched out his arms and dived.

The fall must have taken at least a couple of seconds, but rather than his mind going into slow motion he hit the water with the sense that he'd had no time to ponder its approach. The impact came as a bracing jolt to his body, but not an unfamiliar one. It took another few seconds for the effect of the chain to penetrate his consciousness; he had certainly slowed down once he entered the water, but he possessed no buoyancy, and he was not showing any sign of coming to a halt.

Snatches of sound that might have been distorted singing flowed into Rakesh's skull through the bones of his clenched jaw. He opened his eyes and saw a dozen luminescent blue shapes in the water below: delicate, veiled forms rising up to meet him. Were there sirens here after all, mythical creatures made real to ease his passage?

He fell past them. They were giant jellyfish, propelling themselves along by squirting water from bladders with a flatulent squeak.

Rakesh wondered bleakly just how far Csi wanted to twist the knife. He contemplated deserting the scape to step across the light years in a manner of his own choosing: something involving a stroll across soft grass on a warm day.

The water was pitch-black now. He had gulped air instinctively before submerging, but just how long that lungful would last was entirely in Csi's hands. A mild unpleasantness at the back of his mind was becoming an insistent choking feeling, and his ears were aching from the pressure. He probably could have untangled himself from the chain and made it back to the surface before losing consciousness, but there was no point remaining in the scape at all unless he played along with the scenario, right to the end.

A smudge of silver light appeared beneath him, and Rakesh used what strength he had to swim, or at least steer his fall, toward it. As it grew closer, he suffered a dizzying shift of scale; what had seemed like a small glowing benthic creature was a patch of sea floor twenty or thirty meters wide, strewn with scores of individual white lights.

He put out his arms as he struck the bottom, jarring his elbows and shoulders, burying his face in sticky mud. He rolled upright, sitting on his haunches, amazed that he still had any strength left. There was a hammering at his throat imploring him to inhale, but he wasn't going to breathe water and pull down the curtain prematurely.

As the silt around him settled Rakesh rose to his feet. The white lights scattered across the sea floor were piles of bones. Some were more or less whole human skeletons, others were jumbled assortments of parts. Some bacterial infestation had rendered them all phosphorescent as they decayed.

He must have begun to vocalize something, because he found salt water suddenly burning his nostrils and palate, as if he'd taken a heedless preparatory breath. He rapidly forgot whatever curse he'd been aiming at Csi, and fought desperately to get the water into his stomach instead of his lungs.

As he forced down the mouthful of brine, he felt something hard and smooth under his tongue. He clamped his hand to his mouth and managed to expel the thing without admitting any more water. He didn't need to hold it up to the ghost light to know what it was; his fingertips told him. It was the glass key that Lahl had given him.

And here it opened... what?

Rakesh crouched down and groped through the mud. What had Csi planted? A treasure chest? That might be worth searching for, so long as it contained an oxygen tank and not a pile of worthless coins.

He rose to his feet again and looked around at the graveyard of failed divers. If there was any logic to this macabre metaphor, surely some of them had come close to the prize, even if they'd been unable to unlock it.

Blood was pounding in his ears. Overlaid on a random scatter of remains, there seemed to be a group concentrated on a spot about fifteen meters away.

Rakesh slogged his way toward the hillock of bones. It would have been nice to have Parantham's help at this point, but she seemed to have landed elsewhere, or been shunted right out of his version of the scenario.

As he waded in among the ribs and tibias, he felt a pang of desolation.

What were these corpses to Csi? Hopes? Friendships? After nearly twice as long in the node as Rakesh, Csi was still stranded.

Without leaving the scape, Rakesh spawned an insentient messenger who'd visit Csi after a week had passed and hand him a copy of the key. For all the scorn and derision he'd heaped upon the sirens' call, there was a chance that after a few days' reflection Csi might change his mind and decide to follow them.

His conscience salved, Rakesh put aside his squeamishness and dived into the graveyard of travelers' ambitions. His skull was bursting, but he was determined to find the tin box with the treasure map, or whatever Csi's wry punchline was, before he surrendered consciousness.

His fingers hit metal. Jubilantly, he moved his hands apart to try to span the edges, but the surface just went on and on. The treasure chest was more like a vault, at least a few meters wide.

He probed the metal beneath the mound of bones, scanning back and forth with his fingertips. Streaks of light flashed behind his eyes, followed like thunder by a bludgeoning pain. Finally he held out the key itself and scraped it blindly over the vault's unyielding surface.

Something gave, and his hand moved. Probably the key had just slipped. Rakesh waggled it, disbelieving. It had entered a keyhole, and it fitted snugly.

He tried to plow some of the mound aside, but he soon gave up. He doubted that he'd have the strength to lift the vault's huge door even if he could clear it first. Still, there was something satisfying about getting this far. Let Csi paint his not-quite-triumphant skeleton into the scape and leave it as a signpost for the next traveler.

He turned the key, and felt a click.

The door dropped away beneath him. Mud, bones, Rakesh, and a geyser of water erupted from an opening in the floor of the ocean, into an endless space full of stars.

4

The sense of attachment Roi felt toward her work team had never been a constant, unwavering force. Even in the absence of recruitment efforts it rose and fell, following its own internal rhythm. So it was only when it had reached one of its peaks and she felt confident that her loyalty could survive a few missed shifts that she decided to take a break and travel to the Null Line.

Zak had invited her to come and see his "contraptions" as soon as she'd handed him her first batch of weight measurements, and each time since then when they'd met he'd reminded her that she was welcome to visit, though he'd never made her feel that she was under any pressure. It was, of course, conceivable that he had a team waiting at the Null Line ready to enact a full-blown recruitment, but Roi had made a point of quizzing people for any news they'd heard from the Calm, and she'd turned up no evidence of any such threat. It was hard to believe that an entire team indulging in activity as strange as Zak's could have escaped notice. For a lone, unrecruited person to behave oddly was only to be expected.

When Zak had first invited her, she'd told him an old joke: the easy way to reach the Null Line from the garm quarter was to travel to the shomal quarter, and from there the journey would be downhill all the way. Rather than expressing amusement or irritation, Zak had responded by showing her yet another of his maps.

"These lines are paths that lead neither up nor down," he'd explained. "I call them 'levels'. I've arranged their spacing so that climbing from one level to the next is an equal effort in each case. Counting the lines to be crossed will tell you how much work any journey requires."

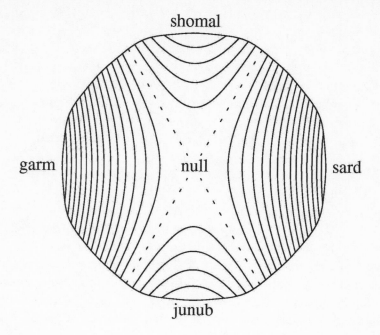

shomal

garm   null   sard

junub

In fact, counting the lines told Roi nothing new; the whole point of the joke was that everyone knew it would take at least as much effort to reach the shomal quarter from the garm as to travel to the Null Line itself. Still, the map made this fact clear at a glance, because the Null Line was *level with* the boundary between the quarters.

Zak insisted that he'd drawn this second map, not by laboriously measuring the weight lines on the first map and marking off increments of effort, but by a kind of reasoning that started with the underlying mathematical rule that described the pattern of weights, and led to a new rule describing the shape and spacing of these levels. Roi was astonished, but when she'd asked for more details she'd found his explanation impenetrable. "When you come to the Calm, when you have time to ponder these ideas at leisure, it will all make sense," he'd promised.

Roi planned the journey to take twelve shifts in all: four spent traveling up to the Null Line, five visiting Zak, and three for the easier return leg. She'd been with the team long enough for an absence like this to be acceptable; everybody needed to recuperate sometimes, and travel was a common form of recreation. If it also made you vulnerable to recruitment, the unspeakable truth was that a certain amount of turnover kept the teams fresh, and if a tired or restless worker was ambushed it was not the end of the world.

It was easy to ponder these matters as abstractions, but when Roi woke in the shelter of her crevice and faced the reality of setting out in the opposite direction to all of her team-mates, she realized that she'd chosen the hardest time to leave. By the end of each shift she craved solitude, but on waking all she could think about was company and cooperation. She'd made no close friends in this team, but that wasn't the point: it gave her the same sense of accomplishment to work beside the most taciturn stranger as it did beside someone sociable and garrulous whose history she knew inside-out. Work was work; everything else was superfluous chatter, however delightful that could be.

As she eased herself out of her resting place, she resolved to follow her plan regardless. The more difficult it was to begin the journey, the more she would feel reassured that her attachment to the team was secure.

Zak had given her a series of maps that showed the way between their usual meeting place and a rendezvous point that he'd chosen near the Null Line. Roi had decided not to follow his suggested route precisely; whether she trusted him or not, it would be more enjoyable to take a few detours and keep the journey unpredictable. She'd been in the Calm a few times, and had even worked for a while in the sard quarter, but Zak's haunts were further rarb along the Null Line than she'd ever gone, and there would be plenty of territory along the way that she'd never seen before.

In the first tunnel she entered, she encountered a crowd of workers descending for the start of their shifts. She deferred to their numbers and climbed along the matted ceiling, trying to exhibit an uncomplicated purposefulness with her gait even as she struggled to keep her footing. The tangle of vegetation seemed imbued with malice; among the crops at the edge the same weeds would be proliferating luxuriantly in the unfiltered wind, and she would not be there to keep them in check. Five of her team-mates passed her below, oblivious to her presence. She was alone and useless; no wonder she was invisible to them.

What was she doing? Taking a rest. Satisfying her curiosity. Scratching an itch so she could keep on working, with all the more energy and dedication.

Taking a rest, and walking into an ambush. Zak was probably just the healthiest member of his team, the only one who still possessed enough strength to travel deep into the garm quarter. Once Roi arrived in his territory all the others would float around her, weakened and deformed by their countless shifts of weightlessness, ready to induct her into their deranged schemes.

The crowd below her thinned, but the anxieties and self-accusations kept coming. *She was a traitor, an unrecruitable freak. She would bring on a famine with her selfishness and perversity.* Roi didn't argue with any of it. She just stared straight ahead and kept moving.

The tunnel led into a chamber that was almost empty, except for a group of children playing with their tutors. Roi kept her distance, still feeling guilty and tainted, not wanting to infect these young minds with her treachery. Listening to their exuberant shouts, though, began to lift her spirits. Everyone remembered stumbling into a team like this: their first ever recruitment. She now knew that hatchlings rarely spent more than eight or nine shifts wandering and grazing alone before finding a group of willing tutors, but in her memory it was as if an eternity of desperate searching had preceded that first moment of fulfillment.

Watching the children mimicking pointless, stylized poses and movements for the sheer joy of acting in unison, Roi began to feel, paradoxically, more at ease with her own truancy. The simple truth was that there would always be a team somewhere that would welcome her. She fervently hoped that she would return safely to tend the crops again, but whatever changes her journey wrought, the sight of these contented infants seemed like a promise that there would always be a place for her in the world.

The chamber opened into a larger space, where susk and murche were grazing. The adult susk were about half Roi's size, with a general body shape very much like a person's, each male having six ordinary limbs while the females carried an extra, shorter pair for mating. From certain angles they looked eerily like children. They even made a range of plaintive sounds, scraping their limbs against the underside of their carapace just like an inconsolable child. The murche, in contrast, were barely the size of Roi's claws, and swarmed around the field on twelve busy legs. If the crops ever failed, Roi decided, she would have no qualms about eating them.

Herders moved quietly among the flock, gently encouraging them to graze on the plants that people found least palatable. Roi had heard it claimed that the best herders controlled the susk by a process akin to recruitment. The murche ate what they pleased, but fortunately that included susk droppings.

The ground here was tiered, rising up in small steps along countless jagged edges. To Roi it looked as if one large, continuous sheet of rock had come crashing down, with pieces breaking off the edge where it collided at an angle with whatever lay beneath it. The marks of this kind of violence could be found everywhere, but Roi had never seen the ground fall. If the Splinter really had been torn from a larger world—and if weight had always grown with distance—that world might have encompassed more powerful forces than any to be found in the present.

If all of this was true, though, how had that mother world itself come to

be? That was the trouble with any question about the history of things:
how could you ever reach an end to it?

The wind was brisk, but it blew from behind her as she climbed the steps
of the field. The light from the rock ahead of her was a gentle glow; she
was leaving the raw intensity of the garm-sharq edge behind.

Roi had grown hungry, so she surveyed the area ahead of her for food,
and finally settled on a solid patch of kahu to munch on. As she ate, two
of the herders approached, unaccompanied by any susk.

"To your life and strength," each bid her encouragingly.

"And yours." Roi watched them warily as they ate beside her. If they
wanted a new team-mate, she was outnumbered and surrounded, with
nowhere to run.

"What do you do?" one of the herders inquired.

"I tend the crops at the edge."

"Valuable work."

"As is yours."

"Where are you headed?" the other asked.

"To the Calm."

"That's a long journey."

Roi said, "I need to spend a few shifts seeing the world. It will make
me a better worker."

Both herders chewed on this in silence for a while.

"Travel safely," said the first, moving away, firing a pellet of faeces deftly
into a clump of weeds.

"Thank you."

The second herder lingered. "Work is what makes better workers," he
opined.

"Perhaps," Roi replied.

He rasped disapproval, but followed his team-mate.

Upon leaving the field, Roi came across a series of chambers where teams
worked to render susk carcasses into a variety of products. The soft skin
that lined the internal cavities made an ideal surface on which to write
and draw. The hard cuticle of the carapace was tough and durable, but
when soaked in plant extracts it could be softened enough to work into
different shapes. Some inner organs were edible, and Roi saw a couple of
workers consuming them fresh from the carcass, but most were dissolved
and processed into inks and paints, glues and resins, specialized plant
foods, medicines, and an assortment of unappealing liquids and powders
and gums whose purpose she didn't feel inclined to inquire about.

The end result of Roi's labor spread naturally throughout the garmside
as seeds on the wind, but these products required teams dedicated to

their transport. As she passed the processing chambers, Roi saw couriers coming and going, traveling in twos or threes depending on the size of their load. Roi introduced herself to one pair, Zud and Sia, who were hauling a cart packed with diverse products that had been ordered by a depot almost halfway to the Calm.

"How long will it take you to make the delivery?" Roi asked. Despite their burden, they were easily matching her pace as they ascended a steep tunnel.

"The cargo will be there in two shifts," Zud replied, "but we won't take it all the way ourselves. Our highest depot is less than one shift away; we only work between there and the edge."

"We're used to the range of weights," Sia added. "It's easier than trying to work everywhere."

Roi felt no sense of threat from this pair; their team-mates were widely scattered, and given the nature of their work it seemed likely that they encountered travelers far too often to treat them all as potential recruits.

She asked them what news they'd heard from the Calm.

"The food supply's been low," Sia said.

"But the reservoir's healthy," Roi protested.

"Perhaps there's an excess of mouths," Zud suggested. "Though we're bringing them a remedy for that." It took a moment before Roi realized what he meant; as well as susk products, they were carrying a stack of contraceptive leaves. The plant that produced them was a variety that could only grow in a strong, nutrient-rich wind. Since she was traveling downwind as well as up into the Calm, she was heading for the most barren part of the Splinter. She should stock up next time she had the chance.

"Any other news?" she asked. "No word of new work teams?"

"New teams?" Zud sounded baffled.

Roi couldn't think of an easy way to characterize the notion of a team of which Zak might be a member. "Doing new jobs. Jobs you'd never heard of before."

Without breaking his pace, Zud diverted three legs to a drumbeat of amusement. "Jobs I'd never heard of? Jobs someone made up from thin air?"

In the face of such mirth from a team-mate, Roi's habit was to retreat graciously into silence, but in her new role as a traveler she felt emboldened. "Do you think every job we do now always existed?"

"They're all necessary," Sia said. "If there ever was a time when they weren't being done, it would have been disastrous."

"They're all *useful*," Roi countered. "But we might have done something different in the past, to meet the same needs. Or our needs might have been different."

"Different *needs?*" Zud had a way of making her perfectly reasonable conjectures sound like oxymorons.

"Is your cargo the same for every trip?"

"Of course not," Sia replied. "But it doesn't change so much that you could say our job has changed. And it all evens out in the long run."

"What if there's a serious famine? Then my own job would certainly change: I'd have to keep people from storming the reservoir."

Sia disagreed. "It's still the same basic function: keeping the food supply healthy and intact, whether it's saving it from mites, or from starving hordes."

Roi was exasperated. "What if the ground fell? What if tunnels collapsed? What if the world was ripped in two? Would that be enough to change anything?"

Both her companions fell silent. Roi couldn't decide whether they were tacitly conceding the argument, or whether she'd offended them by speaking so forcefully. Perhaps she'd overstepped the mark.

After a while, Sia explained gently, as if to a child, "Life is hard, things aren't perfect. So we speak of living in a broken world. It doesn't mean that the Splinter was really part of something larger that was literally torn apart. That's just a story, Roi. The world has always been this way, and it always will be."

Roi stayed with the couriers until they reached their depot, then she looked around for a place to rest. She was as tired as she'd ever been after a shift at the edge; even with nothing to carry, she had found it hard work keeping up with Zud and Sia, who were used to following a tight schedule and completing the ascent in a fixed time. The wind was already so much weaker than she was accustomed to that she felt no need to hunt for a sheltering lode; she simply slipped into the first empty crevice she found, and shut off her vision.

Upon waking, Roi's first thought was that *she didn't understand the wind.* In the garmside, it blew in from the Incandescence at the sharq edge and battered its way through the porous rock of the Splinter, finally escaping at the opposite edge. In the sardside, the flow was reversed. Between these opposing winds lay the Calm. The pattern of the wind was somehow related to the pattern of weights, but the nature of the connection was far from obvious: the wind certainly didn't blow the way things fell. The Null Line lay in the middle of the Calm, but the Calm extended far beyond it, encompassing a whole plane that stretched out in the shomal and junub directions, as well as the Null Line's rarb and sharq.

Roi roused herself and resolved to make an early start, all the sooner to discuss this problem with Zak.

Even here, her cycle seemed to be synchronized with many of the locals, but the workers heading for their shifts inspired no feelings of guilt in her. The softness of the light made everything seem slightly unreal, until she made a conscious effort to adjust her vision; she'd accommodated to the change as she'd traveled, but on waking she'd reverted out of habit to the minimal sensitivity more suited to the edge.

There was a pattern to the light too, of course. It seemed only reasonable that everything should be brightest where the wind from the Incandescence struck the Splinter with the greatest force, though she'd heard that the sard-rarb edge was not as bright as the garm-sharq. Was the wind there weaker, or was there another reason? Perhaps Zak would follow up his survey of weights with one of wind, and another of light.

As she continued her ascent, Roi pictured the levels of Zak's map embedded in the world around her, a succession of intangible layers to be crossed before her journey could end. She wasn't carrying a copy of that map, but from her memory of it she could imagine herself picking up pace, each step carrying her further than the last as the burden of weight gradually eased.

Near the end of the second shift, Roi came across a work team taking metal from a vein in the rock. The vein ran neatly along the wall of a chamber, although it was possible that this team, or their predecessors, had shaped the chamber expressly for the purpose of extraction.

The exposed vein made a striking sight. Metal shone with an eerie uniformity that made it unlike any other substance Roi knew: it was impossible to discern any structure within it, or even behind it. If people's carapaces had been made of metal, their inner organs would have been completely invisible, reducing their appearance to an inscrutable surface sheen.

The team was using an assortment of tools to prise the metal from one end of the vein. Roi could see a long, empty cavity extending away from the point where they were working, a roughly hemicylindrical indentation colored with vegetation that grew thicker with distance. There must have been a time when the whole formation had glistened with metal, and perhaps there'd be a time when the entire vein would be empty. People diligently scavenged the rare material, but that never seemed to be enough to fill the need.

There were people who insisted that these veins replenished themselves, by some process too slow for anyone to witness, rendering any shortage a temporary inconvenience. Roi was skeptical about that theory, but even more so about the supposed corollary. Plants were undeniably replenished by the wind, but if the wind carried metal into the Splinter not only was the process too slow to witness, it was too slow to be of any use.

If metal didn't grow from the rock like a weed, though, then there must have been a time when nobody had been extracting it. Regardless of the certainties Zud and Sia had expressed, there must have been a time when no one had heard of such a team.

How long could that time have lasted? There had to be some limit to how long the metal could have lain untouched in the rock before someone had realized how to make use of it. Perhaps a thousand generations, perhaps a million, but the era in which people had failed to use metal could not stretch back forever.

So, what had come before that? If metal couldn't grow, the vein itself must have always been there.

Which meant there must have been a time when there were no people at all.

Early in the third shift of her journey, Roi stopped near a fork in the tunnel and took a weight measurement. The navigation sign told her the lengths of the tunnel's three branches, and where they led. Her measurement told her that she was slightly more than halfway to the Null Line.

At first she thought this meant that she was roughly on schedule, but on reflection she realized that the news was far better: by Zak's count of levels crossed, she was well ahead. She reviewed the maps Zak had given her to guide her to their meeting place. She'd wandered away from his suggested route, but she wasn't far off course. She set off again with her energy redoubled.

Though her eyes were adapting to the ever softer light, they couldn't render the change imperceptible. Roi was used to the rock around her being noticeably brighter when she looked in the garm-sharq direction, with a characteristic drop in intensity as she turned away from that all-pervading beacon. Here, the distinction had become much subtler, and every contrast that depended on it was equally diminished. It was not that people or plants had ceased coloring and complicating the light, but many of the cues she had grown accustomed to were missing. When her team-mates working in the crops came to the edge of a field and changed direction, she could see patches of brightness temporarily imprinted on their carapaces, a record of their earlier orientation that took a few heartbeats to fade.

The vegetation was unmistakably sparser now, but so were the people. Roi could see none of the signs of a serious food shortage, such as unpalatable plants lying around half-eaten; desperate people would chew on anything, but most weeds tasted so bad that it was impossible to swallow them. She had to stay alert to spot enough food for herself, but that was only to be expected when she was moving through unfamiliar territory, away from the abundance she was used to.

As the shift wore on, the pleasant buoyancy she'd felt since the halfway mark began to mutate into something disconcerting. It was no longer just implausibly easy to ascend a steep tunnel; she noticed herself beginning to grip the floor by making her claws adhere slightly, in the same way she would grip the ceiling in order to walk upside-down. Sometimes her lightness even felt like the product of an upward force, the pull of an invisible assailant opposing her weight and attempting to dislodge her. When this happened she'd freeze on the spot, waiting for the bizarre tugging sensation to subside.

She was not yet in the Calm as cartographers defined it, but the air was still and silent to the limits of her senses. The tunnels were not quite barren or deserted, but the flatness of the light magnified the sense of solitude and rarefaction.

As Roi encountered strangers, usually in twos and threes, she greeted them and tried to guess their purpose. Few people stayed long in the Calm. Couriers and other travelers passed through by necessity, and the sick and injured sometimes spent time close to the Null Line in the hope that the conditions there would speed their recovery. The couriers crossing between the quarters were easy to identify, and she met one male limping along with a gash across his side, but many of the travelers remained difficult to categorize. No doubt some were briefly escaping their own work teams and had decided to experience the restorative powers of the region, or even just its novelty. In one small chamber she saw a trio of youths simply playing, clambering around on the ceiling and then releasing their hold and slowly drifting down.

As she approached the rendezvous point, Roi began to wonder how she might locate Zak, given that she'd be arriving a full shift earlier than he was expecting her. Despite having started the journey doubting the motives behind his invitation, she was eager to see him now, and she couldn't bear the thought of merely killing time while she waited.

When she passed through the intersection he'd nominated she was unsurprised to find it deserted. She traveled to the far end of the tunnel along which she'd approached, then doubled back and explored each of the cross branches. There was no one in sight.

She took out the last of the guide maps that Zak had given her. The invisible abstraction of the Null Line was clearly marked, and a chamber that it crossed was just a few dozen spans away. Roi knew that Zak wasn't here for his health; he'd admitted to her that his prolonged stay had actually weakened him. However, he claimed that the absence of weight simplified his search for its nature and origins, which sounded as paradoxical to Roi as striving to learn about the lives of susk by making sure that none of the creatures were around to distract you. Knowing Zak, merely being close to the line of weightlessness would not be enough for him. Whatever he was measuring, he would be measuring at the Null Line itself.

Roi headed for the chamber.

As she approached the entrance, her eyes caught a faint glint of metal, and she thought there might be a vein running along the far wall. After a few more steps, though, she realized that the perspective was wrong. A strand of metal, much thinner than any vein, ran through the middle of the chamber, far from any of the walls.

She reached the entrance and looked around. A fine web of the same material criss-crossed the chamber, supporting the central thread. Anchored at points in the web were various small, intricate devices; at this distance she couldn't hope to fathom their detailed construction, let alone their purpose.

Suddenly she noticed a figure moving across the far wall. Maybe Zak had been resting in a crevice, or perhaps she'd simply been slow to spot him in the chamber's uniform light.

Roi drummed out a greeting with all the legs she could spare without losing her grip. Zak didn't reply, and for a moment she thought he hadn't heard her. Then he sprung into the air and floated gracefully across the chamber toward her. As he approached, Roi saw that he'd given himself a slight spin, and it was soon apparent that this was not an accident but a carefully judged manoeuvre, because he landed nimbly beside her.

"Welcome to the Null Line," he said. "How was your journey?"

"Safe and happy. I'm sorry I'm early."

"Don't apologize! I'm glad to see you. We have a thousand things to discuss."

Roi had never seen him so excited, and she wasn't prepared to flatter herself into thinking it was due solely to her arrival. She said, "You've found something, haven't you? Something simple?"

Zak hesitated. "Perhaps. I've discovered something interesting. But there's a problem as well."

"What have you found?"

"I think I can explain the weights on the map," he said. "I think I've made sense of the pattern."

"How?" Roi was elated. She had suspected that he would succeed eventually, but she'd never imagined it would come so quickly.

"That will take some care to explain properly," Zak said. "You'll have to be patient with me."

"Of course. But…"

"How can there be a problem, if I've done what I say I've done?"

"Yes."

Zak said, "It's beginning to look as if the map is wrong. I think I can explain the weights on the map, but I don't think the map matches up with reality."

5

Twelve thousand years after walking the plank, Rakesh woke on the floor of his tent. He was lying face-down on a blue and gold sleeping mat; he drew in a deep breath to savor the rich scent of its fibers. This was the tent he'd carried with him on all his travels on Shab-e-Noor, and it remained with him wherever he went. His first sight upon waking after any journey was the interior of this elegant cocoon.

He rolled on to his back and gazed up at the apex. As he moved, his joints and muscles felt subtly different than they had back in the node; a proprioceptive cue he'd chosen to let him know when he was not embodied was unmistakably absent now. It was both disturbing and exhilarating to be reminded that this was the first time since he'd left home that he'd taken on material form. Instead of being software linked into a scape, his body—and his tent—had been built to order by this planet's machinery, and left to engage with the physical world. He held a hand up in front of his face; there was no difference to be seen, but when he turned his palm away the tendons in his forearms repeated the message.

Dawn was still a couple of hours away, but the finely woven mesh of the tent's fabric admitted a tantalizing blue-white sheen. It was like the starlight he'd seen before falling asleep while traveling on his home world, except that this light was brighter. Shab-e-Noor's sky was a blaze of spectacular globular clusters. Rakesh tried for a moment to picture the stars that could outshine those desert skies at midnight, then gave up and simply willed the tent to reveal them.

He smiled uneasily, dazzled by the beauty at the same time as his chest tightened with a kind of vertigo. The sheer number, density and brightness of the stars were staggering. Perhaps the wisps of ionized gas that shone in the clusters over Shab-e-Noor were more delicately beautiful, but that was like comparing a handful of flowers with a looming forest. The difference in scale was impossible to ignore; anything that was close enough could fill the sky this way, but there was a richness, a detailed, endlessly varying texture to the bulge that no mere cluster could have mimicked. Rakesh had no trouble believing that he was gazing into the heart of the galaxy, an empire of stars twenty thousand light years wide.

He left the tent and looked around for Parantham, but there was no one in sight. He was in the middle of a grassy field, and the only sound he could hear was a nearby stream. He found it easily in the starlight, splashed his face and took a few mouthfuls of sweet, icy water. He had lived embodied for his first thousand years, and the time he'd spent in the scapes of the node had been less than a tenth of that, but the return to the flesh was still disorienting. This body, like the one he'd been born with, was efficient and flexible, with very modest material needs, so being subject to the laws of physics would not amount to much of an inconvenience. Nevertheless, it felt odd to be on such intimate terms with the physical world again, without a single layer of simulation, mediation, or obfuscation. It was like being naked for the first time in a century.

Rakesh called out to Parantham, and she responded with her location: she was in a small town called Faravani, fifteen kilometers away. Rakesh had never traveled the Amalgam's network with a companion before, and it hadn't occurred to him that their transmissions might end up being routed to different locations upon landfall. It was lucky that the planet, Massa, had been able to fulfill their individual requests for congenial environments without putting them on opposite sides of the globe. He could have asked the local transport facility to take him apart and reassemble him in the town, but he was in no hurry. He pocketed the tent, then closed his eyes, pictured his location on a map of the area, and set out on foot.

Tramping across the dew-soaked fields, Rakesh felt a strange pang of homesickness. It wasn't that the smells and sounds of this unfamiliar world evoked any sharp resonance with particular memories, but the simple act of walking a few kilometers through such prosaic terrain in the predawn light was redolent of embodied life. He had walked for pleasure in the scapes of the node, but his surroundings—whether they were spectacular, soothing, or deliberately difficult to traverse—had always been contrived, chosen with a purpose in mind. Taking this mundane, slightly muddy trek just to get from A to B was a quintessentially corporeal experience.

He reached Faravani just after sunrise. Massa had no native life; its first settlers had traveled four thousand light years, from a world that belonged to the P2 panspermia. Most of the locals still wore the ancestral pheno-type, a quadruped with hairless, leathery skin, their backs about as high as Rakesh's chest. They communicated with sounds well within his own range of hearing and vocalization, so he chose to comprehend and speak their language himself, greeting the quads who were emerging from their shelters for some early morning exercise. In the node he'd grown lazy and simply perceived everyone to be speaking in his own tongue, but it was far more satisfying to deal directly with these real-time hisses and clicks, hearing all of the genuine sounds and knowing exactly what they meant, instead of wrapping the whole experience in an auditory hallucination of an approximate translation.

When he met up with Parantham outside the town's guest shelter, he found that she'd gone one step further.

"I see you've made yourself at home," he teased her.

"Flesh is flesh," she hissed through her quad mouth. "The shape makes no difference to me."

Rakesh had perceived her as human-shaped back at the node, but her précis had always made it clear that she possessed no innate somatic self-perception. Born in a scape, descended from software that had ultimately been authored—rather than translated from any kind of organic intel-ligence—she seemed to relate to bodies the way Rakesh did to vehicles.

"So have you picked up any worthwhile gossip yet?" he asked. The whole point of pausing at Massa rather than just routing their transmis-sions straight into the bulge was to find out if anything had happened to the state of play between the Aloof and the Amalgam in the time they'd spent in transit. Rakesh had already asked Massa's planetary library to brief him on any developments, but there'd been nothing on the official record. That included nothing about Lahl's experience, which showed how much the official record was worth.

"I've told everyone in sight that I'm heading into the bulge," she said, "but then all they want to talk about is Leila and Jasim."

Rakesh emitted a quad laugh, which involved more saliva leaving his mouth than he was entirely comfortable with. Leila and Jasim were the pioneers of the bulge. After discovering that it was possible to eavesdrop on the gamma rays spilling out from the Aloof's communications network, and to inject data of their own into the system, they had made the first ever crossing, traveling from Tassef to Massa.

That had been three hundred millennia ago. Since then, though noth-ing had changed in the basic principles, the machinery that bridged the networks had been extensively refined. The bulge was now encircled by gamma ray transmitters that could hit the nodes of the Aloof's network with pinpoint accuracy, and receivers that monitored the small portion of every communications beam that overshot its target node and spilled out of the Aloof's territory into the galactic disk, making it possible to extract the piggybacked data once it reached its destination. And though Lahl had been faced with the choice of traveling unencrypted or taking the slow road, most travelers had been able to avail themselves of quantum keys, stockpiled over the millennia, ready to be used as the need arose.

The Aloof could not have failed to be aware of this blatant technological parasitism, yet they had acted neither to stamp it out, nor to facilitate the process. Rakesh couldn't help admiring the sheer consistency of their response. They had balanced their wish for privacy with a truly cosmic indifference: swatting probes and spores back into the disk without the least sign of impatience or intemperance, and placidly accepting this trickle of foreign data because it was, quite simply, harmless and irrelevant. Whatever their strange arm's-length interaction with Lahl implied, Rakesh was in no rush to mistake it for the start of some larger, more generalized thaw. If history meant anything, the Aloof would be rigidly pursuing the same dictates as ever, and it was only the extraordinarily rare contingency that the DNA-infested meteor represented that had caused them to drag a couple of citizens of the Amalgam in as bit players. That the invitation was a rarity was undeniable, but nothing more could be read into it: there was no evidence that the Aloof's isolation was an act of fanaticism that would only be compromised in the direst of emergencies, or that their contact with Lahl represented some kind of wilting of long-held cultural norms in the face of an otherwise insoluble crisis. The one pattern to the Aloof's actions, in as much as any could be discerned, was that they appeared to make carefully measured responses, designed to meet very clear goals. If recruiting the help of outsiders for the first time in one and a half million years was necessary to meet those goals, why would they hesitate? Stubbornness? Timidity? Inertia? It was comforting to imagine that only such petty and irrational reasons could have caused them to spurn their neighbors for so long, but a far more humbling possibility remained: they had simply never found the Amalgam the least bit useful or relevant before.

Rakesh said, "Are you desperate to move on? Even if there's no news to be found here, it seems a shame to jump planet after just a couple of hours."

Parantham flicked her ears in agreement. "I've never been much of a gratuitous tourist, but after such a long journey we can surely look around." Rakesh was relieved. Though he'd felt as if he'd steeled himself for anything as he'd departed from the node, having just escaped from

Csi's manipulations he was relishing this chance to catch his breath before delivering himself into the hands of the Aloof.

The town of Faravani was a loosely spaced assembly of shelters, gardens and sculptures. Winding between them were swaths of empty land, covered by the same wild vegetation as grew in the surrounding fields. Rather than suggesting a state of decay, though, as if this unkempt space had been neglected or abandoned, it made the more obviously artificial elements of the town look as if they'd been freshly delivered, carefully laid down in a pristine field just a month or two before.

The quads trotted playfully around this maze in groups of three or four, some racing each other, some moving more sedately. Like most citizens of the Amalgam who chose to be embodied, they clearly relished their physicality, with all of the specific abilities and constraints that came with it. Having one kind of body rather than another was a supremely arbitrary choice, but the restrictions it imposed gave a shape to everything you experienced. Early in his third century, Rakesh had played around with different bodies for a while, but wandering through that vastly larger space of possibilities had made him feel like no one at all.

"Don't you get disoriented?" he asked Parantham. "Four legs one day, two the next?" He swung his gaze from shoulder to shoulder, a quad gesture that referred to his own body. "*This* is part of what unifies me, what makes me feel that the person who wakes up every morning is the same as the one who went to sleep."

"I don't actually sleep, Rakesh," she reminded him.

"Well, no, but that's not the point."

She rolled her neck pensively. "I understand what you're talking about: inhabiting a particular kind of body has its own unique flavor. The way the joints and muscles interact, the way all their degrees of freedom are linked together, paints a beautiful shape in phase space. I enjoy exploring those constraints. But I don't need them to be the same for my entire life. They're not part of my identity."

A trio of quads passed them at a gallop, and Parantham took off after them. Rakesh watched, smiling, knowing better than to try to catch up. He felt a fresh pang of homesickness; it would have been nice to have someone in human form to race against.

After a few minutes Parantham circled back to him, breathing heavily, then the three locals joined them and she made introductions. Sida, Fith and Paba had been friends since childhood. They'd traveled the planet together, but they'd never left Massa. When Parantham had mentioned her plans the trio had been intrigued, and they were determined to learn more.

They found a shaded spot in a nearby garden, and the three friends listened attentively as Rakesh described the encounter with Lahl.

When he'd finished, Paba asked, "Why is it so important to you to find this new DNA world?"

"It's not," Rakesh confessed. "Not in itself. I'm not obsessed with my molecular family tree, or with completing the map of the panspermias. If this putative world hadn't been inside the bulge, and if it hadn't been important enough to the Aloof for them to make contact with a traveler just to pass on the news, then I doubt I would have gone looking for it."

Fith said, "So your real interest is a kind of reflection of the Aloof's?"

Rakesh shifted on the grass. "I suppose it is, partly. But I'd never been all that interested in the Aloof before, either. And I don't really hold out much hope that they're going to reveal any more to Parantham and me than they did to Lahl." He did his best with his human body to make the quads' gesture for conceding imperfection and uncertainty. "Maybe it sounds frivolous, to travel so far and risk so much when I can't claim a lifelong passion for any single element of what we might find in there. Taken together, though, it's a different story. The sum of these parts is exactly what I've been looking for."

"Some people need a mystery to pursue," Sida mused. "Not everyone, though. Some people can turn a pleasurable routine into an art form: food, exercise, conversation, companionship. The same few leitmotifs repeating for decades. Add some travel every now and then to break up the pattern, and you can spin it out into a satisfying life lasting thousands of years."

"Is that your own plan?" asked Parantham.

"No." Sida inclined her head toward her companions. "We might have chosen to ignore the bulge staring down at us, but we're still chasing mysteries of our own."

"I see." Parantham left no doubt that she wanted to hear more.

Fith said, "There are plenty of Interesting Truths to be found, even now."

Though the quad words were slightly ambiguous, Rakesh understood immediately: "Interesting Truths" referred to a kind of theorem which captured subtle unifying insights between broad classes of mathematical structures. In between strict isomorphisms—where the same structure recurred exactly in different guises—and the loosest of poetic analogies, Interesting Truths gathered together a panoply of apparently disparate systems by showing them all to be reflections of each other, albeit in a suitably warped mirror. Knowing, for example, that multiplying two positive numbers was really the same thing as adding their logarithms revealed an exact correspondence between two algebraic systems that was useful, but not very deep. Seeing how a more sophisticated version of the same linkage could be established for a vast array of more complex systems—from rotations in space to the symmetries of subatomic particles—unified great tracts of physics and mathematics, without collapsing them all into mere copies of a single example.

Paba offered them a description of the work that the three friends were pursuing. Rakesh absorbed only the first-level summary, but even that was enough to make him giddy. Starting with foundations in the solid ground of number theory and topology, a glorious edifice of generalisations and ever-broader theorems ascended, swirling into the stratosphere. High up, far beyond Rakesh's own habitual understanding, no less than five compelling new structures that the trio had identified had started to reveal intriguing echoes of each other, as if they were, secretly, variations on a single theme. The elusive common thread had yet to be delineated, but it seemed plausible to Rakesh (albeit with all the fine details glossed over) that sufficient effort would eventually reveal one dazzlingly beautiful and powerful insight that accounted for the subtle fivefold symmetries they had charted.

Parantham said, "So much for the cliché that embodiment is the antithesis of abstraction." She sounded impressed, and Rakesh suspected that she'd looked more closely at the work-in-progress than he had.

"I've always believed the opposite," Fith replied firmly. "You don't need to turn every mathematical space into a kind of scape, and literally inhabit it, in order to understand it. Anchored in three dimensions, obeying mundane physics, we can still reason about any system you care to describe with sufficient clarity. That's what *general intelligence* means, after all."

"How long have you been searching for something like this?" Rakesh asked.

"Thirteen hundred years," Paba replied. Rakesh glanced at her précis; that was most of her life. "Not full-time," she added. "Over the years, for one or two days in every ten or twenty as the mood has struck us."

Sida said, "I've known people who've given their whole lives over to the same kind of search, but if they find nothing in a century or two they usually become discouraged. The only way we could do this was by refusing to make it the be-all and end-all. The only way we could afford to try was by ensuring that we could also afford to fail."

"That sounds like a good strategy," Rakesh said. He had never been drawn to the same ethereal heights himself, but he wondered if travelers could benefit from a similar approach. His youthful vow to leave his home world after exactly one thousand years, as if he'd expected fate to hand him the ideal destination at that very moment, seemed increasingly foolish. He might have passed another two or three centuries happily on Shab-e-Noor, if he'd found some way to make himself receptive to the kind of serendipity that had ultimately rescued him from the limbo of the node, without subjecting himself to the same miserable feeling that every day without success was wasted.

The five of them sat talking until noon, then the quads took them to the guest shelter to eat. Rakesh's body was flexible enough to make use of almost anything—or at the very least to survive its ingestion without harm—but the quads had a garden that was equally flexible. Instructed in his tastes, within half an hour the plants were able to form fruits and leaves that even his wild ancestors would have found nourishing and delicious. Fith insisted on cooking them into a spicy stew, using tools rather than his mouth to manipulate the ingredients, no doubt having been briefed by Massa's library on certain peoples' preference for food wholly unmasticated by others.

This, Rakesh thought, was the Amalgam at its best. Even these citizens who shared no molecular ancestry with him had made him welcome on their planet, in their town, at their meal. They had shared their ideas and discoveries, and listened attentively to his own stories and opinions.

His next hosts would be very different. For one and a half million years, the Aloof had made it clear that they needed no one's company, no one's stories, and no one's opinions but their own.

Nevertheless, it seemed that they wanted something now: some contact, some flow of information. It had started with Lahl, but Rakesh had no idea where it would end, or what the transaction would finally amount to. A disinterested exchange of scientific data? An act of trade, of mutual benefit? Munificence? Misunderstanding? Deception? Enslavement?

He and Parantham stayed with their friends until the stars of the bulge filled the sky, then they prepared themselves to walk among them.

6

"Three," Zak said, "is a beautiful number. Three is what the map shows, which means somebody else who cared about these things believed that three was correct. And three makes perfect sense, if the weights come from something simple."

He fell silent, brooding. He pushed against the wire he'd been holding and began to drift slowly away from Roi, back into the depths of the Null Chamber, but before he'd gone far he reached out and stopped himself.

"And yet?" Roi prompted him.

"And yet three is not what we found. What we found was *two and a quarter*." Zak seemed torn between melancholy and excitement, as if he couldn't decide whether this strange result was simply a failure of his methods and reasoning, or a hint of some kind of deeper revelation, if only he knew how to decipher it.

"I can't be sure that my measurements were correct," Roi confessed. "I was as careful as I could be, but—"

Zak cut her off. "This is not down to you. I took many measurements myself. A few other people helped me, as well. Throughout the Splinter, whoever was doing the measuring, the result was the same: moving garm or sard increases your weight by two and a quarter times as much as moving shomal or junub. Not three times. Nowhere, never, is it three."

"Perhaps there's some error in the navigation signs," Roi suggested. "Perhaps the weight itself distorts the way the signage teams mark out their distances."

"No. I checked that. I found small, random discrepancies, not some systematic distortion. We all make errors: me, you, the signage teams. Enough to mistake two for two and a quarter, perhaps. But not three."

"Apart from the map, then," Roi said, "why can't the true value be two?

If you had never found the map, would you be satisfied with two?"

Zak made a chirp of wry admiration. "That's a good question. Maybe I've been fooling myself. Maybe I've let a mapmaker who I've never even met corrupt my idea of simplicity."

"Tell me," Roi begged him, "why you think it should be three. How can one answer be favored over another? How can anything in the world be more than chance?" This was what she'd come here to learn: the answer to the impossible question that had dragged her away from her work team, away from everything she knew and trusted.

"If I'm right," Zak said, "then weight is all about motion, and motion is all about geometry. That's where the simplicity comes from."

With these cryptic words hanging in the air, he led Roi along the wire, deep into the Null Chamber. She struggled to remain calm; it was hard enough being weightless anywhere, but at least in the tunnels there'd been rock all around her to assuage the feeling that she was constantly falling. Here, out in the middle of the chamber with only Zak's flimsy web to hold on to, the confusion and contradictions were starker. The fact was, Roi had no trouble supporting herself with the weakest of single-clawed grips, and even if she released that claw-hold accidentally she'd easily have time to regain it. She had probably never been in less danger of *falling* in her life. So why did the lack of weight, the very thing that guaranteed her safety, also make her feel that she was forever on the verge of being dashed against the walls of the chamber?

"Here at the Null Line, with no wind and no weight to confuse us, how do things move?" Zak took a stone from his carapace and tossed it gently away from them. "What do you see?"

Roi said cautiously, "As far as I can tell, that stone moved smoothly in a straight line until it hit the wall."

"Good. I don't expect you to be certain about anything from one crude experiment, but for the sake of argument let's suppose that's true: *weightless things move smoothly in a straight line*. And I'll tell you something more from my own experience, which you can confirm for yourself when you feel more confident: once I've given myself a push and started moving across the chamber, it doesn't matter how fast I make myself travel; except for the slight touch of the air passing over me I really can't feel any difference. Weightlessness is weightlessness, as long as you're moving smoothly, and the only thing that stops you moving smoothly is contact with a wall, or a wire."

Zak led her to a small apparatus attached to the wire that marked the Null Line. It was a tube of susk cuticle, containing a spring with a stone at one end, much like the one she used to measure weights. Here, of course, the spring was unstretched, and the stone lay beside a mark on the tube that indicated no weight at all.

The end of the tube opposite the stone was attached to the wire by a small loop that allowed it to pivot. Zak flicked the tube and set it spinning, the free end sweeping out a circle while the other remained fixed. "What do you see?"

"The spring is stretched now," Roi observed. "As if the stone had weight."

"Yes." Zak reached over and gave the tube another sharp tap, setting it moving faster. "And now?"

"It's stretched even more. As if the weight had increased."

"Good. Now let's put some numbers to this."

Zak took a sheet of cured skin from his carapace, and had Roi count while the tube spun around, to judge how quickly it made each revolution. Six times, they spun the tube and recorded both the time it took to complete a circle and the weight indicated by the stretching of the spring. A special kind of pointer that could only move one way under pressure from the stone made it possible to read the weight off the scale after the tube was brought to a halt; squeezing the pointer made it narrower and allowed it to be slid back, resetting the weight.

Zak said, "Multiply the weight by the time, and then by the time again."

Roi stared at the skin, as if the answers might simply leap into her mind, but nothing happened. "I can't do that," she admitted. She understood the concept, but when it came to manipulating actual figures she had only been taught how to add and subtract. "None of my teams ever needed multiplication."

"All right, don't worry, I'll teach you later." Zak moved down the list of figures, rapidly scratching in the results. Although the individual times and weights varied greatly, the numbers produced by his calculation—weight by time, by time again—were all similar, all close to two hundred and seventy.

Roi was mystified. "Two hundred and seventy? What does that mean?"

"Nothing. Ignore the particular value, it's just a measure of such things as how fast you count, and how we assign numbers to weights. The important thing is, we always get the same value, however fast or slow the stone is moving. There's a rule here, there's a pattern."

"Not a very simple one," Roi protested.

"Be patient."

Zak modified the experiment, shifting the spring and the stone further along the tube, doubling the stone's distance from the pivot. Six more times they spun the tube. When Zak calculated the same quantity again, it was no longer fixed around two hundred and seventy, but had doubled to five hundred and forty.

He repeated the experiment again, then again, each time with the spring shifted further.

"Now we divide by the distance. Weight multiplied by time, by time again, divided by distance." All the numbers this new calculation produced were more or less the same, regardless of the distance from the pivot. By combining all the variables in this way, a constant value again emerged.

Roi had no idea why. She said, "Spinning the tube around gives the stone weight, I can understand that much. But these numbers..."

Zak replied, "*Why* does the stone acquire weight?"

She stared at the apparatus, and struggled to articulate the reason why this phenomenon hadn't greatly surprised her. "A stone without weight moves in a straight line. This stone moved in a circle, so it couldn't still be a stone without weight."

"All right, that's logical. But what made it move in a circle, when I struck it? As opposed to the one that flew straight across the chamber?"

"This one's tied to a spring. The spring holds it back."

"Exactly," Zak said. "The spring forces it to follow a circle, frustrating its preference to move in a straight line. And the effort, the toll this takes on the spring, shows in the spring's extension. Just as the effort it takes for the spring to keep the stone from falling, when they're far from the Null Line, shows in the same way."

Roi couldn't see how this comparison explained anything. "The stone following a straight line is simple, for sure. So the spring has to fight to complicate the motion, to make it a circle instead. But what's *simple* about all the different ways that stones fall, all around the Splinter? Keeping them still, keeping them from falling, seems much simpler to me."

Zak chirped approval. "A fair comment. All I can do is ask for a little more patience." He held up the skin. "This is where the numbers start to help us. You say the spring has to fight to complicate the motion of the stone, to bend it away from the straight line it would prefer to follow. How can we make that hypothesis precise, though?" He sketched the spring and the stone, then drew in a circle—the path that the stone actually followed—and a straight line, the path it would have followed had it not been tied down.

"How far would the stone travel in a count of one, if the spring wasn't there?" Zak marked off a small section of the straight path. "And how far does it actually travel?" He marked a similar section of the circular path.

"What is the difference?" He joined the two marks with a third line, an indication of how far the stone had deviated. "The length and direction of this line is a measure of the effort the spring needs to make, to pull the stone away from its natural motion into the path it actually follows. I call this a weight line, because that's what it measures. I believe weight is nothing more than *the difference between preferred and actual motion*."

"So where does the pattern in the numbers come from?" Roi demanded.

Zak said, "Think about the way the weight line changes as we change the two things we can alter in the experiment. If we make the distance from the stone to the pivot greater, everything I've drawn simply grows in proportion to that distance, including the weight line itself. But if we increase the time it takes for the stone to make one complete rotation, then the distance the stone would travel, or does travel, in a count of one gets smaller. However, not only do those two paths get shorter, the angle between them shrinks as well. So all in all, the separation of their endpoints—the weight line—shrinks in proportion to the rotational period multiplied by itself.

"The pattern in the numbers bears all of this out. The value I calculated reverses these two influences on the weight, canceling their effect, yielding a constant result."

Roi found it difficult to follow the details of Zak's calculations, but if she stepped back and looked at the overall picture, it was a startling idea. *Weight is the difference between preferred and actual motion*. What her body felt as it pressed against the floor of a tunnel was a kind of struggle against falling, a struggle she could only perform with the aid of the rock beneath her. What she felt now, *the absence of that struggle*, only seemed dangerous because in a more normal place any such lapse would be punished with serious injury if it lasted more than a heartbeat or two.

"All right," she said. "The principle you're asserting is simple enough, and I think I understand what's happening with the spinning tube. How can this explain the pattern of weights across the whole Splinter?"

Zak said, "For that, we need another experiment."

He led her across the web, to a tube anchored firmly to several wires. "The axis of this cylinder runs from shomal to junub; the midpoint is precisely on the Null Line." He took two stones from his carapace, then placed one gently in the mouth of the tube, and the other beside the tube's midpoint. Both floated where he left them, showing no immediate evidence of motion.

"What do you think will happen?" he asked Roi.

She thought carefully. "The stone that's a little bit shomal will have a little bit of weight, slowly pulling it toward the Null Line. So given time, it will fall down to the Null Line."

"So let's wait and see."

To help pass the time, Zak asked Roi to recount the details of her journey, and they chatted about the different work teams she'd seen, the changes in vegetation from place to place, the rumors of food shortages. As they talked, the first stone did indeed gradually descend into the tube, while the second one remained where Zak had placed it.

As the moving stone approached the fixed one at the midpoint of the tube, Roi said, "I was right, wasn't I?"

"Keep watching," Zak insisted.

The stone didn't stop at the center. It kept traveling slowly down the tube, away from the Null Line.

"But there is no weight at the Null Line!" Roi said. "If you're exactly at the Null Line, you should go nowhere. You don't start falling junub!" She gestured at the other stone, which continued to float where Zak had left it.

"Move away from the Null Line, and throw a stone across it," Zak suggested. He pointed to the slender wire that marked the invisible line, then handed her a projectile.

Roi complied, bracing herself on a cross-wire. The stone didn't quite touch the wire, but it came close before sailing smoothly past it.

"It kept going," she mused. That didn't surprise her; she hadn't really expected the Null Line to magically rob the missile of its velocity. So why had she been surprised that the stone that had fallen under its own weight, rather than being tossed, had also kept moving?

She went back to watching the stone in the tube. Eventually, it reached the mouth opposite the one where Zak had placed it. She waited for it to emerge from the tube, but again her guess proved ill-founded. Moving just as slowly as it had at the start, it now reversed its motion and began to fall back into the tube.

"A little junub," she said, "means a little weight back toward the Null Line again. And somehow, it all balances out. When the stone first crosses the Null Line, the weight begins to act in reverse, but not enough to halt it completely, only to begin to slow it down. Only when it reaches as far junub as it began shomal does it halt completely. And then it starts the very same motion again, in reverse."

"Right," said Zak. "But where does this beautiful pattern come from? The weight, the motion, two stones coming together and moving apart?"

"I have no idea," Roi confessed.

"What comes back to itself, over and over? What repeats itself, endlessly?"

Roi was blank for a moment. "A circle?"

"Yes."

"I don't see any circle."

Zak rummaged in his right cavity and fished out a loop of wire. "When we throw a stone here, it looks as if it follows a straight line. But how can we really be sure? Before long it hits the wall of the chamber, and we can't know where it would have gone if it hadn't been stopped. So imagine that the way things move when there's nothing to interfere with them isn't always a perfectly straight line. Suppose that if they're tossed in the right direction, they travel around and around, in a very big circle."

Roi was perplexed. "How big? As big as the Splinter?"

"Much bigger than that. Imagine a circle so big that you could follow a part of it from one side of the Splinter to the other and not even notice the curve, not even see that it was not a straight line."

Roi's mind reeled. Crossing from one side of the Splinter to the other... then stretching out far into the Incandescence?

She said, "I understand that we couldn't tell the difference from a straight line. But even if it's true, how would we ever know? Why should we believe it?"

Zak said, "Because of this."

He produced a second loop of wire and held it together with the first, in such a way that the two circles shared a common center. They did not coincide completely, though; a small angle separated them, so they only actually touched at two points. "Imagine two stones, moving along two circles like these. They come together, they pass each other, they move apart, then they come together again. Over and over."

Roi pictured it, following two points around the two loops. It was half true: the *separation* of the two points followed the same pattern as the *separation* of the two stones. "But these stones aren't going around in circles," she said. "Not even big ones that might be mistaken for straight lines."

"How do you know that?" Zak countered.

"Because they're right in front of me! They're not moving away from me!"

"And how do you know you're not moving, yourself?"

This was becoming surreal. Roi replied patiently, "Because then I'd slam into the wall of the chamber."

"And how do you know that wall isn't moving? How do you know the whole Splinter isn't moving?"

Roi tensed her limbs ready to reply, then found she had nothing to say.

Zak said, "I believe the Splinter is moving in a very large circle, around a point far away in the Incandescence. When we let two stones, displaced from each other along the shomal-junub axis, move without interference, they come together, then move apart, just as if they were following two such circles inclined at a small angle to each other. And I believe that the time it takes for the stones to complete their cycle tells us how long it takes for the Splinter to make one orbit around that distant point."

Roi looked back at the stones. The first one, the "moving" one, had almost returned to the midpoint of the tube. If Zak was right, though, then they were both moving in exactly the same way. There really was no difference between them.

She said, "Then what's the Null Line? Why is it special?"

"The Null Line is a piece of the circle that the center of the Splinter traces out as it moves," Zak replied.

"But why are things weightless only *there*," Roi protested, "and not along other circles?"

Zak gestured at the two stones. "Both of these are equally weightless, because both are free to move along their natural paths. The only real difference between them is that the one at the Null Line has the whole Splinter keeping step with it, so we think of that one as 'fixed' and the other as 'falling'.

"When you're shomal of the Null Line, your unhindered path would be just like the path of the 'falling' stone, but the floors of the tunnels and chambers won't permit you to follow that path, and their refusal is what you feel as weight. The further shomal you are, the greater the difference between your preferred and actual motion, the harder the rock has to push up on you to keep you shomal, and so the greater your weight."

Roi turned these propositions over in her mind, torn between skepticism and amazement. She was not yet convinced that Zak was right, but she was beginning to see how his grand vision of weight and motion might fit together.

"What about garm and sard?" she said. She struggled to picture Zak's extraordinary cosmology: shomal and junub pointed out of the plane of the circle that the Splinter followed, and the directions along the Null Line, rarb and sharq, pointed along that circular path. "Is the center on the garmside or the sardside?" she asked.

"The garmside."

So garm and sard pointed toward, and away from, the center of the circle. "If I'm garm of the Null Line," Roi mused, "but not shomal or junub, the Splinter will still carry me in a circle around the same point. And the same is true if I'm sard. So why can't those circles count as natural motion, just like moving along the Null Line?"

"This is where things become trickier," Zak admitted. "I claim that following a circle around one special point comprises natural motion, but I believe that's only true if you're traveling at the right speed. That speed depends on how large the circle is.

"The center of the Splinter must be following its natural path—otherwise objects at the Null Line would not be weightless. On the garmside, though, the circle will be slightly smaller, and on the sardside, slightly larger. The natural motion that corresponds to these circles must involve slightly different orbital periods, but the Splinter is a solid object, it has to move as a whole. Because every part of it must complete an orbit in the same time, there's a mismatch between the speed at which things are moving and the speed of a naturally circular orbit. Wherever there's a mismatch like that, the natural path can't be circular any more.

"On the garmside, the natural path must be more sharply curved than a circle of the same size, because the weight there is directed toward the center of the orbit. On the sardside, the natural path must be *less* curved than the circle that's actually followed, because the weight is directed outward, away from the center of the orbit."

"That makes sense," Roi said, "but where does the three come from? Or the two and a quarter?"

"That depends on the precise rule that describes how the natural orbital period varies with the size of the orbit," Zak replied. "If the period multiplied by itself grows in proportion to the size multiplied by itself, then by itself again, weight should grow three times faster when you move garm or sard than when you move shomal or junub."

Roi said, "Why choose that rule, though, and not another one? Is it really the simplest one imaginable?"

"I thought there was a way of seeing it that made it perfect," Zak replied. "So simple it couldn't be otherwise. But now I don't know what to think. The measurements aren't lying, so I'm wrong about something."

Roi said, "What made it seem so simple? 'The period times the period grows in proportion to the size times the size times the size.' Why is the size taken three times? Why not two? Why not four? Why not five?"

Zak held up the skin and scratched a circle. "This is the orbit of the Splinter. Focus on a small part of the curve, so small it looks like a straight line. That's the Null Line. Now tell me what happens to the direction of that line, as you follow it around one orbit."

Roi stared at the picture. "It always lies perpendicular to the direction from the Splinter to the center of the circle. Rarb is always perpendicular to garm."

Zak said, "Yes. But if rarb stays perpendicular to garm, what happens to garm? If you draw a line from the Splinter to the center of the orbit, what happens to that line as the Splinter moves?"

"It moves with the Splinter, it follows it around the circle."

"Its direction rotates?"

"Yes."

"So what happens to the Null Line, which is always perpendicular to it?"

Roi tapped her carapace in self-reproach. "The Null Line rotates! With each orbit the Splinter makes, the Null Line itself rotates."

Zak said, "Yes. So the Splinter doesn't simply travel around this circle, it's also *turning* as it moves. It rotates around the shomal-junub axis, in exactly the same time it takes to make an orbit. If it wasn't doing that, there would be no Null Line: we would not be weightless anywhere, except at a single point, the center of the Splinter."

Roi was growing dizzy. First the Splinter was flying through the Incandescence in a giant circle, now it was spinning as it went. "What about the first experiment, though? The one where you spun the tube and the stone gained weight?"

"Yes?" Zak sounded pleased that she'd raised this. "Tell me what that means for the Splinter."

"We're on the Null Line, but I'm sure we're not precisely at the center of the Splinter. So we're spinning around the center, just like that stone. So why don't we have weight from that spin?"

"I believe we do. But it's balanced by something else."

"What?"

Zak said, "Suppose we're thirty-six spans rarb along the Null Line from the center of the Splinter. If we're spinning around the center, which way should our weight point?"

"Rarb. Away from the center."

"But we feel no weight at all. So if you *took away* the spin, then which way would our weight point?"

"In the opposite direction," Roi supposed. "Back toward the center of the Splinter."

"Right. Now, if we were thirty-six spans *shomal* of the center, which way would our weight point?"

Roi was confused. "Are we spinning now, or not?"

"It makes no difference. The spinning stone had no weight in the direction of its axis. Spinning the Splinter along the shomal-junub axis has no effect on weights in that direction."

"All right," Roi said, "then nothing has changed. Our weight would point back toward the center of the Splinter."

Zak said, "So for any direction other than garm or sard—the directions that take us closer to, or further from, the center of the orbit—our weight would point toward the center of the Splinter itself. And what's more, if you look closely at the calculations, the weight at any given distance from the center of the Splinter would be equally strong, whether you traveled rarb, sharq, shomal or junub. Shomal-junub weight depends on the time for the Splinter to make one orbit, and your distance from the Null Line, in exactly the same way as the weight from spinning depends on time and distance. So if you took away the spin, shomal-junub weight and rarb-sharq weight would be exactly the same."

Roi said, "Where does that leave the garm-sard weight?"

"You tell me. If the spin was absent, would the garm-sard weight be less or more?"

Spin produced weight away from the center, and the garm-sard weight itself was also away from the center, so part of it could be attributed to the Splinter's spin. "Without the spin, it would be less."

"Yes," Zak said. "Less, per span, by exactly the shomal-junub weight."

"So if it was three times the shomal-junub weight with the spin, then without the spin it would be two?" Roi ventured.

Zak chirped with delight. "Yes! And *that* is what makes three beautiful. With spin, we can say the weights for the shomal-junub, garm-sard, and rarb-sharq axes are: one toward the center of the Splinter, three away, and zero. But the hidden picture, if we strip away the complication of the spin, is: one toward the center, two away from it, and one toward it again."

"I can see that garm and sard are special," Roi conceded. "But why should the garm-sard weight be exactly twice the others?"

"Because that gives a perfect balance between the amount of squeezing and the amount of stretching. Take a package of resin and squeeze it in two directions; I promise you, it will burst out in the third direction, with twice the force. It's not free to do anything else."

Roi pondered Zak's mundane analogy for the arcane symmetry he was proposing. She could see the appeal of it, but was that really enough to determine all the laws of weight and motion?

She said, "What if the reality, with spin included, is two, not three? Then without spin, all the weights would be equal in size, but the garm-sard weight would be opposite the others. Wouldn't that be simple, too?"

"Perhaps," Zak conceded. "Perhaps it's too much to hope for the geometry of weight to match the geometry of resin."

"What we need to do," Roi said, "is find some way to check. The map told us one thing, but our own weight measurements disagreed. We have to find another test, another measurement we can perform that will settle the question."

Zak made a sound of concurrence, then sank into contemplation. Roi looked around the chamber. How long had passed since she'd entered? A whole shift? She was hungry, but reluctant to move, reluctant to break her connection to Zak. The most important thing now was their work.

He'd done it, she realized. All alone, without team-mates, with nothing but words, a couple of machines, and some simple ideas.

She was not going back to the crops on the edge. He'd hijacked her loyalty. He'd recruited her.

7

The first thing Rakesh saw upon opening his tent was Parantham, seated in a chair, in human form. Her detailed appearance was not the same as that which he'd assigned to her back in the node, but her identity signal ensured instant recognition. As he stepped out of the tent he tensed his forearm; his body believed it was real flesh. A moment's further introspection told him that he was not modifying his perceptions in any way. As far as he could tell he was simply seeing her as she was.

Parantham said, "Welcome to the bulge." She was even speaking in his own native tongue.

"Thanks."

She must have noticed his puzzlement, because she explained, "I thought it would make things simpler for our hosts if they only had to deal with one phenotype and one language." She gestured at the instruments around them, which Rakesh had barely begun to take in. "Lots of hand-and-eye-driven interfaces, so it looks as if I made the right choice."

Rakesh told his tent to fold itself. They were in a large cabin, inside some kind of space habitat; a window looked out on to a densely packed field of stars, slowly turning, suggesting a centrifugal origin for the gravity he felt. They'd requested exactly the same destination address as Lahl, but her metabolic and ergonomic needs would have been very different, so their hosts must have undertaken some extensive reconstruction. Rakesh had no idea what the Aloof would have done if Parantham had asked to be embodied as a blind limbless blob: maybe piped all the data straight into their minds, which would have been useful. Then again, maybe their hosts would have split them up, requiring them to take turns to examine the meteor with different instruments tailored to their different bodies.

The meteor itself was prominently displayed in the middle of the cabin, encased in a transparent enclosure, protected from contamination. As Rakesh walked over to it Parantham joined him. The object that had brought them all these thousands of light years was a dark gray slab of basalt about four meters across, its surface pitted with small impact craters.

He said, "What do the Aloof think we can do with this, that they can't do themselves?"

"Give a damn?" Parantham suggested.

"They cared enough to summon us here."

"That wasn't difficult," she said. "Though it might not be a question of effort; it might be a matter of what they see as appropriate. They might believe that they have no right to mess with this themselves, but we're entitled to know about it, and make of it what we will." She smiled. "Though maybe that only applies to you, as molecular next-of-kin."

They left the cabin and circumnavigated the habitat, a spinning ring some two hundred meters across. The main corridor led them to a kitchen, storerooms, a bathroom, two bedrooms, an exercise room, and a workshop. It was both gratifying and slightly chilling to see how well the Aloof understood the human phenotype's needs. The fixtures all had a generic quality, rather than the look of something made by humans for humans, but many cultures within the Amalgam would not have done a better job. Rakesh had swallowed a library before they'd left Massa, so it was a moot point as to whether his hosts had read his mind as the source of all this, or had studied other unencrypted human travelers on their way through the bulge, but they certainly hadn't shaped this place from his own memories; there was nothing specific to the culture of Shab-e-Noor, and they hadn't covered the walls with portraits of his family or lovers. They really couldn't win, though, because such tact itself invited its own creepy sense of invasiveness: they'd peered inside him deeply enough to understand how wrong that would have been.

If Rakesh felt naked, he had nobody but himself to blame. He'd known from the moment Lahl had offered him the key exactly how vulnerable he'd be, and he'd poured scorn on his friends' concerns. These were the terms, this was the deal; it was too late to have second thoughts. In principle, the possibilities for abuse were endless: the Aloof could be systematically torturing a billion helpless Rakesh-clones at this very moment. When he'd mentioned this primal fear to Parantham back on Massa, she'd pointed out that, while she'd regret the Aloof making anyone suffer, they could easily construct *de novos* of their own from scratch in order to mistreat them; sufficiently deranged sadists could always manufacture someone to torture, removing any need to lure their victims into a trap.

In any case, Rakesh decided, there was nothing to be gained now from such paranoid speculation. Having handed their minds and bodies to their hosts as open books, the only sensible strategy that remained was to take their pleasant surroundings at face value and assume that the Aloof's hospitality, however narrowly defined, was genuine.

Back in the meteor room, they set to work. Rakesh had never had reason to be much of a materials scientist or ejecta expert before, and as he invoked the aid of the library the knowledge that flowed into him brought a thrill of discovery, a sense of new vistas opening up before him, that stretched far beyond his immediate needs. Imbibing a massive bolus of pre-digested information was not his usual means of educating himself—he much preferred the slow process of building incrementally on his own prior knowledge, testing and interpreting every assertion before accepting it—but there was no denying the rush of suddenly having thousands of new facts and insights jostling in his skull.

The equipment the Aloof had given them could probe the meteor's surface down to an atomic level; elicit and analyze emissions across the spectrum from gamma rays to microwaves; tomograph it in a thousand different ways; strike it, tap it, pound it, tickle it, and listen to the harmonics as it rang like a bell. Its gross chemical composition and its rarest impurities, its crystalline microstructure and the subtlest deformations thereof, were there for the asking. This rock, Rakesh thought, was as naked to them as they were to the Aloof.

He and Parantham collaborated efficiently, discussing the best strategies for the investigation, speaking a dense specialist lingo that would have been foreign to them both just minutes before. The primary interface to all of the instruments was a touch-screen console, but mercifully they weren't limited to reading the screen and tapping menus; the Aloof had tailored the interface to their detailed embodiments rather than a generic notion of the ancestral human phenotype, and the console could exchange data with the infrared ports in their fingertips.

Tomography alone was enough to locate the dead microbes, but it was necessary to send nanomachines crawling through the crevices to extract reliable DNA sequences. A dose of paleogenetic expertise from the library left Rakesh with no doubt that Lahl had been correct: these were not the corpses of any micro-organism, from any epoch, from any of the known DNA worlds. Their ancestors had probably been blasted off one of those planets billions of years before, on an entirely different piece of rock; that earlier meteor must have fallen to the ground somewhere in the bulge, and seeded a whole new biosphere. A billion or so years later this lump of basalt had been flung into the sky; with better luck it might have contributed to the DNA panspermia itself, but it was a dead seed now. At least, no pristine world could have revived these desiccated, shocked, radiation-fried microbes, though perhaps if they'd achieved the unlikely fate of landing on a planet already awash with DNA-based life, the right species of distant cousin might have scavenged a few of these corpses' gene fragments and tried them out for new ideas.

"The question now," said Parantham, "is how do we find the parent world?"

The DNA sequences were enough to assign probabilities to the meteor's "grandparent world": the planet out in the disk whose ejecta had seeded the world from which this rock had been blasted. Even those probabilities were not sharp, though; there were seven candidates that were almost equally likely. Given the chaotic dynamics of the bulge, this did not do much to narrow the search.

If the DNA couldn't help them, what of the rock itself? Three billion years before, lava flowing to the surface of the parent world had cooled into crystals of olivine, a magnesium-iron silicate, and augite, in which calcium, aluminum and titanium were also present. Subtle deformations in the structure of these crystals offered a partial history of the temperatures and pressures experienced by the rock since then.

The sudden heat and shock of the impact that had thrown the rock into space had left distinctive chemical fingerprints as well as physical dislocations. Over time, in the cool of the interstellar vacuum, some of the substances forged during the rock's fiery ejection had slowly decayed, hinting at a date for the event: fifty million years before. At the same time, the high-energy cosmic rays that flooded through the bulge from a myriad of sources had corroded the meteor's surface, left chemical deposits of their own, scoured tracks deep inside the rock, and created trace amounts of new isotopes. As Lahl had claimed back in the node, both lines of evidence converged on the same date: the rock had apparently drifted through the bulge, unprotected by any atmosphere or planetary magnetic field, for about fifty million years.

The same console that allowed them to control the analytic instruments provided access to a star map. When Parantham activated it, it opened with a view showing their own path and present location (labeled with a stylized picture of the habitat's ring), along with several hundred billion kilometers of the meteor's trajectory before capture (labeled just as clearly with an image of the rock). In fact, the meteor had barely been "captured"—it looked as if the habitat had been constructed around it, more or less matching its original velocity—but the map was careful to delineate between the undisturbed object and its present state.

The map labeled the stars of the region solely by their physical characteristics, and despite phrasing this information in Rakesh's language, declined to adopt the catalog numbers or coordinate system that he would normally have used. Nevertheless, by invoking the library he could match the Aloof's descriptions with his own sources. The Amalgam's maps of the bulge were somewhat patchy, but there was more than enough overlapping data to establish a reliable fit.

For the first time, now, they knew exactly where they were. They had traveled some thirteen thousand light years from Massa, and while part of that journey had taken them "west"—clockwise around the galaxy, looking down from galactic north—they had also penetrated deep into the bulge, and had ended up less than a thousand light years from the galactic center. Lahl had reached roughly the same conclusions, though she hadn't been carrying star maps of her own to compare with the Aloof's.

This central region was distinctly more crowded and violent than the outer reaches of the bulge. Packed with massive gas clouds that periodically burst into life with episodes of star formation, as well as a varied population of older stars that had drifted in from the rest of the bulge, it was as different from the galactic disk as a teeming metropolis was from a rural backwater.

Rakesh said, "Where do you think Csi and the gang are now?"

"Dead to us," Parantham replied bluntly. "And dead to each other as well."

"I was inviting light-hearted speculation," Rakesh said dryly, "not baleful philosophical pronouncements."

"Then I'm sure they're having a wonderful time somewhere, sailing the high seas together."

It was true that they were unlikely to have much in common any more; they were not part of a synchronization clan, they had made no appointment for a reunion. They had probably spent most of the past twenty-five thousand years as insentient data traveling through the Amalgam's network, but even if by some extraordinary coincidence they had crossed paths again, the chances were that their various measures of the time that had passed would have been millennia apart, placing the memories of their shared experiences into very different perspectives.

"So long as they're not still stuck at the node, then I'm happy," Rakesh declared.

He shifted his attention back to the map—constructed inside his skull, but shared with Parantham—which pooled data from the Aloof and the Amalgam and annotated it according to the explorers' own priorities. It was easy to rule out all the stars that were younger than the rock itself;

after that, the next obvious step was to try to account for the direction in which the rock was traveling.

The Aloof's map provided current velocities for the stars in the region—and like the stars' positions, these would have to be theoretical extrapolations from the latest data that could reach them at light speed—but it offered no past trajectories, either observed or computed. Rakesh wondered if this omission was a kind of strategic self-censorship; perhaps the Aloof considered that revealing just how long they'd been tracking these stars would grant some insight into the history of their civilization that they did not wish to disclose to outsiders. It could hardly have escaped their notice that the information would have been useful to their guests.

"Do they want us to find this planet, or not?" he muttered.

Parantham was undaunted. "They've had this meteor for at least fifty thousand years now. If their priority was making things easy for us, they could have located the planet themselves long ago, and sent us straight to it the moment we arrived. But that's not the deal. We're going to have to work for this. We knew that."

The best dynamical model in the library couldn't wind back time fifty million years without generating uncertainties many times greater than the average distance between stars. Lahl had mentioned six hundred candidate stars; Rakesh couldn't whittle this down to less than five hundred with celestial mechanics alone.

Factoring in the chemistry of the rock made a difference. The Aloof's map included high-resolution spectra of each star, revealing the chemical composition of its outer layers precisely. Using a model of planetary-system formation it was possible to compute the probability of the rock's parent world being born from the same nebula as any given star. This reasoning was subject to its own uncertainties; nevertheless, the results allowed them to eliminate more than three hundred of their original candidates, and re-rank the two hundred that remained.

Before Rakesh could invoke any kind of high-powered statistical analysis, Parantham said, "That can't be right." The chemistry-based ranking was not at all what might have been expected, with some candidates shuffled slightly down the list while others were promoted a few places. Rather, the second list more or less turned the first one on its head. The chemical profile of the region's stars placed the rock's origins in a completely different direction than that from which it seemed to have come.

"It must have undergone a sharp course change," Rakesh suggested, "maybe even passing through another planetary system on its way."

"Either that, or its chemistry's distorted for some reason," Parantham said.

"So which trail do we follow?"

"Both, I suppose."

Rakesh groaned. "So instead of halving our short list, we've just doubled it?"

Parantham said, "We haven't finished yet."

"Of course not. I'm sure we can add another thousand candidates if we keep trying."

Parantham selected close-up views of one star after another, but the Aloof's map displayed no planets around any of them. The data simply wasn't included, as if mere balls of rock were as irrelevant here as an ant-hill on a roadmap. Rakesh hadn't seriously expected to find the parent world in all its glory, teeming with long-lost DNA cousins, just by sitting here and zooming in on a map of the bulge, but a little more detail might have helped. The Amalgam's maps showed what was known, given the constraints, but if any world within the bulge had screamed "life" loudly enough for an observatory out in the disk to detect it, that would have been old news.

The gene fragments they'd found in the rock gave some tantalizing hints of the kind of proof-of-metabolism signature that the parent world's atmosphere might contain, though as ever there were uncertainties; these rock-dwelling microbes didn't have to be typical, let alone dominant on the planet as a whole, fifty million years later.

Rakesh said, "We need to make direct observations of our own." The workshop had facilities that would allow them to construct a reasonably powerful telescope, but they lacked the raw materials to make anything big enough to analyze a planetary atmosphere from hundreds or thousands of light years away. They would need to travel further; they had no choice.

The console's main menu did not include any category for travel. It occurred to Rakesh that Lahl had never explained to them precisely how she'd got the message through to her hosts that she'd spent as much time as she could with the meteor, and wanted to move on.

After exploring every option pertaining to the habitat itself—including the ability to remodel the bathroom on command—Parantham finally realized that selecting a star on the map enabled a sub-menu with the unassuming option "Go to star". Choosing this did not change the map's viewpoint or magnification; rather, it caused the map to inquire politely, "Are you sure you wish to travel to this star?"

Rakesh said, "No, we're not sure yet, but thank you for asking."

Parantham said, "Travel how? By what method? How long will it take?" The map remained silent. She re-invoked the option and the map asked again if she was sure, but it remained unresponsive to her requests for details.

Rakesh said, "Try some more stars, see if the option's always present." They worked their way through a hundred candidates. In every case, the map claimed to be able to take them there.

"Does this mean they're all on the network?" Parantham wondered. The eavesdroppers out in the disk had only succeeded in mapping a small part of the Aloof's network, near the edge of the bulge. The nodes there weren't closely aligned with particular stars, but the known ones were certainly spread more thinly than the stars themselves. If the Aloof really did have receivers at all of the places where the map said it could take them, then either this was the best-connected region in the galaxy, or they had receivers at every single star in the bulge, period.

Rakesh said, "I doubt it. More likely they've just automated the ability to add new nodes." Out in the disk, getting a receiver built at a new location was a major endeavor. First, you needed permission from the custodians of the local material resources. Then you had to organize the logistics of sending spores to construct the receiver itself. The technology had been streamlined over the millennia—with the need for eavesdroppers to chase the spillage of the Aloof's data around the inner disk providing a substantial boost—but it still wasn't something you did casually, just by pointing at an obscure star on a map and leaving the rest to insentient software.

Parantham said, "I've often wondered if the network we've mapped isn't merely a kind of decoy, which they built to make us think we understood them better than we really do."

"You mean, not at all?"

"We've been telling ourselves that they use the same general communications technology as we do. Gamma rays modulated with data packets. Encryption keys separately distributed. All very cozy and familiar, as if it were the only conceivable way."

Rakesh couldn't argue with her skepticism. Convergent technology was one thing, but in the Age of Exploration travelers had been amazed by the myriad ways other civilizations had found to solve identical problems, at least as often as they'd been startled to find their own culture's inventions eerily mirrored. "You think they were the ones who eavesdropped on *our* network first, and then they decided to build an imitation of it, as a sop to our curiosity?"

"As a sop to our curiosity. As a honey pot to lure us in. I don't know about their motives. But it wouldn't surprise me if all the 'traffic' we've been seeing over the last three hundred millennia has just been gibberish, and the Aloof's real highways are completely invisible to us."

Rakesh said, "I don't know if that's good news or bad. Do you think they're going to let us ride the real highway?" He was past the point of feeling vulnerable, but he couldn't decide if it was somehow demeaning, or simply exhilarating, to imagine being whisked across the light years by a process he didn't even understand.

Parantham summoned up the first of their candidates on the chemistry-based list, a main-sequence star about four billion years old, two hundred and seventy-nine light years away. While it lay further from the crowded galactic center than their present location, the Amalgam's eye-view of it was still compromised by distance and obstacles. The presence of at least three gas giants had been deduced from the star's slight periodic motion, but no further details could be resolved from afar.

She said, "There's only one way to find out."

8

Roi immersed herself in study, determined to reach the point where she could understand every detail of Zak's ideas. Excited as she was by the simplicity and grandeur of his vision, until she could test the fine points for herself she knew that her instinctive sense that he was on the right track needed to be treated with caution. Anyone could thump their carapace and invent a story so big that it seemed to swallow the world. The one thing that made Zak's account of weight and motion different was that anyone willing to make the effort could investigate the logic of his claims firsthand. On that, the whole thing would stand or fall.

Zak helped her to revise and extend her mathematical skills, starting with multiplication, then continuing all the way to something he called "template calculations": manipulating abstract symbols as well as actual numbers, allowing her to perform a generic version of a sequence of computations without specifying all the quantities involved. After a while, it struck Roi that this was far more than a method for saving labor when she wished to repeat the same calculation many times on different sets of numbers. Just contemplating the template for the answer to a problem—without substituting any particular values for the symbols—could illuminate the relationship between all the quantities involved in a way that staring at endless lists of figures never would.

Zak was a patient teacher. Before she'd met him, Roi had thought of the unrecruited as pitiful creatures, lonely failures on the verge of death. Zak's time at the Null Line had certainly damaged his health, but in his own way he had worked far harder than anyone she'd ever known. Roi had rarely been so confident that the respect she felt for someone was deserved, and not just a product of the haze of camaraderie.

Between their lessons, Roi managed to extract some of his story. Like every hatchling, Zak had found tutors to provide him with a rudimentary education, but when the time came to join a work team, he'd drifted from one recruitment to the next. He'd felt the buzz of cooperation every time, but it had never been strong enough to hold him for long.

One shift, while working as a courier, he'd stumbled upon a library out in the sardside. The cargo he was carrying had had nothing to do with the place, but an accidental detour had been enough to capture his interest, and on the return leg of his journey he'd gone back for a closer look.

The library was full of maps, work notes, diagrams of strange machines, fragments of calculations, and scrawls in languages nobody understood. The librarians painstakingly copied the sheets of skin to preserve their contents from loss or damage, and constructed catalogs and lists of cross-references, trying to piece together a larger picture from these bewilderingly disparate parts. Every now and then, they explained to Zak, someone would bring in a new find, a page or even a bundle of pages that had never been seen before.

Wandering through the collection, overwhelmed by the aroma of long-dead susk, Zak had suffered a giddying shift in perspective. People had been thinking and writing for an unimaginable time, and here, right in front of him, lay countless samples of their labors. A whirlwind tour of history, a million tantalizing snatches of overheard conversations, had been etched into these skins. Zak felt the presence of the thousands of generations that had come before him, and understood that it might be possible to join them in a vast endeavor, a project spanning the ages that he could as yet only glimpse.

He'd begged the librarians to recruit him on the spot, and once they'd recovered from their surprise they had agreed, but they were not the ones who had truly captured his loyalty.

"I was recruited by the dead," Zak said. "Not in any rush to join them in their silence, but from the urgent need to understand what they might have thought and done that could survive them, that could speak across the ages, that could be continued even now."

There was no coherent history of the Splinter, no account of one time following another, but everywhere Zak looked he found evidence of change. The language he understood, the language of his contemporaries, accumulated curious additions and alterations as he moved from page to page into the past. Other pages were written in scripts that, so far as his fellow librarians knew, no living person could decipher.

There were stories of the birth of the Splinter, of the old world being torn apart, but like the stories that spread through the work teams they did not agree on the details, and they all had the sound of having been retold over and over, accumulating embellishments and omissions, before being put into writing. Some even spoke of the calamity recurring many times, stretching back into the unimaginably distant past. How vast, how grand, the mythical First World must have been, if after thirty-six divisions even one of the crumbs that remained was inhabitable!

Hard as it was to believe these stories, let alone know which ones to trust, for anyone who'd so much as crossed the Calm the undeniable fact remained that the weight in the garmside tugged the opposite way to that in the sardside, and the further one went in both directions the stronger this discord became. If the Splinter had suddenly been doubled in size, it was not at all preposterous to imagine that the weight might have been enough to tear rock from rock.

The trouble was, this raised the question of how the old world could have held itself together for more than an instant. The most reasonable answer, it seemed to Zak, was that it must have been born under a different regime of weights, which had only later become so powerful.

During shift after shift in the library, he came across fragments of speculation on these matters, but there was nothing whole, and nothing convincing. The thinkers of the past had left many hints and guesses, but if they had ever fully understood the truth about these mysteries, it had not survived. In the end, Zak decided that he couldn't spend his life merely sifting through these skins, searching for one more inconclusive sign that his reasoning was not completely misguided. If weight had dictated the history of the Splinter, and however many worlds that had come before it, then weight was what he needed to understand.

Armed with the Map of Weights, some plans for ancient instruments, and copies of the few surviving notes on his predecessors' methods and philosophies, he'd walked out of the library and headed for the Null Line, ready to begin uncovering the secrets of weight and motion, and to search for something simple that had torn the world apart.

Roi still didn't understand the wind.

On one level, Zak's idea of natural motion seemed to explain it perfectly. If things moved in circles around the distant point in the Incandescence that she and Zak had come to call the Hub, and if the smaller the circle the faster they moved, then everything about the wind made sense. On the garmside—closer to the Hub—the wind was moving faster than the Splinter, and so it overtook the rock, blowing in from the sharq ever faster the further garm you went. On the sardside—further from the Hub—the wind was orbiting more slowly so the Splinter overtook it, ploughing through it, making it seem to blow in from the rarb when in truth it was merely failing to flee with sufficient haste in the opposite direction. And between them, in the Calm, wind and rock moved together at exactly the same pace, leaving not so much as a breeze to be felt.

The trouble was, while Zak's theory gave a simple, persuasive account of the phenomenon, Roi couldn't reconcile it with the mundane reality of weights. If weight was determined by natural motion, why didn't the wind follow the weights? If she stood anywhere in the garmside, and a crack opened up in the rock beneath her, surely she would fall away from the Splinter, garmwards. Notwithstanding the wind's speed in the cross-direction, which might make such motion harder to spot, and the way the rock and the tunnels worked to divert and complicate its flow, Roi's time among the crops left her thoroughly convinced that the wind wasn't *falling* at all.

Shift after shift she struggled with this problem, hoping she might solve it by her own efforts. Finally, she had to admit that the resolution was beyond her. The next time she met Zak, she asked him to defer their scheduled lesson in template mathematics, and she begged him to make sense of the wind before she lost her mind.

Zak was both amused and chastened. "This is my fault, Roi; I should have explained this much sooner. The weights on the map are fine—give or take the question of three versus two and a quarter—but they're not the whole story."

"There's something missing?"

"Yes. There is a kind of weight that the map doesn't show at all."

Roi was baffled. "How can that be? Weight is weight. I've felt it, I've measured it. It's not something you can hide."

"No, but the map only shows weights for objects that are fixed firmly to one place in the Splinter."

"I've moved from place to place in the Splinter," Roi protested, "and the map described correctly how my weight changed."

"That's not what I'm talking about," Zak said patiently. "You moved at a walking pace to a new location, you didn't race the wind. The wind feels something extra, everywhere, compared to the fixed weights on the map, simply because it's in motion, not because those fixed weights change from place to place."

If this was true it had the potential to resolve the paradox, but the idea still struck Roi as very strange. "Why should it feel something extra just because it's moving?"

"Because the Splinter is spinning," Zak said. "Now, I know the map already takes account of that, in part. An object fixed to the Splinter is really turning in a circle—a small one, much smaller than its orbit—which frustrates its natural motion and contributes to its weight. There's one further twist, though. Imagine a stone that's moving in a straight line, as seen from outside the Splinter. Because the Splinter is constantly turning, as the stone moves, we're moving too. If we try to trace the path of the stone against our surroundings—against the rocks and tunnels we think of as fixed, but which in truth are turning—the line we see it following won't be a straight line, because of the way our motion adds to the stone's. Its path will seem bent, as if there were a weight constantly pushing it sideways. And the faster the stone moves, the greater the apparent weight bending its path."

"The faster it moves in reality, or the faster we think it's moving?"

"The faster we think it's moving."

Roi struggled to visualize it. If a stone moved in a straight line away from the axis of spin, then the rotation of the Splinter would make it seem to follow a spiral path, forever turning. And if the stone was sitting completely still? Then the motion of the Splinter meant that it would appear to be moving in a circle, again with its path constantly veering sideways.

"I think I understand," she said. "But the wind doesn't wrap itself into a spiral. On the garmside, it blows straight from sharq to rarb."

Zak said nothing.

Roi struck her carapace. "Of course, that's the whole point! I've been wondering why the weights from the map don't push the wind garmwards, in some kind of curve plunging back out into the Incandescence. But the extra weight from its motion must push it in the other direction, balancing the ordinary weight exactly."

"That's right," Zak said. "The further garm you go, the stronger the garmwards weight, but because the wind is also blowing more strongly, the weight from its motion keeps perfect step, and the two of them always cancel."

Roi was pleased that she'd finally grasped what she'd been missing, but there was still something frustrating about the whole matter. The Splinter was turning, Zak claimed, and this claim turned out to be absolutely vital in order to make sense of the rest of his vision. Without the strange distortions in weight and motion brought about by the spin, it would have been impossible to reconcile a simple concept such as circular orbits for the wind with the ordinary realities of the Splinter.

However, everything about the Splinter's rotation seemed to involve a kind of conspiracy of self-effacement. It contributed to the garm-sard weights on the map, but who was to say exactly how much it added? It balanced a hypothetical rarb-sharq weight exactly, but that perfect balance left nothing behind to be felt or measured. And now it conspired with the garm-sard weights again... in order *not* to bend the wind.

Roi understood that at least some of this was a logical necessity, not a matter of coincidence. The two points of view, one tied to the rock of the Splinter, the other taking a grand cosmic perspective, were describing exactly the same reality, so of course they had to agree with each other, once you knew how to translate between them. Nonetheless, she couldn't accept that the fact of the Splinter's rotation could be both crucial and completely invisible, impalpable, and immeasurable.

She said, "When I throw a stone in the Null Chamber, why can't I see its path being bent?"

"It's a subtle effect," Zak said. "I've made some crude measurements of it, but it's hard to detect just by looking."

"You've measured the Splinter's rotation!" Roi was astonished. "Why didn't you tell me that before?"

"I wouldn't say I'd measured the rotation. My measurements show that the rotation *exists*, but I haven't come close to quantifying the rate of spin."

"But you've seen the effect itself?"

"Absolutely," Zak said.

"Can you show me?"

They went to the Null Chamber, and Zak fished out a device he called a spring-shot from one of the storage clefts. It was a tube fitted with a spring-loaded plunger that could be cocked to varying degrees of compression and then released, propelling a stone from the tube. The projectile emerged in a reasonably predictable direction, with a choice of velocities.

He attached the spring-shot to the wire that marked the Null Line. Then he prepared a "target board", a flat sheet of cuticle that he coated first with resin, then with a kind of powder. If you pushed a stone against the surface of the target, however gently, the powder sank into the resin, changing the way the two of them scattered the light, leaving a visible record of the point of contact.

He fixed the target board to the Null Line with a bracket, six spans or so rarb of the spring-shot.

"We're sending this stone straight down the Null Line, so according to the map it should feel no weight at all," Zak said. "First I'll make it move as fast as possible, and we'll see what happens."

He squeezed the plunger as tightly as it would go, then released it. The stone flew out rapidly, more or less following the wire that marked the Null Line, and struck the target. When they went to examine the board, it was, unsurprisingly, marked at the edge, just beside the wire.

"Now we reduce the speed."

Roi said, "Now I'm confused. I thought this weight was supposed to increase with speed."

"It does. But greater speed also gives it less time to act before the stone hits the target. By making the stone move more slowly, the weight that bends its path becomes weaker, but the extra time the stone spends in flight more than compensates for that."

Zak was right. With the spring half-compressed, the stone emerged less rapidly, but the mark it made was shifted to the sard side of the Null Line by about twice the width of the stone itself. In a third experiment, with the compression reduced further, the sardwards shift was even more pronounced.

Roi could picture what was happening very clearly, now. While the stone was in flight, the Splinter was turning, carrying the wire and the target board a small way garmwards, leaving the un-rotated path of the stone to strike the target askew.

She said, "Why can't we use this to measure the speed of the rotation?"

"It's a crude experiment," Zak insisted. "If I release the stone several times in succession with the spring compressed by exactly the same amount, the point where it strikes the target still varies. And how can I know how fast the stone is moving? It's traveling too quickly for me to time its motion accurately."

"Let it move more slowly, then. You'll get a larger effect as well."

"There's a catch," Zak said ruefully. "The more the stone gets pushed away from the Null Line, the more it comes under the sway of the ordinary garm-sard weight as well. What we're measuring will no longer be one simple thing. When you combine that with the uncertainties in the aim and the velocity, I don't think there's much hope of getting a meaningful number out of the results."

Roi could see how daunting the complications were, but she wasn't ready to give up. "Can I try it? Slowly? Just to see what happens?"

"Of course."

She squeezed the plunger down to the first notch, the smallest compression possible, then released it. The stone emerged at an absurdly leisurely pace, and even as she watched, it veered visibly sardwards. By the time it had traveled less than half a span toward the target its path had turned sideways, and not long after that it had swung around so far that it was level with the spring-shot again, albeit some distance sard of it. While continuing to move sardwards, its velocity along the Null Line had been completely reversed.

Roi said, "This is not what I'd expected."

"It's just following the rules," Zak said.

Roi moved aside to let the stone pass her. Eventually, its sardwards drift seemed to level out, and it was simply moving backward, parallel to the Null Line, much faster than it had been moving when it had left the tube. Its direction continued to change, though; the relentless sideways tug of the weight of motion was stronger for this stone than it was for the wind, and it began to veer back toward the Null Line.

As the stone approached the Null Line, the sharqwards part of its motion slowed, leveled out, and reversed, so it was now heading back toward the spring-shot. This didn't last long, though. When it reached the Null Line itself, almost grazing it, the stone executed a small loop that took it first sardwards, and then—in a replay of its original manoeuvre upon being launched—swung it around sharqwards once more. It was far behind the spring-shot, let alone the target, and showed no sign that it would ever come close to either again. Rather, it seemed to be cycling back and forth between the Null Line and a certain distance sardwards, while it drifted—mostly, though not constantly—ever more sharqwards.

Roi approached Zak. "What's the simple explanation? I suppose I can accept that the sardwards weight combined with the weight of motion did all of that, but there must be an easier way to understand it."

Zak said, "Think about the orbit of that stone. The stone was always on the sardside of the Null Line, so its whole orbit was larger than the orbit of the center of the Splinter. Larger orbits have longer periods, so the stone took longer than we did to go around the Hub. That's why it drifted backward. It wasn't as fast as us."

"But it started out faster," Roi protested.

"That's true. At the same distance from the Hub, where its orbit touched ours, it was faster than us. That's why we weren't constantly outpacing it, and it didn't move backward all the time. But over a complete orbit, we were faster."

This made sense, but Roi still wasn't satisfied. "Why didn't the stones you launched go backward? Was that because they were moving faster than mine?"

"Definitely not!" Zak was emphatic. "The only difference was, they hit the target before they could swing around and go into reverse. If we had taken the target away—and the walls of the chamber too, if neces-sary—then those stones would have followed exactly the same kind of path as your one. The fact that they were moving faster made their paths larger, and we only saw a small part of each path, but other than that everything about them was the same."

"I see." The whole point of Zak's version had been to concentrate on the very start of the motion, before the garm-sard weight could complicate things. "Can I try something else?"

"Anything," Zak said.

She detached the spring-shot, then reattached it pointing in the opposite direction: sharq along the Null Line. Now the stone would be moving backward from the start, making it slower than the Splinter at the point where their orbits touched.

Its path followed exactly the same pattern as before, except that rarb became sharq, and sard became garm. After leaving the spring-shot the stone veered garmwards; halted its leisurely sharqwards progress and went rapidly into reverse; reached a maximum distance garmwards from the Null Line and started back toward it; then, close to the Null Line, performed a small loop that took it back into the same cycle, albeit many spans rarb of where it had begun.

Roi said, "Its orbit was smaller than ours, so it was racing ahead of us?"

"Yes."

"And the way it moved away from the Null Line and then back again, that's because the orbit wasn't a perfect circle?"

"Right," Zak said. "We remain a constant distance from the Hub, but there are orbits like this that draw closer to the Hub and then move away again."

Roi contemplated this. "What if we could put a stone into an orbit that wasn't a perfect circle, but was still the same size as ours, overall? With the same period?"

Zak didn't reply immediately, but his posture made it clear that he was intrigued by her suggestion. "That could be very useful," he said eventually. "We ought to see it execute a fixed, cyclic motion instead of running away across the chamber."

Roi detached the spring-shot from the Null Line again, and attached it pointing sardwards: perpendicular to the Null Line, "halfway between" the two directions she'd already tried. She was acting purely on instinct, and even as she tightened the clips she wondered if launching the stone away from the Hub meant she'd be putting it into an orbit that would keep it perpetually on one side of the Null Line. But then, shooting the stone along the Null Line itself, which seemed more symmetrical in that respect, certainly didn't work, so what she was trying made as much sense as anything.

She squeezed the plunger one notch, then released it.

The stone veered sideways as it emerged, but not as sharply as it had in the previous two experiments. As it moved, it picked up pace, but nowhere near as rapidly as before. Roi was surprised; she'd half expected the sardwards weight to take over and drag the stone into a frenzied spiral as the weight of motion twisted its ever-quickening flight. Instead, the stone continued to turn in a smooth, shallow arc, still progressing sardwards while swinging around ever more to the sharq.

Eventually, its sardwards motion leveled off, about two spans from the Null Line. It was moving perhaps three times faster now than it had when she'd launched it. It continued to swing around gently, coming back toward the Null Line, while its sharqwards speed lessened.

As it approached the Null Line, Roi tensed. It was no longer traveling sharqwards, but it would probably perform the same annoying little loop as the others, and then it would be lost to them, drifting away across the chamber.

It didn't. It crossed straight over the Null Line, at about the same speed as it had left the spring-shot, and veered to the rarb. The symmetry was unmistakable: it was performing exactly the same kind of motion as it had when she'd fired it, only with garm in place of sard and rarb in place of sharq. If that symmetry held true, there was only one place where it could cross the Null Line again.

When the stone finally approached the spring-shot, Roi thought it might collide with it, but her aim hadn't been that perfect. It was close, though. The stone passed less than half its width from the tube before continuing on around the same closed loop as before.

"I can't believe I missed this," Zak said. "A new periodic motion! Congratulations!"

Roi said, "What are we seeing, exactly? Is this showing us the Splinter rotating?"

"What we're seeing is a stone in orbit, moving back and forth between its nearest and furthest points from the Hub," Zak replied. "If we try to explain that from a Splinter's eye-view, the motion will depend on the strength of the garm-sard weight, as well as the speed of the Splinter's rotation. Once I would have said that those two things should combine in a very simple way, but now I'm not so sure. The two and a quarter has taught me to be more cautious."

Roi launched another stone directly sardwards, this one faster than the first. The loop it followed was larger, but the shape was the same—about three times as long as it was wide—and the faster stone completed each circuit in the same time as its slower companion. These stones were spending half their time sard of the Null Line, moving more slowly than the Splinter, and the other half garm of the Null Line, moving faster, so over time they were keeping pace both with the Splinter and with each other. Surely that meant that each cycle they completed marked the time for all three to complete an orbit around the Hub? And surely the Splinter's rotation around its axis shared the same period, too, as a matter of simple geometry?

Zak said, "I know what we should do." He found an empty tube, attached it to the Null Line aligned shomal-junub, then placed a stone in its mouth and let it begin its slow fall. Now they could compare the two kinds of motion directly, without having to worry about the accuracy of their counts to time the periods.

It soon became obvious that the periods were not the same: the looping stones were taking far longer to complete each cycle than the stone falling shomal and then junub. For a while, Roi wondered if the slower cycle might be exactly twice as long as the faster one—and if some simple aspect of the geometry that she'd neglected could make sense of this—but that hope proved misplaced. The shomal-junub stone completed seventeen cycles while the looping stones completed nine. There was nothing simple about that.

Zak seemed forlorn at first, but then he proclaimed, "There's something encouraging about the way these numbers demolish half of my assumptions, yet the whole notion of orbits seems to survive. Watching these stones, can you honestly tell me that you don't believe they're going around the Hub?"

Roi said, "The idea still makes sense, but we're missing something."

Zak regarded the shomal-junub stone. "If orbits still make sense at all, then this stone tells us how much time passes for something orbiting at a small angle to the Splinter's orbit to come back to the same height above us each time. The stone doesn't go wandering off along the Null Line, so the periods of the two orbits must be the same. But what if the place where the orbits are farthest apart isn't fixed? What if that point moves around? Then this need not be telling us how long an orbit actually takes."

He moved to the looping stones. "And when you deform an orbit so it's no longer circular, what if the point of closest approach to the Hub isn't fixed either? That point, too, might wander around."

Roi struggled to picture what he was describing. "So these other orbits wouldn't close up? The Splinter would follow a perfect circle, but these stones would be weaving up and down, or back and forth around that circle, never quite repeating their paths?"

"Yes."

Roi was dismayed. "If the things we thought were landmarks can't be trusted to stay still, how can we ever decide how long it takes for the Splinter to complete an orbit?"

Zak said, "Good question."

Neither of them had the answer to it, so they set about calculating what Roi's looping stones actually did tell them. They worked side by side until the end of the shift, slept, then worked through two more shifts.

Finally, they had templates describing the relationship between three things: the strength of the garm-sard weight, the period of the Splinter's rotation, and the period of the looping stones. These calculations made no assumptions at all about the existence of "orbits around the Hub"; they just followed the effects of the weights directly—though they did rely on a correct understanding of how spin contributed to weight.

When Zak inserted the numbers, the template told them that the Splinter was rotating with a period about one and a quarter times the shomal-junub cycle.

If you believed in orbits, this meant that for a stone in a tilted orbit to return to its highest elevation was the fastest thing. For the Splinter to rotate around its axis took a little longer. And for a stone in an eccentric orbit to return to its greatest distance from the Hub took longer still.

Three phenomena, three different times.

"Where has all the simplicity gone?" Zak lamented.

Curiously, if he fed his original assumptions into the templates—if the shomal-junub weight was equal to the hidden rarb-sharq weight that was balanced by the spin, and if the garm-sard weight was, in total, three times as much—then all three periods would have been identical. The number three really would have made things very simple.

Roi took a break from the Null Chamber, and traveled a short way into the garmside to give herself some weight again, lest she lose too much strength. Even as she headed out of the Calm into the sights and sounds of ordinary life, she couldn't stop thinking about motion and orbits. At the end of each shift, when her mind had once filled with the images of weeds, now she saw stones, bouncing and looping and swerving in front of her. When she woke, her first thought was always of finding a new way to check Zak's conclusions. Their calculations deriving the Splinter's spin from the looping stones could be flawed. Or the weight measurements they had fed into the templates could be wrong.

Zak's simple experiment, when he'd launched a stone along the Null Line, had been compelling: it had made it obvious that the Splinter was turning while the stone was in flight. There had to be a way to measure the Splinter's rotation directly using that effect, without allowing the complications of the garm-sard weight to intrude. If you could keep the stone moving somehow—without ever letting it go too far from the Null Line—its path would act as a reference against which the turning of the Splinter could be judged.

How could you rein it in, though, without stopping it completely?

When Roi found the answer, she turned around and headed straight back to the Null Chamber. Zak wasn't there when she arrived, but she felt no hesitation about helping herself to his stores of material. They were a work team, now. These things were their common tools, not a lone eccentric's hoard.

Zak arrived just as she was putting the finishing touches to her apparatus, trial and error having led to some changes in the original design. Two equally heavy stones were glued firmly to the ends of a small bar. The bar was free to pivot around its center, where it was threaded by a stiff metal wire, which was bent around into a flat rectangular supporting frame large enough for the bar to turn continuously without obstruction. Another pivot, opposite the bar, attached the frame to the wire of the Null Line; this pivot left the frame free to rotate around the shomal-junub axis.

After they'd exchanged greetings, Zak watched in silence as Roi greased the pivots, marked the initial alignment of the frame on a card fixed to the wire above it, then gave the bar a flick to set it spinning.

An earlier version—with the bar spinning around one of its ends, and a single stone at the other—had been unbalanced, shuddering mercilessly, causing the frame to slip back and forth. This design seemed to have fixed that problem. All Roi could do now was wait.

Slowly but unmistakably, the plane of the spinning bar turned. Or, stayed fixed while everything in the chamber, everything in the Splinter, wheeled around it.

Zak said simply, "Who can doubt it now?"

There was no need to measure the speed of the stones. There were no elaborate calculations to perform. One rotation of the frame corresponded to one rotation of the Splinter, if they understood anything at all.

They set up a shomal-junub stone a short distance away, to compare the motions. After a while, no doubt remained that the period of this new phenomenon agreed with their earlier calculations, based on the more complex motion of the looping stones. The plane of the spinning bar took *one and a quarter times longer* to complete one turn than it took for the shomal-junub stone to complete one cycle.

Roi didn't know what to feel. She was relieved to see two lines of evidence converging on the same answer for a change, but she'd actually been hoping that this experiment might yield a different result, one that removed some of the complexity that had begun to infest the theory of orbits.

"Where did all the simplicity go?" she joked, echoing Zak's refrain.

"I think I know where some of it went," he replied. "I didn't dare mention this before, because I wasn't confident in our results. But now that you've confirmed the period of the spin, it doesn't seem so foolish any more."

Roi said, "Go on."

Zak had been forced to give up his beloved three, and the simple assumption that the shomal-junub weight would be equal to the hidden rarb-sharq weight, which the spin canceled out exactly. Since the shomal-junub cycle was faster than the spin, the shomal-junub weight was stronger than both the spin weight and its equal, the rarb-sharq weight.

Call the shomal-junub weight one. The rarb-sharq and spin weights could be quantified now: they were sixteen parts in twenty-five (the square of the ratio of the shomal-junub period to the spin period). The total garm-sard weight was two and a quarter, according to the weight measurements taken throughout the Splinter, and supported by the fact that the looping stone calculations, based in part on that figure, gave the same rate of spin as Roi's new device.

If you stripped away the complications of spin, the hidden rarb-sharq weight was revealed—*sixteen parts in twenty-five*—and the garm-sard weight was reduced, down to *one and sixty-one parts in a hundred*, which was just three parts in a hundred short of *one and sixteen parts in twenty-five*.

The sum of the two weights that pushed things toward the center of the Splinter was, within the limits of the accuracy of their measurements, equal to the weight that pulled things away from it. The forces that squeezed and the forces that stretched were in balance after all. The number three was nowhere in sight, but of all its beautiful corollaries, the one symmetry that Zak had most admired had somehow outlived it.

Zak said, "We don't know when the Map of Weights was drawn, or what its purpose was. It might be nothing but a guess, or a crude approximation, or a record of someone's wishful thinking. But suppose it's none of those things. Suppose it's an accurate record of the truth, of the weights as they once were.

"This map can't tell us if the weights have grown stronger since it was drawn, because we don't know what scale was used to depict them. It does tell us two things, though: first, that the ratio between the weights has changed, and second, that a hidden relationship between them has stayed the same."

As Roi contemplated this she realized how unsettling it was. It was easy to invent stories about the world being torn apart: one time, many times, take your pick, the event happening for no particular reason and making no particular sense. Everything she'd seen or heard on the subject was either six generations removed from a reliable witness, or had many other explanations. But above and beyond the flimsiness of the evidence was the apparently arbitrary nature of the claims. When a disaster could be invoked without cause or constraint—at some fabulist's whim, as it were—it was easy to doubt its authenticity.

Who would have fabricated a map, though, which secretly implied the very same symmetry as all the painstaking measurements that she and Zak had just made? This hidden thread of order didn't yet tell them why or when the weights might have changed, but the hint that they couldn't just shift any way they liked suddenly made the possibility of change seem far more real to Roi than it had ever been before.

"What now?" she said.

"We have a candidate for a guiding principle," Zak said, "but it still needs to be checked, to be verified somehow. And we still don't know how it manifests itself in the rules of natural motion; we know the weights close to the Splinter, but we don't know the precise rules governing orbits in general.

"We also need to discover, or deduce, the rules that govern the history of the Splinter, past and future. We need to know if the weights really could have changed, and when and by how much they will change again."

Roi could have recited the same demands herself, but hearing them spelt out this way made her feel as if she'd been loaded down with an impossible burden.

"It's too much," she said. "Too much for your lifetime, and mine."

"Of course it is," Zak replied. "One solution to that would be to write down what we've learned, put copies in all the libraries, and hope that in the future someone curious, intelligent, and fiercely independent will come along, understand what we've written, and take up the task where we left off."

Roi said, "That might not happen for a hundred generations."

"Then we're left with no other choice," Zak said. "We need to recruit more people to help us, here and now. Then we can both see the job completed, and we can both die happy."

9

Rakesh felt no change in his body, no disruption in the flow of his thoughts, but when he looked up from the console the pattern of stars through the window was different, and the meteor had vanished from its enclosure.

"All right," he said slowly. "I can live with that."

"This means... whatever they just did to us, they didn't feel entitled to do to the meteor?" Parantham frowned. "Or they just didn't want us mistaking a low-fi copy for the thing itself?"

"So now I'm a low-fi copy of myself?"

"Oh, don't get precious on me," Parantham retorted. "We were counting isotopes atom-by-atom in that rock. Hardly the kind of thing your personality depends on. I suspect they maintained the standard we're used to in travel, but you know that falls far short of sending a few tonnes of matter at atomic resolution."

"Fair enough." In fact, as far as Rakesh knew nobody in the Amalgam had ever attempted such a thing. "So how did they send us?" he wondered. "How long did it take?" He checked the console. The map told them that they'd traveled the two hundred and seventy-nine light years from their previous location in three hundred and twelve years. The excess time over line-of-sight distance didn't really prove anything one way or the other, though: those decades might have been spent adding a new node to the Aloof's network, or they might have been nothing but the necessary delay caused by a slightly zigzagged path between pre-existing nodes. "Did we ride mundane gamma rays, or the secret highway?" How could they tell the difference?

Parantham didn't reply, and Rakesh let the question drop. The destination was more important than the journey, and the cabin was flooding with light as their chosen star swung into view.

The window darkened to compensate, but a broad patch of bright sunlight still swept across the floor, bringing a palpable warmth as it touched Rakesh's skin, lighting up motes of dust as it crossed the cabin. He had almost forgotten that until now they'd had no sun to call their own; the starlight here had seemed more than enough for any purpose. Just as he was getting used to the change, a far greater surprise followed. A stark, slate-gray world appeared beneath them, sharply etched vistas of plains and canyons passing by, before the sliver of vivid dayside topography was replaced by a softer starlit version.

"I take back every insult," Rakesh proclaimed. The lack of planets on the Aloof's star map might have been perverse, but they hadn't played dumb with their guests this time. He had been expecting that he and Parantham would be dumped in a remote circumstellar orbit and left to scour the region themselves for specks of light. Instead, the Aloof had placed them just a few hundred kilometers above a rocky, terrestrial-sized world. Even if the system was packed with other planets, this was clearly a good place to start.

Parantham said, "We'll need telescopes, spectrometers, radar…" Rakesh was already summoning up the interface with the workshop, and sending it suitable designs culled from the library.

While the workshop labored, they stood by the window and waited impatiently for each new glimpse of the world below. Twice a minute, the sunlit landscape raced by; Rakesh would gladly have given up the convenience of centrifugal gravity for a steadier view, but he'd already programmed the workshop with designs for instruments anchored to the center of the spinning habitat, so with a little patience he could have both. At least their orbit around the planet was taking them further into the dayside, so the crescent beneath them was steadily growing.

"What should we call this place?" Rakesh asked. The planet had never been detected from the disk, and though its sun had been catalogued a million years before it had never been allocated anything more than a number.

"We haven't even named our ship yet," Parantham replied.

"*Lahl's Promise?*" The name slid off his tongue without a moment's thought, but on reflection Rakesh decided that it had a suitably admonitory ring to it. It would remind him that he'd vowed to treat the search for his cousins as seriously as Lahl had treated the need to find a child of DNA to take up the quest in the first place.

"That's fine by me," Parantham said. "But let's hold off on the planet until we know something about it."

The planet looked arid to Rakesh, though at least it wasn't visibly cratered, and the haze on the horizon made it clear that it possessed some kind of atmosphere. Back in the disk, the DNA panspermia was full of worlds like this, mostly populated with nothing but microbes who'd been hiding meekly in the soil for a few billion years. *Lahl's Promise?* Rakesh felt a twinge of guilt. Noteworthy as it would be to confirm that the panspermia really had stretched a tendril down into this perilous neighborhood, microbes were microbes, and he couldn't pretend that he wasn't far more excited simply to have found an excuse for the Aloof to release him from their usual strictures. According to legend, Leila and Jasim had been given a grand tour of the natural wonders of the bulge, but even if that was true, in three hundred millennia only a handful of travelers taking the short cut had claimed to have been woken *en route* at all, and no one had ever been handed a ship and allowed to go sightseeing.

Within two hours the instruments were online, and solid data about the planet was coming through. It was a medium-sized nickel-iron-silicate world, with a weak magnetic field and a reasonably thick atmosphere comprising mostly nitrogen, carbon dioxide and methane. There was no obvious chemical disequilibrium, no unstable mix of gases in proportions that only ongoing biogenesis could explain. The temperature and pressure on the surface would permit liquid water in the tropics all year round, but there was none visible, and water vapor was present in the atmosphere only in trace amounts. Radar showed no signs of subsurface ice. This was a dry and dusty world, and there was no obvious reason to suspect that it had ever been much wetter. The topography showed evidence of tectonic activity and vulcanism, and such water as the atmosphere contained could easily be accounted for by volcanic eruptions.

Still, the DNA panspermia had been known to gain a toehold on worlds as harsh as this. The microbes in the meteor had certainly appeared to be adapted to water-based chemistry, but that didn't have to mean vast rivers and oceans.

The view from their low, near-equatorial orbit was limited. Rakesh had the workshop build a mapping probe, to sweep over the planet in a polar orbit, imaging the whole surface in successive slices. Parantham ordered the construction of a second telescope, to search the sky for sister planets.

"Some of the isotope ratios look marginal," she noted. "Nothing we've seen here says that the meteor could not have come from this system, but the data we've got from this planet so far isn't as close a match as I'd expect."

Rakesh laughed. "So maybe the Aloof have a sense of humor after all?

They put us into orbit around this desert world, knowing there was a sibling with oceans and forests a few million kilometers away?"

"Let's see if there are any siblings at all."

In fact, they knew from the Amalgam's catalog that there ought to be at least three, and Parantham's search quickly found them all. One was a "baked" gas giant, a ball of methane and hydrogen more than a hundred times heavier than the world below them, orbiting at less than half the distance from the sun. It possessed two rocky satellites, both far too small to hold atmospheres. The second and third gas giants lay in tilted, highly eccentric orbits, further from the sun. One had four significant moons, the other three, but none of these satellites looked promising either as hosts for life, or as geochemically plausible parent worlds for the meteor.

"This is still our best bet, then," Parantham said.

"Assuming we're even in the right system," Rakesh added.

"I wouldn't give up on that yet. If nothing obvious comes from the mapping sweep, we'll have to think about looking for microfossils."

"Yes." Rakesh's spirit sank; the promise was getting heavier by the hour. Here they were in the galaxy's vibrant core, and Parantham was talking about scouring a planet's worth of rocks for cavities that might once have been microbes. Still, if that was it—if this world was a bacterial graveyard, and the Aloof had invited them here merely to pay their last respects—once he'd done his duty they might yet reward him with the chance to see something more.

He toyed with an image of the four planetary orbits. No two of the el-lipses shared the same plane, and the planets' axes were all over the place. That was what came of living in such crowded conditions: a neighboring star must have passed by and wreaked gravitational havoc. Rakesh ran dynamical models, testing the stability of the present arrangement, trying to get a sense of how long it might have persisted. The outer two gas giants were slowly nudging each other's orbits into a resonant configuration in which one world would complete exactly three trips around the sun to the other's two, but the process hadn't yet reached that stable endpoint. This and other signs that the system was still settling down after a profound disturbance suggested that the event had taken place between one and two hundred million years before. The same encounter might well have altered conditions on the world below them, though the geology still of-fered no indication that there had ever been running water.

"Metal!" Parantham announced.

"What?"

She pointed to the console. "The mapping probe just saw a glint of un-oxidised, elemental metal. Mostly iron, with a number of impurities."

Rakesh reviewed the data. High on a plateau in the tallest of the planet's mountain ranges, a metallic patch a few square meters in area had registered on radar, along with other wavelengths. Its detailed structure had not been resolved, but its chemical state alone was significant. In theory, rare geological processes could be responsible for such a deposit, but the surrounding rocks bore no witness to the necessary conditions.

They let the mapping probe continue its sweep of the planet, so as not to miss any further surprises, but they had the workshop build and launch a second probe tailored to investigate the strange glint more closely.

Rakesh said, "There was nothing in the structure or genome of the microbes we saw in the meteor that suggested they could metabolize metallic ores."

"Viva diversity," Parantham replied. "A microbial world is still a whole ecosystem. If this *is* biological, who knows what other niches there are that we haven't yet spotted?"

The second probe swept low over the plateau, and sent back high resolution images. The metal formed a blotchy but weirdly symmetrical patina on the rock, concentrated in six roughly elliptical lobes arranged in pairs around a central axis. It was hard to see how any underlying ore body that might have been metallized by microbes could have taken such a shape, though perhaps microbial colonies could self-organize into this pattern for some other reason. Spectroscopy revealed no organic matter, but that didn't rule anything out; a similarly remote view of the Aloof's DNA-infested meteor would have portrayed it as equally sterile.

They waited two full planetary days before taking the next step, allowing the mapping probe to image the entire surface. They passed the time arguing about the possibilities, cooking, eating, occasionally sleeping. Rakesh felt a strange mixture of urgent curiosity and an equally strong desire to prolong the unfolding process of discovery. Was this how it had been, to live in the Age of Exploration? Every world had held surprises then, when the ancestors of the Amalgam had still been slowly reaching out to find each other. Back in the disk, every planet he'd set foot upon had been visited by a hundred billion people before him, its every feature catalogued in more detail than he could hope to match with firsthand observations in a thousand years.

The mapping probe found no more elemental metal, and no other chemical anomalies at all. To the limits of the probe's resolution and sensitivity, every other structure and substance on the planet's surface could be accounted for by geological effects.

Rakesh knew exactly what he wanted to do next, but he was unsure where his obligations lay. "What are the rules about landing on a world like this? Just because we can't find a trace of life doesn't mean there aren't a billion software citizens buried in a processor somewhere." The disk contained thousands of planets where all evidence of biological ancestry had been carefully wiped from the surface, out of a desire to avoid attracting attention. They were all catalogued now, and their inhabitants left in peace, but the earliest of the explorers who'd chanced upon such places had sometimes triggered substantial animosity.

"If the Aloof don't want us setting foot here, I'm sure they'll intervene," Parantham replied. "If this planet has custodians who are distinct from our hosts, it's the people who brought us here who have a duty to ensure that we cause no offense. As long as we act in good faith, it's their responsibility."

"I can't argue with that," Rakesh conceded, "but it still doesn't feel right. Act at will and then see if you're restrained or rebuked, like a child?"

Parantham said, "They chose their relationship with us. If they want to open up a dialogue, if they want to educate us, they can do that any time. Until then, what choice do we have? We can't intuit every cultural sensitivity from first principles. So long as we do no harm, if we blunder in where we're not wanted it's up to someone with local knowledge to give us a civics lesson."

"If you go back far enough in history," Rakesh countered, "I can think of some civics lessons I'd rather not have."

They argued for hours, but finally settled on a compromise. They would send down a small collection of probes to investigate the anomalous metal. They would not literally set foot on the surface, but telepresence would still grant them most of the same advantages.

Rakesh switched his senses to his avatar as it plummeted through the stratosphere, curled up inside the heat shield that protected the whole exploratory package. There was no light source within the ceramic cocoon, but when he shifted his vision to infrared the differential heating of the shield provided enough contrast for him to make out his immediate surroundings. Parantham's avatar was coiled snugly behind the laboratory/rover, his jelly-baby twin. Both of them were about a millimeter tall, and shorn of unnecessary extras, leaving torsos, pudgy arms and legs, and heads without mouths or noses. The lab's machinery would do all the smelling, and their real bodies could do all the talking.

Rakesh felt the jolt of the chute unfurling, followed by a persistent deceleration. The heat shield slowly dimmed and his weight diminished as the package drifted down into the troposphere. There was some gentle buffeting, but the descent was uneventful, with nothing to presage the sudden thud of landfall. The plateau was some ten kilometers above the average surface elevation, not quite the highest point on the planet, but close.

The shield split open. A whirring sound followed as the chute was reeled back in. Rakesh restored his vision to the usual wavelengths and looked out across the surrounding terrain, a heavily corrugated igneous landscape. It conjured up fanciful images of boiling lava frozen into glassy black rock, sandblasted for an aeon but still not rendered flat. They were about a meter from the edge of the metallic patch. Had he been his normal size, the ground here would have looked merely dimpled.

Parantham's avatar rose to its feet, and he joined her. The rover purred and advanced beside them on its flexible treads. Rakesh doubted that their diminished stature would cut much ice if there were locals watching from hidden strongholds who held some strange reverence for this site; treading lightly or not, trespass was trespass. Still, at least if these avatars were crushed out of existence their bodies on *Lahl's Promise* would stand a chance. The last backup Rakesh had made for himself was on Massa, and he had no idea what, if anything, the Aloof were retaining of their guests as insurance against misadventure.

They tramped across the undulating lava field. According to the rover, the black rock beneath them contained almost no iron, and there was no obvious cavity marking out a distinct body of ferrous ore that the putative microbes might have mined. The layer of dirty metal ahead of them looked as if it had been sprayed on to the surface.

They reached the diffuse edge of one of the six lobes. The iron was stained green and brown, presenting no silvery sheen, but it still looked more like a layer that had been deposited on top of the igneous rock than something created by converting a pre-existing source *in situ*. Models of the planet's surface evolution lent no weight to the idea that this elevated place had once been the bottom of a mineral-bearing sea, though they couldn't entirely rule out six small, iron-rich puddles at the edge of a muddy alpine lake.

The rover probed the layer across the spectrum, then sent an invisible wave of nanomachines forward to gather more information and sharpen its tentative spectroscopic estimates.

Parantham displayed the evolving isotope data in a shared visualization in front of them. "This has been refined by smelting three or four different ores from different sources," she said. "It's not geological in origin, and it's not biogenic. Iron, nickel, chromium… it's an artificial alloy. This is *steel*. Designed to resist corrosion."

"Can we date the smelting?" Rakesh wondered. "Aha!" There were minute traces of radioisotopes. The models suggested that the metal had been refined between one hundred and twenty and one hundred and eighty million years ago.

Rakesh's thoughts hovered between astonishment and bemusement. Had the cousins just become a great deal smarter, or was he staring at a mirage? They had yet to find a single biological molecule here. Could life have flourished on this desolate planet, to the point of giving rise to a steel-making culture, and then shrunk back down to nothing, leaving this single, shriveled artefact as its only witness?

The nanomachines advanced, probing the composition of the deposit in all directions. It was not homogeneous. Time had blurred what might have once been sharp distinctions, but hints of structure survived as complex veins of impurities threading the six lobes.

Parantham said, "What was it? A sculpture of an insect?"

Rakesh glanced away from his avatar's vision to a virtual schematic, a map of the impurities overlaid on an aerial view of the site. "It's a robot," he declared. "A six-legged robot."

"Perhaps." Parantham was pondering the isotope analysis again. She said, "There are markers in this metal that fit the meteor data far better than anything else on this planet." She hesitated. "It's a *probe*, Rakesh. From the meteor's world. This planet isn't the parent world, but the parent world sent this probe."

Rakesh tried unsuccessfully to pull his jelly-baby face into a scowl of disbelief, but then everything fell into place.

The cousins had made steel, and mastered interplanetary flight. They had sent this six-legged robot to explore their barren sister world, more than a hundred and twenty million years ago. Out in the disk, a species with a head start like that might have circumnavigated the galaxy before Rakesh's ancestors had touched a stone tool, and built a civilization to rival the Amalgam before humans had sent a single spore to a neighboring star.

This wasn't the disk, though. Grand histories, here, were prone to truncation. A neighboring star had come too close, and either captured the planet or ejected it into interstellar space.

Rakesh said, "The meteor is about fifty million years old. The interloper passed through this system perhaps a hundred million years before then. That's why the meteor's path didn't match its chemistry; the whole planet had been traveling away from its home star for a hundred million years before the meteor was blasted off it."

"Yet the meteor still bore life," Parantham said. "That DNA was the same age as the meteor itself, not a remnant from an earlier epoch. Whatever the parent world endured for those hundred million years, it wasn't enough to sterilize it."

Rakesh looked out across the stained patina of metal. "Microbes survived. But what about the probe builders?" It seemed too cruel a coincidence to believe that the interloper had come along just as they were developing the technology that might have allowed them to survive the encounter. Perhaps that had even been a trigger; perhaps they had been locked in some kind of cultural stasis until their astronomers realized that their world was in peril.

"We'll scour the system," Parantham declared. "There might be some more clues here, they might have left something on one of the gas giants' moons."

Rakesh agreed. "And then we go after them." They would follow the meteor back to its source, and retrace the path of these unlucky exiles, deep into the crowded heart of the bulge.

10

As Roi launched herself across the Null Chamber, it struck her that she had never seen the place so alive with activity. She counted seven distinct groups, each numbering six people or more, gathered together on the walls and along the web, making measurements, adjusting machinery, talking excitedly, testing ideas.

She and Zak had scoured the Splinter from garm to sard in their hunt for recruits, braving libraries and workshops, abattoirs and storage depots, risking ambush every step of the way. Now the hard times were over; they had built their team, and its numbers bolstered their loyalty in a way that mere reason never could.

Near the Null Line, Ruz and his apprentices were working on their new clock, tinkering with the mechanism as they calibrated it against a cycling pair of shomal-junub stones. Zak had set them a wildly ambitious target: to create something small enough for a traveler to carry anywhere in the Splinter, oblivious to the varying weights and accurate enough to be trusted for thirty-six shifts without recalibration. After trying out many unwieldy designs, they had devised a system in which two spiral coils of metal ribbon were joined at their centers to small shafts. The first and larger of the coils was tightened by turning its shaft with a lever, and then the force as it unwound was eked out slowly and employed to feed a gentle, to-and-fro rocking of the other coil's shaft. Rendering this complex mechanism perfectly regular was a serious challenge, but the team never seemed to be short of new ideas to try, and each refinement so far had improved on the last.

Ruz had been a metalworker for most of his life. It had taken Roi more than a dozen shifts to recruit him, but he had later admitted that the instant he'd seen Roi's "Rotator"—her contraption for demonstrating the

Splinter's spin—he had been hooked in equal measure by a fascination with the idea that the world could be secretly turning, and a conviction that he could do a far better job at making the kind of gadgets needed to quantify that motion. Happily, his conviction had turned out to be entirely justified.

Roi drifted past the clockmakers and landed against the wall, close to the point where Tan was talking with a small group of students. "What is natural motion?" he asked. "Looked at closely, and in the absence of spin, it seems as if a weightless stone is trying to follow a straight path. Yet over large enough distances, that path can curve around into a circle, or other kinds of curves. What's happening?" He lifted up a complicated patchwork he'd made by gluing together dozens of fragments of skin. "See this line, marked across this surface?" He indicated a path he'd dyed in ink. "On every small piece of the surface, it's a straight line. But the line as a whole isn't straight; it can't be, because the surface itself isn't flat. So how can we determine exactly which paths can be made by small, straight lines joined together in this way? That will depend on the way the parts of the surface are connected to each other. We need a precise, mathematical expression of the nature of that connection, in order to understand which paths are as straight as they can be, given the geometry of the surface."

Roi listened closely. She, Zak and Ruz had lured Tan away from the signage team where he'd honed his geometrical skills. Calculating distances through the tunnels of the Splinter had given him both an extraordinary facility with numbers and a powerful sense of how they could be used to analyze paths, shapes and motion.

"Keep in mind," Tan continued, "that there is one ingredient in the idea of natural motion that doesn't show up when we study a surface like this. Zak has argued that the natural path for any stone you throw from a given point depends, not just on the direction you throw it, but also upon its speed. The natural path of the Splinter appears to be a circle, but an object that starts out on that circle and travels in the same direction as the Splinter will still follow a path with a different shape if it's moving faster or slower than the Splinter. So we need to find a way to incorporate that into our geometrical scheme. We need to merge the idea of *speed* with the idea of *direction*."

Roi had to make an effort to tear herself away. She had heard Tan explain these ideas many times, but on each occasion the concepts became a little clearer, a little bit more precise. If he ever reached the point where they were defined with sufficient mathematical rigor to allow her to start making calculations, she hoped she could find a way to merge them with Zak's other principle—that the true weights everywhere summed to zero—and then she might finally be able to start mapping the possibilities for the Splinter's past and future.

She clambered across the wall to the crevice where Zak was resting. She tapped the adjacent rock gently, and after a moment a single claw emerged from the crack.

"It's Roi," she said, "I've brought you some food."

"Thank you." Zak slid out on to the wall, awkwardly. Roi opened her carapace and took out a bundle of food. She'd spent half the shift collecting it, but she did not begrudge the effort. Zak was old, his body was failing, but she had no intention of letting him starve to death.

Zak ate slowly, in silence. Roi no longer asked him what hurt and what didn't; she gathered that almost everything did.

When he'd finished, he surveyed the activity in the chamber with a satisfied air. Roi could see the meal dissolving smoothly inside him, unhindered by the obstructions she'd noticed the last few times. Clearly the rest had done him some good.

"How are you finding things on your travels?" he asked.

"What do you mean?" She'd returned from the last recruiting expedition with two young students, but that had been several shifts ago, and she'd reported the result to him then.

"How do people think of us? Word must have spread out from the Calm by now, that there's a new team here, doing a new kind of work."

"Ah." It was a good question, but a difficult one to answer. "I wouldn't say that there's any particular resentment directed against us. Nobody likes having their team-mates taken, but recruitment is recruitment, it's a fact of life."

"And work is work?" Zak pressed her. "The mere existence of a team is its own justification?"

Roi replied cautiously, "It seems that way. Most people don't consider themselves experts in the history of the Splinter, to the point of declaring 'There has never been a team like that before'. Work is whatever a group of people do, and most of us take it for granted that what other teams do is useful in some way. There might be only five or six jobs that literally everyone knows about and understands, but that doesn't mean people are hostile or suspicious toward all the rest."

Zak pondered this. "I've been wondering at what point we'll need to let some of our own members get poached."

Roi was startled. "Can we afford that? Our numbers are still very low."

"Can we afford not to?" Zak replied. "It's not just a matter of being sure we play the game, being sure our existence is accepted. It would also be of value if some of our ideas could spread outside the team itself. Almost every child learns writing and simple arithmetic; they're parts of the culture that have managed to move beyond the specializations where they originated. Imagine if the facts about weight and motion could acquire the same status."

Roi could see where this was heading. "So by the time the next division of the Splinter is imminent, everyone will have at least a basic understanding of what's going on. It won't be necessary to try to educate them from scratch."

"Is that too ambitious?" Zak wondered.

"I don't know. Tell me when the next division is coming."

Zak emitted a sarcastic rasp. "I have a feeling you'll know that before I do."

"Don't count on it." In truth, the idea of being able to predict the event still seemed almost as strange and metaphysical a prospect to Roi as the thing itself.

"When is the next overview meeting?" Zak asked.

"Two shifts from now."

"I think I'll attend."

Roi was pleased. "It will be good to have you there. You've been away for too long." She hadn't been close to anyone near the end of their life before, and she was never sure what to expect. Zak's strength came and went, and every time it declined she was afraid he was dying, but a few shifts' rest, some good news about the team, and a problem worth thinking about were often enough to revive him. He'd never travel all the way to the garm-sharq edge again, but he might survive at the Null Line for dozens more shifts.

She bid him farewell, and launched herself across the chamber to the point on the web where her own equipment was set up. Every shift, she counted a few cycles of the three periodic motions to see if anything had changed in their relationship. Once Ruz's clock was declared trustworthy as a standard in its own right she'd start using it to measure the absolute durations of the cycles, but until then she was content to record the ratios between them.

She set everything in motion and then watched patiently, counting the passage of the cycles using a trick she'd picked up from Gul, a recruit who'd worked in a storage depot: sliding a series of stones threaded on wires, rather than trusting everything to memory or wasting precious skin by making a scratch for each event. Though all three motions slowly diminished over time—however thin the air the stones were moving through, however well-greased the pivots on the Rotator's spinning bar—the periods she was measuring were unaffected, and as long as each cycle could be clearly tracked this gradual decay caused no problem.

As Roi watched the stones, in her mind's eye she pictured the way their paths might have looked to some impossible cosmic observer, floating in the Incandescence high above the Splinter's orbit. The problem of how these paths wrapped around the Hub entranced and infuriated her. If the Map of Weights could be believed, then long ago—and, presumably, further from the Hub—anything falling freely would have traveled endlessly along the same closed curve. Whether it was simply going around in a circle, or whether it was also detouring up and down or in and out made no difference, because the periods for all three motions were the same. Now, it was as if something had taken that simple pattern and squeezed and twisted it, forcing the different cycles to break ranks, and yet miraculously preserving Zak's balance of weights.

She finished her count. In eighty-five cycles of the shomal-junub stones, the plane of the rotating bar turned sixty-eight times, and the looping stone completed forty-five loops. These numbers hadn't changed since she'd begun measuring them.

Roi recorded the results with the usual mixed feelings. Any change would be the cause of great excitement, the start of a new opportunity to prise apart the mysteries of weight and motion. The numbers had spoken eloquently when she and Zak had first identified the three cycles, but their silence since then had been disappointing.

At the same time, she knew that any change would mean far more than an intellectual impetus for the team. If the weights increased, the strength of the rock beneath her would be tested, and everyone in the Splinter would be at risk. However great her hunger for revelation, she could not deny a powerful sense of relief that the numbers continued to seem immutable, and that she might yet live out a quiet life merely contemplating their mysteries without ever feeling their sting.

The overview meeting was held in a chamber a few dozen spans from the Null Line. This place was large enough for the whole team to fit, clinging to the walls, but not so large that people could split up into individual project groups with the members audible only to each other.

Tan spoke about his group's continued efforts to explain natural motion geometrically. "First, we need to extend the idea of direction to include speed. We can understand the direction 'three spans garm for every one span rarb', so why not also include the idea of speed, and talk about 'three spans garm for every heartbeat that passes'? But then, if we talk about

rock, claw, push

the garm direction, the rarb, and the shomal, there is a fourth simple direction we must add to the list: time. In fact, every path that's traveled includes some component in that direction; we can't travel garmwards a single span without some time also passing.

"Once we can describe both *speed* and *direction* in the same framework, it makes sense to understand *natural motion* and *spin* as two aspects of the same thing. When an object is weightless, that means its velocity is simply following the geometry it encounters: there is no rock, no claw, pushing against it, so the only thing that can influence it is the way empty space itself is shaped. Similarly, when an object isn't spinning, the directions it carries with it must be following that same general rule. We know that the directions tied to the rock of the Splinter aren't following that rule, because of the swerve weight"—the sideways weight of motion connected to the Splinter's spin—"that we see if we treat those directions as fixed. But I believe the directions tied to the frame of the Rotator obey the same laws as natural motion, and *that* is why we can declare that it's the Splinter that is spinning, not the frame, however compelling the opposite scenario must seem to a casual observer."

In Tan's view, at every point in space and every moment in time it ought to be possible to summarise the effects of the local geometry with a simple mathematical rule for the way directions and velocities were "naturally carried" along any given path. Zak had proposed that circular orbits around the Hub, with a certain period that depended on their size, comprised one form of natural motion. Tan wanted to find a single rule that could account for that, and also the behavior of the Rotator: a single template into which he could insert a direction or a velocity in order to calculate how much (if at all) it was changing, compared to the dictates of geometry. Feed in the Splinter's velocity, and the answer would be: this is natural motion, there is no change. Feed in the direction *garm* and the answer would be: this direction is constantly turning, at a certain rate, around the shomal-junub axis. Feed in any direction tied to the Rotator's frame, and the answer would be: there is no change.

If Tan's ideas were dizzyingly abstract, the next speaker proved to be an antidote. Bard had been a miner, searching out and extracting metal, and he had a bluntly practical approach to his new team's work that sidestepped speculation in favor of tangible results.

"We have no way of knowing exactly why the weights changed in the past," Bard declared. "The Splinter seems to have shifted closer to the Hub, but it isn't clear what made that happen. Was it a gradual effect, spread over many generations, or was there a sudden, violent change in the wind that forced us off our earlier path and into our present orbit?

"The wind on the garmside pushes us faster along our orbit, which tends to move us away from the Hub, while the wind on the sardside acts to slow us down and bring us closer to the Hub. If everything about the Splinter was perfectly symmetrical, the two influences would balance exactly. I doubt that the symmetry is perfect, but even if it's not, we've been unable to measure the consequences in the short time that this team has existed.

"However," he continued, "whether these dangerous shifts come slowly or quickly, it seems likely to me that the Splinter would be safer if we could move it further from the Hub. If we could reduce the weights, taking them back to the values they had before the last division, there would be a far greater margin for surviving any subsequent change."

Zak interjected, "I agree with everything you've said, but how do you propose to move us?"

"We cut a tunnel," Bard replied, "through the sardside. Maybe two or three tunnels. If the Splinter now feels roughly the same force from the wind on the garmside as it does on the sardside, we can shift the balance by letting some of the sardside wind pass right through, delivering no force."

"If we empty out a tunnel on the sardside, won't that shift the center of the Splinter garmwards?" Ruz protested. "If the Calm moves garmwards, the sardside will grow larger."

"We can move the rubble anywhere we like," Bard countered. "We won't toss it out into the Incandescence. If we pack it into some small, empty tunnels that already lie sard of the excavation, the center of the Splinter will move sardwards, and it's the garmside that will grow."

Bard unfurled a scroll of skin. He had drawn up a plan, which showed two tunnels piercing the Splinter from rarb to sharq.

Roi said, "The mouths will be open directly to the Incandescence! How could anyone survive working there?"

"For the final few spans we'll simply loosen the rock and then withdraw the workers," Bard explained. "The wind itself will finish the job."

"How wide will these tunnels be?" she asked.

Bard gave a noncommittal rasp. "As wide as possible. As wide as we can make them."

"What's that going to do to the sardside crops?"

"I expect it would reduce them," Bard conceded. "The wind is what feeds us; if we let it pass by untapped, there has to be some cost. But would it be better to see the sardside torn from the garmside, and the broken halves left to fend for themselves?"

Roi had no reply. She was sure that had happened at least once before, but who could say how much suffering, how much death, it had cost?

Zak said, "This plan is ingenious, but recruiting a team big enough to carry it out, let alone gaining the understanding and consent of everyone affected, would take several lifetimes. I hate to admit it, but we might have to resign ourselves to enduring at least one more division. In the aftermath of a disaster people might be willing to do anything to avoid a recurrence, but I can't see it happening while the majority still doubt that there's anything at stake."

His words brought Roi the same guilty sense of relief as she felt after each set of unchanged measurements. *Let the danger and confrontation retreat into the future. Let some other generation deal with it.*

"There could be a problem with that."

Roi didn't recognize the voice immediately. When she searched the chamber to see who had spoken, it was Neth, a young student of Tan's. As far as Roi knew, Neth's only other work since her hatchling's education had been herding susk, but she had taken to template mathematics as if it were the most natural thing in the world.

Neth continued, a little shyly. "If the next division is like the last one, I'm sure many people would survive. The weights would be greater, but both new Splinters would be smaller, and the weights alone would not be enough to harm us. The wind would still blow, the crops would still spread, we would mourn our team-mates and then continue with our lives.

"But it might not be that way."

She hesitated. Zak said encouragingly, "Go on. We all want to hear you."

Neth said, "I've been studying the templates that describe the motion of the looping stones. When you toss a stone directly garm or sard from the Null Line, it follows a closed curve, an ellipse about three times as long as it is wide.

"This looping motion shows that an object that shares our orbit, then is slightly disturbed, won't wander too far. Even if you toss the stone along the Null Line, giving it a sustained motion in that direction, it won't go far garm or sard of us. Any small disturbance of the orbit we're on leads to another orbit which stays more or less the same distance from the Hub."

Zak said, "Agreed."

"The problem," Neth said, "is that it's not the strength of the weights alone that has changed over time, but also the relationship between them. If we can believe the Map of Weights, then when it was drawn all the relative strengths were different. The total garm weight was three times the spin weight. At present, that ratio is more than three and a half. If we'd tossed a stone garmwards from the Null Line when the Map of Weights was drawn, the loop it followed would have been a different shape than the one we see now; it would have been just twice as long as it was wide.

"If the ratio between the garm weight and the spin weight keeps increasing the closer we get to the Hub, then the loop will keep growing longer and skinnier. But the shape changes faster than the ratio, and the ratio only has to reach a value of *four* in order for the loop to stop being a loop at all. If the ratio becomes four, then a stone tossed garmwards will never return to the Null Line. The swerve weight will still bend the stone's path around, but the garm weight will be strong enough to tip the balance, and ensure that the stone never comes back."

There was silence as people absorbed the implications of this. What Neth was describing for a stone tossed in the Null Chamber applied equally well to the Splinter itself. If the ratio of weights changed in the way she described, any slight disturbance that nudged the Splinter garmwards would no longer lead to a small variation in its path, a gentle meandering that never saw it stray far from the original orbit. Instead, it would immediately send it spiraling in toward the Hub.

Ruz said, "Might it not be that this ratio never actually reaches four? Might it not approach that value as we approach the Hub, without ever quite getting there?"

"That's a possibility," Neth replied. "As things stand, though, we have no way of knowing whether that's true or not."

The meeting's attentive silence gave way to a cacophony, as most of the team began talking among themselves. Roi made her way over to Zak, whose body was hunched against the rock in a protective posture.

"Are you all right?"

"I'm fine," he rasped. "Just a few pangs, nothing unusual." After a moment he added, "I can still remember when we first calculated the period of the looping stones. The square of the inverse period was proportional to *four times the spin weight minus the garm-sard weight*. But I assumed that that quantity would always stay positive. I never considered the possibility that it might change sign, or what the consequences would be."

"Let me get you out of here." Roi started clearing a path for him.

Zak said, "Wait." He forced his pain aside and looked up at her. "Let me speak to the meeting first." Roi drummed a call for silence, and when it was finally heeded Zak addressed the team.

"Neth's work changes everything," he declared. "We are a long way from predicting the ratios of weights all the way down to the Hub, and even if we did find some beautiful templates that seemed to fit the handful of numbers we have, we would be foolish to trust them absolutely. We can't rule out reaching a ratio of four, so we have to be prepared for that possibility.

"I believe that we have two priorities now, both of them equally urgent. The first is to continue the experiments, the calculations, and the philosophical speculations that have brought us this far. This is the work that led us to Neth's insight. We must do our best to map the dangers that lie ahead, even if our foresight can never be perfect.

"Our other priority must be to strengthen our ability to act on whatever insights we can gain. We need to recruit, we need to educate, we need to start the whole Splinter talking about these dangers.

"A few heartbeats ago, I declared that Bard's plan would take several lifetimes to achieve. That might or might not be true, but it's no longer an excuse to delay taking it seriously. If we can devise an easier, less contentious way to move the Splinter out of danger, that would be the greatest achievement we could hope for. If we can't, then we need to prepare ourselves to accept the reality: the lives of all our descendants might depend on whether we can recruit enough workers, and win enough support, to carve a tunnel from one side of the Splinter to the other."

11

In the center of the bulge, a billion and a half stars wheeled around in a disk fifteen hundred light years wide. The astronomers of the Amalgam called this the NSD—the Nuclear Stellar Disk—and had long ago resigned themselves to observing it from afar, as just one more example of the kind of structure seen in a billion other galaxies. It was a telescopic object, not a destination for travelers.

Many of the stars in the NSD were infant prodigies: hot, bright, fast-burning giants born a few tens of millions of years ago in the clouds of gas swept inward by the complex dynamics of the galactic core. Others were older, smaller stars that had wound their way in over billions of years, their orbits slowly decaying as they lost energy to chance encounters.

The meteor that the Aloof had captured had managed to climb just beyond the edge of the NSD. Given that the rock had not been melted by the impact that had sent it on its way, there were limits to the speed with which it could have been blasted free of its parent world. If that world had been bound to a star at the time, meteor and star could not have parted company too quickly.

Over fifty million years, the two might have completed as many as ten laps around the galactic center, with their orbits gradually diverging as they came under the sway of different neighbors. However, if the star in question was assumed to be the Interloper that had scrambled the system of the planet that Rakesh had named Touched-by-Steel, then the possibilities became much more tightly constrained. Many of the stars that might have been close enough to the meteor itself certainly hadn't traveled far enough from the galactic center at any time in the last two hundred million years to have kidnapped the Steelmakers' world. According to the models Rakesh ran, only forty-six stars could have captured the planet, sunk down into the NSD, and then been in the right place fifty million years ago to make sense of the meteor's trajectory.

When the remaining siblings of Touched-by-Steel, the three gas giants and their moons, proved to be untouched themselves, Parantham asked the map to take *Lahl's Promise* to the first of the forty-six stars.

This time, the Aloof's hidden travel agent delivered no pleasant twist to their itinerary. The jump-cut in their consciousness filled the sky with hot blue stars that far outshone the sun they now orbited, but as the seconds ticked by and the cabin window completed its three hundred and sixty degree pan, no planet swam into view.

They scoured the region with their instruments, but this star's sole companion was a sparse disk of rubble, with all the fine dust that might normally have been expected blown away by the wind from the neighboring stars. No gas, no ice; just barren rock. With volatiles so rare, Rakesh thought, it must have been a challenge for the Aloof's engineering spores to scrape together the raw materials to reconstruct the whole ship, unless they'd developed femtomachines sophisticated enough to make transmuting the elements more efficient than scavenging for them.

The second candidate on their list had managed to hold on to even less detritus than the first. The winds from the new-born giants were not as strong here, but if any planets or asteroids worthy of the name had once accompanied this star, they had long ago been dislodged from their orbits by interfering neighbors. Rakesh had learned as a child that life could only thrive out in the disk, and however far the Steelmakers had progressed it was growing ever harder to see them as much of an exception to that parochial rule. Maybe life *had* flourished in this region, in some as yet undiscovered niche that had nothing to do with planets sitting in stable orbits around stars for billions of years; maybe the Aloof were descended from such creatures. The fact remained, though, that his cousins seemed to have hitched their fortunes to a way of life that simply couldn't last here.

The third star possessed a substantial asteroid belt, but still no planets. Rakesh thought, *This is how it's going to be: sometimes a few more rocks, sometimes a few less.* Each star's chaotic history of close encounters would sweep a slightly different range of orbits clean, but there'd always be a smattering of junk clinging on.

Parantham said calmly, "The isotope signature of most of these asteroids matches our rock."

Rakesh viewed the data. Point after point coincided, error bars overlapping. What's more, the models he ran rejected the notion that these asteroids had been born from the same gas cloud as the star they orbited.

It looked as if they'd found the Interloper, and the shattered remnants of the Steelmakers' world.

Rakesh was shaken, though he knew he had no right to be surprised that the search had ended badly. The Interloper had dragged this world into ever more dangerous territory; the real miracle was that it had enjoyed such a long era of safety and stability around its birth star. "So this is their graveyard," he said.

"We don't know that," Parantham replied. "We know that the Steelmakers built at least one interplanetary probe. At some point they might have built star ships, or engineering spores. They might have left this world behind long before it was broken up."

Rakesh had his doubts that the Steelmakers—as a species, let alone a technological culture—could have survived their planet's capture by the Interloper. Still, it was possible that in the intervening hundred million years a second intelligent species had arisen in their place. In any case, he'd honor his promise and sift through the ruins. He owed it to the Steelmakers and whoever might have followed them to do his best to learn their history and bring it back to the Amalgam.

Dynamical models indicated that the Steelmakers' world had been tidally disrupted, rather than smashed apart by a head-on collision. A compact stellar remnant—most likely a neutron star—had passed through the system fifty million years before, coming close enough for the difference in its gravitational pull from one side of the planet to the other to tear asteroid-sized rocks right out of the mantle and send them fountaining into the sky. Though common sense made that sound like the work of a monstrously powerful force, the models suggested that the tidal stretching had only exceeded the planet's gravity by a modest amount, perhaps as little as fifty per cent. If there *had* been any hapless descendants of the Steelmakers around, the tidal force itself would have left them unscathed, but that would have been the least of their problems. Some might have survived the initial quakes, as the pressure bearing down on the planet's interior was lessened in places and strengthened elsewhere, fracturing the crust like the skin of a squeezed grape. Some would have felt their own weight growing, but not unbearably, and even where the tidal stretch turned gravity skyward, some might have had the presence of mind to grip something anchored securely to the ground and cling to life for a few more minutes as the air around them grew thinner. In the end, though, *the ground itself* had had nothing to hold it together against its own reversed weight, and the planet had simply disintegrated.

Rakesh worked with Parantham to design a probe swarm to send into the ruins. Each probe would be about a micrometer wide, and would hop from asteroid to asteroid by riding the currents of the stellar wind—not the Interloper's feeble exhalation, but the overpowering breath of the neighborhood giants. On each rock they visited, the probes would gather energy from sunlight to feed a small band of exploratory nanomachines.

The wind couldn't carry the probes all the way from *Lahl's Promise* into the asteroid belt, so they had the workshop build half a dozen delivery modules, driven by ion thrusters, each carrying a kilogram or so of probes to scatter as they arced along the edge of the belt. These delivery modules would also act as information relays, with instruments to track the probes closely and elicit stored data from them.

The modules filed out of the workshop, flung away from the ship by centrifugal force before their thrusters lit up. Rakesh watched their blue exhaust trails through the cabin window. "Do you regret coming with me now?" he asked Parantham.

"Not at all!" she said. She seemed shocked by the question. "Why would I?"

"If the Steelmakers are dead, with no descendants..."

"Then that's sad," she said, "but history is full of sad stories. If there's no chance of meeting them face to face, I'll happily settle for archaeology. Archaeology in the disk is finished: every ruin has been tomographed down to the molecular level, every scrap of ancient language and every artefact has been interpreted to death. I was promised nothing but a rock full of microbes when I signed up for this, remember? And you expect me to be having second thoughts just because the sentient species we've discovered might have lasted less than one hundred and fifty million years?"

Rakesh couldn't argue with anything Parantham had said, but his own sentiments were very different. "Maybe at the back of my mind I thought the worst case scenario would be a thousand-year-long slog that ended with nothing but bacteria, while the best case would take us straight to the Planet of the Long Lost Cousins, who I could invite into the Amalgam to live happily ever after. Now that we've caught a glimpse of the real story, it seems that it's bacteria who would have had the best chance of living happily ever after."

He could easily picture his own village on Shab-e-Noor with a dark pinprick crossing the sky, the ground rumbling, an ominous lightness. Of course, that couldn't happen in the Age of the Amalgam; there was no conceivable cosmic threat out in the disk that could not be detected and neutralized. Such vulnerability had been relegated to history. Nevertheless, the image haunted him in a way that went beyond mere empathy for its putative victims. There was a chill in his bones at the recognition that, in the broadest sense, he'd stepped out from the shadow of the same kind of ax. His ancestors had been luckier than the Steelmakers, that was all.

The first wave of results from the probes came in while Rakesh was in the kitchen, cooking breakfast.

Dead microbes had been found in more than sixty per cent of the asteroids sampled so far. That figure was surprisingly high; either the biosphere of the Steelmakers' world had extended deep into the mantle, or the rubble that originated from the depths of the planet had been cross-contaminated by other debris, from closer to the surface.

The genome fragments and general morphology closely matched those of the microbes they'd found in the Aloof's meteor. Along with the isotope data, this left Rakesh with no doubt that they'd found their target. Half of the Interloper's asteroid belt consisted of rocks virtually identical to the one that had triggered their search.

"The Aloof should give us a treat and a scratch behind the ears now," he told Parantham as he filled her plate.

She stared at him as if he'd lost his mind.

"On my home world," he explained, "we have domestic animals that can find things by scent. You give them a whiff, then they go searching for something that smells the same."

"You don't have machines to do that?"

"Of course we do. But these animals enjoy it, it's part of their ancestry. If they don't get the chance to exercise their skills, they get sick with boredom."

"Like the gang back at the node?" Parantham suggested dryly.

"Well, yes." Rakesh hadn't intended the comparison to be taken literally, but he felt a momentary frisson of unease. "I suppose that's one theory we can't rule out: the Aloof took pity on us and offered us a chance to chase a strange new scent across their paddock."

"It doesn't show much pity if they only do it for a couple of people every million years." Parantham shook her head. "We're not their pets. They've kept a few secrets from us; good for them. It doesn't make them our superiors."

"A *few* secrets?" Rakesh laughed. "We mapped their gamma ray data routes. They get to read our minds, down to the last byte. And you're the one who told me that the gamma ray network was probably just a honey pot."

"I'm not saying that the relationship is symmetrical," Parantham conceded. "They've certainly out-somethinged us…"

"Outwitted?" Rakesh suggested. "Outsmarted? Outmanoeuvred?"

"Out-sphinxed us," she replied. "We stared into the bulge for a million years, trying to get a reaction, and they just stared back out at us, stony-faced. We did much more than blink; we gave up the game completely. I don't believe it's harmed us, though. I don't believe it's a loss on our part, or a victory on theirs. It's just a difference in our natures. We never wanted to keep our nature and our history secret. It's a game we never wanted to win."

Rakesh was woken by the next wave of results. He watched the data and images spinning in his skull as he walked down the corridor to the control cabin, where Parantham was already seated.

"It's alive!" she crowed. "DNA-based, multi-cellular, *engineered*... but then drifting genetically, running wild for tens of millions of years."

The probes had found a scum of fungus-like growth clinging to parts of some of the asteroids. These were not just colonies of microbes; the cells showed specialization, and were organized into distinct clusters. Though the anatomy of the clusters included a protective skin, all of the cells were individually tough enough to retain internal liquid water while exposed to vacuum, over a considerable temperature range, with antifreeze compounds and vapor-reducing soluble polymers augmenting the sheer strength of the cell walls. Their genome showed clear evidence of sophisticated engineering, and although they shared a common ancestor with the dead microbes, most of the traits that ensured their survival in their present harsh environment appeared to have been artificially introduced.

The creation of the species couldn't be dated exactly until mutation rates and generation times had been measured, but on general biochemical grounds it seemed likely that this fungus had been deliberately constructed at about the time the Steelmakers' world was torn apart.

Rakesh immersed himself in a diagram of metabolic pathways. "It lives on the stellar wind," he marveled. "That's its energy source. For raw materials, it's coping on the asteroids, but there are vestigial enzymes that suggest it might have thrived with a slightly different substrate. So it spread to the asteroids from somewhere else, and adapted to them over time, but the original species was happier in a different environment."

Parantham said, "You look up into the sky, and a neutron star is coming. There is no transport network to whisk you away to safety, and you can forget about deflecting this planet-killer. What do you do?"

"Build a spaceship."

"To go where? There are plenty of stars around, but they're all devoid of companions. A hundred million years ago your ancestors visited another planet, but the space program has grown a little rusty since then."

Rakesh grimaced. "So I give up on the idea of running, and make a *fungus* that will outlive me? I know I've been spoiled by high-tech immortality, but that doesn't sound like much consolation to me."

Parantham said, "Perhaps it's just the bottom of the food chain. Make a fungus that will outlive you, then a few species that can eat it, and so on. Then give birth to a child that can live on *them*."

"Maybe." Rakesh ran his fingers through his hair. "Live on them where, though? Those old genes I mentioned were for enzymes that relied on elements that most of the asteroids don't have. If you know that your world is going to be torn apart, and there are no other planets in sight, where exactly do you expect to live, if not on the scrap heap that's left behind?"

A few hours later they had the answer, from their telescopes rather than from the probes. Near the edge of the belt, an object some six hundred meters across with a highly atypical spectrum had been found orbiting among the rocks. The telescope's image showed a gray ellipsoid, pitted and corroded, but clearly too regular to be an asteroid itself. Spectroscopy revealed that its surface contained molecular filaments, carbon nanotubes with elaborate chemical modifications that both strengthened them and protected them against the stellar wind. A variety of the vacuum-hardened fungus they'd detected in the asteroids could be seen in the indentations of small impact craters, where the wind couldn't reach in to scour it off.

"The material is advanced beyond the Steelmakers' technology," Rakesh mused, "but it's not one hundred million years ahead. They must have gone through a long Dark Age before they finally rose up again." *Only to be cut down once more?* That wasn't clear. Their home world was in ruins, but this artefact was in one piece.

Parantham said, "That surface looks as if it hasn't been repaired in fifty million years."

"Not everyone cares about surfaces," Rakesh replied. "There could still be someone home."

They sent a surveyor probe, which tomographed the artefact with ambient neutrinos. Inside was a maze of tunnels and caves. Apart from these empty spaces, there was an intricate pattern to the density of the structure itself: parts of the walls were solid as basalt, while others seemed as spongy and permeable as limestone.

Parantham beamed a radio signal from the surveyor probe down to the artefact, a simple message of greeting repeated across the frequency spectrum. The faint passive echo that came back suggested some long strips of conducting material, but no resonant circuits: electrical wiring, perhaps, but no obvious low-tech receivers or transmitters.

An analysis of the artefact's thermal emissions showed no significant amounts of heat being generated within, beyond what might be expected from a small amount of the fungus, and perhaps other species. There was no obvious stream of waste, organic or otherwise, leaving the artefact, though with the stellar wind as its only input any putative ecosystem would have to cling tightly to all of its materials.

Rakesh said, "It's time to send in the jelly babies."

"Ha! You were far more cautious with Steel Mountain," Parantham reminded him.

"If we trigger some elaborate defensive response," Rakesh said, "then at least I'll die happy. Knowing that this civilization survived."

There was no entranceway into the artefact, but the surveyor probe identified a system of narrow cracks in the exterior wall that ultimately led to one of the internal tunnels. If they made their avatars even smaller than before, about a fifth of a millimeter tall, they would be able to squeeze through.

Rakesh glanced up one last time into the sky full of hot blue stars before following Parantham into the chasm.

As the walls twisted around them, they soon reached a point where the stars were hidden and everything was swallowed by the deep shadows of vacuum; by switching to infrared vision, though, it was possible to grope their way down by the thermal glow of their surroundings. Their avatars sported adhesive pads on their hands and feet, tailored to the chemistry of the bare surface, but the infestations of fungus made their grip less secure.

Rakesh sent nanomachines from a stock in his avatar's arm into a patch of fungus, to sequence it. There were at least nine distinct species present, and they all showed marked differences from the kind found on the asteroids. The vestigial enzymes he'd noted there were being produced in far greater quantities here, and seemed to interact with several components of the wall material. As he pondered the modified diagram of metabolic pathways, he realized what was happening. The walls acted as a reservoir for the raw materials that the fungus needed, but the fungus did more than leech essential nutrients out of its environment. As part of its life cycle, it returned everything it took, with the added bonus that structural flaws in the wall were repaired in the process. The system wasn't perfect, but a few cracks after fifty million years wasn't bad.

It was a tortuous business navigating the fissure, but Rakesh wasn't tempted to disconnect his senses and leave his avatar on autopilot. He didn't know if he was entering a mouldy tomb or a thriving metropolis, but he had no wish to dilute, or distance himself from, the experience. As painful as he found it to be forced to confront the bleak prospects for life in the bulge, this expedition was exactly what he'd been seeking ever since he'd left his home world. Who else on Shab-e-Noor, who else in the whole disk, would be able to tell their descendants: "We climbed down through a gap in the wall, not knowing what we would find inside the structure after fifty million years"?

When they emerged into the tunnel, Rakesh found himself immersed in a featureless glow. The tunnel wall was so close to being uniform in temperature that its thermal emissions rendered everything in contrast-free monochrome. It was almost impossible to interpret what he saw, let alone navigate by it.

"Is it just me who's gone blind?" he asked Parantham.

"IR sensitivity isn't enough. We need to rewrite our whole visual processing system," she suggested.

Rakesh searched the library. Leaving aside olfactory and tactile modes—sniffing or groping your way through the dark—most underground species employed vibration sensors or sonar. The walls here were excellent sound conductors, but even so that would be of limited use. He found a mode of IR-based perception that some asteroid-mining robots and a few tunnel-dwelling species relied upon. It involved extracting and interpreting very small temperature differences from thermal emissions; it was exactly what he and Parantham needed.

The tunnel snapped into focus, decorated with elaborate patterns where the fungus in all its variety grew. Despite the strangeness of the view, the new system felt right: Rakesh knew where he was now, how to move, and what to expect to see when he did. It was unsettling to be reminded that *vision* was a highly refined form of knowledge, a set of propositions about the world that needed to be deduced, not some passive stream of data that simply flowed into his skull as effortlessly as light into a camera.

They set out along the tunnel, which loomed over them like some monumental feat of engineering. It was only about two centimeters wide, but Rakesh had no way of knowing whether its builders would have viewed it as a cramped passageway, a great highway, or something in between.

They'd chosen not to use the avatars' vibration sensors as their primary mode of perception, but that didn't stop them picking up a faint but rising beat conducted through the tunnel wall. "Should we go and explore that?" Parantham asked.

Rakesh said, "It sounds as if it's coming toward us already."

A giant creature came scurrying around a bend in the tunnel. It was moving on twelve legs like a busy arthropod, about a millimeter across. Their mode of vision rendered it translucent, revealing hints of membranes and chambers flexing and contracting within.

When it changed course to charge straight toward them Rakesh suppressed the urge to flee; their avatars were extremely robust, and in any case easily replaced. The creature halted and inclined the axis of its body toward him; it seemed presumptuous to assume that it was lowering its face, when Rakesh could make no immediate sense of the complex mass of bristles, knobs and tendrils that confronted him. A cluster of these organs suddenly sprang forward and made contact with his avatar, wrapping it and holding it firmly; he steeled himself for the shock of being vicariously swallowed, but after a moment the creature unwrapped him and disengaged. It stood motionless for a second or two, as if pondering the need for another taste, then it turned away and continued down the tunnel, as rapidly as it had approached.

Parantham said, "We should follow it."

"Yes."

The avatars had small fusion-powered ion thrusters attached like backpacks; with no gravity or air resistance to overcome, catching up with the creature and flying a few centimeters above it was easy. Having dismissed them as inedible once, the creature seemed untroubled by their presence, if it was aware of them at all.

The creature had shed cells on Rakesh's avatar, and he had the nanomachines sequence them as he flew. They shared the fungus's vacuum-hardening traits, and a large proportion of its other genes, both natural and introduced.

Parantham said, "I'd like to run a morphogenetic model. What do you think?"

"Coarse-grain it, and I think that would be ethical." Software could take the genome and use it to simulate a growing embryo. A fine-grained simulation would necessarily experience everything that a real organism would, but a coarse-grained simulation could provide information about the range of generic experiences that were possible, without anyone actually experiencing them.

"All right."

In a spare corner of Parantham's mind, a sketch of the virtual creature took shape. While Rakesh watched the adult below him scurrying along, pausing now and then to graze on patches of fungus, a second viewpoint showed him an annotated diagram of the developing embryo in its egg case. As morphogen gradients washed over the dividing cells, eight distinct segments formed, the middle six slowly sprouting a tightly folded pair of legs each. Mouthparts, excretory and reproductive organs were whittled out of the growing mass of cells. The developing nervous system was extremely simple, and by the time the egg hatched it was close to hardwired: a handful of innate drives and reflexes would enable this creature to move, feed and mate, but it had no potential to do anything more complex.

Like all DNA-based life it was Rakesh's distant cousin, but it was unlikely to be a direct descendant of whoever had built this ark.

"It doesn't use infrared at all," Parantham observed. "It listens for sounds conducted through the tunnel wall."

"So how did it home in on me when I was standing stock still?" Rakesh examined the model's results more closely. "Aha. Resonances set up by its own footsteps. A kind of sonar, after all." It was impossible to say exactly how this creature's natural ancestors had lived, but the engineered traits it possessed were extensive and ingenious. The Arkmakers might not have had the technology to locate, let alone reach, another planet like their own, but they had worked hard to adapt life to their new environment.

"So where are its designers?" he asked Parantham.

"Be patient," she replied. "We've barely scratched the surface."

When they reached a fork in the tunnel, they launched a small probe to keep following the twelve-legged creature, and they took the other turn, in toward the center of the ark.

Rakesh kept waiting for a riot of new lifeforms to appear before his eyes—to cross some threshold that marked the end of the barren outskirts, and witness a sudden explosion of diversity—but all they saw were the same kinds of fungus and the same spider-like creatures eating it. In fact, the further they went the sparser the fungus became.

"The stellar wind powers the whole ecosystem," Parantham mused. "But it barely penetrates this deep. Parts of the walls are permeable to it, parts are not; it's as if they designed the ark to have a certain flow, a certain set of currents running through it. But the wind must have been much stronger then. These days, it's too feeble to do the job. And there doesn't seem to be any other mechanism for transporting energy in toward the center."

Rakesh didn't reply, but he couldn't help following her argument to its logical conclusion. The Arkmakers had invented a whole new ecosystem to live in after the death of their planet, but the vagaries of the bulge had defeated them yet again. They had relied on the hot winds from nearby giant stars as their new primary energy source, turning their backs on the relatively weak radiation from their small but stable foster-sun. Giant stars had short lives, and while new ones were always being born, in any particular place the stellar wind could ebb and flow dramatically on a time scale of just a few million years. The Interloper might have finished off the Steelmakers, but it could have provided whoever came after them with more or less constant light for another three billion years.

As they flew deeper into the ark, the fungus disappeared completely. The interior was barren. With nothing to repair them, the walls became increasingly cracked; small thermal stresses over the millennia had torn at the structure, in places reducing it to loose piles of rubble. Electro-magnetic probes revealed what might once have been a network of copper wires running through the walls—distributing power, perhaps, or information—but they were just fragmented segments now, worn and snapped by minuscule but relentlessly patient forces.

About halfway to the center, rubble blocked their way. They despatched a swarm of small probes that could squeeze into the interstices, then backtracked and took a turn sideways, to see if there was anything that they could explore "for themselves". Rakesh had grown used to his new body, and he was reluctant to give it up and return his senses to *Lahl's Promise*.

He said, "Fifty million years is a long time to expect anyone to stay cooped up in a place like this. Maybe the Arkmakers finally developed interstellar travel, mined the asteroids for some raw materials, and then headed right out of the NSD to search for a safer home."

"That's possible," Parantham replied. "And if we can't see the hole where they burrowed out of this cocoon, maybe the fungus sealed it off." She hesitated. "The design still doesn't make a lot of sense to me, though. Even if the stellar winds were much stronger when this place was built, I can't see what the flow was optimized *for*. There's a very precise gradation in the density of the wall material; it's far too regular to be accidental, so it's either an engineering feature that I just don't understand, or a reflection of a very weird esthetic. If you chop this place in half along the center of the long axis, there's more flow-through in one half than the other. What's that all about? And I'd swear the local variations are designed to induce turbulence that would scatter the fungus as widely as possible, but the fluid dynamics is all wrong for any plausible stellar wind that might have blown into this system."

The way ahead was blocked by a cloud of rubble again. Rakesh braked and let himself float in the middle of the tunnel.

He said, "This thing has no engine. How do you think they got it clear of the planet when the neutron star came through?"

Parantham shrugged. "They might have taken it up in small pieces, and used the fungus to weld them together."

"That's assuming they had rockets at all," Rakesh said.

"Well, yes. If they didn't, they could have simply built it on the ground and let the tidal force lift it. That would have been a very risky strategy, though."

"Where would the safest launching site be?" Rakesh glanced at a model and answered his own question, "The point furthest from the neutron star at the moment when its tidal force canceled the planet's gravity. Assuming that it survived the quakes, the ark would simply drift up into space."

Parantham said, "It wouldn't have had much of a head start, though, before all the rocks came tumbling after it. Collisions between the debris would redistribute its momentum, creating some fragments that would outrace the pack. You couldn't avoid a serious peppering, at the very least."

"I suppose they could have made more than one ark, to improve the odds," Rakesh suggested. "The others might have been destroyed by debris, or captured by the neutron star."

Parantham let out a long, reproachful moan. "Captured by the neutron star?"

Rakesh was bemused. "You don't think that's possible?"

"Of course it's possible. *And that's exactly what they wanted!* This one's the failure, the one that was left behind!"

"How is it a failure to get left behind?"

"The giants' stellar wind," she said, "has a greater energy density than middle-aged starlight, but there's something that would give it even more oomph: the gravitational field of a neutron star. The neutron star would have drawn the wind into an accretion disk around it, far richer in energy than anything else in sight. The Arkmakers saw this monster coming, and thought: if it's going to pulverize our home, better to learn to drink from that whirlpool than skulk around in the ruins waiting for the next disaster.

"This ark, and everything in it, was designed to survive in an accretion disk. The asymmetrical flow-through would have given it a kind of buoyancy, pushing it back out into larger orbits if it ever sank in too deep." Parantham ran a model, and piped the output to Rakesh. "The wind in the disk would have been strong enough to keep the fungus alive almost everywhere, to support the food chain throughout the ark."

Rakesh absorbed the model's results. Parantham's conclusions were hard to dispute.

"So this place was starved from the beginning?" he said. "When they missed the neutron star, they had no hope?" The children of the Arkmakers, designed to escape the fate of their planet-bound parents, had found themselves stranded with the wrong biology, trapped inside an ingenious machine for extracting energy from an exotic new source that was receding into the distance at a few hundred kilometers a second.

Parantham said, "No hope for themselves. But I can't believe this was the only ark. There could have been a dozen, there could have been a thousand. If they really saw no prospect of fleeing from the neutron star, every resource on the planet would have been used to maximize the chances of hitching a ride."

Rakesh looked around at the ruins of this desperate strategy, and tried to picture the same tunnels teeming with life while the hot wind from a neutron star's accretion disk whistled through the walls. Perhaps the extraordinary gamble could have paid off, if they'd repeated it a sufficient number of times.

"If they hitched a ride, where did it take them?" Rakesh asked. When he and Parantham had first realized what it was that had created the asteroid belt, they had run dynamical models and checked the maps, but they'd been unable to locate the neutron star that had done the deed. The only thing that had been clear was the general direction of its motion.

"Toward the center," Parantham replied. "Deeper into the core."

12

As the work team gathered in the Calculation Chamber, Roi caught sight of Neth and proclaimed hopefully, "Sixth time brings success!"

"Sixth?" Neth replied. "Surely this is the third?"

"It's one task to frame a hypothesis, then another to test it," Roi insisted. "So that's six separate acts."

Neth was too polite to object, and perhaps too serious to understand that Roi was only joking. If the proverb was worth anything, it certainly wasn't worth taking literally. It did encourage persistence, though, and Roi had a feeling that their persistence was finally going to be rewarded.

Since Neth's discovery that orbits around the Hub might become unstable, a dozen or so members of Zak's original team had left to educate hatchlings into the secrets of weight and motion, and a dozen more had headed for the sardside, with the even more ambitious aim of recruiting a new team to build Bard's tunnel. The task of those who remained was to find a geometry for space and time that satisfied Zak's principle, in the hope of learning more about the dangers the Splinter would face in the future.

Tan had refined his ideas for characterizing geometry to the point where he could calculate the natural paths—the closest things to straight lines—on any curved surface. The vital step that remained, though, was to find the correct way to move from the geometry of space alone to a version that included time.

When Tan analyzed a path on a curved surface, he broke it up into a multitude of tiny, straight line segments of equal length. These small straight lines acted as markers for the direction of the curve. The geometry of the surface could then be embodied in a simple mathematical rule that Tan called a "connection". The connection allowed you to take a direction at one point and shift it to another, nearby point, in a manner that respected the geometry of the surface. If a curve was a natural path, then when you broke it up into line segments and used the connection to shift them all one step forward, the shifted segments would coincide with the originals: shifting the first segment one step along the curve would give you the original direction of the second segment, and so on. If the curve was *not* a natural path, then the directions would fail to agree, and the resulting discrepancies would be a measure of how much the curve swerved unnecessarily, as opposed to merely following the geometry.

That the curves were broken into line segments of *equal length* was a crucial part of the recipe, because the analysis had to yield the same verdict if the surface was picked up and rotated, or if two people were viewing it from different angles. If you decreed that the curve should be broken up some other way, such as into segments that spanned equal horizontal distances, then different people would be left arguing over which direction was "horizontal". Nobody would argue as to whether two successive segments were of equal length. With the connection respecting this rule—preserving the lengths of the segments as it moved them from point to point—everything worked smoothly, and everyone agreed on which paths constituted natural motion and which did not.

What happened, though, when you considered the path of a tossed stone, moving forward in time as well as through space? Anyone could draw a picture in which some chosen direction represented time, and the path of a moving object slanted across the skin, but how could people ever agree on the correct scale for such a diagram? Whether one heartbeat, one shift, or one lifetime passed from the top of the skin to the bottom was a completely arbitrary choice.

Nevertheless, suppose you settled on a scale. What would happen if you divided the path of a stone into segments of *equal length?* To Roi, who tossed a stone forward across the Null Chamber at one span per heartbeat, the path she drew would slant across the skin. If Zak happened already to be moving at the same pace in the same direction, the stone would be motionless to him, so he would draw a line that stretched solely in the time direction. Suppose that after five heartbeats, the stone hit an obstacle. Zak's line would be "five heartbeats" long, whatever the scale of the picture made that. Roi's line, though, would have to be longer: it would stretch five heartbeats in the time direction, but it would also cross five spans of space. The accounts of the two experimenters had to be compatible somehow, but they couldn't expect to draw their separate diagrams and then measure the same path lengths.

What could they agree on? The simplest answer anyone in the team had been able to suggest was the time that had elapsed. If you marked off segments of the stone's path representing *equal intervals of elapsed time*, everyone would agree how many segments there were from start to finish. If you looked for a connection that respected this scheme by never changing the amount of time spanned by a segment, then everything would have a chance to work smoothly.

This was what the team had tried first. They had hunted for a geometry of space and time whose connection left intervals of time unchanged, and which obeyed Zak's principle.

In less than one shift, they had found one. In this geometry, everything was symmetrical about a special point, where the Hub could sit. The natural paths of the geometry included circular orbits around the Hub. The square of the period of each such orbit was proportional to the cube of its size. And the ratio between the garm-sard weight and the shomal-junub weight was precisely three. Close to the Hub, far from the Hub, always, everywhere, three.

It was the answer that Zak had guessed long ago, when he'd thought the Map of Weights might still hold true. It possessed an elegant simplicity, but it was impossible to reconcile with the measurements they had made. The current ratio of weights was two and a quarter; that had been confirmed a dozen times.

This failure had cast some doubt on the idea that natural motion could be described by the same kind of geometrical principles that applied to space alone. The team had considered looking for a completely new direction, but the consensus had been that they shouldn't give up on Tan's ideas so easily.

Was there any other rule that the connection could obey that might make sense? Could the idea of "constant length" that worked so well in space alone somehow be applied in the new context, in spite of the obvious problems?

It was Neth who had pointed out that if you drew a space-time diagram with an outrageously large scale for the time axis—thirty-six times thirty-six spans for one heartbeat, say—then the different points of view of people moving with mildly different velocities could be mimicked quite accurately by the very slight rotations of the picture that would be needed to make their own particular paths point purely in the time direction. The problem remained that if lengths on this diagram were taken as fixed, two people moving with different velocities would consider each other's hearts to be beating faster than if their motion was the same, since a line that was "one heartbeat long" would span a smaller interval of time, and seem to pass more quickly, if it was slanted away from the time direction of the person who was measuring it. In reality, though, if the scale was large enough then the effect would be so tiny as to be impossible to measure. Who was to say that this wasn't happening?

It was an audacious hypothesis, but nobody had any better ideas. The team had labored for five shifts to find a geometry in accord with it. Their success, when it came, had been a mixed blessing, but nevertheless it had convinced Roi that they were on the right track.

The second geometry, like the first, was symmetrical about one special point, and allowed for circular orbits. Far from the Hub, the periods of these orbits were approximated by the old square-cube rule, but for smaller orbits the approximation broke down, and the periods became longer than that rule implied.

As a consequence, the ratio of garm-sard weight to shomal-junub weight was no longer fixed at three. It started out close to three for orbits far from the Hub, which was promising; the problem was, as you approached the Hub the ratio became larger, not smaller. The ratio was greater than three, everywhere, and the two and a quarter they had measured was nowhere to be found in this geometry.

The team had spent a further six shifts checking and rechecking their results. A single error anywhere in their calculations might have thrown the orbital periods and the weight ratios in the wrong direction. There was no error, though. The geometry they had found followed Zak's principle—that the sum of the true weights without spin was zero—and its connection respected Neth's idea that different people's space-time diagrams of moving objects should agree on the lengths of their paths. It was more beautiful, Roi thought, than the simpler geometry they'd found before; it certainly offered richer possibilities. But it did not describe the reality of the Splinter and the Hub.

As Roi had scrutinized the calculations, checking for some tiny, subtle mistake, an idea almost as outrageous as Neth's original hypothesis had occurred to her. Among other possibilities, they were hunting for a sign error: an addition in place of a subtraction, or vice versa. A mistake like that could easily be the cause of the problem. If there was no sign error in the calculation, though, might there not be one in the hypothesis itself?

Neth had supposed that the length in space-time that everyone agreed on obeyed the same rules as a length in space alone. The square of a length in space was the sum of the squares of its components in three different directions: garm-sard, shomal-junub, rarb-sharq. Neth had simply added in the square of the time component, after it had been multiplied by the scale factor that converted time to distance.

Why *add* the square of the time, though? Such perfect symmetry suggested that time was exactly like space, that apart from units of measurement the two things were indistinguishable. It was clear to Roi that time was different: you could walk back and forth along the garm-sard axis as often as you liked, but you could hardly do the same between future and past. If the first scheme they'd used to deal with time had set it too much apart, declaring it absolute, universal and immutable, perhaps their second attempt had gone too far in the other direction.

As a compromise, what if they looked for geometries whose connection preserved a slightly different quantity than Neth had suggested: instead of summing the squares of all the components, what if they summed the spatial ones then subtracted the time?

The team had debated the merits of Roi's proposal for more than half a shift. Many people had complained that it seemed arbitrary and ugly. Gul had pointed out that any object was motionless from its own perspective, so the "length" of its path for one heartbeat would be zero spans squared, minus one-heartbeat-converted-to-spans, squared: a negative number. But if, from another point of view, the object happened to be moving faster than the speed defined by Neth's spans-per-heartbeat scale, then whoever saw it moving that quickly would ascribe a positive length to its path. How could these two facts be reconciled, when the path length had to be preserved?

"Perhaps," Tan had suggested, "nothing can ever be seen to move faster than this speed."

"Then what happens," Gul had countered, "when I'm moving shomal at three quarters of this speed, compared to the rock of the Splinter, and you're moving just as fast junub? How fast do *you* think I'm moving?"

Tan had retreated into calculations, then emerged with an answer. "We each measure the other to be traveling at twenty-four parts in twenty-five of the critical speed. You can't simply add velocities in this scheme, the way you could in the first one."

Reflecting on this, Gul had not abandoned his misgivings completely, but he'd mused, "Then in principle the critical speed might be observable. It would not just be some magic large number that we choose for convenience, to turn time into space and make the mathematics work."

In the end, the team had agreed to test Roi's scheme at the start of the next shift. If it failed, as the others had, then they would move away from Tan's geometrical ideas and begin searching for an entirely new theory of motion.

Twenty-six people had gathered in the Calculation Chamber. Roi had looked in on Zak on her way; he'd offered her encouragement, but he'd been too tired to come and observe, let alone participate.

By consensus, Roi and Tan had been appointed lead calculators for this session. They would work independently of each other, while the remainder of the team, split in two, would act as their checkers. Only if both groups reached the same answer would it be trusted.

To save scratching out mathematical templates on skin, a wasteful and physically tiring process, Gul had devised an ingenious system for representing and manipulating templates by sliding stones around on a wire frame. It had taken Roi many shifts to master the system, but now she couldn't imagine working any other way. When each frame full of templates was completed, she copied the last template to a new frame, then passed the full frame to the first of the checkers.

The team had calculated and recalculated the consequences of Neth's idea many times, and the new templates had a very similar structure, so Roi made rapid progress, and each time she glanced around the chamber the checkers seemed to be keeping pace with her. The familiarity of the calculations also brought its perils, though; with the old version still fresh in their minds, the minor variations that Roi was introducing looked "wrong", like small mistakes that needed correcting. Several times Roi caught herself nearly reverting to the old templates.

She reached a template describing a connection that respected the new definition of space-time length, and whose geometry was symmetrical about the Hub. That she had come this far without any new problems emerging was an encouraging sign, but as yet it told her nothing concrete, because everything was still expressed in terms of two unknown templates that remained to be found.

Roi used the connection to analyze the possible circular motions around the geometry's central point. In space-time, circular motion became a helix, constantly advancing in time as it wound its way around the Hub. Only if the pitch of this helix was correct would the connection declare that it was natural motion: the path of a weightless, free-falling body.

Given the shape of a helix that constituted natural motion, she could find the period of any circular orbit. Since the geometry was symmetrical about the Hub, the period depended only on the size of the orbit, and two stones following two identically sized orbits inclined at a slight angle to each other would come together and move apart with exactly the same period as the orbit itself. In other words, she now knew the period of the shomal-junub cycle, and from that the shomal-junub weight.

Next, Roi calculated how the connection carried directions in space along the helix of the Splinter's orbit. The speed at which the garm or sharq direction was turning—relative to the frame of the Rotator—gave the strength of the hidden spin weight which canceled the rarb-sharq weight.

For the third weight, she considered a point tied to the Splinter, but displaced from its center in the garm or sard direction. Such a point would follow a helix in space-time that would wind around the Hub with the same period as the center of the Splinter, but unlike the center its path would not constitute natural motion. The connection told her the weight it would feel; this included the spin weight, but she could subtract that from it easily enough to obtain the true garm-sard weight.

Roi summed the weights that arose in all three directions, and imposed Zak's principle, requiring the sum to be zero.

This imposed a relationship between the two unknown templates, but it was still not enough to determine them individually. So Roi carried out a similar calculation for a different set of circumstances, summing the weights that would have been felt within the Splinter had it been plunging straight toward the Hub, rather than circling it. Again, Zak's principle required the sum to be zero.

Now she could finally solve for the unknown templates, making all of her previously abstract results concrete.

The chamber was almost silent, save for the clicking of stones. Roi had been afraid that her "sign error" would simply cancel itself out, but it seemed to be propagating nicely, spreading its subtle changes throughout the calculations.

She found the template for the orbital periods. They obeyed the square-cube rule approximately, but closer to the Hub they now grew shorter than that simple rule implied, which was the opposite behavior to Neth's scheme.

She calculated the ratio of the weights. It started out close to three, but on approaching the Hub it now grew smaller, not greater.

Roi passed the frame to Neth for checking and let the final template float in her mind. The ratio of the garm-sard weight to the shomal-junub weight was equal to three, minus six divided by the size of the orbit. That size was measured in units that couldn't be determined, because among other things it depended on Neth's unknown scale for converting time into distance. A small enough orbit would certainly have a ratio of two and a quarter, though; all you needed to do was to make its size "eight units", whatever that came to in spans.

The same template made it equally clear that for an orbit of "six units", the ratio would shrink further, to a value of two. The garm-sard weight, then, would be double the shomal-junub weight.

Zak's principle, and the fact that the spin weight canceled the rarb-sharq weight exactly, made it easy to calculate another ratio: that of the garm-sard weight to the spin weight. When the first ratio fell to two, the second would rise to four. And when the second ratio hit four, as Neth had shown, orbits around the Hub would no longer be stable.

If the Splinter's orbit was ever reduced to three-quarters of its present size, from that moment on the slightest garmwards nudge would send it spiraling into the Hub.

"No errors," proclaimed Ruz, the last of Roi's checkers. Shortly afterward, Kal gave the same verdict for Tan's calculations. Their conclusions, reached separately, were brought together and compared.

"No discrepancies," Ruz declared.

Everyone in the chamber, Roi knew, would understand what the results implied, but for a dozen heartbeats there was silence. Roi herself felt wrapped in a kind of protective skepticism: just because their esoteric calculations had finally been prodded into yielding some ratios that weren't at odds with measurements in the real world, that didn't make the whole theory correct.

Ruz was the first to speak. "Orbits of size six are unstable, but I'm puzzled by what happens even closer to the Hub. It looks as if orbits of size three or less are *impossible*, because the object would need to be moving faster than the critical speed."

"At size two," Gul added, "everything becomes peculiar. The direction in space that points in toward the Hub acquires a *negative* space-time length, as if it were a direction in time."

Tan said, "There are many things here that we'll need to study more carefully. And even if this geometry is correct, we haven't shown that it's unique. There might be other geometries that satisfy Zak's principle and also give the kind of ratios we've seen."

Roi was relieved; she couldn't argue with any of Tan's observations. They had made progress of a kind, but it was not yet proof of anything.

The shift wasn't over but the calculations had been tiring, so some people started moving out of the chamber to eat. Roi joined them; she'd promised Zak that she'd tell him the outcome as soon as possible, and she could gather some food for him along the way.

As she was leaving, Neth approached her. "Sixth time successful," she said. "Congratulations."

"Congratulations yourself. It was your idea, I just twisted it slightly."

Neth made a sound expressing modesty and suggesting that they desist from further mutual praise. "I've enjoyed working with you, Roi. I hope we meet again."

"What do you mean?" Roi froze and stared at her, bewildered. How could another team have recruited one of their best workers, right in front of their eyes? "What have you become, a courier?"

"I'm not leaving the team," Neth said. "Not as I understand it. I'm going to the sardside, to help with the tunnel."

Roi chirped polite approval, but in truth she found this even more shocking. While surrounded by her colleagues and immersed in their distinctive brand of work, Neth had summoned up the strength for a solo, self-motivated defection; even if she chose to think of the tunnel builders as part of the same team, it was the theorists who had first captured her loyalty, and who reinforced it shift after shift. "You're our best calculator," Roi lamented. "The best at manipulating templates. The best at understanding what they mean."

"That won't be wasted with the tunnel builders," Neth replied. "They'll need mathematicians there, too."

"Aren't you still curious, though," Roi pressed her, "to see where the theory takes us? To see our ideas refined? To see this geometry understood, to know if it's unique, to map out all its implications?"

Neth hesitated. "Of course I'm still curious. And I hope that the next time we meet, you'll have news about all of those things. But the tunnel is more important to me now. Twice, we've seen the possibility of danger. Twice, the mathematics has failed to rule it out. We haven't proved anything, but what we've glimpsed in the distance is enough of a warning for me. I'm not prepared to wait for a disaster to show that we were right."

13

Toward the center of the Nuclear Stellar Disk the density of stars began a precipitous climb. Within a cluster two hundred light years wide a billion stars sped along a complex tangle of orbits, and the deeper into this swarm you dived the more crowded and violent it became. To Rakesh, it brought to mind the image of a nest of furious ants caught in a steep subsidence, kept from falling into the depths only by the sheer energy of their motion.

At the bottom of the pit lay Goudal-e-Markaz: a black hole with the mass of three million suns, the one place from which you could fall no further. It wasn't easy to reach this nadir: the hole's zone of capture was barely fifty million kilometers wide, and it was rare for a star to lose so much of its angular momentum that it could execute a head-on dive into oblivion.

However, a bull's-eye hit was not the only route to destruction. Once every hundred millennia or so a star would come close enough to Goudal-e-Markaz for tidal forces to disrupt it catastrophically. As it dived toward the hole, the star would be stretched along its orbit at the same time as it was squeezed in the orthogonal directions, a distended streak of nuclear fire growing ever hotter and more compressed. In some encounters the star would merely be torn apart and the debris sprayed across a range of orbits, but if the tidal compression was strong enough to trigger a burst of new fusion reactions, as the star swung away from the hole and the pressure was released it could explode with the force of a hundred supernovas. The remnants of these explosions could still be seen thousands of years later, tenuous but energetic shells of gas spreading out into the galactic nucleus.

Ordinary supernovas were even more common, of course, and the central cluster was littered with their remnants: white dwarfs, stellar mass black holes, and neutron stars. The Aloof's map showed no less than fifteen million neutron stars. That was a daunting census, and the chaotic dynamics of the region made it impossible to rule out more than a few per cent as potential culprits in the death of the Arkmakers' world.

Standing in the control room of *Lahl's Promise*, looking out into the blaze of stars that hid their quarry, Rakesh asked Parantham, "Would you be willing to visit fifteen million neutron stars, one by one, until we found a living Ark?"

She replied without hesitation, "Absolutely."

For a moment Rakesh considered calling her bluff, but he was sure his own will would crack long before hers. When the creators of *de novos* chose their traits, they were prone to excesses that rarely appeared in even the most technologically augmented versions of inheritance. No gene for keenness could ever compete with Parantham's fiat-driven personality.

He said, "I think it's time we built a decent telescope."

She nodded assent, without betraying the slightest hint of relief that he hadn't been serious about inspecting each candidate in person. "Where?"

"Here would be as good a place as any," Rakesh suggested. "At least there's plenty of raw material." They could try to select an observation point even closer to the galactic center, but their chances of finding a closer star that still clung on to a substantial asteroid belt weren't good.

"That's fitting," Parantham said. "To use a little of the Arkmakers' world, in order to find their new home. I don't think they'd begrudge us that."

Rakesh felt his now habitual twinge of discomfort, at the thought that they might be risking an act of desecration. But there seemed to be no-body around to be offended, apart from the Aloof, who he was sure were looking over their shoulders constantly, ready to veto any unacceptable behavior.

From this distance, a six-hundred-meter Ark somewhere in the central cluster would in principle be resolvable with an optical telescope four million kilometers wide, but to obtain a clear spectrum that would unambiguously identify the wall material it would be prudent to aim a bit higher.

"Ten million kilometers?" he suggested.

"That sounds about right."

Rakesh plucked some standard designs from the library and tweaked them for their specific goals and the local conditions. They could mine the rubble of the Arkmakers' world for the raw materials, then stream the refined feedstock into an orbit clear of dust and micrometeors, where the mirror segments would be constructed. With sunlight and the stellar winds as their main energy sources the project would proceed at a leisurely pace, taking more than a year to complete. Still, that was nothing to the time they'd already spent in transit within the bulge, let alone the time it would have taken to hop from neutron star to neutron star.

Rakesh initiated the process, sending twelve delivery modules into the asteroid belt to sow the rocks with engineering spores.

"No veto from the Aloof," he noted. "They won't allow spores in from the outside, but they don't mind us spreading these ones around."

"Which either means that they trust us," Parantham replied—making it clear from her tone what she thought of that proposition—"or they're watching us so closely that they know exactly what these spores will and won't do."

Rakesh mused, "What if we tried to build a node here? Conforming to the Amalgam's standards? We'd have our very own short cut through the bulge."

Parantham responded cautiously, "I'd say we're too far from the edge to establish a reliable link with the Amalgam's network."

"Perhaps," Rakesh conceded. "That's not the point, though. What if we tried it?"

Parantham said, "I think the moment we so much as formed a serious intention to contravene the rules they've spent the last million years enforcing, our hosts would turn our bodies into dust and feed it to Goudal-e-Markaz. We're here on their sufferance. We shouldn't even think about pushing our luck." She smiled. "Do you dream, Rakesh?"

"Yes."

"Then draw up a list of topics for your dream censor. We wouldn't want the Aloof getting the wrong idea."

Rakesh followed one of the mirror spiders, hovering beside it as it drank from the feedstock streaming down from the asteroid belt. Though the milky flow resembled a liquid, it was actually composed of tiny granules, each one consisting of a core of volatiles wrapped in a distinctive mineral shell that both protected it and labeled its contents. The spider's acute vision and nimble mouthparts allowed it to extract exactly what it needed, leaving the rest for other users further downstream.

Once the sac of its belly was full, the spider launched itself back toward its web with a barely visible burst of ions. It had already constructed a rigid, skeletal frame for the mirror segment it was building. Each segment was a kilometer wide, but even when the planned ten billion segments were completed they would only fill one ten-thousandth of the eighty trillion square kilometers spanned by the telescope's total width. Seen as a whole, the mirror would be mostly empty space, but the individual segments lost none of their light-gathering power by being spread out like this, and it increased the resolution of the instrument by a factor of a hundred.

The spider started at the rim of the frame and began secreting a glistening polymer film, more like a metallic-looking tape than a silken thread. Mobile electrons in the polymer made it as reflective as silver, but it was lighter and stronger than any metal. The precise molecular structure of the polymer was being constantly tweaked as it was synthesized, tailoring the natural curvature of the film to fit the parabolic shape of the mirror to within a fraction of a wavelength.

The frame was rotating, so the spider only had to inch its way slowly toward the center, depositing the film in a tightly wound spiral while the growing mirror turned beneath it. Rakesh watched patiently as the annular strip finally reached a sufficient size for him to glimpse the blaze of the central cluster reflected back at him, a view so sharp that it looked more like some kind of rift in space than a mere reflection.

When this segment was completed and moved into position, an array of precision accelerometers measuring the phase difference between counter-rotating superconducting currents would track its orientation, and a faint breath of ions from its attitude thrusters would keep it perfectly aligned. The insect-eyed instrument package that sat at the telescope's focus was already complete, and undergoing testing and calibration. Once a million or so of the ten billion segments were in place, some worthwhile data collection could take place, albeit far more slowly than it would when the full light-collecting area was brought into play. At that point, the telescope would be imaging the accretion disks of thousands of neutron stars simultaneously, hunting for the telltale spectrum of an Ark's synthetic walls.

Probes had scoured the rubble-strewn center of the sole Ark that remained in this system, but had found neither artefacts nor the mummified remains of its original inhabitants. Though the higher tiers of the wind-fed ecosystem had probably collapsed quite quickly, there was a sufficient population of microbes even now to make short work of anything organic, and the slow grinding of the rubble over the millennia had milled any remnants of the inhabitants' material culture down to dust. Rakesh didn't dare to guess what the chances were that any of the Arks captured by the neutron star had thrived—even briefly, let alone for fifty million years—but he had written off the cousins prematurely before, and he was not about to make the same mistake again.

He turned away from the mirror and let his avatar drift, spinning slowly. He shifted his vision down the spectrum, into the infrared and microwave bands, dimming the fierce stars but revealing the eerie world of gas and dust in which they were embedded, full of structures more subtle, delicate and diffuse. Shells of plasma from thousand-year-old supernovas hung in space like the smoke from some slow-motion fireworks display. Half a dozen glowing filaments lined up perpendicular to the galactic plane shone with the synchrotron radiation of electrons spiraling along magnetic field lines. From a ring of gas a dozen light years wide that circled the galactic center, a surreal double helix stretched across the sky: the infrared glow of dust trapped by a wave in the magnetic field that was anchored to, and twisted by, the orbiting gas.

Somehow, the Aloof had mastered this beautiful, perilous place and claimed it as their own. While Rakesh's hapless cousins had been hammered relentlessly by the forces of nature, perhaps to the point of extinction, the Aloof had overcome or circumvented the same hardships, to make this their jealously guarded home. Whether they'd matured in the disk first and only come here once they were armed with sophisticated technology, or whether their whole mode of existence had rendered them impervious to the dangers of the bulge from the start, was anybody's guess. Rakesh did not expect answers from them, at least not directly, but he couldn't entirely surrender the naive hope that merely being allowed inside the fence and permitted to see what the Aloof had seen, to steep his body in the same radiation and feel the same stellar winds and tides, might yet crystallize some insight about their nature that could never have formed from idle speculation back in the disk.

Parantham spoke, puncturing his reverie.

"We have company."

This assertion was so bizarre and unexpected that Rakesh simply floated in silence for a while, refusing to abandon his sanctuary among the spiders to see if she was joking.

"What do you mean?" he finally replied.

"Someone has sent us a messenger. I've already asked it what it wishes to say, but it insists on speaking to us together."

Rakesh took his senses out of the avatar, back to his body slumped in a couch in the control room of *Lahl's Promise*.

Standing beside Parantham was a figure resembling Csi, as Rakesh had perceived him back in the node: the same bald head, the same serious demeanor, the same barely visible hint of a smile. Unlike Csi himself, it was meaningless to ask what this messenger really looked like; as an insentient courier it had no self-perception, let alone any need for a physical embodiment. Their hosts had simply loaded it into one of the habitat's processors and let it communicate with them via Amalgam-standard protocols.

Rakesh rose to his feet and embraced the messenger. "Welcome to the bulge!" This was not his old friend, but it was designed to communicate as if it were, and perhaps to take a reply back to the sender. Some people became self-conscious in the presence of messengers, but Rakesh's policy was to treat them as if they were the sender, and only to retreat from that stance if it led to real absurdities. To embrace this insentient hallucination was no more foolish than responding with warmth and sincerity to a written letter or a video message. "What's been happening? Where have you come from?"

"Darya-e-ghashang. A few years after you and Parantham left the node, a traveling festival came through: the Ocean of Ten Million Worlds. I fell in with them, and I've been with them ever since."

"The Ocean of Ten Million Worlds?"

"Every month, we swim, sail, or dive in the waters of a different planet."

Rakesh smiled, recalling his sodden farewell from the node. "That sounds wonderful." These festivals were really just large groups of friends traveling together, but they were usually dressed up with some kind of distinguishing paraphernalia: claiming to offer some new social structure or artistic milieu, or to choose their destinations in order to celebrate some particular aspect of life. Their real attraction was that they offered a satisfying mixture of stability and novelty. As long as you stayed with the group, you didn't have to cut ties with everyone you knew just for a change of scenery.

Parantham said, "So what made you think of us, out of the blue?"

"I heard some news about Lahl," the messenger said.

"Lahl?" Rakesh was almost as surprised by this as he had been by the messenger's arrival. "What did she do to become famous?"

"She came out of the bulge without entering it."

Rakesh said, "I see." If that was true, it was worth a degree of notoriety.

"The inter-network traffic report from the node she'd claimed as her entry point finally reached the node where she'd emerged," the messenger explained. "It took a while, because she'd told the truth when she'd said there'd been a temporary shortage of encryption keys linking the two. When that shortage was remedied and the two nodes compared data, it was clear that she'd lied about her origins."

Parantham said, "Does that really mean she never went into the bulge?

She might have entered at a different point, and the data just hadn't been brought together for matching, the last you heard."

"That wasn't literally impossible when I left Darya-e-ghashang," the messenger conceded, "but even then the remaining opportunities for that were slim. It's widely believed now, around much of the western inner disk, that the Aloof created her: that they used their knowledge of all the unencrypted travelers they've been able to study over the millennia to manufacture a plausible citizen of the Amalgam, and then they sent her out to do, well... who knows what?"

"So where is she now?" Rakesh asked.

"Nobody knows. There is no record of her departing from the node where we met her."

Rakesh laughed. He was not convinced that Lahl was anything but an ordinary traveler who preferred not to leave behind detailed records of her movements; perhaps her story about the synchronization clan had been a cover for something more complicated and nefarious. And even if she really was a messenger from the Aloof—whose lack of social skills might have led them to phrase their request for a "child of DNA" to investigate the meteor in this mildly dishonest fashion—was that anything to worry about?

"I'm glad that you decided to share this news with us," Rakesh said, "but it's not going to change our plans. I don't approve of deceit, but Lahl's basic message was genuine. Has Parantham told you about our discoveries?"

"Yes."

"So what should we do? If the Aloof meant us harm, it's already too late to prevent it, and the very fact that you've reached us to pass on these suspicions makes it seem even less likely that they do."

"I didn't come to warn you about the Aloof," the messenger said. "I came to warn you about the Amalgam."

"Oh." Rakesh felt a real twinge of unease now.

"Unencrypted, unauthenticated travelers taking the short cut through the bulge have always done so at their own risk. It's not just a question of what the Aloof might do with them; the receiving nodes on the other side of the bulge are actually under no obligation to embody, or re-route, unauthenticated data. Since the days of Leila and Jasim, and the first wave of excitement when they discovered the Aloof's network, it's been the common practice for the people of the inner disk to make exceptions for data taking the short cut. With rumors spreading that the Aloof aren't dealing with us openly—that they're manufacturing impostors and spitting them out into our networks, to act as spies and saboteurs—that easy-going policy is being questioned."

Parantham said, "So when we're finished here, and the time comes for us to leave—"

"It might not be as simple as you expected," the messenger said. "The Amalgam might not be willing to take you back."

14

"Thirty-three," Roi counted, vigorously waving her back left leg, followed by her front left leg.

"THIRTY-THREE!" the hatchlings replied in unison, mimicking her actions precisely.

"Thirty-four." Roi waved her back left leg, then her middle left.

"THIRTY-FOUR!" echoed the hatchlings.

"Thirty-five." Back left leg once, then once again.

"THIRTY-FIVE!"

"Thirty-six." Roi leaped off the floor as high as she could, struggling to wave her front right leg twice, clearly and distinctly, before she touched the ground again.

"THIRTY-SIX!" The hatchlings couldn't jump as high as she had, but they were all nimble and energetic enough to repeat her gestures before they had even begun to descend.

Roi rolled over on to her back, exhausted. The hatchlings, of course, copied even this unintended flourish. They really were infuriating sometimes.

"I'm getting too old for this," she rasped to Gul.

"You just need to spend less time at the Null Line."

"Maybe."

While she rested, Gul took over the class, pouring a fine colored powder on to the floor and scraping furrows in the shape of simple words. As Roi watched the hatchlings copy him, her tiredness and irritation faded. She knew it would be a joy to teach these children, to bring them to an understanding of the world.

It was also a daunting responsibility, but she believed she had grown better at the job. She had tutored seven groups of hatchlings so far, and from the last three groups she was sure that everyone had left her class with a clear understanding of the basic facts about the Splinter. They would carry that knowledge with them throughout their lives, and spread it among their team-mates.

The great tunnel that Bard had planned, to unbalance the force of the wind and drag the Splinter to safety, remained unbuilt. While Bard, Neth and a few dozen others continued to survey, and recruit, and try their best to explain the tunnel's purpose to the people of the sardside whose factories, storerooms and grazing areas they wanted to turn to rubble, so far they had failed to recruit a workforce large enough to make a scratch in the rock, and the locals remained largely hostile to the whole idea. Roi couldn't see the situation changing while the threat of the Splinter descending into an unstable orbit around the Hub remained an incomprehensible notion to most people. She suspected that it would take at least two generations for Zak's vision to permeate the culture to the point where everyone could understand the danger, but at least she and Gul, and a dozen other teams, were nudging things in the right direction. Move the people, and the rock might follow.

The hatchlings completed tracing the words for "left" and "right" and began smoothing the powder into its blank state again, ready for the next word. Suddenly the weight changed, and Roi, Gul, hatchlings and powder were flung high into the chamber. An instant later, the Incandescence brightened, sixfold, thirty-six-fold, searing everything into invisibility.

Roi thought: *This is the end. So soon. No warning, just death—*

She struck the floor, right way up. After a moment she flexed her legs cautiously; she was sore from the impact, but she had not been injured. She heard the hatchlings mewling in distress beside her; still blinded, she instinctively chirped out words of comfort and reassurance. "Everything is fine! We're safe! Don't worry!"

As her vision began to return, she could see that the walls around her still bore an afterglow from the burst of light, a lingering radiance far stronger than anything she'd witnessed before, even at the garm-sharq edge. She could feel the rock creaking ominously beneath her. Was the Splinter about to be broken in two? Or was it on the verge of plummeting into the Hub? This was not how she'd imagined either disaster beginning. As far as she could judge, once the disturbance that had tossed them from the floor had passed the weight had returned to normal.

Gul limped over to her. "Any idea what's happening?"

"None at all."

"Do you think we should head sardwards?" That was one plan that had been mooted as a response to an impending division: head for the sardside, in the hope that the sardwards fragment of the Splinter would end up further from the Hub.

"We're a long way from the Calm," Roi pointed out, "and the hatchlings can't move as quickly as adults. It would take us two shifts, at least. If we're breaking up, we might be heading into danger." If the Splinter divided symmetrically, the Calm was the last place you'd want to be when the halves violently parted company.

"That's true," Gul said. "And if we're going to get thrown around again, travel is probably unwise unless we're sure our lives depend on it. Let's wait and see if we can make sense of the situation." The hatchlings were milling around them making plaintive sounds, but their small bodies were resilient and none of them appeared to have been harmed by the fall. Gul chirped soothing words to them at his most reassuring pitch.

The walls around them were growing darker now. At first, Roi had thought it was just the afterglow from the flash continuing to fade, but as she increased the sensitivity of her vision to compensate, she realized that she was straining at the edge of her ability.

"Am I going blind?" she asked Gul. "Or is the Incandescence fading?" Maybe the flash had damaged her sight.

He said, "Either we're both going blind, or it's fading."

The hatchlings fell silent, as if the darkness itself was a source of tranquility for them. Perhaps it was lulling them to sleep, just as the voluntary cessation of vision induced drowsiness. Roi could think of no other experience with which to compare it; the Incandescence might penetrate the rock more weakly in the depths of the Splinter than it did at the edge, but for the all-pervading glow to change before her eyes was unprecedented.

As the darkness grew deeper, Roi tried to stay calm. Whatever was happening to the Splinter was not a fate that anyone had predicted, but it was better to be perplexed and alive than to face those long-anticipated cataclysms.

"Can there be a hole in the Incandescence?" Gul wondered. "A gap, a void?"

"If there is, why did we never pass through it before?"

"Perhaps it moves, perhaps it wanders around," he suggested. "And that flash of brightness was... a concentration of the Incandescence at the edge of the void, heaped up like the rubble dug from a hole."

Roi had no idea if that made sense; she had never thought of the Incandescence as something you could make a hole in by any method. "Can you feel the wind?" It was a measure of how disoriented she was that she had to ask, that she couldn't trust her own senses.

"No. There's nothing. The rock is making a sound I've never heard before, but it's not from the wind."

Roi was relieved by this small sign of consistency. "I suppose that means we're not simply going blind. Wind and brightness, gone together." *With the Incandescence gone, how would they eat? How would they survive?* If the hole they had entered was not too large they should emerge from it soon, as the Splinter continued its orbit around the Hub. If it enclosed their whole orbit, though, they would remain in darkness until it moved away of its own accord.

Roi said, "How long do you think it's been, since the darkness started?"

Gul rasped amusement. "My mind's not that clear. I wouldn't like to guess."

"Less than half a shomal-junub cycle, I'd say." Roi had watched the cycling stones so many times, the rhythm of it was stamped into her mind. "We don't know for sure that the Splinter's orbit has the same period, but that's what the simplest geometry implied. So if there's a gap in the Incandescence that's smaller than our orbit, we ought to emerge from it in less than one shomal-junub cycle."

"That sounds reasonable," Gul said cautiously. "The gap itself might be moving around, complicating things, but if it's moving slowly then everything should repeat about once every orbit."

Just a few heartbeats later, the walls began to brighten. Roi tensed, preparing herself for a recurrence of the violence that had preceded the onset of darkness, but the light from the rock climbed calmly and steadily back to its normal strength, and the wind resumed its usual susurration, unaccompanied by any sudden shifts of weight or blinding flashes.

The strange creaking and rasping from the rock did not abate, though.

"Half a shomal-junub cycle," Roi said. "Almost exactly half."

Some of the hatchlings began to stir. Gul made soothing noises and drew them close to his body. "Why would a void in the Incandescence be half the size of our orbit?" he said. "That seems like too much of a coincidence."

Roi took advantage of the normal light to survey the chamber. All the hatchlings were accounted for, and the basic structures around her were intact—the entrances to the chamber were clear, the ceiling hadn't fallen—but there were some cracks in the walls that she was sure she'd never seen before. The rock continued its maddening groan. If she could feel no change in weight, what was tormenting it?

She could hear people in the distance, calling to each other, fearful and confused. "Where should we go for safety?" she asked.

Gul said, "We're as safe here as anywhere. There's nowhere to go."

The light and the wind began to fade again. Why were some things repeating themselves, while the flash and the jolt had happened only once?

Roi said, "*We were pushed.*" The pattern was unmistakable; she'd tossed enough stones in the Null Chamber to know how to set things cycling back and forth. "That's what threw us off the ground. It wasn't the fact that we entered the void that did it: the push came first, the disturbance came first. Whatever struck us changed our orbit slightly, enough to knock us into the void."

"Why is the void half as big as our orbit, though?" Gul protested.

The darkness thickened, the wind fell away. Roi pictured the orbit of the Splinter, and the motion of the stones in the Null Chamber. What happened twice in every shomal-junub cycle? The "falling" stone passed by the "fixed" one. First it passed it on its way shomal, then it did so again on its way junub. Twice in each cycle, the stones were close together. And twice, they were far apart.

"The void's not half as big as our orbit," she said. "It's far bigger than that. And it hasn't wandered up to us by chance; it hasn't moved at all. It's been right beside us all along."

Gul was silent for a while, contemplating her cryptic remarks. Then he said, "If the Incandescence isn't *everywhere*, but we never left it before, then maybe it's confined to a thin layer around the plane of our old orbit. Now something's disturbed the Splinter, and we're moving shomal and junub—above and below that plane—for the first time."

"Exactly!" Roi said. "Out of the Incandescence, then back. Twice every shomal-junub cycle. The whole Splinter has become the falling stone."

She waited, picturing the stones in her mind's eye. As one imaginary stone ascended from its low point and approached the other, the walls began to brighten.

Gul said soberly, "We're lucky we survived this. And lucky we can understand it." Then he let out an ecstatic chirp that woke half the hatchlings. "We're not going to die!" He scooped up two bewildered children and tossed them on to his back, then started running around in a circle. "Darkness, light, it doesn't matter! We're safe, we're fine. Everything is perfect!"

Roi watched him, dizzy with relief herself, if not so exuberant. This was not the end of the Splinter, not the plunge into the Hub that Neth had foretold. The crops would suffer, though. There would be food shortages, and everyone would struggle to complete their work as the darkness came and went.

The strange event had shown them something new about the Incandescence, even as it had confirmed Zak's picture of the Splinter orbiting the Hub. It might even persuade some people to accept his ideas and agree to the tunnel. The loss of crops was a hard price to pay, but in the end it might change things for the better.

The one thing that worried Roi most was that she still had no idea what dazzling thing had flown past and knocked them out of their orbit. Where had it gone? To the Hub? Into the void? Could it cross their path again?

And if it did return, which way would it push them next?

Zak stretched his legs out across the wall of his chamber, trying to ease the pain in the joints. "I have a plan," he said. "But I'm going to need your help."

"Whatever you want from me, just ask." Roi had left the hatchlings in Gul's care to travel to the Null Line and check on Zak's condition. He had survived the Splinter's Jolt and the aftermath, with members of the theorists' team still bringing him food regularly, in spite of their own problems and distractions. His health had been fading for a long time before the event, though, and Roi suspected that his death was close now.

Zak said, "When I was working in the library, I heard about a crack in the wall at the junub edge. Some people had climbed right through it and reached the Incandescence."

Roi was skeptical. "Are you sure that's not just a story?"

"I have a map."

"You always have a map. Did anyone come back?"

"Of course not. The Incandescence killed them; nobody has ever walked into it and survived. It's not just the strength of the unfiltered wind: even at the Calm, there's something fatal, something that the rock protects us from."

Roi could see where this was heading. "You think it might be possible to survive there, now? In the times when our orbit takes us right out of the Incandescence?"

"It's worth trying," Zak said. "We don't know how long the new orbit will last. This might be our only chance to look into the void."

There had already been measurable changes in the orbit. Although the period of the complete light/dark cycle remained the same, with Ruz's clock it had been possible to detect a small reduction in the time the Splinter spent in darkness. This suggested that the total distance they were traveling away from the old orbital plane had diminished slightly.

Other experiments in the Null Chamber had shown that the Null Line had, strictly speaking, vanished; although the weight throughout the chamber remained very small, there was no longer a line of perfect weightlessness running through the Splinter. The small weights that were present now were difficult to measure, but they seemed to undergo cyclic changes. Tan had suggested two possible explanations for this: either the Splinter's rate and axis of spin had been disturbed in such a way that the spin weight no longer canceled the rarb-sharq weight, or the rarb-sharq weight itself was no longer constant throughout each orbit, and hence could no longer be canceled by *any* constant spin.

In either case, the ceaseless groaning of the rock was probably due to the fact that the weights throughout the Splinter were no longer fixed; the precise forces were always shifting, repeatedly tightening and relaxing their grip on the rock. Tan believed that the price to be paid for this restlessness would be a gradual return to a state of alignment, whether that meant a change in the Splinter's spin, its orbit, or both.

Roi said, "This journey will be hard for you. Someone younger and healthier should go instead."

"Someone younger and healthier might climb out through the crack in the wall and never come back. It makes far more sense for me to risk the last few shifts of my own life than to allow someone else to throw away the best part of theirs."

"You can barely walk," Roi protested. "How are you going to reach the junub edge?"

"I've arranged for some couriers to bring me a cart."

"Are they going to deliver you to your destination as well?"

Zak said, "I want you to pull the cart. You and Ruz. Ruz has already made some instruments for me, to allow me to take measurements of whatever's there to see."

"So you want Ruz along to fix them if they break?"

"Yes."

Roi didn't ask what her own purpose would be, apart from sharing the load. She said, "You should have peace and ease at the end of your life, not a dangerous journey like this."

Zak rasped irritably. "If I knew that the Splinter was safe, I'd have peace. But I'm sure that it's not, so the best I can do is keep struggling to make that happen."

Roi made a sound of acquiescence. "What do you think it will tell us? Looking into the void?" The thing that had lit up the rock when it touched them seemed to have vanished, but then, from inside the Splinter the whole Incandescence seemed to vanish when they were no longer immersed in it.

Zak said, "We've been half right about a lot of things, but there's something missing from our theories, something whose nature we haven't even guessed yet. If we don't learn to understand it, it will kill us."

When Roi returned to the hatchlings' chamber to explain her plans, she found Gul in pain, full of ripe seed packets. She had helped him dispose of them many times before, but she was surprised that he hadn't found someone else while she was gone.

"I've been busy with the hatchlings," he said. "What was I supposed to do? Walk the tunnels begging for a mate, with the children lined up behind me copying every move?"

The hatchlings were asleep, so there was no danger of that now, but Roi had no contraceptive leaves. She was too tired to go hunting for the stupid weed, but she couldn't bear to see Gul in so much pain.

"Open your carapace," she said. "I'll take them."

"Are you sure?"

"Quickly, before it gets dark. If I can't see what I'm doing you'll be sorry."

As she snipped the seed packets free and loaded them into her egg cavities, the pleasure that spread through her body felt muted. Without the contraceptive to compete with them, the packets were producing far weaker secretions than she was accustomed to. She had never been entirely sure why it had always seemed right to keep her eggs from being fertilized; she had understood that the Splinter could only feed so many mouths, but other people made hatchlings all the time. Now, with the crops diminished, that should have been a stronger reason than ever, but even as the rush of contentment faded she felt no regret for what she'd done.

She had planned to stay for less than a shift before returning to the Calm to meet up with Zak and Ruz, but she found herself lingering, waiting for her eggs to be ready to lay. Six had been fertilized, and when their cases finally hardened she found a snug crevice close to the chamber where Gul worked, and she packed the eggs carefully into the gap in the rock.

She was aware of how strange it was that she was arranging for these hatchlings to be educated by their father, rather than leaving it to chance. The job itself was the thing, and every member of every work team, not to mention every hatchling, was supposed to be interchangeable. Still, in these dangerous times everyone's children needed to learn what Gul could teach them. She would have counselled any stranger to do the same.

Although Roi was late returning to the Calm, when she arrived she found that the cart Zak had hoped to receive several shifts before had only just been delivered. That the metalworkers, couriers and depot operators had managed to fulfill Zak's strange request at all—while the food around them became ever more sparse, and the world of constant brightness they had known all their lives flickered in and out of existence—was testimony to the robustness of the work teams. Some people, Roi suspected, would not miss a shift even if the Splinter itself was torn apart.

The cart was big enough to hold Zak, the instruments Ruz had built for him, and a reasonable amount of provisions. Roi had already collected some food on her way back from visiting Gul, but she spent another shift foraging until she had as much as they could carry. Although the Calm supposedly became less barren as you moved away from the Null Line, and so in theory they'd be traveling into a more bountiful region, Roi had spent so long around the Null Chamber that she knew a dozen places where the seeds that drifted in tended to settle and grow. She would not have the same local knowledge once the journey was under way.

There were two harnesses for the cart, strung together one behind the other, so she and Ruz could share the load if they wished, but the cart would not be unbalanced if they chose to take turns pulling it instead.

The whole team of theorists came to bid them farewell; Tan addressed Zak on behalf of everyone. "We wish you a safe journey, and clear observations," he declared. "Our frames are ready for your numbers and templates. You built this team from nothing; perhaps you will return to us with the knowledge that will make our work complete." Zak replied simply with a murmur of thanks, but the send-off seemed to lift his spirits.

Roi took the harness first, leaving Ruz free to walk ahead of her, checking for hazards and clearing obstacles. The Jolt had left debris almost everywhere, and the less-traveled the tunnel the more chance there was that nobody had yet moved it aside.

Their journey would take them rarb and junub, uphill all the way, but it would be a while before their weight made much difference. Even in near weightlessness the cart was unwieldy, but by far the greatest irritation was the darkness. In her earlier trips between the hatchlings and the Null Chamber, traveling alone with no burden, Roi had found it impossible to make progress once the light fell away and her vision failed. The path ahead could be clear for dozens of spans and she could declare to herself that nothing terrible would befall her if she simply advanced at a leisurely pace through the darkness, but her body would still refuse to obey her after the first few halting steps. Attempting the same thing with Zak swaying on the cart behind her was inconceivable, even if Ruz had been in the harness to remove him as an unknown. The periods of enforced rest might have been welcome if not for the fact that they came so much more frequently than they were needed, making them more frustrating than recuperative.

"What *is* light?" Roi wondered, waiting for the darkness to end.

"A very fine part of the wind, perhaps," Zak suggested. "That would explain why it can penetrate more deeply through the rock than any other component. It seems it can penetrate anything but metal."

"It must be easily scattered, though," Ruz said, "or there'd be no light at all here in the Calm. The rock can't block it completely, but still manages to change its direction."

"Yes." Zak seemed intrigued by this observation, but unsure how to pursue it further.

Roi said, "If light is part of the wind, how can we hope to see anything at all once we're out of the Incandescence?"

"Some light might be scattered up to us from the Incandescence," Zak replied. "But the void itself might contain a faint wind."

"Including light?"

"Let's hope so," Zak said. "All we know for sure about the void is that it's a *thinning* of the Incandescence, to the point where nothing can reach us through the rock. That need not mean that there's absolutely nothing there."

The tunnel began to brighten again. It always took a while for the walls to begin glowing with their full intensity, though how much of that was due to the time it took for the light to penetrate the rock, and how much might be the product of a gradual transition between the void and the Incandescence, was hard to say. From outside the rock it might be possible to judge how sharp the border between the two regions was, though it would be risky to stay outside beyond the periods of full darkness.

It was only after they'd been traveling for nearly a shift and a half, according to Ruz's clock, that they decided to stop and sleep. Before the Jolt, most people had more or less agreed on the length of a shift, growing tired after a similar period of wakefulness. The stretches of darkness had led to an increase in that time, but not always an equal one for each person.

When they woke, Ruz was first in the harness. After a dozen light/dark cycles Roi took his place, and this time she finally felt the burden of pulling the cart uphill. The junub weight grew less than half as rapidly with distance as the garm and sard weights—and they were also traveling rarb, which contributed nothing—but beyond those excuses it was a measure of how slow their progress had been that it had taken so long to reach the point where they really cared which way was up.

The Calm appeared more sparsely populated than ever; apart from occasional couriers that Roi glimpsed in the distance, their role made obvious by carts of their own, the tunnels seemed deserted. The expeditioners passed the time with light-hearted speculation, eschewing any grim predictions about the fate of the Splinter. By the end of the journey's second shift, Roi and Ruz were dragging the cart together, with the lead harnessee also keeping a lookout for obstacles. It was hard work now, and Roi was beginning to feel that their enforced breaks didn't come a moment too soon.

Halfway through the third shift, as they slowed for the onset of darkness, Roi noticed a flicker of light ahead. At first she thought it was merely a lode in the rock that was dimming more slowly than its surroundings, but as the darkness deepened the contrast only grew stronger. A reddish patch of light stood out against the blackness; it was an unsteady glow, but it never failed entirely. It was moving slightly, with a rhythm that reminded her of a person's gait, as if someone was carrying the source of the light toward them.

Ruz said, "Can you hear footsteps?"

Roi listened carefully. "Yes."

"There are five people," Ruz declared. "And some kind of machine."

"I'll take your word for it." A dozen heartbeats later, she could make out two people in the front of a small group. The light was coming from an object strapped to one of their backs.

Zak said quietly, "That I lived to see such wonders."

Roi called out a greeting, unsure if the three of them would be visible by this strange illumination. A reply came back, cautious but friendly.

When the group drew closer, Roi could see that Ruz was correct: there were five people. They made introductions; the light-bearer was called Lud, and the others were Jos, Rud, Cot and Sad.

The light that emerged from the machine on Lud's back was weak, rendering the group sketchily. Their bodies were merely hinted at by a glimmer of surfaces, as if their carapaces had turned to metal. Seeing your companions' beating hearts was not the point, though; this modest light would still be enough to allow you to spot obstacles and walk through the darkness with confidence.

"Where are you headed?" Ruz asked politely. Roi was sure that he was twice as eager as she was to hear how the light machine worked, but it would be discourteous to raise the matter immediately.

"We have no destination yet," Jos replied. "We want to know what's happening to the Splinter, so we've left our teams to search for answers."

Roi could hardly believe what she was hearing. They'd left their teams?

How? Had the Jolt shaken them free, like the rubble it had torn from the solid walls?

She said, "We have some ideas about what's happening to the Splinter. We believe something has pushed it, and now it's falling back and forth, in and out of the Incandescence."

Lud said, "Falling back and forth?"

"If you throw something shomal from the Null Line," Ruz explained, "it will reach a certain distance, fall back to the Null Line, go past it some way junub, fall back again, and so on. We think the Incandescence ends if you go far enough shomal or junub, and that's why the light comes and goes."

The group talked this over among themselves, then asked to hear more. Zak remained quiet, which usually meant that he was tired or in pain, so Roi explained his idea of the Splinter orbiting the Hub, and the experiments in the Null Chamber that seemed to support it.

While they were talking the light from the machine faded, and its whirring sound died away. But the walls were already beginning to brighten, and soon Roi had a normal view of everyone. They had a small cart with them, full of metal parts.

Cot climbed on to Lud's back and began turning a handle attached to the machine. Ruz could no longer contain himself. "It's spring driven, isn't it?"

"Of course," Lud said. "Trying to crank it smoothly and walking at the same time would be impossible."

"*But what makes the light?*" Ruz's tone was drenched with such longing that he might have been a starving child begging for food.

Lud chirped with amusement. "Just two rough surfaces scraped over each other, under pressure. Rough enough to make a disturbance, but not so rough that they'll stick."

Jos added, "I found the effect completely by luck. I was grinding plants into a powder between two stones, and I grew tired of stopping work every time it grew dark. When I ground stone against stone with nothing between them, a faint light seemed to come from the point of contact. At first I thought I was just going mad from the darkness, but the more effort I applied, and the less of the mush there was to smooth the stones, the stronger the light became."

Roi said, "So you've left your old teams now? You've formed a new one, and you're looking for recruits?"

"Not exactly," Cot replied, working briskly to ensure that the spring was fully wound before the darkness returned. "We still don't know what's the best thing to do. We'll form a team if that's necessary, but we're willing to join an existing one if they can make a good case that they know what's going on and that they're doing something useful about it."

Every time Roi thought she could no longer be shocked, these people outdid themselves. It had taken a great struggle for her to tear herself free of her work team to join Zak. On that first journey to the Null Chamber she had never been able to admit her intentions, even to herself. Now here were five people roaming the Splinter, challenging every passing stranger to make a *reasoned bid* for their labor, as if the whole idea of recruitment had been turned inside out.

Zak spoke softly. "Some people are trying to build a tunnel that will change the way the wind pushes on the Splinter. If they succeed, they hope it will carry us to safety. I'm sure they could use your skills."

Lud said, "I can make no promises, but we'd be happy to talk to them, to hear their case."

Ruz said, "We can draw you a map, give you directions."

"You're not going there yourself?" asked Sad.

"We have another task." Roi explained about the crack in the wall, and the observations that they hoped would clarify both the Splinter's ordinary motion and the nature of the Jolt.

The idea struck a chord with the light-makers, and they seemed torn between joining Zak's expedition and heading for the sardside and the tunnel-makers. Zak, however, explained that he would be making the observations alone and that his two assistants were all that he needed.

Cot said, "Then at least take this with you to help you on your way." He opened the cart and produced a second light machine. "We brought two spares, and plenty of parts. If you take this one, we will still have no trouble reaching the sardside."

Zak said, "Thank you." Roi would have preferred an extra body or two to help pull Zak's cart; this was more weight to carry, and now they'd have no excuse to rest when darkness came. Still, at least this way they could choose their own pace.

Roi drew a map for the light-makers showing the way to Bard's team, and the two groups parted. Ruz agreed to carry the light machine on his back; he took the rear harness so as not to obstruct Roi's view ahead.

They toiled on toward the junub edge, resting as they wished and using the machine to enable them to travel through the darkness. At first Roi found the strange, shallow illumination it cast disorienting, but after a dozen cycles she was accustomed to it, her mind switching easily between the two ways of seeing.

It was hard work winding the spring, though. "I want you to improve on the design," she told Ruz.

"In what way?"

"I want a version that works unattended, filling itself with light when there's light to spare, then releasing it in the darkness."

As they approached the edge the tunnels became increasingly strewn with rubble and the walls ever more fractured. Some of this might have been due to the Jolt, but Roi had heard descriptions of the area that long predated that event. It was easy to believe in a crack in the outer wall here, if not so easy to reach it.

Ruz, who had been timing the lengths of each stretch of light and darkness, reported that he'd finally started to detect a small asymmetry between successive times spent in the dark. Now that they were a significant distance away from the Null Line, when the Splinter moved junub of the Incandescence the darkness came earlier, and lasted longer, than when it moved shomal. Roi had already noticed a difference in the way the light penetrated the rocks, with the onset of brightness coming faster when it started from above than from below, but every sign that confirmed their guesses about the Splinter's motion through the Incandescence was important. Apart from anything else, they would be relying on the rock of the Splinter to protect Zak from any dangerous emanations; they did not want to misidentify the phases of the cycle and send him out in the wrong period of darkness, to find the Incandescence looming directly above him.

Shifting enough rubble to allow them to steer the cart through the tunnel became an impossible task. Roi helped Zak pack the instruments into his cavities, then had him climb on to her back. According to Zak's map they did not have far to go, but the map contained no annotations about the ease of travel along the tunnels it portrayed—let alone an up-to-date account that included the damage wrought by the Jolt.

Roi noticed a slight thickening in the sparse vegetation on the walls before she felt the faint hint of a wind, rising and dying with the light. This close to the Calm, that could only mean that the feeble wind had almost no rock to penetrate. She moved ahead cautiously, afraid that they might all be caught by surprise with no roof above them, but as they approached the intersection marked on the map as lying directly beneath the crack, the onset of light brought no blinding revelation. If anything, this place seemed less bright than the garm-sharq edge.

Still, the vegetation on the roof was the thickest Roi had seen since they'd set out from the Null Chamber. She set Zak down and clambered up the wall to explore it. She hadn't walked upside down in weight like this for a long time, and the encrusted surface didn't make it any easier.

She probed the surface gently with her claws. "The rock feels strong," she reported. "No gaps, no cracks."

Ruz said, "Maybe the vegetation's repaired it."

"All my maps are too old," Zak lamented. "We should have brought tools to cut our way out."

"Tools, and a very large work team," Roi suggested. She'd heard it said that the outer wall was at least a dozen spans thick, though like much common knowledge that claim might not have had much grounding in solid information.

Ruz said, "If there's a system of cracks, there might be other openings. Even if the vegetation got to all the old ones, the Jolt might have broken a way through somewhere else."

Roi climbed down to the floor. "Stay here with Zak," she said. "I'll take a look around."

She continued along the tunnel by which they'd reached the intersection. When the darkness came she froze and looked back, but there was no faint glow in the distance; she hadn't bothered to rewind the light machine, and apparently Ruz hadn't either.

As the light returned she advanced slowly, listening to the wind. The sound had an odd, resonant beat that she'd never heard before, and as she approached the next intersection it grew louder.

She turned right into the cross-tunnel, pursuing the sound. The floor of the tunnel was piled high with rubble, and it reached the point where it became easier just to climb on to the ceiling and stay there. When darkness fell once more it hardly seemed to matter; there might be cracks here, but at least she couldn't slip on a loose stone. She inched her way forward through the blackness.

When the wind rose up again, Roi could hardly believe that she was in the Calm. Even at the garm-sharq edge she'd felt nothing like this; her carapace tingled beneath the assault as if she was being pelted with fine sand.

The light now was brighter than she'd ever seen it. Brighter everywhere, but ahead, opposite the mouth of a side tunnel, a patch on the wall was almost blinding.

She dimmed her vision as much as she could, and approached the intersection cautiously. As she turned to peer into the side tunnel she saw the floor ahead awash with radiance, blazing too brightly to bear. She retreated, her heart racing.

When the next cycle of darkness came and the light ebbed from the surrounding rock, the intersection did not lose its strange radiance entirely. Roi approached the entrance to the side tunnel again, and looked toward the place that had been intolerably bright before. She could see a hole in the ceiling, with a ragged patch of the floor illuminated beneath it. The Incandescence was far away now, but it seemed that a part of its light was still reaching through that hole.

No doubt remained in Roi's mind: this was a crack in the Splinter's edge, leading out to whatever lay beyond. The next time darkness fell the Incandescence would lie safely on the other side, and the secrets of the void would be rendered visible to whoever dared step outside.

15

Rakesh was dreaming that he was a child on Shab-e-Noor, diving into a river with a group of friends, when Parantham appeared among them. She stood on the riverbank, smiling. "We've found an Ark," she said.

"Is this real, or am I dreaming?" he asked.

"Both," she replied.

His friends seemed troubled by the news. "Don't worry," he told them, "I'll be back as soon as I'm finished with this." A sense of panic was rising in his chest. Why couldn't he remember any of these children's names?

"If we let you come back," one said darkly.

Rakesh woke. He had not imagined the claim about the Ark; the telescope's report had entered his skull and the discovery had seeped into the dream's scenario.

He walked to the control room. Parantham said, "I was about to wake you."

"The news did that itself."

"What do you think?"

Rakesh scanned the data. The neutron star where the Ark had been found was twenty light years from the galactic center. Even with ninety per cent of the telescope's mirror in place the image of the find was just a tiny dark blur against the glow of the accretion disk. The spectrum was unmistakable, though; the object in question was made from the same material as the failed Ark that had been left behind.

This Ark would be immersed in powerful winds from the differences in orbital velocity across its length. In spite of the turmoil of its surroundings it had apparently managed to remain in place for fifty million years, kept from spiraling inward by a passive asymmetry in its structure that allowed it to gain energy from the wind if it ever sank too close to the neutron star. It was in precisely the environment for which it had been built. If its makers survived anywhere, surely it was here.

"Is there anything to keep us here?" he wondered. They had already built a communications link that would allow the telescope to convey any further discoveries to *Lahl's Promise;* before departing they could aim it at their destination, and if they moved again from there they could leave a relay behind.

"Nothing I can think of," Parantham replied.

Rakesh felt a twinge of anxiety. "What if this one's empty, too?"

"Then we wait for the telescope to find another one." Even if this neutron star had captured all of the successful Arks initially, that didn't mean it had held on to them all. If there had been enough of them to start with—or if the Arkmakers had flourished in their new environment and found a way to build more—then viable Arks might have ended up orbiting several different neutron stars.

"And if it doesn't find another one?"

Parantham walked up to him and put a hand on his cheek, an almost maternal gesture of tenderness mixed with exasperation. "Then our time here will be over. We'll move on." She took her hand away. "But it hasn't come to that yet, so can you please stop fretting? Whatever this Ark contains will be fifty million years removed from its makers, so I'm not offering any bets about the nature of its inhabitants. But even fifty million years of energy starvation didn't finish off the other one completely. We've already faced the worst-case scenario. We've seen the desert; now we're heading for an oasis."

When their hosts rebuilt and woke them at their destination, the sky had turned from dazzling salt to luminous milk. Fifty times more crowded than before, it had lost every perceptible trace of black. The closer stars still outshone the bright backdrop formed by the crowd behind them, but the contrast was greatly diminished. Night had become day; it was almost as if they were back on Massa, where the stars of the bulge could be seen against the pale twilight sky long before darkness fell.

When the accretion disk came into view it outshone the sky around it, but it was not the kind of spectacle that it would have been against the black night of the disk. Then again, it could never really have existed out there. This was not a blazing X-ray binary, where a neutron star actively tore strips off a closely orbiting companion, but no star was truly isolated here, and the combined exhalations of thousands of neighbors kept the accretion disk aglow. The neutron star itself was almost lost in the bright center of the disk, where a narrow jet of plasma shot up from the plane.

Its days as a conventional sun were long gone, but the chances were that it had never hosted life until it traded its own thermonuclear glow for this gravity-powered renaissance.

The Ark was far too small to see with the naked eye from their distant vantage point, so Parantham aimed the shipboard telescopes while launching surveyor probes. The gray ovoid was six hundred meters long, the same size as the one they'd left behind, but its surface appeared far smoother. That might have meant better repairs by better-fed fungus, or it might just have meant that it had avoided more of the debris from the destruction of the home world.

The Ark's rotation was tidally locked: it spun around its axis in exactly the time it took to complete an orbit, fixing its orientation with respect to the neutron star. This froze the stretch and squeeze of tidal forces into a stationary pattern, allowing the material of the Ark to respond to those stresses once and for all rather than suffering endless cycles of flexing; no doubt this had not always been the case, but the process of flexure would have stolen energy from the rotation until the spin finally did fall into synch. The fixed stance the Ark had achieved did not aim its long axis directly at the neutron star, though; the torque from the orbital wind produced a perceptible slant on the telescope's annotated image.

Rakesh wondered if this leaning tower had been crafted to take account of its inevitable inclination. The interior of the Ark they'd visited had been essentially weightless, but here the orbit, fifty thousand kilometers from the neutron star, was small enough for tidal forces to be felt. While they waited for the surveyor probes, he summoned up a map of that other Ark to see which directions its makers had expected to be "up" and "down". It looked as if they'd hedged their bets: most chambers tended to be almost spherical, with no special orientation required to make particular surfaces work as floors. Similarly, the tunnels sloped in all directions. The makers had been prepared for some uncertainty, but they had clearly not expected the tidal gravity to grow strong enough to dictate the lives of the inhabitants. They had trusted the wind-based buoyancy to keep the Arks in comfortable orbits, and in this case they'd been proven right: the strongest that the tidal gravity would reach here, augmented by centrifugal force from its spin, would be about one sixth the surface gravity of the home world.

The surveyor probes reached their target. Rakesh watched anxiously as the neutrino tomograph slowly accumulated details, a solid labyrinth emerging from fog. The layout was not a tunnel-by-tunnel copy of the interior of the other Ark, but it was very similar, as were the density gradients in the walls. Here, those gradients could achieve their purpose: models showed the wind being scattered into the interior, spreading nutrients deep into the dead zone around the Ark's center where the plasma orbited at the same velocity as the habitat itself. In fact, the main difference the scan showed from the Ark they'd left behind lay in the center; where the last one had been full of rubble and unrepaired cracks, this Ark was in pristine condition.

The probes added an analysis of the Ark's thermal budget, which showed that a substantial fraction of the energy from the wind was being degraded into heat, in a manner that turbulence alone could not explain. On that basis, the biomass within appeared to be at least ten thousand times more than its barren sibling had contained.

Parantham said, "Let's see if anyone wants to talk to us." She broadcast a greeting from one of the probes, sweeping across the spectrum from the longest practical wavelengths down to far infrared. The plasma of the accretion disk stirred by the neutron star's magnetic field would not make for ideal radio reception, but shorter wavelengths would have no chance of penetrating the walls, and there were no visible external antennas or detectors that they could target. The other Ark had contained stretches of conductive wire, but if they had been part of the original design here they must have been broken up and dispersed. Perhaps that was a sign of technological change rather than decay or disrepair, with the old infrastructure being cannibalized for other purposes.

Rakesh said, "I'm loath to barge in until we've given them a chance to respond. It's hard to know how to warn them that we're coming when they don't seem to be looking outward at all, but we should at least try."

"That sounds reasonable," Parantham agreed.

Was it reasonable to enter this place at all? Rakesh tried to step back from his own agenda and ask the question objectively. Whether or not the Ark contained the descendants of a single cultural lineage stretching all the way back to the Steelmakers, these creatures or their ancestors had already suffered greatly from forces beyond their control. Weren't they entitled to do their best to shut out the universe and make their own lives inside this cocoon? It was true that the Amalgam could offer them far greater security than the most stable orbit in this perilous neighborhood, but it would be naive to think that contact itself would be a neutral experience. Out in the disk, the Amalgam had usually waited for cultures to develop interstellar travel for themselves before making contact with them; the exceptions had often been messy.

He turned to Parantham. "Assuming there's someone in there, why can't the Aloof keep them safe? Do you think they could really have been unaware of this place until we came here?"

"We don't know that they're not looking after them," she countered. "Maybe they're tweaking all the local stellar orbits, even as we speak. Maybe they've wrapped their giant hands around this spark of life to shield it from harm, just as meticulously as they've shielded the bulge from intruders."

"Then why are we here? What do they expect us to do?"

Parantham shook her head. "I could spin some half-plausible theory about them hunting for companions for these lonely foundlings, but the truth is I really don't know. It's not our responsibility to read their minds, though; our responsibility is to whoever is inside that Ark."

"To do *what*, exactly?" Rakesh hadn't realized quite how tense he was until he heard it in his own voice. He didn't want the fate of a civilization resting on his shoulders, but nor could he simply turn and walk away. Any people who'd survived their world being dragged from star to star and then torn apart deserved sanctuary. What he did not want to do, though, was blunder in and destroy their paradise, if they had already found it right here.

Parantham said, "Whether the Aloof are pulling our strings, or whether they really don't give a damn what we do, in the end we only have our own judgment. All we can do is tread carefully. I say we wait a few weeks to see if anyone answers our message. If they don't, we go in as unobtrusively as possible and take a look around."

Standing on the surface of the Ark at the point closest to the neutron star, Rakesh could feel the plasma wind and the tidal gravity trying to peel him off and fling him away into the accretion disk. It was like hanging upside down in a stiff breeze, albeit in low gravity and very low pressure. The adhesive pads on his jelly-baby feet could easily resist his avatar's minuscule weight, but the insistent tug was still disconcerting. It was no wonder that in all of their time watching the Ark they had seen no locals foolish enough to venture outside.

Parantham said, "Come on, it's this way." He followed her across the gray plain; the surface felt rough to his clinging feet, but it was flat to the eye and bore no visible cratering. The plasma around them was extremely hot, but also very thin; its temperature in Kelvin made it sound like it would fry anything instantly, but if you calculated its energy density it suddenly seemed a whole lot tamer. The inner edge of the disk and the plasma falling on to the surface of the neutron star were emitting hard radiation that would not have been too healthy for an organic body, but it was nothing to their avatars, and the Arkrock would block it once they were inside.

The crack they'd found was even narrower than the last one, and they'd had to shrink their avatars accordingly. Parantham entered first and Rakesh followed, reaching up by bending sharply at the waist to get a handhold before unsticking his footpads. They could have used their ion thrusters and let the autopilots navigate them through the crack without even touching the sides, but to Rakesh that would have ruined the whole sense of presence; he might as well have sent in a surveyor probe and merely watched the feed from its cameras. Whatever the Arkdwellers might think, he felt far more comfortable making an uninvited entrance in this form than he would have about sending in an autonomous spying device; this way seemed respectful, rather than sneaky. No doubt that reflected his own cultural bias, but until he had something better to go on it was as good a basis for choosing his actions as any.

As soon as they reached a point sheltered from the direct force of the wind, fungus began appearing on the Arkrock. Rakesh took some samples and sequenced them; they were recognizable cousins of the species on the other Ark, though there were significant genetic differences relating to the different environments. As they clambered up the walls, the winding of the crack soon blocked out the starlight, but this time as well as the thermal radiation of the walls themselves they had another kind of light to see by: the Arkrock was translucent to a band of terahertz radiation being produced by electrons spiraling around the magnetic field lines of the plasma. This window appeared to have been tuned to the predominant frequency in the plasma surrounding the Ark's natural orbit, so it was almost certainly a deliberate part of the design. The Arkmakers had not built a dark world of subterranean tunnels and caverns; they had made a world of glass and set it swimming in a sea of light.

Combining the visual processing techniques they'd used in the previous Ark with sensitivity to this new illumination was remarkably effective; although the kind of information they were receiving was very different from that yielded by the usual scattering of light from surfaces, making use of the right cues still generated a rich, detailed sensorium. Rakesh found that he could distinguish most of the species of fungus by sight, and even spot one kind buried beneath another. It was a shock at first to realize that almost nothing was completely opaque across this new spectrum, but once you accepted that fact the potential confusion abated. It was still possible to determine which of two things in your line of sight was the closest; it was just a matter of abandoning the old expectation that the nearer would obscure the farther as a matter of course.

They passed through a point where the fungus was exuding tendrils that criss-crossed the width of the break in the wall. As Rakesh understood the organism's behavior from genome-based simulations, this structure would develop into a net that would trap drifting material—both the "sand" of eroded Arkrock and the mineral-rich corpses of micro-organisms—and use it to reconstruct the wall. Perhaps within a century or two the fissure would be completely sealed.

They emerged from the crack and clambered up on to the floor of a small tunnel; though it dwarfed their tiny avatars, it was less than a centimeter wide. Dozens of varieties of fungus were growing on the walls, inflecting the Arkrock's crystalline translucence with a rich spectrum of colors. If this place turned out to be empty of higher lifeforms, it would not be for want of food. Rakesh could feel the plasma wind even now, flowing right through the walls.

Parantham said, "We don't seem to have sprung any alarms yet, but I suspect they don't have a big problem with intruders."

"No."

"So what now?"

"We take it slowly," Rakesh suggested. "Give them a chance to react. Wait here a couple of hours, to avoid appearing hostile or impatient. If there's no response, we go a little deeper and do the same again."

They waited. Rakesh was sure that certain kinds of fifty-million-year-old civilizations could not have avoided noticing their presence the instant their feet touched the Ark, but then, they were also the kind most likely to have left this place behind completely. The various possibilities were not mutually exclusive, though: even a technologically advanced culture with the power to travel far from the Ark need not have deserted it, and the fact that he and Parantham were not yet facing a welcoming party was no proof that the Arkdwellers had died out or migrated elsewhere.

After two hours with no sign that they'd been noticed, they started walking along the tunnel.

As they approached an intersection the sensors in Rakesh's avatar began to pick up a faint, complicated set of vibrations coming through the rock. It didn't match the footfall of the twelve-legged creatures they'd found in the other Ark; if it was being caused by any kind of animal, it was a large group of a different species altogether.

At the intersection they turned into a wider tunnel, following the vibrations. Their own footsteps didn't seem to be attracting attention, but then even if they were audible in principle this crowd's own noise might have been drowning them out.

The tunnel veered sharply, then opened up into a large chamber. At first all Rakesh could see was the far wall, thickly layered with fungus, but as they drew closer to the entrance the view took in the chamber's floor. Dozens, perhaps a hundred, creatures were moving through the fungus. They were each about a centimeter wide—ten times the size of the curious arthropod that had greeted them in the first Ark. Some had six legs, some had eight. The trunks of their bodies were flattened ovoids, encased in smooth, bilaterally segmented exoskeletons. Within, Rakesh could see small, pulsing organs pumping fluid through a series of cavities surrounding the other viscera, whose functions were less immediately apparent.

They stood at the mouth of the tunnel and observed the creatures in silence. Their motion seemed purposeful, systematic. After a while Parantham said, "They're not feeding on this stuff, but I think they're tending it."

Rakesh agreed. They were crushing some of the rarer plants with their claws, and doing the same to some much smaller animals living among the fungus, but they did not seem to be ingesting anything. They were favoring a handful of species, which were visibly flourishing under this attention, while killing what amounted to weeds and pests.

That didn't prove that they were sentient; agriculture was a fairly common form of innate symbiosis. Would such skilled genetic engineers as the Arkmakers have sentenced their descendants to toiling in the fields? Surely they could have devised maintenance-free crops. Was this proof that the genetic infrastructure had fallen into disrepair? Or perhaps the whole idea that this was a failure was cultural bias; perhaps for them this was enjoyable toil, as exhilarating as running could be for Rakesh's own phenotype.

Parantham said, "You see how they're drumming their legs against their torsos?"

"Yes."

"The vibrations are making it through the rock, so it could be a form of communication. I've been searching for correlations with their surroundings and behavior, but nothing's emerged so far."

"So either it's not communication at all," Rakesh concluded, "or it's playing a more sophisticated role than coordinating this task."

"It looks that way," Parantham agreed. "I was thinking that these might be domestic animals, engineered to tend the crops, but if they're talking to each other about matters far from the here and now, I would hope that means they're the farmers."

"What else could it mean?"

"They could be sentient, but enslaved in some fashion."

Rakesh was dismayed. "Where *do* you get these charming hypotheses?"

"It's been known to happen," Parantham replied dryly.

If the "farmers" had noticed their presence, there was no sign of it. Their avatars were a hundred times smaller than these creatures, and though they were culling pests barely larger than that out of the tangles of fungus, that was at close range. Rakesh couldn't help feeling that if he and Parantham wandered down into the cavern, their most likely reception would involve a similar treatment. In any case, trying to introduce themselves at this point would be premature; they needed to learn the creatures' language, if they had one, and determine exactly what could be expressed with it. Translating "we come in peace from another star" might be tricky if nobody in the Ark had braved the hard radiation of the exterior for several million years. It would be unwise to prejudge the matter, though; for all he knew these farmers could be passing their time debating cosmology and wondering whether life could exist outside the perfect conditions of the galactic bulge.

The two travelers continued to observe, patiently. Just as Rakesh was beginning to suspect that nothing was going to change however long they watched—there was no diurnal cycle here, after all—the farmers broke off traversing the crops and began milling toward the chamber's exits. None approached the tunnel where he and Parantham were standing; they were all heading in the opposite direction, deeper into the Ark.

Rakesh exchanged glances with Parantham; even with their unexpressive jelly-baby faces they didn't need to speak to confirm the decision. They switched on their thrusters and flew across the chamber. As they approached the far side the unspoken consensus continued; they flew together into one of the tunnels, then hovered in the middle to observe the exodus. The farmers jostled beneath them, crowding the small corridor, sometimes climbing the walls and ceiling to get past each other; with their claws splayed against the rock they seemed to have little trouble supporting their weight, but it could not have been entirely effortless as they weren't disregarding gravity completely. In the near vacuum and with no contact with the walls, Rakesh could no longer detect the vibrations of their putative language directly, but everyone in the torrent of bodies surging around him was visibly engaged in the drumming gesture, even more so than when they'd been among the crops. The creatures still showed no interest in the avatars; with the faint glow of the ion thrusters far outside the frequency range of the ambient light, they probably looked like nothing more than specks of dust thrown up by the stampede, and it would have taken an unlikely second or third glance for anyone to wonder why they weren't settling to the floor.

When the last of the farmers had surged past them, Rakesh and Parantham pursued the tail end of the crowd. When the tunnel forked, they split up. It was impossible to follow everyone, so Rakesh chose a group of five among his quarry who seemed to be sticking close together. One by one, though, in side tunnels and small chambers, each of the farmers dropped out of the group. They wedged their bodies into crevices in the rock, and simply stood there, dormant.

When Rakesh had no one left to follow he backtracked along the tunnels, not waiting for his avatar to meet up with Parantham's before filling her in on what he'd seen.

"The same here," she replied. "Perhaps the Arkmakers were constrained by a need for activity cycles in the ancestral biology, so they put in some internal, or social, cue to take the place of the diurnal triggers that would have been present on the home world."

"Sleep, glorious sleep," Rakesh rhapsodised. "These truly are my cousins."

Their avatars returned to the fork where they'd parted. "So is everyone dormant now," Rakesh wondered, "or is this night someone's day?" He was about to suggest that they go hunting for signs of activity when he saw two creatures, identical to the farmers, approaching along the tunnel where Parantham had just been.

They were moving quite briskly, but pausing now and then to scrutinize the tunnel wall. Looking for pests, like the farmers in the chamber? Or hunting for some particular food?

The pair stopped completely, and Rakesh flew closer to see what they were doing. One was scraping fungus from the wall with its claws, while the other opened up the side of its body and removed a small, detached sac or bladder full of dark fluid. The contents were not literally opaque, but came as close to it as anything Rakesh had seen so far.

When the first creature had finished cleaning the wall, the other one punched a hole in the bladder with the tip of one claw, and began squeezing the fluid on to the wall in a slow, painstaking fashion. As Rakesh manoeuvred himself into a better vantage point, he saw that a complex pattern of intersecting lines was already present, marked on the wall with a thinner, paler version of the bladder's dark contents. Line by line, this Arkdweller was repainting a faded sign.

Parantham caught up with him, then hovered beside him, watching in silence. When the signwriters had finished the two travelers remained, gazing at the strange symbols.

16

Zak called out, "Just a few more spans, and I'm there!"

He sounded exhausted, but utterly determined to complete the arduous climb. Roi circled anxiously around the edge of the crack. When she'd helped him up to the entrance, he'd struggled to maintain his hold on the steep, jagged surface, and she had doubted that he would make it all the way through the outer wall. She had underestimated his reserves of strength. He hadn't taxed himself needlessly on the journey; he hadn't even forced himself to stay awake to make polite conversation with his bearers when he'd felt like resting instead. He had been saving everything for this moment, and now it seemed that his strategy was about to prove its worth.

The light machine stopped chugging but it was out of reach, so Roi left the darkness undisturbed. On Zak's instructions she and Ruz were clinging to the ceiling, the idea being that if whatever had killed those who'd ventured out before was present in the void as well as the Incandescence, they would be less exposed to it here than anywhere on the floor nearby. In fact, as Roi had helped Zak into the entrance, she had seen by the glow of the light machine that the crack was twisted in a way that allowed no direct line of sight. Still, during the shomal dark phase some light from the Incandescence had nonetheless made its way right down to the floor, so she couldn't fault Zak's logic.

Zak exclaimed suddenly, "I'm outside!" A moment later he added, "There's an arc of light. I don't understand this."

"An arc?" What did he mean? "Zak?"

There was a long silence, then he replied in a labored voice, "I need to take some measurements. I'll explain everything when I get back down."

"All right." Roi was desperate to hear exactly what he'd witnessed, but she knew it was unfair to expect a running commentary. Zak didn't have much time, and he needed to concentrate on setting up the instruments and collecting the crucial data.

Whatever else there might be to discover in the void, the one possibility in which they had invested the most hope—and planning—was that Zak would be able to locate a distant object that he could track for a while, in order to obtain an independent measurement of the Splinter's motion. From inside the Splinter, there were really only two distinct numbers that could be measured: the ratio of the garm-sard and shomal-junub weights, and the ratio between the periods of the shomal-junub cycle and the turning of the plane of the Rotator's spinning bar. Those numbers were in agreement with Zak's principle, but beyond that they revealed nothing about the geometry through which the Splinter was moving. If the simple geometry that the team had found in their calculations was the right one, then the time it took the Splinter to orbit the Hub would be identical to the period of the shomal-junub cycle. If all orbits at a given distance from the Hub were the same, regardless of their angle of inclination—the assumption of symmetry on which the simple geom-etry was based—then a stone moving shomal and junub of the Null Line would take the same time to complete its orbit as the Splinter itself, and so it would return to its greatest distance shomal of the Null Line after exactly one orbit for both.

How could you mark a fixed point on an orbit, though, in order to measure the time it took to return to it? The idea that two orbits at an angle to each other always intersected at the same two points was the very assumption they were trying to test, so it could not provide the signposts. The only method anyone on the team had been able to come up with was to rely on a different assumption—that objects far from the Hub moved on slower orbits—and then to hope that, with the Incandescence out of the way, it would be possible to observe something in the void so distant that it was as good as fixed. The apparent motion of that distant beacon would then be due—in the most part—to the Splinter's motion around the Hub.

While Roi had paced, Ruz had been still, but now she heard him shift-ing, consulting his clock. "Zak?" he called. "It's halfway through the dark phase!"

A few heartbeats passed, then the reply came back, "I know."

Roi said, "We should have tied a rope around him. Then if he cut it too fine we could have just dragged him down."

Zak hadn't taken the light machine, because of its weight, but they had never imagined that such a device would be available. Ruz had made three clocks that could easily be read by touch, and Zak had practiced in total darkness setting up the most important instrument, the one that would allow him to measure the passage of an object across his field of view. Once that was in place, then so long as there was a beacon worth aiming at, he only had to be able to time the moments when it passed behind a series of metal wires. However dim or bright an object might be, whatever the color of its light, you always knew when it passed behind metal.

"An arc of light?" Roi said. "Do you know what that could be?"

"No," Ruz replied. "But be patient. We'll have the whole journey back in which to interrogate him. In fact, we should extract every detail and write it all down, so if the Splinter sinks back into the Incandescence and never leaves it again, we'll have a record of what lies beyond."

Roi struggled to imagine what it could be like, looking out into the void. "If the Splinter really did break in two, long ago, do you think we could ever find the other half? Ever see it, even if we couldn't reach it?"

Ruz pondered the question. "It's hard to know how far away its orbit might be. Until we know, *in spans*, how far away the Hub is, it's difficult to quantify anything else. At the moment, we're not even sure that our orbit is 'size eight', let alone what that would mean in terms of actual distances." He paused, then called out, "One-quarter of the dark phase remaining! Zak, you need to move *now!*" It had taken Zak almost a quarter-phase to ascend through the crack, and though it would be easier coming down they needed to keep a healthy margin of safety.

Roi waited for his reluctant assent.

There was nothing.

"Zak?" She pressed her body against the rock, straining to hear anything, a word or a footstep. "*Zak?*"

She climbed up into the mouth of the crack. "I'm going up there. Something's happened to him, I need to bring him back."

Ruz said, "If the void's harmed him, it will do the same to you."

"You know what his health is like! He's been sick even back at the Null Line. The effort of the climb would have been enough to weaken him."

"When we planned this trip," Ruz insisted, "we all agreed that only Zak would take the risk—"

Roi seethed with frustration. He was right, they had agreed, but she didn't care. She said, "I'm not going to waste time arguing."

She clambered up the inside of the crack as quickly as she could, forcing herself to ignore the instinctive urge to feel her way slowly through the darkness. The rock was sharp in places, and slippery with weeds, but she kept her footing, and kept advancing. She didn't try to judge the distance or the passage of time, she just willed herself forward.

When a hint of light appeared ahead, she made no effort to make sense of it. Moments later, she tumbled on to the surface of the Splinter.

A band of light was wrapped across the blackness of the void, an arc that stretched from a point high above the rock and swept around a quarter-circle before the Splinter interrupted it. The color of the light varied smoothly across the band from inner to outer rim; within it, small points of brightness slowly drifted, changing color as they moved. Roi looked away; the spectacle was baffling and hypnotic, but this was not the time to sink into the morass of questions that it posed. The illumination it cast on the rock around her was weak and shallow, barely more than that cast by the light machine, but she had no trouble spotting Zak.

She ran to him, and drummed directly on his body. "What happened? Can you move?"

He stirred feebly, but there was no reply.

"Climb on to my back. Can you do that?" She placed herself beside him and flattened herself against the rock.

Nothing. She waited a few heartbeats, but he didn't move.

"All right. I'm going to try to lift you. Relax your grip on the rock." She nudged his body and it shifted slightly; whether he'd heard her and complied, or had simply lost his hold along with his strength, he wasn't sticking.

Roi tilted her carapace and managed to get all four claws on her right side beneath him. The edge of her body was too blunt simply to slide under him, so she tried to raise him with her claws first. She was not so old and weak that his weight should be immovable, and she was sure that once she got him on to her back she would be able to move quickly enough.

She strained against the rock. The very posture that she was forced to adopt undermined her strength, but if she couldn't raise him she could at least make it easier for Zak to complete the action by his own efforts.

She kept pushing, clinging to the hope that in a few more heartbeats the balance of forces would shift, he would slide into place, and they would dash to safety together, but whether or not Zak was striving to assist her, between the two of them he was barely moving.

She'd made a joke to Ruz about a rope, but it was exactly what she needed. She looked up at the tracker that Zak had assembled, wondering if she could use it somehow to lever him up. Then she noticed a sudden brightening, an aura of true, strong light seeping around the rock in the distance.

Roi hesitated, trying to imagine some way in which she might yet save them both. If they both died here, then it would begin to look as if the void itself was fatal, and Ruz would not be so foolhardy as to try to make the measurements himself. The chances were that nobody would leave the Splinter again.

Zak twitched, then tapped one claw against her.

"Run, you fool!"

She bolted for the crack and skidded over the edge, losing her grip by accident but then understanding that it was better this way, better to fall. She bounced painfully against the jagged rock, but kept her claws tightly closed, refusing to slow herself. The rock around her was brightening, and she could feel the heat of the raw, unfiltered Incandescence growing above her.

She hit the floor, bruised and aching, but forced herself to limp down the tunnel away from the searing light. Ruz appeared beside her and she climbed on to his back. She clung to him tightly as he sprinted to the intersection and around the corner.

He kept running until it was clear that they were sheltered by the rock, immersed in nothing but ordinary brightness. Roi listened to the pounding of their hearts. Ruz sounded almost as shaken as she was.

After a while, she spoke. "He was too weak to move. I couldn't shift him."

Ruz said gently, "He might have died in the Null Chamber instead, but it would have been soon, whatever he did. This was the risk he chose."

"I know."

"He did a lot in one lifetime. More than any of us. What he learned, what he taught, what he changed."

"That's true." Roi let the sadness sweep over her. In the end, there was only work, only the Splinter, only the next generation of hatchlings, and the next, on and on into the future. Nobody could live forever. But Zak had woken them all from a daze, woken them to a new kind of thought, a new kind of work, a new kind of happiness. Even if the Splinter itself had not been at stake, he deserved to be remembered for that.

Ruz said, "Are you badly hurt?"

"No. Give me one shift and I'll have my strength back."

"You want to go back there?" Ruz's tone was neutral; he wasn't going to pressure her to take Zak's place, but nor would he try to dissuade her.

"I've walked beneath the void once, I can do it again. And I'm sure there's something out there that we can track, something we can measure." Roi pictured the strange ribbon of colors stretched across the darkness; she had no idea what it was, but she had seen lights moving within it.

"There must be something simple," she said. "We have to keep searching for it."

Zak's body had been seared beyond recognition. Roi had seen many corpses in her life, most of them half-eaten by murche, but she had never faced a choice before about the fate of a friend's remains. Though everyone expected to be consumed by scavengers, as it was normally as inevitable as death itself, was it her duty to Zak to ensure that end? It seemed more fitting to leave him here, where the Incandescence had claimed him.

The tracker, made of metal and susk cuticle, was pitted and tarnished but appeared to have survived intact. Roi went to it and adjusted the aim, sighting a bright point of light at the edge of the colored arc. She took the clock Ruz had made for her from her right cavity, and held the moving wheels against her claw so she could time the occultation of the light by the tracker's wires.

As the light moved, its color changed smoothly. It didn't take long for it to cross the whole width of the band and vanish completely. Roi had no idea how to explain this peculiar behavior. Was the light now being hidden by something in the void—something opaque, like metal—or had it been destroyed?

She recorded the time it had taken for the light to cross a small portion of the view, but she didn't trust that number to tell her much about the Splinter's motion. The lights weren't merely changing color, they were moving apart as they flowed across the band. To expect the time it took for them to cross one thirty-sixth of a circle to be directly proportional to the whole journey seemed absurdly optimistic.

Ruz called to her anxiously, and she returned to the interior with plenty of time to spare. When she was safe in the shelter of the side tunnel she explained what she had seen.

"I have to go out again," she said. "Maybe we'll think of an explanation for all of this, and find some way to calculate the Splinter's orbital period from this data, but since we don't really know what we're measuring, the more observations I can make, the better."

Back on the outside, Roi confirmed a hunch that she'd had before: if she confined her measurements to one part of the band, all the lights took the same time to move through the same angle; when she reoriented the tracker and looked elsewhere, though, the time was different.

Halfway through her second stint, Roi thought she recognized some familiar patterns among the points of light, appearing again in the same part of the band. She wasn't sure, though; she hadn't made an effort to commit the patterns to memory.

The third time she returned, she was certain that some patterns were re-curring. By the fifth time, she was convinced that everything she could see in the void was following the same periodic motion. Her first impression of the lights drifting across the band had been that they were like motes of dust, never the same twice. That wasn't true, though. Notwithstanding the strange distortions of color, angle and speed that accompanied their passage, and the fact that they regularly disappeared from view, she was seeing the lights arranged in exactly the same patterns, again and again. The view as a whole was as cyclic as clockwork.

The period was certainly longer than the window of time she was able to spend making observations during each junub dark phase; it was not, however, equal to the shomal-junub cycle itself, as the lights were not the same each time she returned. Her first guess was that three cycles of the moving lights was close to two shomal-junub cycles, and once she knew what she was looking for her observations bore this out. The two-thirds ratio was not exact, though; it was closer to thirteen parts in twenty.

So much for the simple geometry.

"If we understand anything about orbital motion," Ruz ventured, "then this period has to be coming from the Splinter. There's no way that the orbits of all these other objects could conspire together to give the same result."

Roi would have been happier about attributing everything to the Splinter's motion if the pattern of lights had moved rigidly across the sky, like the view when she leaped from one side of the Null Chamber to the other, tumbling as she went.

"If these things really are motionless," she said, "then why does their appearance change all the time?"

Ruz pondered this. "If they're very distant from us," he said, "then the natural paths of the light that's reaching us from them might be affected by the geometry. This isn't like seeing something that's right in front of us, when we can reach out and confirm by touch that what we're seeing is what's really there. If the geometry can bend the Splinter's natural path to wrap it around the Hub, why shouldn't it bend light as well?"

"Ah." Roi couldn't see how this could explain the whole strange vision that the void presented, but it did make some sense. They'd been used to thinking of light as traveling in straight lines, like a rapidly flung stone crossing the Null Chamber before anything could divert it. It seemed the void was too big, and even light was too slow, for the comparison to be sustained.

"We're going to need to do a lot more calculating," she said. Ruz's sug-gestion was both daunting and encouraging; daunting because it complicated the way they needed to interpret the observations, but encouraging because it meant that the same data provided a far richer means of checking new theories about the geometry than the single number—the Splinter's orbital period—that they'd anticipated gathering.

The eighth time she climbed out into the void, Roi felt her body beginning to falter. Though she'd given herself time to recover from the battering she'd received after fleeing the Incandescence, she hadn't rested again since she'd started making observations.

Her work here was almost complete. Although the motion of the lights wasn't rigid, and varied in a complex way across the band of color, there were only so many measurements required to characterize it; she believed she was getting close to the point where further data was merely confirming what she had already recorded.

She chose a bright light that would be easy to follow, and aimed the tracker toward it. It was only halfway through the measurement, when the times for the successive occultations were beginning to diverge from those she'd seen before for this part of the band, that it struck her that she should have noticed this bright object before. She recognized the pattern of lights around it, and she was sure that in the past they had not included this luminous interloper.

Which meant what?

Perhaps this object was not as distant as the others. It could be orbiting the Hub closely enough for its own independent motion to show up against the synchronized rotation of the background.

Could this be their lost half, the other Splinter?

It was an appealing notion, but why should another Splinter moving through the void be bright enough to see at all, when their own was in darkness? Roi fought her tiredness and tracked the object carefully, until Ruz shouted a timely reminder.

When Ruz heard the news he was excited. "I have to see this for myself," he insisted. Roi was too tired to argue; it was still possible that the void was causing her harm that would only show up in the long run, but it seemed overly cautious to deny Ruz one quick trip when she had survived so many herself.

"When I've rested," she said. "I think I know when it should be visible again. We can go up together."

Roi found a comfortable crack in the wall and shut off her vision, leaving images of the arc of lights wheeling through her mind. The understanding they needed seemed to be forever retreating beyond their grasp, but if she thought about how much had been learned since Zak's first experiments in the Null Chamber, she felt a surge of optimism. Even the Jolt, the source of as much threat and disruption as anything she'd known, had brought them this rich new vein of information.

Sometimes she felt as if there were two people fighting inside her. One longed for the time when she'd tended the crops, basking in the uncomplicated bliss of cooperation, and wished for nothing more than a return to that changeless routine, and a sense of belonging so strong that it extinguished everything else. It was like the Incandescence itself: endless light, endless sustenance.

The other part of her recoiled from that memory. She still reveled in the joys of belonging to a team, but the work she had chosen was utterly different. Instead of being blissfully content with the same healthy crop at the end of each shift, she could only claim success now from something new: a revelation, a contradiction, a twist that turned their old guesses inside out. If they ever did reach the end of the mysteries of weight and motion—and if Zak's legacy finally granted his people the power to steer their fate—she would welcome the return of ease and safety like everyone else, but she did not know how that second part of her would go on living.

Ruz was younger and far more rested than she was, so Roi let him climb ahead of her. She heard his exclamation of delight when he emerged on to the surface. By the time she joined him, he was already beside the tracker.

"Let me get oriented," he said. "This way is rarb, around the Splinter's orbit." He swung the tube of the tracker toward the center of the arc. "And this way is garm, toward the Hub." He turned it to the left, away from the arc. "So the garmside of the void appears completely black, while on the sardside this arc of light is wrapped around the rarb direction." He had heard the same basic facts from Roi, but finally seeing the void's peculiar geometry for himself seemed to compel him anew to seek an explanation. "A quarter of a circle. Why a quarter? The Splinter beneath us is blocking half the view, but why should we be seeing light in only half of what remains?" He hesitated, then answered his own question. "The missing half is in the direction of the Hub. So the Hub must be responsible."

Roi said, "Do you seriously believe that we're almost as close to the Hub as we are to the Splinter—to the rock beneath our claws?" That was a terrifying prospect. She had always imagined the Hub as something small and distant, not a looming presence they were on the verge of swiping, like some careless runner scraping against a tunnel wall.

"Maybe not the Hub itself," Ruz replied. "But suppose we're close to the point where orbits become unstable. Imagine that region as a huge ball around the Hub. There's nothing solid in it, but presumably light can't cut across it to reach us, because it spirals in and hits the Hub instead. There's no rock, no metal, beside us the way the Splinter is beneath us, but *the geometry* still blocks the view."

"That does make sense," Roi admitted. She tried to picture the paths that the light might take as it flowed in from the distant reaches of the void. "The light's not moving in circular orbits, though, so where it gets caught by the Hub might not correspond to the point of instability for the Splinter. I wish I knew *exactly* where rarb and garm lay from here; if we measured the angle from rarb to the start of the arc, that might tell us something."

"Tan can probably think of a way to do that; the signage teams make trickier calculations all the time." Ruz surveyed the arc. "And that's the bright light you mentioned? To the far right, just above the Splinter?"

"Yes."

"We need to get some new recruits here," he suggested, "making measurements constantly, shift after shift. Between the orbit of this Wanderer, and the paths of the light through the void, there must be enough information to pin down the geometry exactly."

"Let's hope so." Roi wasn't sure how complicated the geometry might yet turn out to be. Now that they knew that it lacked the perfect symmetry they'd hoped for, in principle it could be as messy and irregular as the walls of a tunnel.

Ruz timed the Wanderer as it moved across the width of the arc. Roi looked out into the void, freed of the tracker's narrow view, wondering what these lights might be. Small pieces of the Incandescence, severed from it somehow? She didn't understand why the Incandescence was confined to a plane at all, but perhaps there was some way that parts of it could break free, over time.

Or perhaps it was the other way around. Perhaps these points of light began by moving freely, their orbits aligned in all manner of directions, and over time the geometry around the Hub gathered them together and dragged them down into the plane. If that was the case, then these lights were not the offspring of the Incandescence, but its source, its replenishment.

Roi felt giddy, but she could almost picture it: a void full of lights that spiraled in toward the Hub, which swept them together into a plane of wind and radiance. That was the world the Splinter had been immersed in before the Jolt, and from within it had seemed boundless and unchanging. Gradually though, even particles of wind would drift close enough to the Hub to fall, irretrievably. So there would need to be more of the lights coming in, endlessly feeding the Incandescence.

She was tempted to share her ideas with Ruz, but that could keep until they were inside again; better to let him concentrate on his measurements. As she watched the lights drifting across the arc, the Wanderer suddenly grew brighter. A luminous spike transected it, and a second point of brilliance blossomed at the tip of that spike and moved away.

Ruz said, "Did you see—?"

"Yes."

"What was *that?*"

The smaller bright point had vanished; Roi wasn't sure if it had traveled beyond the band of visibility or simply become lost in the crowd, but she couldn't see anything moving.

"The weight must have torn a piece off it," Roi said. "Like the Splinter dividing."

"It's still there," Ruz said. "As bright as ever."

"It's not rock," she said, "it won't break up the same way. Rock by itself is dark; this is wind and light, it's all the things that become the Incandescence."

"What strength does wind and light possess, to hold together at all?" Ruz protested.

"I have no idea," Roi said. "There's still too much we don't know."

The dark phase was almost over; they made their way to the crack and began the descent.

They agreed that it was time to return to the Null Line, to tell the rest of the team the sad news about Zak, and to start working together to make sense of their observations. They put the light machine inside Zak's cart, and took turns in the harness.

The downhill journey was easy, and with the light machine to keep them going they made good progress. As they trudged through the tunnels in the shallow light, Roi found herself wondering if her eggs had hatched, if her children were already taking lessons from Gul. Let there be another Zak or two among them, she thought. The Splinter was going to need them.

Suddenly the tunnel was drenched in brightness. Roi tensed, gripping the floor, prepared for another Jolt. Ruz was behind her, dragging the cart; she heard him take a few unwilling steps from sheer momentum before he froze too.

The light peaked, then faded. After a few heartbeats there was darkness; the light machine was still grinding away, but Roi's eyes were too dazzled to register its effect. There'd been no Jolt, no change in weight.

Ruz spoke first. "What we saw break free from the Wanderer..."

"Just passed us by," Roi said. "The Jolt must have been the same kind of thing, only a bigger piece, or a more direct encounter." She was certain now that her guess about the lights was correct: they fed the Incandescence, and it was not a gentle process. "The geometry is tearing the Wanderer apart, and some of the splinters from it will fall toward the Hub. We're so close to the Hub that it's inevitable that we'll be in the way of some of them."

The light machine fell silent.

"Then which way does safety lie?" Ruz asked. "We need to move away from the Hub, or the next Jolt could push us past the point of no return. But if Bard's tunnel is ever completed, and we succeed in making the Splinter spiral outward, how can we be sure that we won't collide with the Wanderer itself?"

Roi said, "We can't be sure of anything. All we can do is what Zak taught us to do: measure, calculate, try to understand."

Ruz shifted nervously in the darkness. "How many generations will it take us to understand enough to climb out of this trap, without killing ourselves in the process?"

"Maybe one," Roi said hopefully, thinking again of her own children. If they grew up juggling templates and calculating the geometry of the void, it might not be the same struggle for them as it had been for their elders.

Ruz said, "We might not have that much time."

17

Rakesh said, "There's no question that they're sentient. And there's no question that the bulge is a dangerous place. The question is, would they understand what it is we have to offer them?"

Parantham gazed back at him across the control room. "Probably not. Not straight away. Perhaps we could work up to it over time."

"How much time do we have?"

"This Ark's not in any kind of imminent danger."

Rakesh said, "We can't do much for them if we're exiles here ourselves."

"You mean Csi's story? You're afraid the Amalgam won't take us back if we don't get out before the news about Lahl spreads around the inner disk?"

"Do you think I'm being paranoid?"

"I don't know." Parantham thought it over. "The Amalgam has a strong tradition of hospitality, but it also has a strong tradition of cutting off those who abuse it. I think it will come down to whether or not people will believe that Lahl was an act of bad faith by the Aloof, or just a genuine traveler who covered her tracks."

"Or in the absence of conclusive evidence either way," Rakesh suggested, "it will come down to where they want to place the benefit of the doubt, how they want to weigh the risks."

"What risks? The Aloof have no more power to harm us by posing as citizens of the Amalgam than they have skulking down in the bulge."

"Maybe, but they shouldn't have lied to us. That's the part that's hard to forgive. That's the part that makes it hard to trust them."

"Maybe they had to lie." Parantham spread her arms. "Is this my body? Was I born with it? Am I lying to you by pretending to inhabit it the way you inhabit yours?"

"If they were capable of pretending to be Lahl, surely they were capable of saying, 'By the way, we're not quite who we seem to be.'"

"Just because *we* can imagine Lahl saying that doesn't mean *they* were capable of doing it—or capable of understanding why we wish they had."

Rakesh put his head in his hands. "Forget the Aloof. What are we going to do about the Arkdwellers?"

Parantham said, "Keep studying them until things become clearer. If you'd let me run some simulations—"

"They're sentient, they have a right to privacy. We can't do anything like that without informed consent."

"But we can spy on them as much as we like?"

"There's a difference," Rakesh protested heatedly, "between sending avatars in discreetly to observe their public behavior and stealing DNA samples in order to run simulations."

"Public behavior, as distinct from what? They don't seek privacy from each other for anything they do."

"It's about consent, it's not about social taboos."

Parantham raised her hands in a gesture of resignation. "You're their cousin, you're the child of DNA. You decide, I'll just keep my mouth shut."

Rakesh knew he was being inconsistent, but he had to defend the compromise he'd struck. If they had ruled out clandestine observations, then there was simply no point being here; making their presence known to the Arkdwellers without studying them first would have been ineffectual at best, and at worst disastrous. But he would not countenance sequencing them without their permission; that would be treating them like animals.

The Arkdwellers had language, spoken and written. They had tools, they had agriculture, they had industries. They had specialization: each one of them performed a particular role to keep the Ark running smoothly. Rakesh had at first suspected that these roles were innate biological castes, but that had turned out not to be the case. Rather, workers were inducted into teams by a kind of socially mediated bonding mechanism, which was powerful but not irreversible; they could be press-ganged into another team, if the right circumstances arose.

Similarly, their agricultural and technological practices seemed to be culturally transmitted rather than genetically hardwired. The cultural legacy included a small amount of written material along with the predominant mix of oral instruction and learning by imitation, but did not contain anything that Rakesh recognized as history, or natural science. They did not seem to know about the Arkmakers, or to have any comprehension of what lay outside the Ark.

How could he invite them into the Amalgam, when they had never even seen the nearest stars? How could he offer them sanctuary, when they had no idea how close to extinction their ancestors had come? They were not in any immediate danger; even in this crowded, chaotic place, it was possible to predict that nothing would tear them from their orbit in the next few millennia, and given how long they'd survived already they might remain unscathed for millions of years.

In the long run, though, they couldn't rely on the Ark's design to protect them from all the perils of the bulge. Should they be left to live in peace, then, isolated and ignorant, until the inevitable finally happened and they were incinerated in a supernova or ferried by some new Interloper all the way to the singularity at the heart of Goudal-e-Markaz?

Rakesh had made a promise to Lahl, and whether she'd been a citizen of the Amalgam or some kind of construct sent out by the Aloof was beside the point; what he had accepted was an obligation to take the responsibilities of any discovery seriously, and not treat these creatures as a mere trophy, a curiosity to be catalogued and then abandoned.

He turned to Parantham. "I think we should leave before we risk getting stranded, but we should try to make contact with the Arkdwellers first. There's a chance we'll be able to come back eventually, but we have an opportunity now to plant some information that might help protect them, even if we can't return."

Parantham considered this. "Contact can be disruptive."

"So can being blind-sided by a neutron star that you never even dreamed existed."

"We could go out," she suggested, "come to some arrangement with the eavesdroppers in the inner disk to normalise our status, then return to do this at our leisure."

Rakesh said, "And will we come to some arrangement with the Aloof whereby they promise to let us in again? Or just take our chances and hope this wasn't a once-in-a-million-year opportunity?"

Parantham wasn't happy. "If you're resolved to do this, I can't stop you, but I'm not going to participate."

"I see." Rakesh was surprised by the strength of her disapproval. He hesitated, weighing up the options again.

Every choice was risky; there was no perfect solution. But he would not leave the bulge until he'd done his best to help the Arkdwellers understand their history, and regain control of their fate.

There were no cracks in the Ark large enough to admit his new avatar, so Rakesh took it through in pieces and assembled it in the tunnel. It was the size and shape of a typical adult Arkdweller, with the six legs of a male, but none of the Ark's inhabitants would mistake it for one of their own. The imperfect imitation was intentional; he wanted to communicate with the Arkdwellers effectively, not deceive them about his nature. He wanted his strange body to act as evidence, to back up his extraordinary claims.

He and Parantham had gathered enough data on the Arkdwellers' leg-drumming to assemble a comprehensive picture of the language, and Rakesh had tweaked his mind not only to enable him to speak and understand it, but also to acquire new vocabulary, and grasp any other nuances or novelties that had eluded their survey so far. When he switched his senses into the new avatar, he drummed a few phrases softly, accustoming himself to the mode.

"Wish me luck," he said, in his native tongue with his real mouth, addressing Parantham across the control room. She didn't reply, but Rakesh knew she would be watching everything. He would be glad to have her looking over his shoulder; even though she wouldn't actively participate, he hoped he could rely on her to warn him if she thought he was pushing the Arkdwellers too hard. Sharing a replicator with these people gave him no special insight into their nature, and he'd welcome a second opinion any time she cared to offer one.

He set off down the tunnel.

As he approached the farmers' chamber he slowed, and strained his hearing. The last time he'd been here the vibrations reaching his avatar had sounded like meaningless noise; now the hubbub was imbued with the unmistakable cadences of speech, even though he could not make out any individual words.

He reached the entrance to the chamber and stood in plain sight of the whole work team, waiting expectantly for a shocked silence to descend, or a commotion to arise. He was sure that if an ambulatory scarecrow had approached the edge of a field full of farmhands on Earth, in the days before machinery, there would have been a dramatic response.

The farmers ignored him. It was hard to judge their lines of sight, but Rakesh knew he was clearly visible in principle, and he believed that at least a dozen of the workers had looked his way and then continued tending the crops.

This was, he decided, an encouraging sign: the mere sight of him wasn't going to spark a riot. If the Arkdwellers' lack of curiosity was alien to him, their lack of volatility could only make it less likely that Parantham's fears would turn out to be well-founded.

He clambered down the sloping wall of the chamber, into the thick of the crops, and approached one of the workers.

"To your life and strength," he drummed.

"And yours," the worker replied, continuing past him.

Rakesh turned and followed her. "Wait, please."

"I'm busy."

"Can't we talk while you work?" The farmers talked among themselves all the time.

"I'm busy," she repeated. To the extent that Rakesh understood her tone, it was not unusually cold or hostile, merely emphatic. He wondered what, exactly, she thought he was. Some kind of grossly deformed member of her own species? He did not belong to her current team, of course, and that was the most important distinction.

Another of the farmers was heading his way. Rakesh greeted him, and he received the same standard reply.

"My name is Ra," Rakesh said.

"I'm Neb," the farmer replied.

"I've come from outside the world," Rakesh announced boldly.

"We have enough workers," Neb explained. "We're not seeking recruits right now."

"I want to talk with you, that's all."

"You didn't hear me?" Neb admonished him. "You should return to your own team, or find another one. We have all the workers we need here."

Neb moved away from him, sifting purposefully through the fungus.

Rakesh kept trying, but each time he received the same perfunctory response. The fact that he could speak and was roughly the right shape seemed to be enough for the Arkdwellers to treat him as one of their own kind, but having made that categorization they had no interest in his actual words. If the team had been short-handed perhaps they would have sought to recruit him, but it was not, so he was irrelevant. Beyond the curt exchange of greetings that even a stranger merited, conversation served only as an adjunct to social bonding, and they had no need, or wish, to form any kind of bond with him.

Rakesh stood motionless in the chamber and let the farmers pass him by. Nobody took it upon themself to say a word to him, to ask him where he was from, how he had arrived, what he wanted. A walking scarecrow from beneath the edge of the world was surplus to requirements.

So be it. These farmers were not the only team in the Ark; there had to be one that would welcome a new recruit.

Rakesh left the chamber by a tunnel opposite the one he'd come in by. At first there was no one else in sight, but as he ascended deeper into the Ark he started glimpsing people moving in the distance, crossing ahead of him through side tunnels. He thought of running after them, but he'd observed enough of the Arkdwellers' normal behavior to know that the hot pursuit of strangers, followed by begging for recruitment, lay right off the spectrum. The strangeness of his body had not proved to be the icebreaker he'd hoped; eccentric behavior was unlikely to open any more doors.

He reached a T-junction in the tunnel he'd been following; he took a right turn, since that was the branch that continued to slope upward. Ahead of him was a female Arkdweller, pulling a wheeled cart loaded with animal hides.

He greeted her, and introduced himself. Her name was Saf, and she proved to be far more responsive than the farmers; when he asked where she was going, she explained that she was carrying the hides to a depot about one shift's journey away.

"Can I travel with you?" Rakesh asked.

"Why should I stop you traveling wherever you wish?" she replied.

Rakesh trudged beside her in silence. He was less inclined than before to blurt out a declaration of his origins, and risk rupturing this tenuous relationship.

Saf said, "You don't look very healthy, but you move as fast as I do with very little effort. I can't even see your heartbeat."

"I'm much healthier than I look," Rakesh agreed.

"What work do you do?"

"I have no team. I'm looking for a new one."

"I see." Saf fell silent. Rakesh was beginning to wonder if it was a bad thing to admit to being unemployed; he had never actually seen an Arkdweller ejected from a team, and it would be understandable if that lowered his chances as a potential recruit. If he wanted to be headhunted, he should have claimed some high-status occupation that would have had everyone trying to poach him.

"My colleague was recruited by susk herders on the way down," Saf confided. "If you want to pull the cart with me, we can be team-mates."

Rakesh emitted a whoop of delight from his real mouth, then calmly and politely accepted the offer. Saf stopped and showed him how to take the cart's second harness, then they continued together.

18

"Seventy-two more shifts and we'll be done!" Bard said proudly.

Roi stared down the length of the giant tunnel. It vanished into the distance, the far end lost in the glow from the walls. She could hear the din of workers chipping away at the rock face, but she couldn't see them, and it probably would have taken her half a shift to reach them. There might have been other tunnels in the Splinter as long as this, but there were none as wide, or as straight. In a way, she found the sight of it stranger than anything she'd seen in the void; you expected to be shocked when you climbed outside the world, but in this ordinary place the simple rearrangement of rock and empty space had created something unprecedented: a structure with the power to move the Splinter itself.

"Just seventy-two? Are you sure?" They were standing in the middle of the tunnel's longest segment, but there were a dozen others still growing out from their starting points, reaching toward each other but yet to join up.

Bard retreated slightly. "Something close to that. I can't say exactly. The team's been growing steadily ever since the Jolt, but if the numbers level off we might take longer to complete it. We have as many workers as we can fit at the rock face, but we can always do with more shifting rubble."

Word of Bard's project had spread throughout the Splinter. In ordinary times that would have counted for nothing, but it seemed that everyone who had been shaken free of their loyalties had come to take a look at the tunnel, and to hear the arguments its builders had to offer. Roi had encountered more than a dozen such travelers on her journey into the sardside, and they had all been willing to listen carefully to the case she'd made on Bard's behalf. People who, she was sure, would once have turned away in boredom and incomprehension at such useless metaphysical talk had striven patiently to come to terms with the subtleties of weight and motion, the nature of the Jolt, and the way the wind's free passage through this sardside tunnel might unbalance the Splinter and allow the garmside wind to carry them to safety.

Bard wasn't even sure of the number of workers he had at any moment; he'd appointed supervisors to take charge of the various stretches of the tunnel, all the way from the rarb edge to the sharq, and they recruited new arrivals for themselves. When a segment was completed earlier than expected, as sometimes happened because the rock turned out to be softer than usual, the workers moved along until they found another place where they were needed.

Roi had come to break the news to Bard that the tunnel was going to require some modifications. With the Wanderer orbiting further out from the Hub, they couldn't simply open the tunnel to the wind and then trust in their luck to carry the Splinter to safety. They would need to be able to block and reopen the tunnel at will, providing some control over the Splinter's outward spiral.

Bard listened carefully as Roi explained what she and Ruz had observed. She knew he had lost interest in the fine points of space-time geometry, and he had nothing to say about the strange appearance of the void, but the prospect of a more complex role for his cherished creation seemed to delight him.

"We can build cross-tunnels with plugs we can roll across into the main shaft," he suggested. "There are plenty of lodes of dense rock that we had to move whole, because they were too hard to break. In fact, if we build a whole system of movable plugs with different kinds of rock, we ought to be able to set the flow to any level you like."

"That's a good start," Roi said. "I was wondering, though, what would happen if we needed to block or unblock the tunnel while we were in the Incandescence?"

Bard was startled. "You think we might need such fine control that we can't wait for the next dark phase? Isn't it going to take a shift or two just to get word here that the tunnel should be blocked?"

"I don't know what we're going to need," Roi admitted. "We still don't know how we're going to do this: what path we'll require the Splinter to take, and how we can ensure that we follow it precisely. But even if we don't need to alter the tunnel at short notice, there's a chance that as we move out from the Hub we might lose the oscillation the Jolt gave us; we might sink back into the Incandescence permanently. So we need to be able to open and close the tunnel, whether we're in the Incandescence or the void."

Bard pondered this new challenge. "We could build some kind of system of ropes. Mount the plugs on wheeled carts, and have people in the side-tunnels—sheltered behind fixed, dense lodes themselves—who can operate the ropes and slide the plugs into place."

"That sounds perfect."

Bard pressed himself against the rock, a posture jokingly suggesting that she was putting him under stress. "I hope you theorists know what you're doing."

"I can assure you that we don't. The geometry is still beyond us. All I learned in the void was that our best guess so far is certainly wrong."

"That's comforting." Bard looked down the tunnel and rasped frustration. "So when this magnificent work is finished, you'll want us to keep it plugged up for another thirty-six shifts while you do your calculations?"

"At least," Roi agreed. "Maybe longer."

"So what are we honest workers supposed to do while we're waiting for you to judge the shape of space-time?"

Roi said, "You had plans for a second tunnel, didn't you?"

Bard replied wryly, "On skin, a second tunnel costs nothing. It was on the drawing I made, when I first had the idea. But I spent so long failing to get the first one started that I gave up thinking about anything so ambitious."

"You should build the second one if you can," Roi said. "Then a third, then a fourth. There's every chance we're going to need them. When we go ducking and weaving around the Wanderer, the faster we can move, the better."

Roi's second task on the sardside was to visit Neth, and see if she could persuade her to return to the Null Chamber. The theorists would need all the help they could get, and the battle Neth had come here to fight, to win people over to the cause of the tunnel, had been resoundingly won.

Bard had given her directions to the place where she could find Neth, but nobody could keep track of all the obstructions and detours surrounding the Great Project. The signage teams had probably all gone mad, or disbanded. As Roi passed among a group of workers shifting rubble from the tunnel's construction, she recognized one of them as Jos, the light-maker she'd met when she was traveling with Ruz and Zak.

Jos was happy to see her, but didn't want to stop working, so Roi walked beside her, helping her to carry a heavy piece of stone. Ideally, everyone doing this job would have had wheeled carts for their loads, but there probably weren't that many carts in the whole of the Splinter.

"This must be hard work," Roi said. "Shift after shift." She was struggling beneath the weight of the stone, even with two of them sharing the burden.

"It's not so bad," Jos said. "We're always taking the rubble downhill, sard of the tunnel. Bard told us that every rock we move shifts the Calm a small way sardwards, strengthening the garmside winds."

The darkness descended, but Jos insisted that they keep moving. "I've traveled this route so many times that I know it by touch."

Roi had little choice but to trust her. "What happened to your light machine?"

"It's at one of the rock faces. It's more useful there, where they can leave it in one place for a while. If I tried to carry it with me everywhere, I'd have no room on my back, and no strength for any rock."

"Fair enough." Roi hadn't brought the one that Cot had given her, even though she had little else to carry; this deep into the sardside the weight would have been too much.

"I still think about light all the time," Jos said. "What it is, how we can make it and use it." She added, almost apologetically, "There's nothing else to think about when you're carrying rocks."

Roi was no longer surprised by statements like this. Once, it had gone without saying that work and companionship, loyalty and cooperation, were more than enough to fill anyone's mind. Now the strange urges that had made people like her and Zak such aberrations were infesting half the Splinter. The strangest thing of all was that it had not brought anarchy and chaos, famine and death. People still carried out their work, still made sure that every necessary thing was done. There was a restlessness, though, a fluidity, reshaping the organization of the Splinter, faster than any tunnel builders could reshape its rock.

"What kind of ways could we use light?" Roi asked her. "Apart from the obvious."

"Imagine a flat sheet of metal at one end of a tunnel," Jos said. "An ordinary tunnel, not the one we're building. You could see it clearly from a very long distance: until the bend in the tunnel took it out of sight. Now if someone turned it edgeways to you, you'd notice straight away. In the dark phase you'd need a light machine beside it, but with care you could keep it visible all the time."

"I don't doubt that, but what use would it be?"

"Suppose you needed to get a message to someone on the other side of the Splinter. If we had a team of people positioned in the right locations, watching for changes in each other's sheets of metal, they could pass the message faster than anyone could run. Like couriers for words."

Roi was bemused. "Words need drumming or writing. Where are the words?"

"We agree on a list of simple words," Jos said. "Then we divide the list in half, in half again, and so on, until the last half is a single word. Tilting the metal once can tell us which half of the list the word is in, twice which half of that half-list, and so on."

The light was returning. Roi said, "You've thought about this for a while?"

"It passes the time."

If they needed to change the plugs in Bard's tunnel quickly, a system such as this might help. Roi had been struggling to imagine how they were going to navigate their way safely out to the Wanderer's orbit and beyond, when the one place where they could see into the void and the one place from which they could change the Splinter's motion were so far apart. She'd thought of trying to construct a platform for observations closer to the tunnel, but the directions of the weight made that a daunting prospect. Having to cling upside-down to the Splinter's exterior—when there was nowhere to land if you should fall—was not a situation likely to be conducive to accurate measurements.

Roi explained all of this to Jos.

"So you think it could actually be useful?"

"Absolutely! You need to start work on this immediately," Roi said. "See if you can persuade some of your team-mates to join you. Work out the details, smooth out the problems. Then come and meet me at the Null Line and let me know how things are going." Roi gave her directions to the Null Chamber.

Jos seemed overwhelmed by the sudden turn of events. "I believe you when you say this is important," she said. "But my job here, with the rocks… I came here, I listened to Bard…" She trailed off, confused. The Jolt had changed her enough to bring her here, and enough to make her restless with ideas, but she hadn't entirely lost the sense that the best thing to do was to stick with your team as long as you could.

"When will it end?" she implored Roi. "I want the old way back."

"You'll get it back," Roi said. "But first you have to do this."

Jos signaled to her to halt, and they came to a stop together. With a rasp of reluctant acquiescence she eased the rock down between them.

Roi said, "You're just going to leave that here?"

"It's not my job any more," she replied.

Roi found Neth alone in a chamber, surrounded by template frames. Neth greeted her warmly, and listened to all the news.

"I'm sad to hear of Zak's death," Neth said, "but I expected it long ago."

Roi didn't want to dwell on that. "So how are you spending your time here?"

"I'm trying to understand the wind," Neth said. "Even before we've cut open the mouth of the tunnel, moving all this rock has changed the flow. This whole thing is not as simple as Bard suggests."

"What do you mean?"

"If the Splinter simply wasn't here, the wind would blow straight from rarb to sharq; we can all agree on that. I'm not convinced, though, that cutting a long tunnel through the Splinter will necessarily have the same effect. The surrounding rock will still be diverting and complicating the flow of the rest of the wind. It will all mix together in the tunnel. The result isn't easy to predict."

Roi was dismayed. She had thought the hard part would be persuading people to help build the tunnel; now Neth was suggesting that it might not even work.

"What can we do if the flow isn't strong enough to make a difference? Build more tunnels?"

"That could help," Neth said. "But the important thing will be learning how to shape and control the flow through however many tunnels we have. What you say Bard has planned, with the varying plugs, will make a good start, but we'll need to study the effects of that arrangement, experiment with it, fine-tune it."

"And make calculations?"

"Of course."

Roi struggled to reconcile herself to this new setback. She couldn't be sure that Neth was right, but she appeared to have thought about the problems of the flow more deeply than anyone else. Bard would certainly get the rock shifted and the machinery in place, but without Neth's aid, there was a chance it would all be in vain.

She could not ask Neth to leave and join her in the Null Chamber.

"Tell me," Roi said, "given what I saw in the void, how do you think we should approach the calculations now?"

For a few long heartbeats Roi was afraid that Neth was going to modestly demur that it was not her place to offer advice on the matter, now that she'd left the theorists' group. *Not my job any more.*

If that was her inclination, she managed to overcome it. "Try to hold on to as much symmetry as you can," she suggested. "You've shown that there isn't perfect symmetry around the Hub in all directions. But for all the time we sat in the plane of the Incandescence, nothing in the weights changed while the Splinter completed each orbit. In fact, the period of the orbit was impossible to discern without looking outside the Splinter. That tells us that the geometry as we moved around the Hub was completely unvarying."

"We were moving through just one plane, though," Roi said.

"Yes," Neth replied, "but the simplest way such a symmetry could arise would be if it held true for *all* planes parallel to the Incandescence. So if you rotate the whole geometry around an axis passing through the Hub, perpendicular to the plane of the Incandescence, it should be left unchanged. Instead of the symmetry of a sphere, look for the symmetry of an ellipsoid."

As Roi departed, she thought irritably: *That's obvious. I didn't need Neth to tell me that.*

Everything simple was obvious in retrospect, though. What remained to be seen was whether the void itself had any interest in the kind of simplicity that might let their minds reach out and grasp the truth about the world, or whether Zak's principle was just a beautiful, but misguided, statement of hope.

When Roi returned to the Null Chamber, she found to her delight that it was crawling with hatchlings. Gul was among them, orchestrating their exuberant play.

She climbed out along a wire to reach him.

"I heard the news about Zak," he said. "I thought you'd probably be too busy to come back to us for a while. Then I thought, why not let them experience weightlessness and see some experiments, instead of just hearing about everything second-hand?"

Roi didn't recognize any of the pupils; this was a new class. Her and Gul's children would almost certainly be among them, but if they were she had no way of identifying them. She watched the scampering hatchlings with an uneasy, almost guilty, thrill. Just as Jos had found it hard to defect for a second time, even Roi had her limits, and it was difficult to view the secret obsession she'd developed with her own offspring's fate as anything but shameful and perverse.

Since the Jolt the Null Chamber was no longer perfectly weightless, but though the changes were enough to ruin long-term measurements it was still possible to demonstrate the basic cycles here, not to mention indulging in the pleasures of simply floating around and throwing things to see how they moved. The place brought back memories of Zak, but Roi could feel no sadness at that when two dozen hatchlings were being steeped in his ideas before her eyes.

Gul said, "If you have a moment, later... I'm in pain."

Roi had seen the seed packets inside him, but he'd hid the discomfort so well that she'd assumed they weren't yet ripe. She felt no inclination to berate him, this time, for failing to find someone else to deal with his burden. The simple truth was, she wanted the two of them to have children together. As many as possible.

She turned the baffling notion over in her mind. *Why?* He was a good teacher, but he didn't have to be the father of a hatchling, she didn't have to be the mother, in order for him to teach it. Did she imagine, absurdly, that their individual skills had somehow seeped into their seed and eggs, and would collide within their children to imbue them with a preternatural ability to endure the struggles ahead? None of the hatchlings here were dishing out lessons in space-time geometry and template manipulation. If her children were special in any way, why couldn't she even pick them from the crowd?

It was a mystery, but she didn't feel like fighting it; she didn't even have the energy to ponder it for long. If the next generation turned out to be so brilliant, they could work out the reasons themselves; she'd be content just to see them survive.

She said to Gul, "There's a machine someone gave me that turns darkness into light. When the children are asleep, come and see me, and I'll show you how it works."

Roi met Tan, and they began preparing the way for the calculations that they hoped would lead to the true geometry.

Zak's principle remained their most trusted guide, but it was a curious thing. Once you knew certain aspects of the space-time geometry it allowed you to deduce the rest, but if you started with a blank skin it could not tell you anything definite. It was less a prescription for a single, self-contained world than a kind of style or constraint that left room for a multitude of possibilities. Before you could apply it, you needed to weed out all but one small, manageable portion of that overwhelming bounty.

As Neth had suggested, their best hope of success was to retain as much symmetry as possible. At the same time, if they pruned away too much of the geometry's freedom just to make the calculations simpler, they would risk failing, once again, to capture the true richness of the space-time around the Hub.

"I believe in rotational symmetry," Tan said firmly. "We have evidence for that, and not just in the plane of the Incandescence. Since the Jolt, we've been moving periodically out of that plane, and your observations show that each time we've entered a shomal or junub dark phase, we've actually been at a different place along our orbit. Yet apart from the different view of the lights you saw, nothing else is different from phase to phase. The weights change slightly as we ascend and descend relative to the plane, but at a given point in each cycle, everything *feels* the same."

"We're not going very far out of the plane," Roi cautioned. "It's hard to quantify, but I doubt that we're rising by more than a tiny fraction of our distance from the Hub."

"No, but the lack of spherical symmetry you discovered manifests itself in the length of the shomal-junub cycle, which we first measured in the Null Chamber with stones that never went further than *one span* from the plane of the orbit! It was only the fact that the Incandescence and the Splinter were blocking our view of the lights in the void that stopped us from comparing the shomal-junub cycle to the orbital period."

"That's true," Roi conceded. "In any case, even if we can only pin down the geometry close to the plane and use it to explain the Splinter's motion, that will be a start." The Wanderer's orbit appeared to be inclined, taking it high above the Incandescence, but with the strange distortions of the light to account for, making sense of those observations remained a distant ambition.

"We're agreed then," Tan said. "We look for a geometry unchanged by rotation around a fixed axis."

The other symmetry they were committed to retaining was the assumption that the geometry around the Hub was unchanging over time. Though the Splinter and other objects might be nudged into different orbits, it was the fact that they had shifted in space that altered the geometry they experienced; the geometry itself was not melting beneath them.

"The question then," Tan said, "is how are the two symmetries related? In our last calculation we assumed that the symmetries of space always acted in a direction perpendicular to the time symmetry. But do we have any evidence for that?"

Roi hoped Gul was filling their children's minds with ideas that would prepare them for questions like this. She had been raised with an understanding of three perpendicular directions in space—garm/sard, rarb/sharq, shomal/junub—and if you added time as a fourth, it seemed obvious that it ought to be measured perpendicular to all three. Certainly, any clock you carried with you would measure time that way, and even in the abstract world of Tan's geometry, at any given time and place you could simply *pick* four perpendicular directions.

However, the directions of symmetry weren't a matter of choice or convenience; they were properties of the geometry itself. And while the framework for the calculations would become more complicated if the two symmetries were allowed the freedom to slant against each other, it would be even worse if they could not rely on a measure of time in which the geometry was unchanging.

Roi said, "What would count as evidence?"

Tan couldn't answer that immediately. He took a sheet of skin and started doodling. "Throw out one dimension of space, the one that takes us out of the plane of the Incandescence, and use that instead to picture time." He drew a point for the Hub, then sketched a circle around it for their old, un-Jolted orbit. "The symmetry in time takes this circle into another one in the future, tracing out a cylinder." He sketched in the cylinder, drawing lines rising straight up from the circle to indicate the direction in which it could be pushed without its geometry changing.

Roi said, "And if the time symmetry isn't perpendicular to the rotational symmetry?" She scratched a second diagram beside the first, in which the lines that carried the circle forward in time wound around the cylinder in helices. "But wouldn't we always be able to straighten out these lines?" she said. "The geometry doesn't change, whether you move around the cylinder as you travel along its length, or just slide straight up and down. It's all the same."

Tan thought for a moment. "With *one* cylinder you could always do that, but don't forget the rest of the geometry." He drew in a second, larger orbit on Roi's diagram, then sketched in helices with a different, steeper pitch. "Suppose the time symmetry makes a different angle with the rotational symmetry at different distances from the Hub. We're free to combine this whole motion with any fixed amount of rotation around the Hub, but we're *not* free to rotate around the Hub by different angles at different distances, and that's what we'd need in order to straighten everything out."

Roi said, "So there'd be a kind of unavoidable twist in the geometry?" She pondered this. "Then wouldn't motion around the Hub in the direction of the twist be different from motion in other directions?"

"That sounds plausible," Tan said.

"When we throw a stone out of the plane of the Incandescence," Roi said, "it completes the orbit in much less time than it takes to fall down and rise up again. It's almost as if it's being swept around the axis of symmetry, forcing it to go around faster than the other cycle it's completing, the shomal-junub cycle."

Tan said, "I think you've just answered the question. There might turn out to be some other explanation, but for now we definitely can't assume that the symmetries are perpendicular."

That would make the calculations harder, but at least they were doing it for a reason. Roi felt buoyed; the idea that they could anticipate a feature of the geometry that might allow it to conform to the new observations was encouraging. Most of what she'd seen in the void remained utterly mysterious to her, but they were moving in the right direction.

"There's one more thing we need to decide before we call in the calculating team," Tan said. "How are we going to measure distances from the Hub now?"

In the previous calculation, they'd described each point's relationship to the Hub by the size of the sphere on which it lay. You didn't need to worry about the actual, messy curved geometry all the way from the point to the Hub itself; instead you imagined rotating the point *around* the Hub in all possible directions, sweeping out a sphere whose surface area would increase the further the point was from the Hub.

With the spherical symmetry gone, they could no longer do this. They could replace the spheres with circles—rotating each point around the axis of symmetry and then considering the circumference of the circle it swept out—but away from the plane of the Incandescence it wasn't clear how those circles would be related to each other.

Ruz appeared at the entrance to the Chamber. He greeted them politely and apologized for interrupting, but Roi could tell from the way he hunched against the wall that he had something he urgently needed to say.

"We're seeing more flares from the Wanderer," he announced. "Nine, in the last report I've received." While Roi had been visiting Bard and Neth, Ruz had arranged a group of new recruits to stay at the junub edge, with pairs climbing up through the crack in the wall each time it was safe, to make observations.

"We've felt no new Jolt," Tan said.

"No," Ruz replied, "we've been lucky. But if this continues, it's only a matter of time before another one strikes us. We're also seeing the Wanderer's orbit changing: it's losing its inclination, coming closer to the plane of the Incandescence."

Roi felt a crushing sense of hopelessness descend, but she struggled to fight it off. One tunnel was almost complete, and Neth would help Bard sort out any problems with the flow. They were tracking the Wanderer heartbeat by heartbeat. Now it was up to the theorists to find the way forward, to draw the map that showed the way to safety.

She addressed Tan. "We should assemble the calculating team, next shift."

"All right," he said. "But what about the question of distance from the Hub?"

Roi thought for a while. "There's one symmetry that's always present, that we forgot to mention: the geometry really doesn't care how we describe it." You could wrap space-time in numbers in countless different ways, but the underlying shape was oblivious to the packaging. "We don't know the best way to express distance from the Hub, and even if we make a certain guess now it might turn out to make things harder. So we should give ourselves room to manoeuvre: we should set up the templates so we can choose the easiest scheme at any point in the calculations."

Tan concurred. He said, "I'll go and tell the calculating team."

When he'd left, Ruz said, "I'd better go and send the messengers back to get the next report."

Roi said, "Remember Jos?"

"Jos?"

"One of the people we met with the light machine?"

Ruz looked tired. "Vaguely. Why?"

"She's had an idea for something much faster than any messenger. I think you need to talk to her."

19

Rakesh spooned chillied dhal into his mouth with an urgency that had nothing to do with hunger. The longer he spent among the Arkdwellers, the more he needed to reinforce his sense of presence in his own neglected body, and the familiar taste and aroma brought him back to himself like nothing else did.

"I'm going mad," he announced. "One more month of this, and you can erase me and break the news to my backup."

Parantham said, "Don't expect my sympathy. Just because the Arkdwellers' culture turned out to be resilient, it doesn't mean you were right to take a risk with it."

"*Resilient?* I think the word you're looking for is catatonic." Sweat was pouring down the back of his neck from the spices, but he kept eating without pause, and without diluting the heat with bread or rice.

Each time his Arkdweller colleague Saf slept, Rakesh took his senses out of his avatar, leaving it dormant in a crack in the rock close to the one she'd chosen. Each time Saf stirred, his avatar would notice and summon him back. It was a summons he was beginning to dread.

His job had allowed him to tour the Ark, and at first the experience had been fascinating. The Ark's biosphere was bottom-heavy in fungi and bacteria, but it had a few niches for larger organisms. A genetic analysis of the five varieties of herd animals the Arkdwellers farmed showed that they'd been created by selective breeding from an earlier inventory of just two species. Whether the Arkmakers had initially stocked the place with more and the others had been lost at some point was unclear; it was also unclear just when the Arkdwellers had lost their ancestors' ability to engineer the animals' genomes, and had to revert to patient observation of traits and restrictive mating or manual fertilization. Both the larger animals and the Arkdwellers themselves reproduced in more or less the same way, which involved excruciating pain for all fertile males and more pity than pleasure on the part of the harassed females who put them out of their misery. Rakesh fervently hoped that it was something the ancestors had passed down from their own biology only because it was too technically difficult to change. The possibility that they might have freely devised such a scheme didn't bear thinking about.

The flow of stellar winds into the neutron star's accretion disk was a powerful and relatively constant source of energy, and even the tiny portion siphoned off by the Ark was enough to allow a technologically unsophisticated culture to rise above subsistence agriculture. A range of simple goods was manufactured, mainly from animal products, but also from a small amount of scrupulously recycled metal. Services ranged from courier rounds like Saf's to the curating and restoration of repositories of documents, written on animal skin, bearing recipes for such things as inks and glues, and drawings of useful tools and machines.

It was all very practical, but it seemed a long way removed from the kind of knowledge their ancestors must have possessed. Though born on the surface of an ordinary planet, the Arkmakers had mastered the plasma hydrodynamics of a neutron star's accretion disk in sufficient detail to construct a whole world that could flourish in this radically new environment. Rakesh couldn't see the current inhabitants coping with even the mildest disruption to their routine.

Parantham said, "It need not be pathological, to respond to stability with stasis. Perhaps this is what the Arkmakers longed for: after all the turmoil they'd faced, they didn't want to have to look over their shoulders for the rest of eternity. They didn't want to be fretting about how they'd escape the next unpredictable disaster."

"This is *the bulge*," Rakesh replied. "You have no choice but to look over your shoulder."

"In the long run, maybe not, but they've managed to survive for fifty million years. Perhaps they calculated the odds, and said, if we burrow down deep into this neutron star's gravity well, it will be a long, long time before anything else wanders by that's strong enough to prise us out." Parantham spread her hands. "Once you make that decision, what's the point in being outward-looking, or in seeking constant change? Some cultures have thrived on uncertainty, but for some species there's nothing more stressful than the need for vigilance."

Rakesh could see her point, but he didn't like where she was heading. "So when the Arkmakers faced the prospect of the neutron star tearing up their home world, you think they willingly rid themselves of the very traits that allowed them to survive that event? They resented the unpredictable universe so much that they consciously stripped away all their curiosity, all their powers of abstract reasoning, and gave birth to this nest of sleepwalkers?"

"Are they happy?" she asked.

"They're not miserable," he replied, begrudgingly. "But only because they don't know what they're missing."

"Are they happier than you were back at the node?" Parantham countered. "Going mad with frustration because the whole galaxy had been tamed a million years before your birth, and there was nothing left for you to do with your own redundant curiosity and vigilance? Is that what the Arkmakers should have wished upon their children? Fifty million years of safety—tainted by fifty million years of resentment because their sanctuary was not exciting enough?"

Rakesh closed his eyes and let the sweat from his forehead trickle down and sting his eyelids. He said, "I don't know if their way of life is a good thing or not, but if they want to reject the outside world, let them make a conscious choice about it. The Arkmakers had very few choices; I'm not giving up on these people just because their ancestors faced some hard decisions fifty million years ago, and did what they thought was best. I don't want to force any changes on them, but I'm not leaving until I find a way to get through to them."

By the time Rakesh and Saf reached the depot, he was worn out. As part of a new program to improve his social skills in this milieu—with nothing in the library to guide him, let alone the usual package of time-tested tweaks to provide instant cultural fluency—he had decided to experiment with plausible feelings of fatigue induced by his avatar's actions. While he couldn't conclude anything with certainty without sequencing and simulating the Arkdwellers themselves, studying the physiology of the larger animals had provided him with some reasonable clues. The tidal gravity was quite small even at the Ark's periphery, but a sustained "uphill" slog like the one they'd just completed seemed to leave Saf in need of recuperation, so it looked as if he'd set his response at about the right level.

It was the role of the depot workers to unpack the cart while he and Saf stood by, offering occasional gratuitous complaints about the way the goods were being handled. As this was happening, Rakesh noticed one of the workers looking at him with surprise. Lacking anything corresponding to a primate's mobile face, the Arkdwellers expressed their emotions in their posture, gait, and length and duration of gaze. Rakesh's odd appearance had occasionally caused an involuntary moment or two of staring, but this worker kept looking back, as if she couldn't quite believe what she was seeing.

Rakesh introduced himself, and the worker, Zey, did the same. After these pleasantries the conversation went no further, but when the cart was unloaded Zey emerged from the depot's chamber and approached them.

Saf drummed softly, "Be careful, I think they might be looking for recruits."

Rakesh didn't want to break the news to her that, grateful as he was that she'd employed him, he really wouldn't mind moving on. "I'll be careful," he promised.

Zey said, "Forgive me, but I couldn't help noticing the differences inside you."

"There's nothing to forgive. I know how strange my appearance must be."

Saf said, "Ra tells us he was hatched 'outside the world'. This is not his real body, he just wears it to get along with us." Rakesh still couldn't quite gauge the intent behind her tone of amusement; he didn't know if she was inviting Zey to mock him, or imploring her to deal gently with his delusions.

"Are you our cousin, then?" Zey asked.

Rakesh felt goose bumps rise on the back of his arms, back in the control room; there were some things he simply wasn't equipped to feel viscerally through the avatar itself.

He replied carefully, "It depends what you mean by that." Although the Arkdwellers had terms to describe the relationships between adults and their offspring, they rarely knew who their various relatives actually were. You could respectfully call any stranger of the appropriate age "father", "mother", "brother", "sister", "daughter", "son". The term he was mentally translating as "cousin" was—as far as the data the probes had gathered could reveal—a negation of siblinghood that carried a connotation of distance. It was not unfriendly, but if someone had traveled from the other side of the Ark for the first time, you were more likely to call them "cousin" than "brother" or "sister", as if to acknowledge that it really was stretching plausibility to suppose that you might have shared a parent.

Zey said, "I heard that once there were six worlds, not one. People used to travel between them, but then something happened to the cousins, and all the journeys stopped."

Rakesh was torn between pressing her for details of this story, and taking care not to misrepresent himself as something he was not.

"My people have never been here before," he said. "I don't know the whole history of this world, but I believe I've traveled farther than the cousins you describe."

Zey took a few moments to digest that.

"You don't know the six worlds?"

"Far away there are many more than six. But I haven't seen any world, nearby, from which a traveler could have reached this one." Rakesh hesitated, then added, "The worlds you mention might have been closer, in the past. But I have no direct knowledge of these matters; I can only guess what the fate of these worlds might have been."

"I see." Zey seemed confused and disappointed, but then she said, "You've been outside, though?"

"Of course."

"What is there to see?"

"Bright lights. Long distances." Rakesh had never reached the point of someone asking him even this much before. "Where I come from, we live on the outside of the world, the surface of the rock."

"Everyone would get sick and die!" Saf scoffed.

"It's different, it's safe."

Saf was growing impatient. "We need to sleep, then reload for the return journey." She started walking away.

Rakesh said, "You should look for someone new to go with you."

"Why?"

"I'd like to stay here a while and talk with Zey," he explained.

"Talk with Zey?" Saf seemed to find this suggestion far more surreal than any of Rakesh's baroque cosmic fantasies. "You're going to join this team, after three words with one member? When were you hatched?"

"I'm sorry to let you down," Rakesh said, "but this is part of my job, part of my duty."

Saf rasped a word with no simple translation, but the gist of it was that Rakesh was a damaged infant simpleton who could not be relied upon to perform any task, and his loyalty was so promiscuously offered and so easily withdrawn that he might as well have been a flake of excrement drifting on the wind.

Zey said, "We have all the workers we need."

Saf drummed contemptuously, "They don't even want you, you fool!"

"I'm staying here," Rakesh replied firmly. "I'll find work somewhere nearby." For a moment he caught himself worrying about his prospects, as if he actually needed a job. Still, it was the right thing to say; Zey had been beginning to look alarmed, and the news that at least he wouldn't try to foist himself upon her team seemed to reduce her anxiety.

Saf walked away, rasping to herself.

Zey said, "There's work for me to do, I should join my team-mates."

Rakesh said, "I'm going to rest here, but I don't feel like sleeping. When you're finished, if you want to talk—"

Zey turned away and went back into the chamber. Rakesh waited, wondering what was going on in her mind. His strange appearance and unlikely claims had been met with little more than indifference before. No one else had been curious enough to question him about his origins, let alone make an effort to fit his answers into some larger framework. How reliable these fragments of oral history were was beside the point; what mattered was that Zey remembered the story, and could conceive of it as more than a myth. She could imagine the cousins returning. She could believe in other worlds, and accept the idea of traveling between them.

She might not provide a link to the past, but she could still help build a bridge to the Ark's future.

20

As the Calculation Chamber filled, Roi realized that she barely knew the names of half the people around her. It was an encouraging sign. While Bard and Neth, Ruz and Gul were all busy with their own work, Tan and the other theorists had managed to keep recruiting. Even as people grew hungry, they had been driven not to ransack the diminished crops at the edge, but to gather around the seeds that Zak had planted, to tend and protect a very different crop.

Tan approached her. "Are you ready?"

Roi felt sick. She remembered the time at the junub edge, when Zak had gone silent. If they failed now, it would be the very same feeling played out in slow motion for everyone in the Splinter. Worse than a new division, worse than anything that had happened before.

"Absolutely," she said.

In silence, side by side, she and Tan plunged into the world of geometry.

This time, there were not two but five unknown templates to feed through every step of the calculations. One was tied to the way the symmetries slanted around the Hub; another to the freedom they needed to express the size of orbits; another to the way the shape of space-time varied as you moved out of the plane of the Incandescence. Along with the other symbols they needed to wrap the whole space-time in unknown numbers, the total was so great that Gul's beautiful frames had all needed to be hastily rebuilt.

Roi lost herself in the process. She worked slowly, satisfying herself that every step she took was valid before moving on to the next, so that when it came time to pass each frame to her checkers she felt no hesitation. As the dark phases approached, the newest recruits wound the light machine and kept the work going.

The stones clicked gently, the templates grew longer and more intricate. The third of her checkers called an error to her; she accepted the frame back, and corrected the mistake.

As well as the Splinter's old circular orbit, it would be necessary to apply Zak's principle to at least three other paths through space-time in order to unravel all the unknowns. To provide an extra degree of confidence in their results, she had not conspired with Tan on the choice of paths; the two of them would make their own separate decisions, and then see if their final answers still agreed.

Final answers? The prospect still seemed impossibly remote. The templates thickened like weeds. Someone brought Roi some food. She had lost count of the number of dark phases they had passed through. She finished her first analysis of the Splinter's orbit, and chose the next path: an orbit that went backward around the Hub. In the simple geometry that would have told her nothing new, but with the strange new twist they'd added, it became an entirely different kind of motion.

Tan called a break; they all needed to sleep. Roi clipped protectors over the wires of her frame to keep the stones in place. She didn't speak to Tan, to anyone, she just found a crevice in the wall of the chamber and shut off her vision.

When they resumed, she felt refreshed, but the intervening time melted away; it was if she'd never put the frame down at all. The templates were too big to be considered beautiful, but she was beginning to recognize similarities in some of the ugly knots writhing around within them, and she clung to the hope that these knots might meet up in a way that would allow them to untangle each other.

A chance came to use her own tool to unravel some of the ugliness: the free template linked to the size of the orbits. She hesitated, wondering if she was acting too soon; how could she know if a different choice, delayed, might not spare her even greater effort?

The knots were crowded around this one point right now, though. She let them join up, loosen, vanish.

She finished her third path, her fourth. She had applied Zak's principle four times, and now there were no more decisions left for her to make; all she could do was keep smoothing the templates, following the internal logic of their forms.

Sleep again. *Already?*

Roi woke before anyone else, and walked softly back to her frames. She stared at the template locked on the wire, and saw in her mind's eye what three or four steps would produce. Her tactic with the orbit-size template had paid off: the period of the Rotator, the period of the Splinter's spin when judged against the path of a tossed stone, obeyed the square-cube rule exactly. The same had been true for the simple geometry, but she had never dreamed that such a relationship could survive all the complications they'd thrown into the mix.

Her checkers stirred, and patiently resumed their places. She dared to cast a glance at Tan; his posture seemed optimistic. She was not fooling herself, then. They had not become lost in this maze of symbols.

Roi pushed on to extract the other results. The period of the orbit, the ratios of the weights were much more complicated templates than before. Roi found them ugly, but that didn't prove that they were wrong.

This time, as well as determining the size of the Splinter's orbit—compared to a still unknowable natural unit—she would need to quantify the twisting of the geometry around the Hub. The two were entangled in the templates, but taken together, their newest observation, the ratio of the Splinter's orbital period to the shomal-junub cycle, and their oldest, the ratio of the weights, could unlock the numbers.

Roi finished the calculation, but couldn't bring herself to pass on the frame for checking. She was sure she had made a mistake. The amount of the twist, in natural units, was very close to one. She had no real idea what that meant, but at least it was simple.

The size of the Splinter's orbit, though, was not eight, as before, but barely more than *two*. It was true that the orbits could not be compared directly between the geometries, but surely an orbit four times smaller was impossible. Wasn't an orbit of size six unstable?

The answer turned out to be: not any more. In this new geometry, orbits in the direction of the twist remained stable right down to a size of one unit. The marker for danger remained the behavior of a looping stone, but the link between the shape of the loop and the size of the orbit had changed completely.

Roi didn't know if this was good news or bad. They were four times closer to the Hub than they'd imagined, but they could survive a further halving of their distance, rather than losing a quarter of it.

She passed the last frame to her checkers and stretched out against the rock. She looked over at Tan; he'd finished too.

She waited for the final verdict. There was some confusion; she and Tan had expressed their results differently, because his way of describing the orbit size was not the same as hers. The checkers worked through the conversion, then announced a perfect concordance.

Roi was elated that they'd made it through the ordeal and emerged with answers that made sense, but she needed to remain cautious. They had shown that a geometry with rotational symmetry, and which obeyed

Zak's principle, was possible. That was a beautiful result that they had never been certain of before. However, the freedom to set the twist in the geometry to whatever number they wished meant that they hadn't really subjected their theory to a meaningful test. One new observation, the period of the orbit, had been absorbed entirely by the need to pin down that new unknown, the twist.

Tan approached her.

"Well done!" he chirped.

"You too."

"I'm glad we made different choices," he said. "We should keep the two systems; it will allow us to cross-check everything between them."

Roi said, "We need to start thinking about the other observations from the void: the lights, the motion of the Wanderer. Once we've thrown all those numbers at this geometry, we'll know if it's real."

Tan let his legs sag comically. "I need a break," he pleaded. "At least one shift doing nothing."

The checkers dispersed to gather food. In spite of his protests, Tan lingered, poring over the templates with her, trying to understand what the new geometry meant.

He said, "When you carry the direction of the Rotator's plane around a loop in curved space-time, it comes back changed. So the period of our spin is different from the period of our orbit; even the old geometry predicted that. But in this geometry, *even if the Splinter didn't orbit*—if it was held at a fixed position, with the garm-sard axis pointing toward the Hub—we would still feel a spin weight, and the Rotator would still turn!"

Roi checked; he was right. If you took a direction pointing toward the Hub, and simply carried it forward in time, it turned away from the Hub. The only way to feel as if you were *not* turning was to spin along with it, like the Rotator.

"It's all very strange," she said. A little later, she noticed something else. "If your distance from the Hub is two or less, it becomes impossible *not* to move in an orbit! To try to stay still means moving faster than the fastest possible speed!"

Roi followed the geometry inward, closer to the Hub. At a distance of one, as she'd already calculated, the looping stones would stop looping: the smallest disturbance would topple you from your orbit. But something else happened there, too: staying at a fixed distance from the Hub became, not just unlikely, but impossible. Orbits weren't merely unstable, they ceased to exist at all. The only kind of motion that was allowed was inward. Every path, natural or otherwise, led inexorably straight to the Hub.

Tan said, "It would be a quick death, I think. The garm-sard weight would grow so fast that our bodies would be torn apart before we could feel much pain."

"Better than burning in the heat of the Wanderer?" By moving the Splinter outward, that was the fate they were risking.

"Where did this madness come from?" she asked. "If we work hard, our lives should be good. Some sickness, some famine, that can't be avoided. But for all of us to die, how could that be possible?"

Tan said quietly, "Nobody can understand these things."

"I won't let our children live like this!" Roi declared. "When this is finished…" She trailed off impotently. She would do what? Banish every future Wanderer that might disturb their tranquility? Build a wall across the void?

"If we keep working," Tan said, "our lives will be safer. We need to keep thinking, calculating, watching the void. But this work will never be finished. There will never be a time when we can go back to the old ways and expect to be safe."

After a rest shift, Roi met with Tan again to plan the way forward. Their ultimate goal was to understand the geometry well enough to be able to map out a safe path past the Wanderer, but they still lacked the mathematical tools to calculate anything except for circular orbits in the plane of the Incandescence.

The observations of the void held the key, both to validating the new geometry itself and to understanding what kind of paths were possible. If they could fit the motion of the Wanderer into the picture, Roi was sure everything would become clearer. But to make use of their observations, they needed to understand the paths that the light they were seeing had taken through the curved geometry, which was every bit as hard a problem as working out the path of the Wanderer itself. It wasn't quite a vicious circle, but the way to break in was not easy or obvious.

Three shifts later they were still getting nowhere, when a young recruit appeared at the entrance to the chamber.

"Excuse me," she said. "I think I've found something."

Her name was Kem; Tan introduced her to Roi. He'd given copies of Roi's observations from the void to all the recruits who'd finished their studies in template geometry, and set them the task of finding a way to interpret them.

"I've been thinking about symmetries," Kem said. "If you look at the relationship between the direction of a natural path and a motion of symmetry, it should be the same all along the path." The idea, she explained, wasn't tied to the particular geometry they'd discovered; it followed from the very definition of symmetry.

A simple example made Kem's proposition more persuasive. On the surface of a perfectly round stone, the natural paths were great circles: the circles whose centers were the centers of the stone itself. The symmetries were rotations around any axis you cared to name. If you chose a particular great circle to be your natural path, then chose a diameter of that circle as the axis of rotation, the motion of symmetry—the way points on the surface shifted when the stone was rotated—would be perpendicular to the direction of the path, everywhere. If instead you chose an axis of rotation perpendicular to the plane of the great circle, the motion of symmetry would agree with the direction of the natural path, all along its length. And if you picked an axis that lay between those extremes, then although the angle between the motion of symmetry and the direction of the path would change, the *size* of the motion would also change, growing ever larger as the two drifted away from being parallel, in just the right way to compensate. Between the two effects, a number could be computed that would remain identical all along the path.

The stone was just an illustration, though. Kem shuffled templates that applied to any geometry, and made her case in all generality.

Roi was excited. The geometry they were testing possessed two distinct symmetries, and every natural path, every orbit, would have a constant relationship with them all along its length. For circular orbits in the plane of the Incandescence this told them nothing new, but within three shifts they had characterized the shapes of two other kinds of orbits in the plane: those whose distance from the Hub varied periodically, and those that came in from afar and then spiraled right down to the Hub.

It was beautiful mathematics, but was any of it true? Roi's observations of the void were still useless, because although they knew the angle at which the light had reached the Splinter, they had no way of measuring how fast it had been traveling. She'd joked with Ruz on the journey back from the junub edge that he should make that his next task, but for all his ingenuity she couldn't imagine how he could succeed.

"The problem is twofold," Tan mused. "It's not just the speed of light we need to discover, because what matters is the ratio of that speed to Neth's unknown speed, the speed for turning time into space. Knowing the first without the second is useless."

Kem said, "But we don't need both, we just need the ratio?"

"It would be nice to have both, but we could make a lot of progress with just the ratio," Roi replied.

"Light travels so fast," Kem observed, "that we might not be far from wrong if we suppose that the ratio is one."

Tan rasped disapproval. "Nothing can travel at Neth's speed. Anyone doing so would have a heart that never beat, a sense of time that never advanced, and a notion of distance that squashed the whole world flat."

Roi couldn't deny those absurdities, but she wasn't sure that was the point. "As an approximation, though, would it necessarily mislead us? We won't calculate anything from the light's point of view; what we're interested in are our own measurements. And if we make this choice, the calculations become easier." That was an understatement. Neth's speed had the gloriously simple property that everyone agreed on it, regardless of their own motion. If they imagined that the speed of light was Neth's speed, then the light they were seeing would not gain or lose velocity at all as it traveled from the void toward the Hub.

"Eat stones, excrete stones," Tan rasped sullenly. "If we start with non-sense, what should we expect at the end?"

Kem looked dismayed, but Roi was not dissuaded.

"I think it's worth trying," she said.

Tan left them, to pursue ideas of his own. Roi worked with Kem, carefully setting up the calculations. Strictly speaking, they could still only deal with the paths taken by light that remained in the plane of the Incandescence, but Roi had many observations from the void where she'd followed lights that appeared to be skimming the surface of the rock. The paths that linked her eyes to those distant objects were so close to the plane that the difference scarcely mattered.

They spent half a shift calculating, then they called in some helpers to check the results.

Roi took Kem with her and went in search of Tan. He was alone in a small chamber, surrounded by frames, scraping his legs distractedly against his carapace.

"This is going to take me a while," he admitted. "I can't seem to find the way forward."

Roi said, "Try eating what we ate."

She passed him the final template that she and Kem had derived, and let him check it against the observations. "Correct," he murmured after a while. He put down one skin of data, copied from Roi's time and angle measurements, and picked up the next. Each time, the verdict was the same.

"Nothing can travel at Neth's speed," he insisted. "But perhaps light can get very close. Too close for us to see the difference."

Kem spoke shyly. "I have some ideas about orbits that go out of the plane. There's a trick I think we can use to understand them."

For a few heartbeats, Roi gazed at her in silence. Before the Jolt, Kem had been cleaning susk carcasses. Tan had taught her well, giving her the tools every geometer needed, but he had not fed her any of these insights himself. Whatever mysterious skill it required to take the knowledge of your teachers and double it had blossomed across the Splinter at precisely the time it was needed. Where had it been hiding? How had it emerged? Roi couldn't begin to imagine how such things could be explained.

When they'd dealt with the Wanderer, she could worry about that. She'd look forward to spending her final shifts cataloguing her ignorance.

"Tell us your ideas," she said to Kem. "Tell us how we're going to understand the Wanderer."

21

Shift after shift, Rakesh returned to the depot and waited for Zey to finish work. Sometimes she was too tired to speak with him, but more often she would spend a few minutes chatting before she went to find a crevice to rest in.

Zey talked about her life, and the things she'd heard about the history of her world, and the cousins'. The various jobs she'd done had all been important to her at the time, but she had little to say about them; even the time she spent in the depot moments before they met seemed to pass in a kind of pleasant daze, and left almost no impression once the shift had ended.

She talked about the ideas that had crept into her life in the cracks between these episodes of dutiful sleepwalking. The story of the six worlds had been passed on by a fellow worker as idle chatter, three jobs past, but it had resonated deeply with Zey, and since that time she had viewed her surroundings in a new light, always trying to guess the age and origin of things, always trying to fit them into a coherent picture. Who built the first cart? Who carved out the tunnels? What kind of machine could carry you between worlds?

It was not that her fellow Arkdwellers were simpletons in comparison. They could all master complex tasks, and juggle equally sophisticated concepts, if and when the need arose. They were, however, monumentally indifferent to their history, their circumstances, and their prospects. Every question that to Rakesh seemed most compelling struck them as, at best, a frivolous diversion.

As they traded stories, Rakesh tried to find a balance between misleading Zey and confusing her. How could you tell someone who had never seen the stars about the size of the galaxy, or the scale of the journey he'd made? He spiraled out gently from the things she knew or imagined—her guesses about the cousins, criss-crossing the all-enveloping warmth and light of the accretion disk—into the swarming emptiness beyond. She was interested to hear about the way he'd lived, on the surface of a rock that was far from its own source of warmth and light, but what really galvanized her were the hints he'd found of her people's history. As he unwound the story, all the way back to the Steelmakers' fossilized spacecraft and their missing world, Zey soaked up every word, every detail, and begged him for more. That this was a need no one around her shared, let alone had the power to fulfill, only made the situation more poignant. Rakesh had never seen anyone lonely in quite this way before.

Parantham watched through the probes that filled the Ark, though she really didn't need to spy on them that way; if she'd asked, Rakesh would have let her take the data stream straight from his avatar's senses.

"So where exactly is this seduction leading?" she demanded.

"Seduction? If you want to call it anything, call it a recruitment."

"Instead of dreaming about her long lost cousins, now Zey can spend her life dreaming about the Amalgam. And this has helped her... how?"

Rakesh said, "If she wants, she can come with us to the disk. Imagine seeing ten thousand new worlds with fresh eyes, after spending all your life buried in a rock." And never mind that their own ability to return to the disk was far from certain.

"You want her to trade one kind of loneliness for another?" Parantham retorted.

That had not been Rakesh's plan. He did not want to tear Zey out of her world; he hadn't even offered to take her to visit *Lahl's Promise*. He wanted to kindle her innate curiosity and excitement to the point where it began to spread to those around her; he wanted to use her as an ambassador, as a bridge between their cultures.

The trouble was, however successfully he engaged with her, it was the gap that separated Zey from her fellow Arkdwellers that remained the hardest to bridge. Her instinct, she'd told him, had been to keep his revelations to herself, because she knew how they'd be received, but she hadn't been able to control herself. Her instinct had been right: nobody wanted to hear about her "distant cousin", or the thirty-six times thirty-six worlds. Nobody wanted to discuss the perils that their ancestors had survived, or to debate their options for evading the unknown catastrophes that the future might bring. They wanted to listen to inconsequential chatter as they worked, and when they were finished working, they wanted food, sex and sleep.

"Why am I sick?" Zey asked Rakesh. "Why is my mind so damaged?"

They were doing their usual circuit of tunnels close to the depot, walking and talking until she needed to sleep.

It would be meaningless to reassure her that most of the galaxy was on her side, that the qualities that made her an anomaly here were almost universally valued and admired.

"I don't know," Rakesh said. "But if you allow me, I can try to find out."

"How?"

"If you let me take a small part of your body, I can study it carefully. I might not be able to answer your question, but there's a chance I can tell you something about the reasons that you're different."

Zey was alarmed. "I'm using every part of my body. I'm not a male, to offer a portion to be removed."

Rakesh chirped amusement. "I'm talking about a part so small that you lose thirty-six times thirty-six in every shift, without even noticing."

"I lose parts of my body *without noticing?*" However dazzled she'd been by Rakesh's stories, Zey retained a healthy skepticism toward his wilder claims.

"Absolutely. They're too small to see."

"Then how will you study them?"

"With machines too small to see."

"So all of this happens, invisibly, and you believe what these machines whisper to you at the end?"

"That's about it."

"I think your mind is damaged more than mine."

This wasn't banter; Zey was deadly serious. Rakesh had to spend the next four of their meetings explaining the atomic nature of matter, and trying to make it plausible without setting up a demonstration in chemical stoichiometry. Then they moved on to cellular biology, and the eleven known molecular replicators. If Rakesh had had any qualms about her ability to give informed consent to being sequenced, she seemed determined to make it clear that she would not allow him to perform his technological magic and then pronounce upon her nature like an oracle. When she understood his proposal well enough for his claims to seem plausible, she would consider it, but not before.

As they toured the basic sciences, Rakesh could see Zey building a picture far bigger than the subject at hand, integrating everything piece by piece into an ever more sophisticated world view. It was firmly anchored to the familiar things around her, but her mind was stretching to encompass the distant, the small, the abstract. Shift after shift, he was making her "sickness" worse, "damaging" her even more. Her co-workers didn't care; they might tease her when she couldn't keep quiet about her strange ideas, but they wouldn't ostracize her as long as she kept doing her job. This was not a culture that could be scandalized by her dalliance with Rakesh, or her heterodox notions of history and reality; the only sacred thing was work. Zey was the one who would feel the separation; it didn't have to be imposed on her by her peers. If Rakesh failed to bring the other Arkdwellers along with her on this intellectual journey—if he transformed her and then abandoned her, with nobody else who thought the same way—she would be lonelier than ever.

Thirty-six times thirty-six.

22

One of the children Gul had taught, a young male named Haf, approached Roi with three claws full of food. She accepted the gift gratefully, but he retreated before she had a chance to talk to him. As he rejoined his team-mates, she heard him whisper to one of them, "She was Zak's first student."

"She must be very old," his friend replied.

"She saw him die," Haf announced solemnly.

"That means she'll die soon herself," the friend explained. "That's the way it happens."

Roi was amused. Gul had sent his former students here to do fetching and carrying while they learned more about the intricacies of the project, and were gradually recruited into more specialized teams. She listened to their innocent gossip for a while; it made a welcome diversion. Then she turned her full attention back to the task ahead of her.

The control post she'd set up lay on the border between the junub and sard quarters, halfway along the line of light-messengers that Jos had established between Ruz's void-watchers at the junub edge and Bard's control post. From there, Bard's own separate network of light-messengers branched out to reach all the tunnel-plug operators.

Twelve shifts before, Bard and Neth had reported success. They had developed a system of movable baffles to tweak the shape of the tunnel, and after some laborious trial and error in conjunction with Neth's calculations, they had finally achieved a smooth flow. The tunnel had been opened on more than a dozen occasions, but only for a single bright phase each time. The wind would pass through it cleanly now, but the question that remained was whether Bard's ambitious scheme could actually achieve its purpose: whether the free passage of the wind really could change the orbit of the Splinter itself.

Roi consulted the clock beside her, made a note of the time on a sheet of skin, then took the handle of the metal signal-sheet on her right and cranked out the code to have the great tunnel opened. Many spans away along the ordinary tunnel that sloped down into the sardside, the light-messenger watching her sheet would note the sequence and repeat it. Then the watcher for that sheet would do the same; on and on the message would go, all the way to Bard, and then to a dozen plug operators, who would call on their teams to drag on the ropes that pulled the wheeled stone plugs aside. A part of the sardside wind that had once forced itself from rarb to sharq through the rock's reluctant pathways, losing all its strength along the way, would now make the same journey entirely unhindered. The force it had once imparted upon the rock of the Splinter would vanish.

Of course, the remainder of the sardside wind would still exert a powerful force, but on the garmside the opposing force would not be diminished at all. If the perfect balance of the winds really had kept the Splinter in place for generations, that balance would no longer hold.

Roi turned to Kem. "Now we wait."

"Can we calculate while we wait?" Kem asked anxiously.

"Of course."

Kem took her frame and started working through a fresh set of path calculations. There were some problems they could only treat in the most general fashion until they had data from the void-watchers to tell them how the Splinter was responding, but Kem seemed determined to pre-calculate every result they could possibly need.

Up at the junub edge, the void-watchers no longer needed to scramble back and forth through the crack that led to the surface. Inspired by Jos's light-messengers, Cho, one of Ruz's team, had invented an elaborate system of polished metal plates that allowed them to observe the lights in the void from the safety of the tunnel below. Each time the junub dark phase ended, the plates were retracted part-way into the crack, shielding them from the full savagery of the Incandescence, while a stone plug, like a smaller version of Bard's tunnel-plugs, was wheeled into place below to provide some shelter for the void-watchers themselves. The system did not afford them the sweeping views of the whole quarter-circle that Roi had seen, but now that they had mapped the fixed pattern of lights in detail, and knew how to follow the Wanderer against that background, their sighting and tracking of individual lights would yield enough information for the theorists to calculate both the Wanderer's shifting orbit and any hoped-for change in the Splinter's own motion.

Roi passed the time by checking Kem's results. She did the work scrupulously, but it scarcely demanded her attention; it was like walking now, pure instinct. These were not new template calculations, replete with symbols for unspecified values; rather, she and Kem were feeding a range of numbers into existing templates, making earlier, abstract computations concrete.

Kem was, in effect, mapping out dozens of possible futures for the Splinter, attempting to distinguish the safe paths from the hazardous. Shuffling the numbers in a single case was a straightforward process, but it was impossible to prepare for every combination of circumstances that might arise along their journey. Roi was almost certain that they had found the true geometry, but they still could not predict how the strength of the wind would change as they moved out from the Hub; its speed was dictated by the curvature of space-time, but its density was not. Anticipating the Wanderer's behavior was even more difficult. Though it followed a comprehensible orbit for short stretches of time, its motion was subject to unpredictable changes, and only some of these could be clearly linked to its visible eruptions.

Nobody could understand the Wanderer's nature. It appeared to be a ball of wind and light, but what could hold such a thing together? Nothing in the long run, apparently, since the wind and light were spilling out ever more violently the closer it came to the Hub. Whether the old stories of the Splinter's origins were true or not, the Wanderer was fragmenting in a very different way; instead of being torn brutally in half in one cataclysmic moment, it was forever being stripped of small portions. If the Splinter's mythical parent really had divided, that would have eased its plight for a very long time, halving the greatest of the weights until some ancient Jolt, or some generation-spanning drift toward the Hub had eventually increased them. The Wanderer's losses seemed to make no difference, as if each small excision only gave it a chance to offer up something more, like a fast-growing crop eager to be pruned.

Haf and the others kept bringing food. Sometimes Roi caught herself trying to guess who among them were her children, but even when that urge passed she was surprised at the strength of her feelings toward them all. Her sense of duty had always been directed toward her team-mates; of course she had never been indifferent toward hatchlings, and would have aided any child she found in need, but the idea that the well-being of the next generation was as important as the completion of her next shift had always been a remote one, with little emotional force and even less need to be acted upon. Eggs hatched themselves, and the hatchlings found teachers; this didn't require any attention from her. The clearest lesson on the matter she had received from her own teachers had concerned the need to practice contraception with sufficient diligence to avoid playing her part in bringing on a famine.

Now the sight of Haf, Pel, and Tio brought a warmth to her mind that was as strong as the buzz of cooperation. The hope she felt at the prospect of navigating the Splinter to safety was still, in part, the same kind of longing for a successful shift that she had known all her life, but that familiar emotion was increasingly overlaid with a compelling sense of what it would mean for the ultimate beneficiaries. The thought of her own premature death, of Gul's, of Ruz's, of all her team-mates', was dismaying, and more than enough to drive her, but the extraordinary idea that they could carry the hatchlings into a transformed world where this danger would finally lie completely behind them was imbued with both more urgency, and more prospective joy, than anything else she had ever contemplated.

Leh, who watched for light-messages from the junub edge, came to Roi with a written transcript. Ruz's team had measured a small increase in the Splinter's orbital period. It was tiny, but it stood out above the usual variations due to uncertainty in their observations and the imperfections of their clocks.

Roi waited three more shifts for the next report to arrive, before letting herself believe it. The second set of timings confirmed the earlier result: the Splinter was moving, drifting outward very slowly.

She sent the news on to Neth and Bard, then asked Kem to tell the other theorists. In no time at all there was a riot of delighted chirps coming to her from the surrounding tunnels.

When Kem returned, Tan was with her.

"It's good news," he said, "but I'm worried by how slowly we're moving. It doesn't give us much flexibility if we find ourselves in a dangerous situation."

Roi concurred. "Bard and Neth understand that. They'll make the new tunnels their priority now."

Kem said, "If the Wanderer continues to behave as it has been, I believe that with three tunnels we'd have enough control over our ascent to pass through the Wanderer's orbit on the opposite side of the Hub. The problem will be if that orbit shrinks rapidly without warning."

"There's something else we might need to consider," Tan said. "One of my recruits, Nis, came to me two shifts ago with a new idea about the Wanderer. I don't know how seriously we should take it, but he's working on the details, trying to make it more precise."

"What's the general idea?" Roi asked.

"The strength of rock is what holds the Splinter together," Tan said. "But the Wanderer doesn't seem to be made of rock. So why doesn't it simply fall apart from the usual weights? Spinning in different ways from the Splinter won't do the trick. Without strength of *some kind*, it ought to be smeared all along its orbit by now."

"So what kind of strength can it have?" Kem asked.

"Geometry," Tan replied. "The same thing that keeps us close to the Hub holds the Wanderer together. But now the Hub and the Wanderer's geometry are fighting each other for the Wanderer's wind and light."

Roi allowed herself a moment of pure exhilaration. It was a beautiful, audacious proposition. Who ever said the Hub was the only object in the void that could be wrapped in curvature? It might be the strongest thing in sight, powerful enough to twist the Wanderer's path around it, but that didn't mean the Wanderer itself was a mere passive follower of geometry, as the Splinter seemed to be. Why couldn't it carry its own curvature? The Hub had the glory of the entire Incandescence, but the Wanderer, at least for now, held on to its own portion of wind and light. The two were alike, one smaller, one greater.

Unfortunately, if this elegant solution to the mystery was true, it changed everything. If the Wanderer was wrapped in space-time shaped as it was around the Hub, then in turn the geometry around the Hub itself could not be described perfectly by the rotationally symmetrical solution that she and Tan had found. The presence of the Wanderer was like a dent hammered into a smoothly curved sheet of metal; it could be ignored from afar, but the closer you came to it, the more significant it would be.

Kem appeared dazed. "Two Hubs fighting? We need the geometry for two Hubs fighting?"

Tan said, "It's just one possibility. It needs to be thought through in a lot more detail."

"But how will we know?" Kem demanded. "*When* will we know?" Her careful preparations had always been in jeopardy from the Wanderer's erratic behavior, but this new unknown threatened to render half the calculations meaningless.

Roi said, "We need to observe something in motion close to the Wanderer. That's the only way to understand its geometry." If they waited for it to have a measurable effect on the Splinter's own motion, all their questions would be answered too late.

"What is there close it?" Kem asked forlornly. "Just its wind and light erupting chaotically every now and then. How can we make sense of that?"

Roi fought against a sense of panic. It seemed almost fortunate now that their progress outward was less rapid than they'd hoped; if it had been faster, she might have had to call a halt until they were certain this problem could be solved.

"What moves close to the Wanderer?" Tan mused. "Nothing stays, but many things pass by."

Roi said, "This is no time for riddles."

Tan chirped amusement. "After her victory over me, I would have thought Kem might find the solution first."

"Victory?" Roi had lost track of all the minor squabbles and disputes among the team; once things became clear, she had trouble remembering who had first thought of each idea.

"Light travels at Neth's speed," Tan replied, "or as close to it as makes no difference. As fast as that is, though, its natural paths still respond to geometry."

Roi thought she knew what he was hinting at now, but it was Kem who put it into words.

"The Wanderer moves against the background of lights," Kem said. "We need to observe and record the positions of a small, closely spaced group of lights very carefully. We do this once when the Wanderer is among them, then once again when it's far away. If there's a change in the angles between them, it will tell us that the geometry has changed. It will tell us that the Wanderer is like the Hub, wrapped in curvature of its own."

As the Splinter spiraled slowly outward, Roi traveled with Kem and Nis toward the junub edge. This was too complex a matter to explain to Ruz through messages, whether sent in writing or by flashes of light. There was nothing to keep her at the control post; they would not be dodging and weaving around the Wanderer for many shifts yet.

The light-messengers remained at their posts, though, ready to get word swiftly to Tan and the others if anything suddenly changed. As Roi greeted each one along the way, it struck her that the whole Splinter was almost like a single work team, now. In a sense that had always been true: couriers had worked with depot organizers, susk herders had worked with cuticle-wrights, and even those teams that had not directly cooperated had shared a common goal: the welfare of the Splinter as a whole. There was no denying, though, that since the Jolt the old borders had melted, and the old system had been twisted into a new shape, far richer and more contorted than even the Hub's strange geometry.

When the delegation of theorists reached Ruz, he called his best recruits together and they listened to Kem's proposal.

"There's one problem," Ruz said. "We've already made the kind of measurements you've described, and to the limits of our ability we've found no changes."

Kem said, "Can you check the data? If you weren't expecting this effect, you might have dismissed it as just part of a background of observational error."

"Perhaps." Ruz sent someone to carry out that task.

Cho said, "There's a way we might be able to improve the accuracy of our measurements. It involves curving the metal plates, bending and polishing them to systematically distort what we see."

"Distort?" Roi was skeptical. "Isn't that just going to make the errors greater?"

"If we didn't know the shape of the plate well enough, then of course it would," Cho conceded. "But if we can calibrate the shape with enough confidence, we might be able to exploit a system of such plates to magnify the angles we're able to discern."

Ruz seemed displeased; Roi wondered if Cho had proposed this system before, and Ruz had ruled it out as too complex and uncertain. She tried not to let her loyalty to Ruz sway her; she had to be ready to judge the ideas of every team member on their merits.

"Can you explain in more detail?" she said.

Cho believed he'd found a simple geometrical principle governing the paths that light took when it struck metal: the angle it made with a line perpendicular to the surface when it hit the metal was the same as the angle when it departed. For a flat plate, the consequences were straightforward, and they lay behind the contraption the void-watchers were now using to observe the lights from the safety of the tunnel below the crack.

For a curved surface, Cho's principle had more complex ramifications. He had templates to show that if the shape followed a certain curve, light from distant objects could be brought together sharply on a certain plane; using the opposite side of the same shape, the light could be made to appear as if it was coming from a plane *behind* the metal.

By combining elements of these two kinds, Cho believed he could construct a system that, while bringing the light down from the surface, modified the geometry of its paths in such a way as to make it seem as if the observer was closer to the distant lights. With one of his designs, all the angles would become larger by a factor of twelve.

Roi looked to Ruz, to hear his objections.

"The principles appear sound," he said. "But we can't be sure that we can shape the metal to the necessary precision. And how can we test it, when our one passage to the surface is taken up completely with the system we need, and that we know is reliable? How can we disrupt all our observations to gamble on this?"

"I understand."

Roi struggled to weigh up the risks. They desperately needed to understand the nature of the Wanderer. If Nis's idea was right then the geometry that wrapped it would influence the Splinter's path, and while as yet she had no idea how to combine the Hub and the Wanderer's geometry into a single shape, the sooner they learned exactly what the geometry close to the Wanderer was, the better their chances of making sense of that complex interaction before it was too late.

At the same time, the present system was certainly running smoothly for the void-watchers. If they disassembled Cho's first invention to make room for his second, they would have to resort to observers clambering back and forth from the surface every junub dark phase. They would lose observations, or even people, in the rush.

She could always ask Bard to close the tunnel, to buy them more time. The Wanderer had its own schedule, though. If they kept delaying their ascent, the Wanderer would come to the Splinter, she was sure of that. To pass it by in its present large orbit was one thing; to be wedged in by it, this close to the Hub, would almost certainly be fatal.

"How thoroughly have you explored the area around here?" she asked Ruz.

Ruz knew exactly what she was asking. "There are no other cracks," he said.

"When we first came here," Roi recalled, "the one we were looking for, the one from Zak's map, was closed. It was sheer luck that we found an open one. But how much work would it take to reopen the old one?"

Ruz's posture shifted slightly, growing defensive, as if she had accused him of neglecting his duty. "I don't have enough people to do that job, to open it up."

Roi said, "Stop thinking the old way, my friend. Everyone is your team-mate now. We don't have to lure them away from their colleagues and recruit them, one by one. We just have to explain the need, and the urgency. We just have to make sense."

23

"You can have what you asked for," Zey told Rakesh. "You can take a part of me to study."

She had just finished her shift and had come out from the depot. The other workers were still milling around, talking among themselves before heading into the tunnels to sleep.

Rakesh felt no need to ask if she was sure; everything they'd spoken about for the last dozen shifts had been for the sake of informing her decision. He did feel he owed her a small moment of drama, though, so rather than admitting that, thanks to their long proximity, his own avatar was already plastered in her cells and he had no need to collect a sample, he reached out with one claw and gently scratched a soft part of her nearest leg.

Nanomachines inside his avatar swarmed over the cells, dissecting some destructively, infiltrating others to watch their components in action. The DNA sequences were only part of the analysis; they would be meaningless without the full context of cellular biochemistry.

Parantham spoke to him, back in the cabin. "You might have done this when I first suggested it, instead of elevating your own need for customary formalities over the real ethical issues." Rakesh ignored her.

He took the nanomachines' data and ran coarse-grained simulations of morphogenesis, precise enough to give a clear picture of the way the Arkdwellers' bodies were shaped generically, and to map out the strongest genetic and environmental influences on each individual, but not so precise that the simulation itself would experience anything.

The generic map of the Arkdwellers' brain that the simulation produced made visible what Rakesh had long suspected: their ability to form and manipulate abstract symbols was powerful enough to grant all of them general intelligence as a birthright. Though the data came solely from Zey's DNA, there were far too many genes involved for her to have mutant variants of *all* of them; the generic map encompassed the whole species. As for every human born since the Stone Age, as for the ancestors of every member of the Amalgam, there was nothing the universe was capable of doing that the Arkdwellers were not capable of comprehending. They were not mere clever-looking animals, with some hard-wired repertoire of impressive but inextensible skills. With sufficient motivation and freedom from distractions—and perhaps a modest boost in longevity—they could have grasped anything. Apart from the subjectivities of art and language, where everyone needed tweaking to cross the species barriers, there was nothing in the Amalgam's million-year-old storehouse of knowledge that would have been beyond their reach.

That was the ability, the potential in every one of them. There was, however, no drive to realize it: no curiosity, no joy in discovery, no restlessness, no dissatisfaction. The Arkdwellers needed their full intellectual toolkit in order to master the complex tasks allotted to them in the present social order, so it was *not* a useless vestigial genetic fossil. It was the living, breathing embodiment of matter's ability to comprehend itself, but it was tamed and caged in a manner that Rakesh had never encountered before. It could rise to the occasion to overcome a limited range of mundane setbacks and challenges, but it would never soar.

Rakesh was not surprised by any of this, inasmuch as it applied to the Arkdwellers as a whole. It fitted his observations of their behavior perfectly. He did not yet understand Zey, though. Her team-mates could not be too different from her genetically, but he'd expected her to carry two copies of some rare, recessive gene that could explain why she alone was compelled to make full use of her intellectual abilities. If that had been the case, though, the coarse-grained simulation would have had no way of knowing what the ordinary version of the gene was, and erasing Zey's atypical urges from the generic map.

This proved that whatever had made her different could not have been entirely genetically determined. The simulation had smoothed out the possible environmental influences on brain development into a plausible average, but in doing so it had clearly missed something that had made all the difference to Zey.

Rakesh probed the data more deeply, looking for genes that might have been triggered only rarely, rather than being rare themselves. He simulated the chemistry of the developing embryo in more detail, looking for possible surges in morphogens, and the wave of changes they might bring. When he found what he'd been looking for, it was like an elephant stepping out of the wallpaper. There was a vast network of linked genes and proteins that could influence neural structures *both in the embryo and in adulthood*, and it bore the clear fingerprints of an engineered design. The Arkmakers had had their hands all over this part of their children's genome.

If there was a vital spark missing from the generic Arkdweller, these genes were designed to light the fire. Without imaging Zey's brain, Rakesh couldn't say just how far from the average the random biochemical detour she'd experienced in the egg had taken her, but a one-in-ten-thousand surge would have triggered a cascade of events that guaranteed a thirst for knowledge comparable to all of her other basic drives. The frequency of such individuals in the population would obviously be low, but Rakesh did not believe for a moment that Zey was an accident. The Arkmakers had wanted people like her, but not too many.

He was sure she had been born, or hatched, this way, because if the other trigger he'd found had been the cause then there was no explaining her team-mates' apathy. Extreme stress could bring on the development of the same neural structures in an adult's brain. Mild hardship wouldn't start the cascade, though; it would require a sustained, dramatic change in the environment. Depending on the circumstances, and the exact range of individual susceptibilities, it looked as if anything from thirty to sixty per cent of the population could be transformed by that route, but only if the Ark itself was subjected to a massive upheaval.

From there, the process would snowball, with an ever greater proportion of each subsequent generation driven by an urge to understand the crisis they were facing. If the threat subsided then the *status quo* would eventually return; the simulations suggested that a few dozen generations of tranquility would be enough to put out the fire. Then, as before, only a handful of individuals would exhibit the trait, until the next emergency.

Rakesh had performed the whole analysis in a couple of Zey's heartbeats, but she already had an air of impatience.

"What's your answer?" she said. "What's the nature of my sickness?"

Rakesh explained everything he'd found, as clearly as he could. He'd already told her all he knew about the Arkmakers, so the idea that her distant ancestors had shaped her people's nature did not come as a shock in itself.

"Why am I here now, though?" she said. "If the world was falling apart, of course it would be good to have people who tried to repair it, instead of just tending their herds and waiting to die. But why did they arrange for people like me to be hatched when there is no need for us?"

"I don't know," Rakesh confessed. "I can't read their minds, I can't know what they were thinking. Perhaps they wanted a kind of sentinel, a small group who would be vigilant enough to notice the first signs of danger and prepare the way, while the evidence was still below the threshold for the rest of the population. Or perhaps they wanted a route for the cultural transmission of some crucial ideas that everyone else would consider too impractical to retain."

"As long as the world is safe, though," Zey replied despairingly, "I'm useless, aren't I?"

Rakesh said, "Knowledge is good in itself. Understanding is good in itself."

Zey chirped amusement. "I can't argue with that sentiment, can I? I've been built to think like you. But you come from a world where the ones who disagree with you are the sad, strange few. You haven't spent a lifetime as the only one with that point of view."

Rakesh didn't know how to reply to her. The chasm between her and the other Arkdwellers was not something that any of them were capable of bridging. She could never be his ambassador, and he couldn't hope to enter into any kind of dialogue with them himself, slowly coaxing them out of their shells, opening them up to new possibilities, turning their faces to the stars. Without a calamity to throw the switch, they were physically incapable of caring about such things.

Zey's mind was working faster than his now. She said, "I would never ask you to bring trouble to my brothers and sisters, to damage the world, to sow fear and death. But is that the only way to bring change?"

Rakesh asked nervously, "What do you mean?"

"These genes, these molecules, these signals in our bodies... my ancestors built them to work one way, but I believe you are more powerful than my ancestors. These are all just made from atoms, aren't they? Your little machines can move them around the way I move cargo from one side of the depot to another. If you wanted to, you could ask them to make these signals appear in all of our bodies, without any reason, without any danger.

"If you wanted to, you could wake us from our sleep."

24

"Any progress?" Haf asked, as he wound the light machine.

Roi looked up from her template frame. "Not really," she admitted. "Be patient, though. We haven't followed this to the end yet."

She had come to the sardside for the opening of the third tunnel, and to confer with Neth and Bard. Haf had tagged along as her helper, gathering food, providing light, and checking her interminable calculations. Even as they waited in this small chamber for their hosts to call them to the big event, Roi could not put her frames aside.

Since Cho and Nis had measured the Wanderer's curvature from the tiny angle by which it bent the incoming light, she had been spending most of her time trying to discover a template for a geometry that could encompass both the Wanderer and the Hub. Without any of the old symmetries to rely on, though, the templates became vastly more complicated.

The curvature that wrapped the Wanderer was about six to the eighth times weaker than that around the Hub, so it might have been simpler to take the idealized geometry of the Hub alone as a guide to their calculations, and then rely on the observations of the void-watchers to tell them when their true position was deviating from their predictions. Like someone sliding down a steep tunnel that had been crudely mapped but never actually traversed, they could try to avoid the smaller hazards by sight, rather than aspiring to a mathematically perfect foreknowledge of every bump that lay ahead. The only problem with that eminently practical approach was that the dark phases were shrinking, so the observations of the void-watchers were already being curtailed. If it ever came to the point where the dark phases vanished, they would be skidding down the tunnel blind, entirely at the mercy of their calculations.

As the natural light dimmed, Roi handed Haf her last frame and started on a fresh one.

"Your templates are like weeds," Haf remarked helpfully. "No shape at all, they just grow where they like."

"Thanks for the encouragement. How about checking whether they're true or not, and then you can weed out all the false ones to your heart's content."

As Haf set to work, Roi stared pensively at the stones of the blank frame. Sometimes the problem really did appear to be impossible to solve, but the geometry that twisted around the Hub had once seemed almost as intractable, and now the Splinter was spiraling out along a path that was confirming that solution, shift after shift. The weights, the cycles, the view of the void, all fitted together exactly as the templates decreed. Ruz had been up to the surface a few times, and he'd told her that the strange quarter-circle was expanding: the angle of the arc, its radius and its thickness had all grown visibly larger. Part of this change was due to the Splinter traveling more slowly around its larger orbit, and part to the gentler space-time curvature as they moved away from the Hub bending the incoming light less severely.

"I have a friend called Tio," Haf said, without looking up from his frame. "He told me that the best way to think about curved geometry is to imagine it as lots of little flat pieces stuck together. I mean, a cube is just six flat pieces, but it's not that far from the shape of a sphere. And if you use more pieces, you can get closer."

"That's true," Roi said. "You can shift all the curvature into the corners between the pieces. But I'm not sure where that gets you. Who did Tio study with? Kem? Nis?"

"I don't think it was either of them. He spoke to a lot of different people. Picked things up here and there."

Roi kept staring at the frame, but her mind was blank. Having exhausted all the elegant tricks she knew, she had finally attacked the problem directly, with no subtlety but all the diligence she could muster, hoping that somewhere along the way an opportunity to simplify the mess would appear before her eyes. It hadn't happened yet. *There must be something simple*, Zak had declared. But he'd found that once already, in the principle of the weights. In a void full of Jolts and Wanderers, and countless distant lights that for all Roi knew could be wrapped in curvature of their own, how much more simplicity could they expect?

Sen, one of Neth's students, appeared at the entrance to the chamber. "We're opening the tunnel now," she said.

Roi put down her frame. Haf made ready to heft the light machine on to his back, but Roi said, "I don't think we'll need that." The dark phase was almost over, and Sen knew the area so well that she'd come to them without any light of her own. Roi was getting better at following people by the sound of their footsteps, even when she was in an unfamiliar place, a skill that seemed to come naturally to Haf and the others hatched since the Jolt.

They followed Sen down a narrow, sloping tunnel toward the rarb-sard edge.

By the time they reached their destination, there was enough light to see Neth, Bard, and a few dozen others gathered in the plug chamber adjoining the new tunnel. The outer wall where the tunnel approached the surface had been thinned and weakened to the point where it had almost certainly broken apart during the last light phase. From this chamber, the first of the sets of stone plugs that were keeping the tunnel sealed would be pulled aside, at the same time as eleven others further downwind were withdrawn. If everything went as planned, the wind would flow freely across the width of the Splinter and strike the sharq end of the tunnel with enough force to break through the thin crust that had been left by the workers there, opening up a third unimpeded channel from Incandescence to Incandescence.

Roi approached Neth. "Surely your work's done here now," she joked. "We'll be waiting for you to join us at the Null Chamber." In fact the Null Chamber was empty of theorists and Roi had no reason to visit it any more, but no other place had the same ring to its name.

"When the tunnels have steered us past the Wanderer, I might take you up on that," Neth replied, in all seriousness. "I want to work with someone who's interested in a deep understanding of the changes we've seen in the density of the Incandescence as we've moved away from the Hub. There are many mysteries there. We understand weight and motion pretty well for rocks like the Splinter, I think, but when it comes to anything else we're still just gathering data, and guessing."

Bard consulted a clock, and called out to the plug operators. There was no need to send a light-message to the operators in the other chambers; they'd be following prearranged instructions and clocks of their own.

The plug operators, lined up in rows, began hauling on their ropes, which ran through a system of pulleys to the huge stone sitting at the far end of the chamber. Although this single stone was probably close to the limit of what could be moved with a wheeled cart and metal tracks, it was only about a sixth of the size of the tunnel's aperture; six separate plugs inserted from their own separate chambers came together to block the tunnel at this point alone.

As the stone moved Roi could see a halo of light shimmering around it; though she wasn't gazing directly into the Incandescence through the small gap between the stone and the chamber's walls, even the reflection from the tunnel wall was dazzling. There was scarcely any wind leaking out through the gap, though; the path straight ahead through the great tunnel was so much easier for it to take.

The halo shrank and dimmed as the plug came closer, though the light remained visibly brighter than that flowing through the stone itself. It occurred to Roi that they could have put void-watchers here after all, in spite of the inconvenient direction of the weight; with one of Cho's contraptions poking out into the void, the observer would not have needed to cling to the surface. It was only the historical accident of the order in which various things had been invented that had kept the void-watchers at the junub edge. With the present system working smoothly, though, and all the teams accustomed to it, she couldn't bring herself to suggest rearranging everything for the sake of efficiency. Light-messages reached their destinations quickly enough.

It would be a few shifts yet before the void-watchers could tell them precisely what the new tunnel had achieved. The further they moved from the Hub, the less powerful the wind became, but they were also ascending a gentler slope as they struggled toward the fateful distance of the Wanderer's orbit.

As they headed toward the exit together, Haf said, "We should find a way to capture the wind and then push it out ourselves, with a strength that suits us. Why should we be hostage to the speed it travels naturally?"

Neth assumed a posture containing a mixture of respect and amusement. "That's a nice idea, but where does the 'strength that suits us' come from?"

"Give me time," Haf replied. "There must be a way."

Roi heard a deep groaning sound coming through the rock. She had no idea what its cause was, but she had never heard anything like it when she had visited the other tunnels. Perhaps they were experimenting with a new configuration of flow-control baffles, but if that was the case then this ominous noise suggested that the wind was making short work of them. She looked to Neth for an explanation, but it was Bard who shouted for all of them to run.

The noise grew louder as they reached the exit tunnel, and as they clambered up the slope an intense light rose up behind them. It could not be the baffles; Roi hoped it might just be a single plug coming loose, but she didn't waste time looking back and trying to weigh up various scenarios. She saw that Haf was far ahead of her, his youthful vigor carrying him to the front of the pack. Amid the chaos and fear, and her own determination to outrace the danger if she possibly could, a small part of her relaxed, resigned to anything so long as he survived.

As they passed the chamber where she'd waited with Haf, the ground rasped and screamed like a susk in agony. The tunnel flattened, making progress easier, and the light from behind dimmed even as the sound became unbearable. Roi finally paused to look back and saw a fissure opening in the rock behind her, separating the tunnel they'd ascended a few heartbeats ago from the one they were now following. It was the kind of terrible spectacle that she had once imagined a division of the Splinter might bring, but the weights had done nothing but ease as they'd moved away from the Hub. If rock was parting from rock, the curvature of space-time was not to blame. As she bolted on down the tunnel, she understood that the most likely cause was not a fresh Jolt from the Wanderer, either; the timing would have been too much of a coincidence. This was a disaster they had brought upon themselves.

They ran until the rock fell silent and the glare of the Incandescence was left behind. When they finally paused to take stock of the situation, Neth was nowhere to be found. Roi couldn't remember seeing her at all during their panicked flight, but it was possible that she'd split up from them at some point, taking a different turn once they'd had a choice. More than a dozen other people from the chamber were missing.

Bard led them to a point where a terrified light-messenger was still standing at her post, though the next station to her rarb was now deserted. It was still possible to send queries skirting around the tunnel in the other direction, and Bard was slowly able to build up a picture of what had been lost and what remained.

It seemed that a large piece of rock had sheared off the side of the Splinter. What was gone included the original mouth of the new tunnel, and all six of the first set of plug chambers. The next set, downwind from that, remained intact. Many dozens of people had certainly been killed, some of them carried off into the Incandescence inside the fragment that had broken away, others seared by exposure. The ordinary system of tunnels was now open to the Incandescence, but that in itself wouldn't cause any more harm if people kept away from the damaged region.

Roi had sent Haf to search for Neth, but he returned with no news of her. She tried to set aside her fears for her friend, and think through the other ramifications of the disaster. The tunnel was still open, and could still be controlled by the remaining plugs and baffles. If the cracks caused by the construction ran deeper, if more of the Splinter's rock was threatened, it was hard to imagine any easy solution to that now. Leaving this tunnel open, and closing down the other two instead if they needed to adjust the balance of forces, was about the only strategy Roi could think of to minimize the risk; shutting off the flow was just as likely to trigger another failure in the rock.

Haf said, "Why is the wind blowing from rarb-junub?"

"What?" Roi had become disoriented. She looked to the nearest wall sign; Haf was right. She found Neth's student, Sen, huddled against the rock and asked her if she could explain the anomaly in terms of the damage, the local density of the rock, the possibility of a redirection of the flow.

Sen had trouble concentrating; she was still in shock from their brush with death, and Neth's disappearance. She did her best to analyze the problem, but she couldn't rule anything in or out.

Roi asked Bard to send a message to the void-watchers, asking them if they'd noticed any changes in their latest observations. When the reply came back from Ruz, it was exactly as she'd feared:

"The Splinter has gained a spin around the garm-sard axis. Direction is junub to rarb. Period about seventeen times shomal-junub cycle."

The slow spin would be rotating the tunnels in and out of alignment with the wind, slashing their effect to a fraction of what it had been. If it could not be corrected, they would be left with far less speed and manoeuvrability than when the first tunnel had been opened.

Bard said, "If we have to cut more tunnels, we can do that."

"And lose more rock? More people?"

"What choice do we have?" he replied. "Can we pass the Wanderer safely in this state?"

"I don't know. I don't know how much power we will have lost, I don't know how the whole picture will have changed."

Roi sent a message to Kem, to be sure that she knew exactly what had happened, and was thinking about these problems. Then she approached Sen again.

"I need your help," Roi said gently.

Sen still couldn't get out of her flattened defensive posture; she wanted the walls to hide her, to swallow her.

"The Splinter is spinning," Roi told her. "The only way I can think of to correct that is to use the baffles in the tunnels, and try to modulate the flows to provide a torque to bring us to a halt."

Sen struggled to focus. "I think the most stable alignment for the Splinter with respect to the wind would be with the tunnels running rarb-sharq again. In time, we should settle back to that naturally."

"That sounds likely," Roi said, "but we can't rely on it happening in time. We need to get stabilized as soon as we can."

"We never planned for this," Sen replied. "Neth and I. We never did the calculations."

"But you understand her ideas? You can work it out?" Roi had only the crudest notion of Neth's work herself. Even if she found the written notes, it would take her thirty-six shifts to begin to master the theory of wind flow.

"Perhaps I can do it," said Sen. "Perhaps."

Bard found a chamber for them to work in, close to an existing light-message route, and set up a control post with Roi, Sen, Haf, and a dozen checkers.

As the great tunnels swung around, the wind would strike first one side wall, as they approached rarb, and then the other as they turned away from it. If there was any natural effect that would favor one wall in a manner that could halt the spin, Roi couldn't see it operating on the kind of time scale they needed. They would have to try to take control of the flow, using the baffles to ensure that the wind hit the rock with the maximum possible force when it could retard the spin, but passed through the tunnel as smoothly as possible at all other times. Like the imbalance between the garmside and sardside that had carried them away from the Hub, they could try to break the natural symmetry of the situation to work to their advantage.

Sen struggled with the calculations. There was no shortage of people around her to help with the raw template manipulation, but she was the only one who really grasped Neth's ideas. When her mind grew stale and she needed a diversion to clear her thoughts, Haf did his best to cheer her up, babbling away about his schemes for the future.

"When we're past the Wanderer, we should build a wall around the Hub," he suggested. "To make sure that whatever happens, no future generation ends up where we are."

"A wall around the Hub?" Sen made a sound of delighted incredulity. "Made out of what, exactly?"

"I don't know yet," Haf replied. "But we should move right outside the Hub's curvature, and put the wall so far out that there's no chance of the Hub capturing anyone again."

"How can we go past the Hub's curvature?" Roi protested. "Even if the Incandescence stretches that far, the wind will be too weak to move us."

"We'll capture it and push it out ourselves," Haf insisted.

"How?" asked Sen. "What can push the wind, if not curvature?"

"What moves our legs?" he countered. "Curvature's got nothing to do with that."

"So we'll capture the wind… and push it out with our legs?" Sen asked.

Haf said, "Now you're just being silly."

Sen's confidence grew, and she completed her calculations. They tested a set of configurations for the baffles, switching between them as the tunnels swung in and out of alignment with the wind. They would have to wait several shifts for the void-watchers to notice any change in their motion compared to the distant lights, but there were people stationed close to the tunnels' walls who could measure the difference in flow coming through the rock, and the general plan did seem to be working: the wind was striking the walls at the right times and places.

Roi began to feel hopeful again. The deaths and the damage had scarred them all, but it was not the end of the Splinter. If they could realign the tunnels, Kem's calculations gave them a good chance with the Wanderer; they would not need to add to the existing three tunnels, risking more fissures in the rock.

Confirmation arrived from Ruz; the wayward spin was growing measurably smaller. In each report from the void-watchers that followed, the news became ever more encouraging. They would have to take care as the spin approached zero to ensure that the tunnels ended up in the right orientation, but since each successive prod was only delivered when they were already more or less aligned with the wind, it would take a combination of very bad luck and very poor judgment to end up with the tunnels stranded in a position where they could deliver no power at all.

It was many shifts after the accident before Roi began thinking about her own work again. There had been too many distractions and responsibilities; a part of her had also been hoping that a long break from the calculations would see her return to them with fresh ideas.

It was not a new insight that set her back to work, though, but a worrying postscript to one of Ruz's reports on the dwindling spin. "Dark phase shrinking faster than ever," his message said. "Perhaps eighteen shifts left."

Roi had expected more time. Whether the accident, or their response to it, had somehow hastened their re-immersion, or whether the plane of the Incandescence itself had grown thicker as they moved away from the Hub, the opportunities the Jolt had granted them were about to come to an end.

The power the tunnels could extract from the wind would be a little stronger, and their worries about food a little less. Since she had no choice in the matter, Roi tried to dwell on the benefits that would flow as the

Incandescence reclaimed them.

The greatest change that was coming, though, was too stark to ignore. The void-watchers could pack up their instruments and start tending crops and herding susk. However great Cho's ingenuity, once the dark phases were gone, surely nothing could enable them to see into the void through the glow of the Incandescence itself.

One part of their fate was clear now. By the time they approached the Wanderer, the Splinter would once again be blind.

25

Rakesh sat in the kitchen of *Lahl's Promise*, rearranging the rice in front of him with his fork, unable to bring himself to eat. He'd already missed three of his usual after-shift meetings with Zey, and the fourth one was looming. Without a clear answer to her plea, he did not know how he could face her.

"The Aloof knew all of this, I swear," he told Parantham. "Maybe they followed the trail from the meteor, like we did, or maybe they already knew where it would end. But I don't believe they brought us into the bulge because of dead microbes in a rock. They brought us here to see the state of the Arkdwellers. They brought us here to resolve this problem."

"That might be true," Parantham conceded. "But what does it change?"

"It makes me feel used, that's what it changes." Was this the reason Lahl had singled him out, back at the node? She had drilled straight into his soul, seen to the heart of his boredom and frustration, and known how powerfully a request like Zey's would resonate for him?

"Used, how?" Parantham replied. "You think the Aloof are so morally finicky that they'd decline to throw this genetic switch themselves... but so morally bankrupt that they don't mind contriving a situation where you feel pressured to do it for them? If they wanted to do it, they'd do it. If they were capable of understanding the Arkdwellers' plight, they'd be capable of fixing it."

"I'm not talking about technology," Rakesh retorted. "Of course they could throw the switch if they wanted to. But they preferred to wash their hands of the matter, and make it someone else's responsibility."

Parantham seemed genuinely puzzled. "You mean, they asked for a second opinion on a difficult ethical question, from someone who they hoped would be better qualified? From a cousin of the Arkdwellers, a child of DNA?"

Rakesh wanted to strangle her.

Actually, what he wanted most of all was for Parantham to tell him that he had no right to intervene, and that he should leave the Arkdwellers to sleepwalk in peace. It was what he'd expected her to say when she heard Zey's plea. Unfortunately, she'd failed to oblige.

He tried to back away from all the things that were frustrating him, and analyze the situation calmly one more time.

"The Arkdwellers had this genetic mechanism forced on them by their ancestors," he said. "But it wasn't done blindly or gratuitously; it carries some very clear advantages. It keeps them satisfied with the *status quo* when the *status quo* is working. It spares them the boredom and claustrophobia that they'd otherwise suffer, cooped up in a rock, orbiting a neutron star, with no other safe place to go. But when something comes along to threaten them—a challenge of cosmic proportions, the kind of thing their ancestors faced all the way back to the Steelmakers—their intellectual powers come out of hibernation, and they get the Enlightenment on overdrive."

Parantham said, "Which is fine as far as it goes, but if some other kind of opportunity comes along—a chance to enlarge their horizons that isn't accompanied by stress and danger—how can they even assess it properly, let alone take advantage of it?"

"They can't," Rakesh replied. "It's impossible."

"Except for Zey, and those like her."

"Yes."

"But the question then," Parantham said, "is do *the exceptional cases* have the right to speak for the whole Ark? Zey has her own interests. If she wants to come visit the Amalgam, we can try to oblige her. But is she entitled to drag the whole of her society, without their consent, into her own state of mind?"

"Were the *Arkmakers* entitled," Rakesh replied, "to sentence their children to fifty million years of docility? Yes, their intentions were impeccable, and yes, they were acting under pressure, desperately hunting for a way to keep their children alive while a neutron star was bearing down on them. But they couldn't anticipate everything that the future would bring. Maybe they thought that when the next apocalypse-cum-renaissance arrived, their descendants would figure out everything and make a new set of choices for themselves—reengineering their own genome as they saw fit, to suit the next set of challenges. Maybe it was never their intention that their children would end up stranded with this *ad hoc* solution for so long; they just did their best and hoped that it would tide them over for a couple of million years."

"Can we be sure, though," Parantham wondered, "that this situation is entirely artificial? What if a similar mechanism had already evolved long before the neutron star approached the home world, and the Arkmakers were merely fine-tuning it?"

Rakesh said, "So if it's natural, that changes everything?"

"No, but it's not entirely irrelevant," Parantham replied. "All your drives, all your values, all your priorities come from your biological ancestors. You've removed some drives, and strengthened others, but you didn't sit down one day and say, 'From first principles—ignoring all my inherited traits—what should I be like? How should I live? What should I value?'"

"All right, I take your point," Rakesh said. "There are no such *first principles*. I risk plastering my own values all over the Ark. But if the Arkdwellers inherited this long winter of the mind—and some deep part of them cherishes it, the way I cherish various human things for no great, universal reason—they must have inherited the intellectual spring as well. I gave Zey a few simple science lessons; I didn't colonize her brain with nanoware and turn her into something alien. What she represents is a part of everyone's birthright, just as much as the alternative, docile state. It's an accident of circumstances that's put them in a place where that birthright can never be realized again, short of almost certain death. I mean, what's going to tear them away from a neutron star, and still give them time to reboot their culture into a state that will let them defend themselves?"

Parantham fell silent. Rakesh pushed his plate aside. He could curse the Aloof all he wanted, he could listen to Zey, he could listen to Parantham, but Parantham could debate the pros and cons for a thousand years without coming down on one side. However much he hated it, this was in his hands alone. He could not walk away and pretend that he simply hadn't seen the Ark, or go begging all around the disk for someone else to take responsibility.

He said, "What if we wake them all to the point where we can communicate with them meaningfully—the way I can communicate with Zey—and then let them choose for themselves? We can grant them an easy way to switch back to the docile mode, individually, if they want to. They can't give consent for what I'm proposing, but putting them in a state where they can understand the question isn't forcing them to remain that way. Zey's state isn't hermetically self-affirming: merely entering it doesn't guarantee that you prefer it. Every individual will still have the power to reflect on their situation, and choose."

Parantham considered this. "Suppose we do what you suggest. Then what happens next? Those who choose to revert remain in the Ark, obviously, but can they tolerate sharing it with a thousand restless Zeys, when their life *doesn't* depend on that?"

"The rest explore the bulge, or come out to the disk with us."

"Explore the bulge *how?*" Parantham demanded. "Do we have some promise from the Aloof that they'll have access to the local network?"

"Well, no," Rakesh conceded.

"Do we have a promise from the Amalgam that they'll be allowed out into the disk?"

"You think they'll be refused membership of the Amalgam, just because of the stunt the Aloof pulled with Lahl?"

Parantham said, "I think it will take a while to negotiate exactly what's going to happen between the bulge and the disk. I think we need to go back and sort out that mess, before we start triggering an intellectual renaissance in a small, crowded place with no escape hatch."

Rakesh couldn't argue with her central concern. They couldn't light this fire and then walk away, leaving the Arkdwellers to sort out the ensuing conflict. These people were stuck deep in a gravity well, with no planet to mine for materials, and no resources save the meager contents of the Ark itself and the thin plasma of the neutron star's accretion disk. The Arkmakers had envisaged the switch being thrown in a time of crisis, but also a time of opportunity. Without a bridge leading away from the Ark itself, there was no opportunity. Leaving them to stew in their own frustration would be unconscionable.

"All right," he said, "we have to clear the way to the disk. Go and come back. Hope the idiots in the disk let us out, and then hope the idiots in the bulge let us back in again."

Parantham nodded, then started laughing with relief. "So that's it? We're agreed? This is your final decision?"

Rakesh hesitated. It would be thousands of years before they returned. The Ark would survive, and little would have changed, but Zey would be long dead.

If he went to her with this plan, this promise for the distant future, he knew what she would say. She would beg him to locate the spark in her mind, the thing that made her different from her team-mates, the thing that he had spoken to, nurtured and encouraged, shift after shift.

Then she would ask him to reach inside her and extinguish it.

26

The darkness was gone; the Splinter was immersed in constant brightness again. The light was softer than that in which their journey had begun, its colors less fierce. Everything was gentler, further from the Hub: the wind, the weights, the light. Roi thought: if we'd done this long before the Wanderer came, it might have been a simple, peaceful journey.

"I never really believed you and Gul," Haf confessed, "when you said you'd grown up without dark phases. How could anyone imagine such a thing?" Roi wasn't sure if he was joking; sometimes it was difficult to tell. "I wonder how it will be for the next generation."

"Wait and see," Roi replied. Sometimes she felt like playing along with Haf, joining him in his wild speculations, but lately she was afraid of too much talk about the future, as if any hope put into words was more exposed, more vulnerable, than everyone's unspoken longing for safety.

In the last few dwindling dark phases, Ruz's team had snatched their final observations from the void. Just as the Splinter sank back into the plane of the Incandescence, the Wanderer's orbit had lost its own traces of elevation; they were confined to the same two dimensions now, locked into a closer, more dangerous dance. If the only thing to fear had been a head-on collision with the Wanderer itself, then the problem would not have been so difficult, but mere proximity could be as fatal as contact. The Wanderer was far hotter and brighter than the Incandescence; if they drew too near, or were struck by one of its flares at close range, the heat could sear right through the shelter of the rock and kill them, as surely as if they'd been standing unprotected on the surface.

Kem had computed the trajectories for both light and flares, and sketched out the safest passage past the Wanderer's orbit. The twisted curvature of the geometry had a pernicious effect, focusing the danger into places where a simpler analysis might have anticipated safety; the

Hub *did* act as a kind of shelter, but the points to which it offered the greatest protection did not lie directly opposite the Wanderer.

Kem's laborious calculations had identified the path of least danger; the only problem now was to follow it, without a glimpse of the void to confirm their position. Roi had set up systematic weight measurements, and cycling stones and Rotators in a new Null Chamber; all of this helped quantify their distance from the Hub, but the most crucial information, their angle from the Wanderer, could not be measured this way.

Sen and her team were monitoring the strength of the wind, and had done their best to calibrate a model linking the characteristics of the flow through the tunnels with the last of the solid data that the void-watchers had been able to gather on the Splinter's changing orbit. The varying density of the Incandescence could not be anticipated, but it could be measured in the wind, moment by moment, and fed into the templates to derive a range of estimates as to the effect the tunnels were having on the Splinter's position and speed.

These efforts gave them a far better chance than they would have had by merely trusting in luck, but two things remained to elevate the uncertainty. One was the Wanderer's erratic orbital shifts, which they had never been able to understand and no longer had any hope of observing. Roi had accepted that there was nothing to be done about that. The other complication was the influence of the Wanderer's curvature, and that was a flaw she could not accept without a fight.

They could never hope to track the Wanderer's proximity with a change in the weights; the differences it made from one end of the Splinter to the other were too tiny. But that lack of detectable influence did *not* mean that as the two of them swept around the Hub, the Wanderer was incapable of advancing the Splinter in its orbit, slowly dragging them out of the safe zone that Kem had delineated.

With Haf and Pel as their checkers, Roi, Kem and Nis stood with their template-frames, shift after shift, trying to merge the geometries in a way that satisfied Zak's principle. Having failed to make progress before, Roi had them try the simplest approach: imagining that both the Hub and the Wanderer possessed the twistless curvature of their first, incorrect guess for the Hub. Such an answer would not have been the true geometry, of course, but it might have opened up a crack leading in the right direction.

Roi's vision as she fell into sleep at the end of each shift was filled with images of smooth, bright surfaces colliding, grating against each other, refusing to meld. Each time she woke, the problem filled her thoughts again immediately. *How could they pass the Wanderer, blinded by the*

Incandescence, without slipping unknowingly into danger? The geometry of space-time was the only guide left to them, but while their knowledge of its shape remained imperfect, that guide was uncertain, and perhaps even treacherous.

Kem put down her frame. "I can't think any more. I'm going to get some food."

"Haf can bring you food," Roi suggested.

"Pel can do it!" said Haf. "She's not doing anything!" Pel was lying on her back, gazing at the ceiling. No one had passed her a frame to check since the start of the shift.

"I can get it myself," Kem replied. She left the chamber.

Nis had paused while they were speaking; now he looked to Roi, almost accusingly.

"We're all tired," he said. "I think we're going nowhere."

"You're giving up on this?" Roi felt a stab of bitterness. "To do what?" If there'd been some other urgent task she would have sent him to it with her blessing, but Sen's team had their calculations under control; they didn't need a new recruit to train in their methods.

"I'm not giving up," Nis replied. "I'm losing my mind. These calculations aren't leading anywhere. Nothing simplifies; they just grow more tangled with every step. Someone smart enough could probably *prove* that we're never going to find this geometry."

Roi thought of Tan, who was sick now, as Zak had been. If he'd been healthy, maybe he could have done just that: proved that she was wasting her time.

"The geometry exists!" she rasped. "It's there around us. It's what we're moving through, even as we speak."

"I didn't claim it doesn't exist," Nis said wearily. "But not everything in the world fits a template. Can you write a template for the shape of the Splinter? For the shape of your own carapace?"

Roi fell silent. Nis's analogy had to become right at some point, but she had hoped that they could reach this small step further with the mathematics. Two "Hubs", two centers to the curvature; it didn't seem like such a complicated thing to capture with a template.

Nis said, "Space-time does what it does, following Zak's principle over and over, fitting together perfectly, everywhere, all the time. Without sliding a single stone along a wire. Without knowing the first thing about templates. That's how it defeats us at this game. It doesn't need to capture the details of everything it does across all of space and all of time in a few elegant symbols. It just does what it does."

He put down his frame.

Roi pushed herself against the rock, stretching her aching joints, struggling to clear her mind. There was something wise in Nis's words, but it wasn't the message of pessimism.

She said, "You're right, it's not trying to do template mathematics. It doesn't need to. But if it doesn't, then why do we?"

Nis answered dutifully, as if he were her student. "Because we need a template to distil everything that happens into a simple, compact form. How else could we calculate anything?"

"How does *space-time* calculate anything?" she replied.

"I don't understand," Nis said.

"I understand," said Haf. "We should do as Tio said."

"What?" Roi was confused now. "What did Tio say?" Tio was a friend of Haf's who had wandered from teacher to teacher among the theorists, learning a great deal but then arguing with everyone, refusing to perform the calculations they expected of him.

"I told you thirty-six shifts ago," Haf said reprovingly. "He treats space-time as lots of small, flat pieces. When you make them small, the templates describe what happens at the corners, how you join the pieces together. But the templates are easy, not like these weeds." He shook the frame of Roi's that he'd been checking.

"You just need a lot of them," Roi said. For a few heartbeats she was simply dazed, unsure if this was some false promise that her weariness had caused her to misjudge. But Haf's words made perfect sense; Tio's idea was the only way forward.

She asked Haf, "Can you find him? Can you bring him here?"

"Sure." Haf prodded Pel and they left the chamber together.

Nis said, "I still don't see it."

"Wait for Tio," Roi suggested. "If I try to explain it, the way I'm feeling right now I'll probably just end up confusing us both."

"But who does he work with? What's he been doing?"

"He's been working by himself," she said.

"A team of one?" Nis scoffed.

"Zak was a team of one," Roi said. "A long time ago."

Nis was unimpressed by the comparison. "Not everyone who thinks they're like Zak is actually correct in that perception."

"That's true," Roi conceded. "So let's just judge his ideas on their merits."

Haf and Pel returned with Tio. For a moment he seemed nervous and resentful, but when Roi addressed him respectfully and said that she needed his help, his posture softened and the words spilled out of him.

He had reformulated Zak's principle, he explained, in a way that suited a picture of space-time built up from many small, flat pieces. The result was not perfect, like Tan's geometry, which could be trusted down to the finest detail. But the calculations, though laborious and repetitive, were extremely simple. You couldn't fail to find an answer.

Roi asked, "How many divisions would we need to make, how many pieces of space-time to cover everything from our last known orbit to the Wanderer's, and a short way beyond?"

Tio fell silent, calculating something, or guessing. "Perhaps six to the eighth pieces. Six to the ninth for more accuracy."

"And what kind of team would we need? To calculate all the geometry before we reach the Wanderer's orbit?"

Tio said, "Six to the fourth, if they're good calculators. Maybe double that if everyone needs checkers."

Six to the fourth. Ruz's void-watchers, and all the theorists combined, would come to less than a quarter of that. Sen's team could not leave their work, but perhaps some of Jos's light-messengers could be diverted for a while; with no observations to bring in fresh information, there was little news to be relayed.

"Can you set up this problem in a simple way, that everyone will be able to understand?"

"Yes," Tio replied confidently.

"So that anyone who can manage arithmetic can learn what to do in half a shift?" Roi pressed him.

Tio said, "I'm sure of it."

Roi looked around the small chamber, trying to picture a much larger one nearby where they could put everyone. She noticed, distractedly, that Pel was now carrying four seed packages inside her, and that Haf's body was empty. He'd shown no signs of pain; Pel had taken the packages pre-emptively, without even needing to witness her friend's suffering.

Everything in the world was strange, but Roi didn't care. The last thing that was in their power to change had finally shown signs of yielding. She believed they would survive now.

Tan was staying in a small chamber, not far from Tio's geometry-calculators. Before starting her shift Roi brought him food, and they spoke for a while.

"Where are we now?" he asked.

"All the measurements put our orbit close to size twenty."

"Twenty!" Tan marveled. "No wonder I feel like I'm back in the Null Chamber."

"The weights are nothing," Roi agreed. "Even at the garm edge now, people can cling to the ceiling for a whole shift if they want to."

"I don't want to cling to the ceiling," Tan said. "I just want to live a few more shifts. I want to see this through."

"I understand." Roi had never asked him about his children, whether he caught himself hunting for them in the crowds. Everyone's gaze had shifted, though, whether it was focused on their own hatchlings or just the generation as a whole.

"Either that, or we'll all go out like Zak did," Tan chirped, making a joke of it.

"We've worked hard," Roi said. "There'll be ease and safety for the next generation."

"Let them have safety," Tan said, "but not ease."

"Why?"

"Do you want them to go back to the old ways?" Tan looked at her searchingly. "You do know that's what will happen, don't you? If they have nothing to push against, nothing to understand, nothing to explore."

Roi didn't know how to answer him. She knew, now, that she could never go back herself, but she wouldn't have to face that; she would not live a great deal longer than Tan. Did it matter, though, if Haf and Pel and Tio slipped gradually from their adventurous youth into a world where the generation that followed would once more live for nothing but the buzz of cooperation, whatever the team, whatever the task?

"Do I have any say in it?" she replied. "Is there anything I can do that will determine how much they'll struggle?"

Tan said, "Nothing at all. But you can still hope for the right thing."

Roi left him to start her shift, entering quietly and taking her place in the chamber from Leh; the two of them shared a position, working alternate shifts. Tio had arranged the geometry-calculators in a carefully designed pattern, so that each one exchanged information with just five of their neighbors. There was no need for messengers to weave back and forth between them; the results each person needed in order to continue always came from someone beside them.

Numbers washed back and forth across the chamber, but Roi could stay focused on her own simple tasks, ignoring the wider picture. Compared to battling the templates for a space-time connection, it was almost as mindless as weeding a crop. She let herself fall into a happy daze, thinking of nothing but the details of each calculation.

Halfway through the shift, she emerged from her trance; Tio had called a halt. A dozen people walked across the chamber, moving from calculator to calculator, asking them about the numbers associated with the piece of space-time they had just analyzed. The answer they were given decided which of the calculator's neighbors to move on to. In effect, Tio's path-walkers were letting an imaginary object fall in a straight line across each small region of space-time being modeled, and seeing where it emerged. By keeping track of a few simple details, they could follow it into the future—across a region that was effectively curved by the way the many flat pieces were joined—building up a fair approximation to a natural path.

The orbit of the Splinter. The orbit of the Wanderer. The light and flares that might pass between them.

Kem and Nis studied the results, and shaped them into instructions for Sen. The changes made in the tunnels, ever finer now, steered the Splinter closer to their best guess for the safest possible place to be.

When her shift was over, Roi went to see Kem and Nis.

"Where are we?" Roi asked. It was a question that no one could stop asking.

"Twenty and three-quarters," Kem replied. "That's the latest from the Null Chamber."

Roi echoed the number. "And now I have to sleep?" At its last sighting, the Wanderer had been in an orbit at a little more than twenty-two, but everything in its history made them believe that it would be down to less than twenty-one by now. The path they were following tried to steer down the middle of the uncertainty, putting some bounds on the danger without them being sure exactly where their nemesis lay.

"We might have passed it already," Nis said. "It might all be over, and we just don't know."

Roi said, "When we cross twenty-two, I'll believe it's over."

"There can still be flares," Kem reminded them. "We have to stick to the course."

"For how long?" Roi had never really confronted the question before; just crossing the Wanderer's orbit safely had always been hard enough to imagine. "We keep moving out, the Wanderer keeps moving in. Until there's a healthy distance between us. But what happens to the Wanderer?"

"The Hub tears it to pieces," Nis said. "Its own curvature has been holding on to less and less of... whatever it's made of. There'll come a point when there's simply nothing left, when it's all bled out into the Incandescence."

"And that's it?"

Nis said, "That's how weight and motion work. What else can happen?"

When Roi woke, she found Tan's chamber empty. She searched around frantically for anyone who might know what had happened to him.

Finally she met up with Pel, who would sometimes wake earlier than Roi and visit Tan herself.

"I saw him," Pel said. "I gave him the news."

"What news?"

"Everyone believes we've crossed the orbit," Pel said. "We're not at twenty-two, but the Wanderer can't have stayed in the same orbit all this time. We're past it, we're going in different directions now."

"That's good news," Roi said. "But where did Tan go?"

"He said he needed some exercise," Pel replied.

Roi hunted for him, until she could no longer leave Leh doing her job. As she shuffled the numbers, she pictured her old friend, finding a comfortable fissure in the rock somewhere, shutting off his vision, letting the long brightness fade from his mind.

27

"Be careful coming through," Rakesh warned Zey. "It's quite a squeeze at the end."

She climbed down through the habitat's entrance and dropped on to the deck beside him.

"I'm outside the world," she marveled. "But I'm not dead."

"The walls shield us from the radiation," Rakesh reminded her. "You couldn't survive unprotected outside."

Zey said, "How can we make the place outside the world our home, if we always need to be shielded from it?"

"It's not that big a problem," Rakesh assured her. "My ancestors needed a special mix of gases with them, everywhere they went. So did yours, but you've already been tweaked to live in vacuum. There are adjustments you can make to your bodies, if you want to. Matter is matter; many things are possible."

Zey wasn't listening to him; she'd discovered the view. The habitat was a bubble joined to the Ark over the crack in the wall on the neutron-star side; Rakesh had had nanomachines enlarge the passage through the rock to a size that any Arkdweller could climb through. As well as shielding them from the hard radiation that came from the innermost parts of the accretion disk and its flow on to the neutron star, the walls of the habitat screened out most of the terahertz synchrotron radiation coming from the plasma around them. This was the glow that suffused the whole Ark, the frequency at which the rock was translucent, and to which the Arkdwellers' vision was most sensitive. However, they could also see far enough into the infrared band that if the terahertz glow was removed, they were not left blind. Instead, the dazzling foreground fell away, and they could see beyond it. Bright infrared sources dotted the sky. Zey was looking out at the stars.

Using the workshop on *Lahl's Promise*, Rakesh had built the habitat and equipped it with everything he'd need. Then he had upgraded his Arkdweller avatar, hard-coded himself into it, and trashed his body back on the ship.

Docked to the habitat was a small ferry. It could exploit the winds and magnetic fields of the accretion disk for some journeys, but it also had a separate, fusion-powered drive. There was a halo of rocky and carbonaceous detritus around the outer parts of the accretion disk, well within the ferry's range; it was not exactly a mother lode of riches by Amalgam standards, but the Arkdwellers were small creatures, and their needs were likely to remain modest for a while.

It would not be an easy life, but the choice would be theirs to make. Rakesh wasn't offering them a cornucopia, a highway straight to the Amalgam's dazzling riches. It was possible that everyone he awakened might decline the chance to leave the Ark behind, when the alternative was so spartan.

Still, he had kept his promise to Lahl, whoever she was, and he had kept faith with Zey. He had neither ignored his cousins, leaving them to sleepwalk into eternity, nor obliterated their present, stable culture and robbed them of all meaningful choices.

Rakesh asked Zey, "Are you ready for a small journey?"

"A journey where?" Zey's body tensed nervously.

"It's not far, I promise. I just want to say goodbye to my friend."

They crossed into the ferry. Having no need for airlocks simplified things enormously. Rakesh was almost beginning to enjoy his new embodiment: crawling around in vacuum, clinging to walls and ceilings, and knowing that it wasn't an act of puppetry, but a benign metamorphosis. He hoped, he believed, that he could live this way until Parantham returned.

Rakesh started the fusion drive, and the ferry arced up out of the disk. Zey scuttled around the cabin, confused, not knowing which way to orient herself. "What's happening to my weight?"

"Acceleration. Get used to it."

"I don't understand."

"Be patient," Rakesh implored her. "Just enjoy the view."

Even with the limited range of frequencies that the combination of the hull's filters and their vision afforded them, the neutron star made a majestic sight. Parts of the disk and the central jet shone brightly, and the narrow band brought out complex structures woven into the jet that would have been much harder to discern in the glare of a full-spectrum image.

As the spinning ring of *Lahl's Promise* came into view, Rakesh's anxiety began to rival Zey's. With the sight of his last fragile link to the Amalgam looming in front of him, the prospect of renouncing it, of cutting his ties, was beginning to seem a thousand times more daunting than leaving the node had been. He had not felt the same vulnerability since the day he'd left Shab-e-Noor. In the bulge, nothing would be certain. He did not understand the Aloof and their whims. There was no guarantee that he'd ever see Parantham, or any other citizen of the Amalgam, again.

So be it. That was what backups were for.

He brought the ferry to a halt a hundred meters from the ship.

"This is the cart I traveled in," Rakesh told Zey. "Though not all the way from the place where I was born."

"I don't understand," Zey complained. "How you traveled, where you've been."

"Don't worry," Rakesh said. "Forget about those things. Think about this place, and your own journeys."

He spoke to Parantham as she sat in the cabin, through a radio link bridging the vacuum between them.

"I've found Tassef's star on the map," she said. "If I ask the ship to go there, I suppose the Aloof will try to inject me back into the Amalgam's network."

Tassef was on the far side of the bulge from Massa, where they'd entered. Parantham would be re-enacting Leila and Jasim's first journey in reverse. Assuming the Amalgam let her back in.

"Safar bekheyr, my friend," Rakesh replied. *May your journey be blessed.* They had said their goodbyes, and he had made it clear to her that he was resolved in his decision; he didn't know what else to add.

"I'll see you again, Rakesh," she promised. Whether or not that was possible, he knew she meant it honestly; she would try to return.

For a few long heartbeats nothing happened to *Lahl's Promise*, and Rakesh wondered if that was the way: the Aloof simply rescanned the ship's contents each time, and left the latest incarnation behind, intact, as a kind of fossil.

Then the spinning ring began to smear out before his eyes, each speck of material cut loose from its neighbors and set free to follow a separate trajectory. Before long it was a faint, diffuse cloud of dust.

Zey was running in rings around the cabin now. "The people who did that? Where do they live?"

"I don't know," Rakesh replied. "Don't worry, though; they're not going to do that to us."

"How do you know?"

Rakesh chirped amusement. "I don't know anything about them, for certain. But I'll tell you what I'm thinking right now."

Zey managed to calm herself, and she stood beside him, waiting for him to compose his reply.

"I think they might be sleepwalking," he said. "Like your team-mates. I think they've done many things, learned many things, seen many things, but now they've had to find a way to live without needing what the world can no longer provide for them." He could understand the attraction of a strategy like that, for the Arkdwellers, for anyone. It was better than going mad with boredom. "Maybe there are one or two among them who are a bit like you, but a lot less restless. Sentinels, not quite awake, who can watch the world go by, and even intervene in it a little, but who can't, or won't, reengage with the universe until it has something new to offer them."

Zey absorbed this. "But they brought you here, just to wake us?"

"That's what I believe," Rakesh said. "But I'm not certain about any of this."

He waited until the last traces of *Lahl's Promise* had drifted out of sight, then he started the ferry's drive.

"Forget the Aloof," he said. "Let's go and find out if any of your team-mates are ready to engage with the universe."

28

The message from Ruz began, "Cho has found the Wanderer."

Roi read on, amazed.

While most of the void-watchers had given up their old job and come to join the geometry-calculators, Cho had refused to accept that the act of observation had become impossible. The junub edge *had* become useless; not only had the Incandescence hidden all the ordinary, distant lights that might have been used as guides to the Splinter's motion, once the Wanderer was orbiting in the same plane as the Splinter, the rock of the Splinter itself blocked any chance of a view of it from the junub edge.

So Cho had gone first to the sard edge, hunting for another crack in the rock through which he could extend his light-gatherer. He'd had no luck, though, in finding such an opening, or even a promising site where one could be made.

Once the Splinter crossed the Wanderer's orbit, the garm edge, facing in toward the Hub, became the only feasible observation post. Cho had journeyed back across the length of the Splinter, carrying all his metal plates, to search for a new vantage point.

He had found a suitable crack in the rock, and lowered his light-gatherer through to the surface. By blocking the aperture with punctured metal sheets to limit the amount of light transmitted, and then projecting what remained on to a smooth stone surface backed with roughened metal, he had been able to form an image which could be viewed safely.

The image was not sharp, but even through the Incandescence a dazzling smear of elevated radiance could be seen. It was the Wanderer orbiting the Hub, its intensity cycling dramatically. The emission of a flare or some other misadventure had apparently knocked it into an elliptical orbit, and on its closest approaches to the Hub it was now shining with an unprec-

244 •   GREG EGAN

edented brightness, which fell away again as it moved further out.

Roi conferred with Kem and Nis. "What does this mean?" she wondered. "How strong can this new light become?"

"I have no idea," Nis confessed. "I don't understand what's happening. The weight is squeezing the Wanderer, agitating its material somehow, but this effect is out of all proportion to that. It's as if... a child had teased a susk a dozen times, always getting a response as mild as their teasing, but then they found they'd crossed some kind of threshold and driven it into a fury."

Roi did not like the sound of that. What could the Wanderer do to them, *in a fury?*

Kem said, "We have two choices, I think. We could simply keep moving out, trying to put as much distance as we can between us and the Wanderer."

"That's getting harder, though," Roi replied. "And more perilous." Not only was the slower wind and the thinner Incandescence limiting their pace, if they ended up too far from the Hub there would be no hope of sustaining the crops. To survive the Wanderer only to die in a famine would be the worst thing she could imagine.

"The other choice is to take a different gamble," Kem said. "It's not too late to put ourselves in an orbit where we're constantly shielded by the Hub. The Wanderer's closest approach to the Hub is closer than we are now, but its furthest distance is still outside our present orbit. We can match orbital periods with it, and try to lock ourselves into a relationship where the Hub protects us as much as possible."

"Then what do we do when the Wanderer's orbit shrinks further?" Roi said. "We can't follow it back down toward the Hub in order to keep our orbital periods the same." She had had the idea, long ago, that perhaps Bard should have carved tunnels through the garmside as well as the sardside, granting the Splinter the ability to travel in either direction. If it came to a slow, drawn-out famine because they were too far from the Hub, that might yet be their only salvation, but there wasn't the slightest prospect of creating those tunnels in time to chase the Wanderer.

Nis held up the message sheet that contained Cho's observations. "Look how much brighter it's becoming already, just from the slight increase in weight when it reaches the closest point to the Hub along its orbit. When its orbit *shrinks*..."

He trailed off, but Roi didn't need him to complete the prediction. Either the process that was driving this radiance would come to a halt by destroying the Wanderer, or it would keep growing in the same spectacular fashion, and it would make no difference where the Splinter was.

Unless they were shielded by the Hub, this light would be strong enough to outshine the Incandescence and sear them all to death.

Roi rejoined the geometry-calculators for one more task. Since the Splinter's orbit was essentially circular and the Wanderer's was not, they couldn't hope to track its motion perfectly, keeping themselves always in the center of the safe zone that lay roughly—but thanks to the twist, not precisely—on the opposite side of the Hub. However, they could find the orbit that gave them the greatest protection possible, given that the Wanderer's brightness was reaching its ominous peaks with perfect regularity.

In effect, they would try to hide the Wanderer behind the Hub, to make it disappear from view. As the instructions flowed from the calculators to the sardside tunnel, and the observations flowed from Cho to the calculators, Cho's data began to reveal a modified cycle. As well as dimming and brightening from its own mysterious dynamics, the Wanderer was now growing more or less obscured by the Hub, which was swallowing varying portions of its light. As the Splinter eased into its new orbit, the two cycles slipped into the desired, antagonistic relationship: the Wanderer's dazzling bursts were cut short by the Hub's intervention, and when the imperfect alignment of the orbits most prevented the Hub from hiding the Wanderer, it was, of its own accord, at its least radiant.

Roi signaled Bard to close the tunnels, and told Tio to let the calculators rest. There was nothing more to be done. If the orbits started slipping further out of alignment, moving further from the Hub would only worsen the disparity. Their fate was at the mercy of the Wanderer now.

Roi sent word to evacuate the edges, to bring everyone as close as possible to the center of the Splinter. Her first instinct had been to move people to the sard edge—doubling the amount of rock between them and the Wanderer compared to the center—but Kem had pointed out that while pure light straight from the Wanderer couldn't reach them from the opposite side, a flare might wash behind them while radiating heat and light of its own, rendering the sard edge vulnerable.

Cho refused to leave his observation point, as did the light-messengers who linked him to the center. Roi sent a message to him.

"Let me replace you." She was older, it was her time.

Cho replied, "This is my work, not yours."

It was a bad argument, his skills might yet be needed for some future task they could not imagine, but Roi lacked the strength to make the journey to the garmside to plead with him in person.

The evacuees poured into the crowded center, bringing stores of food, pushing carts, herding susk.

Roi left her post and moved from chamber to chamber, seeking out people she'd known. Gul had come with a new class of hatchlings. She greeted him fondly, and played for a while with the children, but some restlessness drove her on. Ruz was nowhere to be found; eventually she heard that he'd taken the place of one of the light-messengers.

She stumbled across Bard in a crowded tunnel, pressed against the rock, his heart laboring despite the lack of weight.

He was dying. She said, "You moved the world, brother. You gave us our chance. Be at peace." He was too weak to reply. She looked around for food to bring him, but the influx of people had scraped the rock bare.

She had wanted to find Haf, but the crowd around her had become impassable. What could she have done for him, anyway? Sheltered him beneath her carapace? Offered him words of comfort, which would only have made him more certain that death was upon them?

Roi found a place beside Bard. She had planned to return to her post to wait for news from Cho, but the only news that mattered now would come to them all, soon enough, without the need for instruments and calculations.

She looked around at the people covering the walls and ceiling. They had worked hard, all of them. What was the nature of the world, what was the meaning of work, when so much struggle could end in obliteration?

She was tired now. She wished she could have gone as Zak had, when there was still so much hope. This was unbearable.

Bard stirred, and drummed something faintly.

Roi said, "I missed that."

"I think we've all been *recruited*," he said.

Roi caught his meaning and chirped softly. They really were one big team now. She turned the bleakly funny notion over in her mind, and felt the answering buzz of cooperation. Living or dying, she'd be doing the same as everyone around her. How could she not be happy with that?

Light replaced the crowds, the rock, the world. Roi ramped down her vision as fast as she could, fleeing from its intensity, trying to burrow into the safety of her mind to reach a painless black sleep. The light wouldn't let her escape: it overtook her, then reached into her eyes with lacerating claws.

There was only pain, heat, and brightness. She willed death, but the light kept slicing into her, playing with her, refusing to deliver mercy. Every time the sameness of it softened the blows, the thing turned her over and cut her somewhere new.

I can't do this, she pleaded, though she didn't know what she was addressing. Something broke, something weakened, and there was distance between her and the brightness. *Finally.* She relaxed. This was death: like sleep.

The pain welled up again, but the darkness remained. She thought she slept, three or four times, but there was no waking into light, either savage or gentle. Only waking into pain.

Roi flexed her legs, and felt her claws scrabble against rock. It hurt her to move, but it was not impossible. The only thing impossible was vision.

She waited, and heard movement around her, then plaintive drumming. She was blind, but she was alive, and others had survived alongside her.

There was work to do; she had to learn everything about the new situation. She called out to her team-mates, "Can someone tell me if the light is gone?"

Haf said, "I have some interesting news."

Roi put down her template frame.

"There's rock in our orbit," he announced. "I think we should stay here, or at least close by."

"*Rock?* What do you mean?"

"The void-watchers can see it with their light-gatherers. Pieces of rock, orbiting the Hub."

"You mean… *other Splinters?*"

Haf hesitated. "I don't think so. The shape's not the same. And the rock isn't exactly like our rock."

Roi let the puzzling news sink in. No mythical cousins, but that had always been a fanciful notion. To have rock, or something like it, not far away might be useful. She had no idea how they would reach it, but she was sure Haf would find a way eventually.

The death of the Wanderer had replenished the Incandescence, thickening it to the point that they were threatened not with famine but corrosion from the wind. They had reopened the tunnels and started moving out again, searching for the right balance. They had reached a point where the wind was not too strong but the crops would still be plentiful, and now they had this unexpected boon.

"I agree," she said. "We should stay here."

The Wanderer had killed a third of their people, and blinded another third. Bard, Cho, Ruz, Nis, Tio and Jos were all gone. Nobody understood what had happened, what had given the Wanderer's disintegration such force. Perhaps in a dozen generations someone would find a way to explore such mysteries; there might yet be something simple beneath it all.

Haf mused, "Rock's a good start, but I really don't think it will do for the wall."

"What wall?" Roi knew exactly what he was talking about, but she enjoyed teasing him.

Haf rasped annoyance. "The Hub is a dangerous place. Once we've left it behind, nobody should get close to it ever again. If they come this way we should send them back, the way you guide a hatchling away from danger: just pick them up and turn them around."

Roi chirped with delight. "First a wall, and now... what? A great machine for herding hatchlings who are hurtling through the void! Do you know how many spans it is *around the Hub?* In thirty-six times thirty-six generations, we could never build anything that began to do what you describe."

"Perhaps you're right," he conceded, but he didn't sound the least bit sincere.

She heard him approach and pick up one of her frames.

"Can I check your calculations?" he asked.

"That would be good."

The Wanderer's death-throes had given their orbit some elevation again: a return to light and dark, she'd been told, and a chance to see out into the void once more. She had been calculating a manoeuvre that she hoped they could perform with the tunnels to maintain the tilted orbit indefinitely. The opportunity to look out at their surroundings was too precious to lose again.

Haf worked in silence. Roi listened to the clicking of his claws against the stones, and felt herself drifting into sleep.

AFTERWORD

The "weight and motion" of objects in the Splinter follow from Einstein's theory of general relativity; many of the effects described also occur in Newtonian gravity, but observations within the Splinter are sufficient to discriminate between the two theories. The best general reference on this subject is:

> *Gravitation* by C. W. Misner, K. S. Thorne and J. A. Wheeler,
> W. H. Freeman, New York, 1970.

The most comprehensive treatment of the particular space-time geometries discovered by the protagonists is:

> *The Mathematical Theory of Black Holes* by S. Chandrasekhar,
> Oxford University Press, Oxford, 1992.

"Zak's principle" is essentially Einstein's equation in a vacuum, that is, the version that applies when the matter in your immediate vicinity has no significant gravitational effect. The general equation, which allows for the presence of matter, is described in terms that are almost as simple in this excellent account:

> "The Meaning of Einstein's Equation" by John C. Baez and
> Emory F. Bunn, **math.ucr.edu/home/baez/einstein/**

Some events in this novel depend on the detailed behavior of the plasma accretion disks that are present around black holes, and several aspects of this subject remain uncertain. For example, precisely if and when an accretion disk with given physical characteristics would be forced to lie in the equatorial plane of a rotating black hole (a phenomenon known as the Bardeen-Petterson effect) is a matter of controversy, because determining this theoretically depends on complex computer simulations, and direct observational data is inconclusive. See, for example:

"Spin-Induced Disk Precession in Sagittarius A*" by Gabriel Rockefeller, Christopher L. Fryer, and Fulvio Melia, **www.arXiv.org/abs/astro-ph/0507302**

A comprehensive discussion of the possible fates that can be suffered by stars that encounter black holes is given in:

"Tidal Disruption of Stars by Black Holes," by Martin J. Rees, *Nature*, Vol. 333, 9 June 1988, pp 523-528.

In charting Rakesh and Parantham's journey, I drew on:

"The Nuclear Bulge of the Galaxy. III. Large-Scale Physical Characteristics of Stars and Interstellar Matter" by R. Launhardt, R. Zylka, and P. G. Mezger, **www.arXiv.org/abs/astro-ph/0201294**

Panspermia—the spreading of viable biological material from one planet to another—is almost certainly possible between planets in the same system, but the prospects of such material achieving, and surviving, interstellar journeys is far slimmer. Interstellar panspermia is an interesting idea, and I don't believe it has been shown to be impossible, but I wouldn't argue with anyone who considers it to be highly unlikely.

Supplementary material for this novel can be found at **www.gregegan.net**